I0742375

THE KING'S FEAR

THE BRASS MACHINE: BOOK TWO

ISAAC GRISHAM

Also by Isaac Grisham

The King's Sun
The Brass Machine: Book One

Cooper Blue Books, LLC

www.isaacgrisham.com

Edited, formatted, and book design by Kristen Corrects, Inc.
Cover art design by Dissect Designs
Author photo by Eric Mackiewicz

First edition published 2019

ISBN: 978-1-7321406-4-6

for Celeste

the Lady of the Mountain

BEFORE KITSUNE

MYOBU

Screams resounded over the peaceful beaches of Urel, and the young fox's ears pricked up in interest. Lifting his head from oversized paws, his sleepy eyes cleared as he peered out of the den, scanning the nighttime surroundings. The howls were those of his mother and father. Though he had heard none of his kind cry out in such a fashion, he had hunted enough prey within his short lifetime to know his parents were cornered, frightened—and in pain.

A flash of muted purple light from farther down the beach illuminated the nearby ocean. The water, which normally sparkled like blue sapphires even on cloudy days, was now dark and murky. Despite a lack of wind, mixtures of water and sand spiraled about the shoreline like small waterspouts.

At the center of all the commotion, holding the source of the colored flash, stood a monstrous creature.

The purple light disappeared. His mother's yelping barks cut through the new darkness, but those were summarily silenced.

More of the beach's white sands were kicked into the air as the fox leaped from the den and raced down the coast toward the unfolding scene. As he ran, he tried to make sense of what he had just witnessed. The beast looked to have the mass of a horse and stood upright on its hind legs with a practiced dexterity not seen in any other animal. It was covered with thick hair colored black with flecks of red. Its most striking features were the massive horns protruding from its head and reflective, pearly white fangs.

The fox wondered if the animal was one of the humans he had heard tell of, but he quickly discounted that. Humans had always been described as softer, slender creatures with little hair. Their closest settlement was over fifty leagues away, well beyond the fox's realm of exploration. They knew of Urel, desired its rich mineral deposits and bountiful game, but its geographical location made it difficult to access.

The purple light flashed again as he drew nearer, its subdued glow revealing its source to be a massive sword wreathed in colored flame. Though not ornate, a string of glyphs was etched into the side of the blade. The fox could not understand them. Even if he'd been able to decipher their meaning, he was far more concerned with the horrid scene the sword had revealed.

His mother lay still on the ground. The light, reddish-brown fur along her side had been slashed open by either the weapon or one of the monster's long, sharp claws. Blood still poured from the wound, but her eyes no longer had the light of life in them. Despite that, his father was standing guard over her, his hackles raised as he snarled at their opponent.

Surprisingly, the horned creature looked distraught at what had transpired. It reached its free hand out toward the slain fox, palm open and expectant. Nothing happened, and it eventually threw back its head and howled in anger. The surrounding waterspouts expanded into a single transparent cyclone of sandy water, swirling around the perimeter.

After a few heartbeats, the beast turned its attention to the fox's father, its eyes burning a ghastly green. The remaining mate ceased his bristling. He turned away from his opponent, leaving himself open to attack, and looked back toward the den. Back to where the young pup was supposed to be sleeping.

"Myobu, my son," the elder fox expressed telepathically. *"RUN!"*

Myobu ran as fast as his natural Yokai form would allow him. Not away from the battle as his father meant, but straight for it. He was still too young to fully comprehend the meaning and consequences of losing someone, of their no longer being there, but he knew for certain what had happened to his mother was atrocious. He would not turn tail when a similar fate could befall his father.

Besides, he expected his father to flee, to run toward him and lead him to a safe place. To Myobu's dismay, the elder Yokai swung back around to the monster, crouched, and then leaped upward. His body underwent a radical transition as he went airborne, morphing from a sleek, agile fox into a bulkier, ferocious wolf. Larger fangs sprang from his jaws, which were ready to snap shut on the throat of his target.

Neither the increased weight—meant to knock the creature to the ground—nor the larger set of teeth served their purpose. The beast appeared as shocked as Myobu by the attack. It swung its weapon in defense. As the youth watched in helpless terror, it cleaved the wolf nearly in two. Death came even before the body fell to the ground with a heavy thud.

"Father, no!" Myobu shrieked, not realizing he simultaneously let out an animalistic scream.

The monster again appeared perplexed by the bloodshed, its eyes blazing in anger at the fresh carnage at its feet. It stamped about, swung the blade, and roared at the sky. The weapon pulsed again with a brighter intensity. The flames looked as if they were straining away from their wielder, and they disappeared when Myobu skidded to a stop within the beast's field of vision.

Myobu saw intelligence and understanding in the creature's fiery green eyes. The beast calmed and set its sights on him. He knew with sudden certainty this was not a mere animal like those he and his parents had hunted and eaten. This was not a monster blessed with horns, claws, and a flaming sword. The massive, abhorrent being had thoughts and goals. It had come here for a reason. This entire encounter was not by chance.

Now it was looking at him with a singular drive.

Just as it had done with his mother, the creature reached its free hand toward him through the hazy mist of water and sand. It was a friendly gesture, probably meant to calm him. Myobu cocked his head, looking at the clawed hand quizzically. He had just decided to leap forward and bite it with his tiny jaws when he was knocked back in blinding pain. It felt as though the sword had been driven deep into his skull, creating a chasm through which his very being was spilling out. His mind was torn asunder. In his agony, he only saw white light and heard a piercing wail.

Then it stopped. His senses were still screaming in reaction, but whatever force had ripped through his head was gone. He tried to get up, to bolt as his father had demanded, but all he could do was lay on his side, twitching and panting.

Despite his vulnerability, no further harm came to Myobu. As his acuity of the surroundings normalized, however, he knew the danger had not yet abated. Strangely, he felt and heard water all about him. Not the sandy mist that had been streaming through the air, but the ocean itself rushing up the beach as though the world itself had been turned on its side.

His vision finally cleared, and Myobu saw another creature had dared step into the fray. He recognized the scent of Kirin, a Yokai who had recently taken up residence in a nearby den. Kirin was in another form Myobu had never seen before. This guise had to be a human male, he thought. Not nearly as hairless or soft as he had imagined, Kirin would have been an imposing sight if not for the snarling beast he faced.

Both of Kirin's hands were held out, much like the creature had been doing moments before. In contrast to the thing's calming gesture, Kirin was visibly straining with effort. His focus was not on his hairy opponent, but rather on the churning ocean itself. Using forces invisible to Myobu's senses, Kirin drew the salty water out from the depths, up the sandy beach, and pooling it at the beast's feet. As the young fox watched, the water rose off the ground, clinging to the thing's legs.

Myobu realized what his neighbor was attempting to do: encase the monster. Slow it down. Drown it. He could also see it wasn't going to work. The creature was so powerful it had killed his parents almost by accident, though there was little doubt death would've been the result of its nefarious intentions. Despite the onslaught of accumulating water—now up to its waist—it was still slogging its way toward Kirin. His large, hoofed feet made horrible sucking sounds as they were driven into and out of the wet sand.

As it neared Kirin, the thing raised the giant sword, making to slash it down upon the chest of the human form. It burst into flames again, the purple colors straining in the opposite direction of their handler. Myobu thought himself delirious, but he would have sworn he could perceive souls within the fire. The souls of his kind.

The moment this impression crossed Myobu's mind, his perception of time slowed to a crawl. The purple flames turned to him and reached out with enticing, translucent tendrils. Wrapped about him, they pierced his consciousness, drove deep into his mind. Quite suddenly, he understood fire. Not just that of the sword, but all fire. He knew its properties, its strengths and weaknesses, and what fueled it. Fire was within him, an integral part of his very being. As such, he could control it just as though it were his leg, jaw, or tail.

The translucent tendrils dissipated. Without even knowing he was moving, and despite the pain and exhaustion he was suffering, Myobu jumped to his feet. Using a power he had never before practiced, he reached out to the sword with his mind. The weapon was halfway through its swing toward Kirin, and the flames were about to vanish once again. Before they could, Myobu wrested control of the fire, causing it to explode outward and engulf the creature's hairy arm.

Bewildered, the beast let the sword slip from its grasp. It went completely dark before embedding itself into the sand by Kirin's feet. Myobu still had control of the flames that crackled along their foe's appendage, and he used his newfound power to spread it quickly over the rest of its body.

Kirin appeared to double his own efforts. Somehow, his water assault did not lessen the effects of Myobu's flames. Riddled with both elements, the monster whirled about in a frenzy, attempting to find its lost weapon and roaring loud enough to awaken half of the beach's inhabitants. It wouldn't be long before others came to investigate.

The monster appeared to sense this. Having been overpowered and disarmed, it knew it had to make a quick escape or else risk its own life. It spun about even faster, causing a cyclone of fire, water, and sand. Its form looked as though it was dissipating, becoming a black smoke that diluted the interior of the cyclone. Even when its figure became completely obscured, Myobu could still discern two blazing green eyes staring right back at him with malice and hatred.

A fissure in the ground cracked open underneath the cyclone, and the screaming mass of smoke descended straight down into the jagged hole. Intent on tormenting their target as long as possible, the fire and water rushed down with it.

Myobu and Kirin were plunged into darkness. The only sound that now disturbed the early morning quiet was dry sand spilling into and filling up the pit in the earth.

*

"Are you injured?" came a low, gravelly voice. It belonged to Kirin, and the words were sent telepathically.

Myobu walked in a circle one way and then the other before falling to the ground in fatigue. *"My head aches terribly from that thing's attack."*

"I do not doubt you," Kirin said, placing one of his human hands on Myobu's head. On one of the fingers was a ring adorned with a large white stone. The stone itself was a hoshi no tama, capable of storing its Yokai owner's power. It was used when they took on a form that wasn't entirely compatible with their magic. *"I suspect you wouldn't be able to do anything at all if it had procured what it desired. The headache should subside with time."*

"What did that thing want? What was that thing?"

"That was a demon," Kirin responded. *"A particularly powerful one, too. Hundreds of sun cycles old, at the very least. As for what it sought, I could not say. Just as other species have trouble understanding the motives of our kind, I cannot begin to comprehend what would cause a being to act so violently toward others."*

Myobu knew many species in the world considered the Yokai to be spirits, not living creatures. Others of their kind, collectively known as yako, helped perpetuate the misconception that they were a kind of ghost or spirit. They mischievously played on those notions for their own amusement. Mostly, though, the misunderstanding was due to the unique powers of the Yokai. Their abilities to see and interact with the natural world, shapeshift, and communicate telepathically appeared to be magic. Perhaps it was. To Myobu, still just a pup, it was natural and completely organic.

Before he had known what he was, understood he was more than just a mere fox, he had trouble grasping what his parents were. They seemed otherworldly, like spirits. That was probably how most humans, who were like children in their relationship with the natural world, felt of the Yokai. It was certainly how he felt of the demon.

"What was the demon holding?" Myobu asked, pointing his furry snout at the sword sticking out of the ground near Kirin. *"My parents spoke of devices designed to kill, but never one that possessed the power of flame."*

"This," Kirin said with an inordinate amount of wonder, pointing at the glyphs that ran along its side, *"is Tsukumogami."*

"It's…alive?"

"Yes and no," Kirin replied, reaching his jeweled hand out toward the weapon, yet not taking hold of it. *"Countless sun cycles ago, back when even we were a primitive race, this truly was nothing more than a sword. Legends say its first owner, the one who forged it, was Inari herself."*

Myobu's jaw fell open. If he hadn't already been lying down, he would have fallen back on his rump. Inari was by far the most well-known of the Yokai. Her name was known throughout the lands by nearly all sentient species. Numerous myths and stories told of her agricultural knowledge and how she spread that information throughout the known world, increasing health and prosperity for all.

Though few now believed in the historical accuracy or existence of Inari, she'd been worshipped as the Yokai's goddess for millennia. As the Yokai became more harmonious with the natural world and enlightened on how their powers could manipulate it, they lifted concepts behind the ideology of their ancient religion and applied it to their more nature-centric lives.

"She was renowned for her powers in cultivation, but there are theories she had a secondary gift in metallurgy," Kirin explained. *"She hid this fact while attempting to spread peace and harmony throughout the lands, wishing not to be a beacon of death."*

Myobu blinked in surprise, but then reminded himself these were all stories. The Yokai had several innate abilities, such as shapeshifting and telepathy. Half their kind was blessed with a more specific and unique gift. Kirin was one of these individuals, able to control the flow of water. His own, discovered just now under distress, was apparently the manipulation of fire. The idea that one of the Yokai would possess *two* specific skills was virtually unheard of outside of fantasy.

"Stories say that when Inari died, her powers and soul were absorbed into the blade. Her followers, believing it had taken on a life of its own, named it Tsukumogami. Since then, the rare individuals who possessed two unique abilities found themselves drawn to the sword. So long as they could demonstrate their gifts, they were granted permission by Inari's followers to wield it. When each passed on, their souls did not ascend to a higher plane as others do. Instead, they and their powers joined Inari's within Tsukumogami. Over time, the blade became the most powerful object in the known world. As it grew stronger, so did its draw on those with dual abilities."

Kirin paused, glancing down at Myobu. The man looked a bit at odds in regards to what he had already revealed and whether he should continue. *"As our species turned its back on gods, goddesses, and hero worship, the sword was handed to fewer and fewer individuals. It eventually disappeared altogether—probably lost when its bearer died in a distant land. As time passed, many questioned whether it, like Inari herself, actually existed."*

"Until now," Myobu said, thinking of how he had thought Yokai souls resided within the purple flames. He had the impression they did not regret their eternal lot, being trapped within a sword, though they had not cared for the being that had recently found them.

"Until now," Kirin agreed. *"Though it is too soon."*

"Too soon?"

"I have heard from one of our kind—someone so old and wise they can sense the future—that Tsukumogami will once again play an integral part in shaping our world's future." Kirin grasped the hilt of the sword and pulled it deftly from the sand. No flames burst forth. It was inanimate. Just a piece of metal. *"The time is not right, however. Other foretold signs have not yet come to pass. No known Yokai has had two gifts in generations, and with no remaining followers of Inari, there is no one to keep it safe from others who may be drawn to it. For that reason, I think it best Tsukumogami remains lost to history for now. To that end, I must take the weapon far from here."*

"You're leaving?" Myobu exclaimed, suddenly panicked. The emotion surprised him. Kirin was truly just an acquaintance. A friendly neighbor.

Then the reality of Myobu's situation set in. Both of his parents had been murdered. They were not going to trot down the beach, take him back to their den, and lay next to him until his heart and mind calmed and he fell asleep. They would not be around when he awoke in the morning to accompany him on a breakfast hunt. They would never know his special power involved fire and would not witness his first shapeshifting.

Without them to guide and teach him, would he even be able to learn such things on his own?

In lieu of his parents, those he had been closest to, there was only Kirin. They were bonded together by virtue of surviving and defeating the demon.

"What will I do?" Myobu asked, more to himself than Kirin.

"*Though the night is quiet, you are surrounded by your own kind,*" Kirin said. Myobu was not comforted and, upon seeing this, the elder continued, "*I do not know what your immediate future holds, but I am certain you will rise above this night's transgressions. Do not give me that sullen look. You see, I am not here by chance. The same Yokai who spoke of Tsukumogami insisted I come to Urel.*"

"*Why?*" Myobu said, puzzled.

"*To save you,*" Kirin answered, pointing down at him with a human finger. "*The Harbinger—that is how many refer to this wise one—has made me privy to bits and pieces of what might come to pass. I barely understood most of what was revealed, so I cannot tell you much. What I can say is you are important: You are as integral to our future as Tsukumogami. You will come to know the one who will wield it and, together, you both will destroy the very demon we fought off today. You will keep safe the brass machine and, in doing so, save our world.*"

MEMORIES OF HATE AND LOVE

Kirin's words had dripped with importance, but Myobu was still too young to fully comprehend their meaning. He didn't care about a legendary sword or who would wield it, though he was thankful it was no longer in the clawed hands of the demon. The creature—that monstrous thing from the depths of nightmares—was something he wished never to encounter again.

Myobu was but a pup. He should still be asleep, curled up between his parents. He needed to be comforted, not burdened with the fate of the world.

"I don't know anyone," he admitted, looking up at Kirin from the sandy ground. *"Why can't I come with you?"*

Kirin appeared startled by the question, then gave Myobu a parental look. *"I am journeying well beyond the borders of Urel. Far to the north is a wild region, and there I will hide Tsukumogami. Once that task is complete, I will not be returning here. Instead, I will travel to the Kingdom of Gaav, where I have spent many sun cycles."*

Dejected and unsure of what to say, Myobu remained quiet.

"I understand how you are feeling. I grew up without my parents, and I've lost many others throughout my sun cycles. That is the way of life and death, but that truth does not make it any more palatable."

Kirin's human eyes were distant for several moments before he continued. *"I would like to share some memories with you. Some of them may be rather painful, but they might help you process what has taken place here today and appreciate your parents' love and sacrifice. Your mother and father would have passed along their own memories to you, albeit fewer at a time, and it's something I would have done with my own son."*

Another silent pause was accentuated by the lulling waves. Kirin gave a pained expression. Myobu was about to inquire when the older man went on. *"Seeing as you saved my life as much as I saved yours, that you have no parents to receive memories from and I have no offspring to give mine to, this makes sense. Would you agree?"*

Myobu pondered that for a few moments. He knew the transference of remembrances from parents to their progeny was part of the maturation process of their species. As a Yokai youth became capable of understanding who and what they were, the feats of which they were capable of, and the interactions they might face in the world beyond, memories were used to illustrate oral lessons. It helped prepare them for the complex webbing that intertwined nature, their power, and emotion. As he was of age and asking questions, his parents had recently broached the subject with him.

But now his parents and their recollections were forever lost to him.

"I agree," Myobu said, grasping at anything that would keep his mind off what had been taken from him. He would have to deal with it eventually. Their mangled remains were on the beach for all to see. Questions would come as the sun rose and others awakened. But for now, he just needed to keep his mind occupied.

"Very well," Kirin said, appearing simultaneously pleased and anxious. Closing his eyes, he held a hand out toward Myobu. *"The transference is traditionally performed one memory at a time to facilitate training. Depending on the loquaciousness of the teacher, passing along everything can take dozens to hundreds of sessions, possibly taking many sun cycles to complete. We do not have the luxury of time, so I will give you what I can. It will take time for you to*

process. You will not understand it all at first. When you do, and with the help of others, you will fully realize your potential."

Silence fell between them for several heartbeats. Myobu wondered if something was wrong, but then he heard hooves beating frantically upon the ground and the braying of horses. When he turned to peer at the source, he saw the ocean and beach had disappeared, replaced with an open field of grass. Upon this new sea of green were two teams of horses, each one topped by a human. The two groups galloped toward one another at a frightening speed.

The humans atop the animals were clad in crude metal armor. Each held a sword or a long pike with a sharp, pointy end. Ugly, angry looks were on their faces, and battle cries and obscenities were thrown across the narrowing grassy gulf between the two groups.

Directly in the middle of the opposing forces were three foxes, two adults and one pup around the same age as Myobu. For a moment, he thought they represented his own family. Then he remembered this was a memory and guessed they were a young Kirin and his parents.

The canids were panicking, running back and forth to escape the oncoming collision. With nowhere to go, the two adults shielded their offspring with their own bodies at the last moment. As Kirin's field of vision was cut off, so was Myobu's, but his other senses were still intact.

The thundering of the horses' hooves jolted the earth with a ferocity greater than any earthquake he had ever felt, shaking his body as well as assaulting his eardrums. Had Myobu experienced an earthquake before, or was this Kirin's memory mixing with his own? He couldn't remember, and it was suddenly becoming difficult to differentiate between personas. Clear thinking was arduous with the screams of those same horses being stabbed by pikes or having their legs broken by a sword. Their pained shrieks easily outmatched those of their human counterparts who met similar fates. All their blood mixed, and the smell of it and broken flesh invaded Myobu's—no, Kirin's—nose, disorienting him even further.

The worst part was the screaming of his parents as they were trampled, followed by their silence.

As the sounds of clashing metal and human voices faded, Kirin emerged amid the carnage. The senseless death of his parents befuddled and incensed him, filling him with a new emotion he would come to know as hatred. The humans had done this to his family. They had done this to him.

Having already discovered his specific gift was the manipulation of water, he reached out with his mind to the pools of blood staining the once serene sea of grass. Plasma was the liquid property of blood, and it was mostly water. Using this source, he attempted to lesson his grief and anger by exacting revenge on the human survivors that littered the field. So many of them had been left behind, though most were critically injured or incapacitated and wouldn't have lasted the day. Drowning them had probably been more a mercy than a torture.

With the wounded now dead, he went off in search of the remaining armies.

*

The upsetting memory faded away, which suited Myobu just fine. An hour ago, his only concept of death was hunting lesser animals for food. Now he had witnessed Kirin taking so many sentient lives in vengeance. Worse, as he became familiar with this new emotion, he found he wanted to track down the demon and make it pay for what it had done to his family.

Other recollections tumbled into Myobu's head as Kirin continued the transfer. True to the elder's word, they were a confusing mess Myobu fought to understand. He grasped at them, suddenly finding himself in a wholly unfamiliar scene. It was as if he were in a massive den, although not a hollow of nature. The room had been made perfectly square. Planks of wood were laid out across the ground. Several holes had been cut into the walls, though they were small enough that their purpose was only to allow in light and fresh air. It had to have been an example of human habitation.

Kirin was slightly older now and had learned to shapeshift. He was now in the form of a surly-looking human male. The rage and hatred that had taken root that day on the battlefield consumed his soul. These feelings manifested externally as a roiling sphere of water hovering at his side. It hung there midair, four footfalls tall and across. Noisily spouting steam and water droplets, it looked menacingly ready to do his bidding.

Kirin failed to act upon his revengeful impulse. A new emotion had suddenly sprouted within his consciousness, corrupting the hate. It was shame.

Across the room were three other individuals. Two of them were a king and queen, leaders of the Kingdom of Gaav and commanders of one of the armies that had killed his parents. It had taken time and cunning to find them and make his way into their residence, but his quest for retribution had fueled him to succeed. At least until now. Upon his dramatic entrance, smashing his way in with the ball of water, they had thrown themselves protectively over the third human, their daughter.

It occurred to Kirin that in his quest to reach this point, through the act of killing all those he had come across—which had not been a few—he had become the very destructive force he despised.

The boiling globe lost cohesion as he released it from his grip. It splashed harmlessly to the ground. In turn, he sank to his knees in disgrace and anguish. What had happened to his family was an unknowing consequence of the actions of others, but his response to it had been abominable. How could he even begin to pay the price for that sin?

*

Myobu shook his head as the memory faded into the ocean of Kirin's life and another came into focus. Many sun cycles must have passed, for the weight of maturity that saturated this recollection far surpassed his own. Kirin was still in human form, albeit one with different physical features than the previous incarnation. He was again in a large, square den. It was one of many conjoining rooms, and how he felt in the setting made it clear this was his home.

Another human was in the room with him—a young woman with strong features and a beautiful smile. Her eyes were tired but filled with a look Myobu could not yet identify. She was holding a bundle of cloth to her chest. Wrapped in the blanket was a pup…no, a baby. A human baby boy.

The same emotion Myobu had seen in the woman's eyes now exploded throughout Kirin's mind, accompanied by pride and joy. The woman was his partner, and the child was their offspring, created through mutual…love. It was a glorious feeling that made Myobu feel as though anything was possible. He wanted to experience this himself. Was it something that came naturally to all creatures, or was it a part of interacting with humans?

"Love is something both humans and the Yokai feel, though in fundamentally different ways," Kirin's voice cut through the memory. "Humans tend to associate love with a concept they call passion. Passion is another emotion which should not be taken lightly. As wonderful as it is to spend your life with another, to share and feel and bask in each other's feelings, it can be a destructive force. It can be a poison, ruining all it touches."

Despite the warning, Myobu wanted nothing more than to bask in this human version of love. It felt so pure and good, and it washed away so much grime from his mind. Even the hatred he had felt for the demon just moments ago diminished to the point of being nearly forgettable. He had to pursue this passion, experience it for himself. Not just another's memory. With an odd sense of certainty, he knew this would define his life.

Kirin began to remove his mental tendrils from Myobu's mind. The youth wanted to remain within the memory. It was peaceful and comforting, like a good sleep, and he didn't want to wake up. Heeding the warning, though, he let go.

Before the stream of recollections completely faded, another scene was passed on to him. It had to have been an accident on Kirin's part, for the man let out a frightened curse as soon as it happened.

Myobu's ears were ringing from a fresh round of mortified wailing. Everyone was crying out. Kirin. His partner. Their baby. Except their offspring wasn't a baby anymore. He was a young man—short and slender, although he had a toughness about him. His jaw was square, a feature that accompanied a heart-shaped face and high cheekbones. What was left of his dark hair was thick and disheveled. Most of it, though, had been burned away.

They were all on fire, burning alive. The smell of charred flesh filled the air as flames ate away at their beautiful faces. Muscles, now clearly visible, were contorted in anguish. They were screaming. He was screaming.

And though it could not be seen in the memory, the presence of the ferocious, green-eyed demon was more than palpable.

Then there was utter blackness.

*

Kirin thought he had perhaps been too liberal with his words and memories. Whereas so many individuals underestimate the abilities of youth, he may have overestimated what the pup could handle.

"I must apologize for that last recollection. It was not something you were meant to see," Kirin said out loud. Still in human form, he was sitting on the ground next to Myobu, stroking the young fox's reddish-brown fur. The youth was unconscious, a reaction to the onslaught of mental and emotional stimulation. Speaking telepathically would have been no more effective than doing so audibly, though he wasn't sure to whom he was truly apologizing. Thankfully, it helped assuage Kirin's own feelings.

"The woman you saw was my wife," he continued. "The young man was our son. His name was Acro, and he elicited such pride and joy from me that I believed myself the happiest man in the world, having finally contributed something that made it a better place."

Despite the blissful words, Kirin found he had anxiously driven his free hand deep into the sandy ground. The fine granules scraped against his skin. Attempting to relax, he gazed into the sun in the east, its early rays already causing the ocean waters to sparkle. It was a beautiful sight, or at least he knew it was. He rarely recognized beauty anymore, and he often wondered if he ever would again.

"When I realized what I had done in the wake of my parents' deaths, that I had snuffed out innumerable and innocent lives with my magic, I was beside myself with a different kind of grief. I gave myself to Gaav's king, fully expecting death as punishment for my actions. He certainly looked as though he desired to personally remove my head. Yet after consulting his family and advisors, he instead created a new role for me on his council. Under the title of Ninko, I was to take the guise of a new man, one learned in agriculture, and use my magic to benefit his kingdom and people.

"This was long ago. The citizens of Gaav were mostly nomadic. They roamed their lands as the seasons changed, following migrating herds for food. The royal family knew if they were to become a competitive economic force in the region, to keep their lands and resources from the growing militaries of their neighbors, their people would have to change how they lived their lives, essentially putting down roots. I was to teach a people ignorant in the management of crops and fields how to feed themselves throughout a sun cycle while remaining in one place.

"The city of Hawte became Gaav's new permanent capital, and it sprang up as citizens heeded the call of their king for societal reformation. Thousands of families and tribes settled there over many sun cycles, shedding their traveling ways. Surrounding land proved fertile, capable of producing enough food for all. I covertly used my magic to bring moisture to the plants while the people learned about crop rotation, irrigation methods, and how to tend fields."

One of the sun's warm rays caressed Kirin's human face. He forced himself to relax, pulling his hand from the sand and smoothing the granules across the ground. Myobu remained unconscious, though his breathing was beginning to calm.

"I eventually met a pretty young lady. She was a barmaid, and I suppose her charm and grace kept many patrons coming around. Not that the folks needed the reason. Taverns were a novel concept to them. One of many, but one they particularly liked.

"The woman—Abby was her name—made such an impression on me that I drank myself into a stupor trying to impress her. While I don't believe that worked, she was kind enough to put me up for the night while I recovered. That was the inroad, and our conversations the following morning over breakfast *did* capture her attention. We were courting within a month. A sun cycle later, I asked her father, the owner of the tavern, for his blessing to marry her. He graciously allowed the match, though I suspect his knowledge of my connections to the royal family may have partially swayed his thinking.

"Acro was born to us within the following sun cycle, a beautiful baby boy. My life had never been so complete and full of meaning. That feeling did not abate for over two decades. As Abby and I watched our baby grow into a man, I observed him carefully for any signs of magic. The children of Yokai and human relations can possess the power of our species. Though their blood isn't pure, their magic can be just as powerful. While he was a bright and curious individual, Acro never displayed magical abilities. Perhaps it did not have the time to manifest."

Kirin clasped his hands in his lap, not trusting himself to hold anything as he came to the next part of his story. Despite the pain, it was best to remember, to keep Acro and Abby alive in memory.

"I was out in the fields late one night, using my abilities to call water from a nearby river to the vegetation, when a fire caught and raged through several neighborhoods. My home was among those in its destructive path. By the time I noticed the flames piercing the night sky and rushed back, it was too late. My return was met with their screams. Abby and Acro had been asleep when the fire caught, and there was no way to escape. It was…the most awful thing I've ever had to endure."

Pausing a moment, Kirin took a deep breath and then went on, "Beneath the smoldering buildings and stench of death, I could sense something else had been present. Not human or Yokai, but something malevolent. I can't shake the feeling it was waiting for me, but I don't believe it was responsible for the fire that ravaged my neighborhood. The fire probably scared it away.

"I could not say why the thing was there, nor could I ever produce proof that it wasn't my grieving imagination. It left no scent or physical evidence. Still, something indescribable lingered in the air. Even the humans could sense it." Kirin shuddered, looking at where the demon had disappeared into the sand. "I feel that same presence now."

While most foxes hunted at night, the Yokai preferred the day. Kirin could sense them as they emerged from their dens in search of water and a rodent breakfast. None of them had yet noticed four figures on the beach, one in human form and two dead.

"Gaav's king was very old by then, and his plans for creating a sound future for his kingdom were panning out. The people had learned to grow and maintain crops and fields on their own. Without my family, there was little reason for me to remain. Being reasonable and empathetic, the king released me from his service.

"In my grief, I roamed the lands as a field fox for many sun cycles. It was easier to trade my conscious thought, self-awareness, and intelligence for a relatively dumb mind than to deal with my loss. As such, I cannot recall much of that time. I survived, obviously, and only came out of my stupor at the insistence of the Harbinger."

Kirin gave Myobu one last pat on the head before pushing himself up. He stretched his human muscles, the feeling like an old memory. He took hold of Tsukumogami, only then realizing that he was stark naked.

"Though I was sent here to protect you, I regret my failure to help your parents. It is ironic," Kirin said with a troubled cough, "that while I was unable to save my son from fire, I was able to rescue another whose power is control over it.

"My apologies for leaving you with your mind in disarray, but I think it best to depart before anyone recognizes Tsukumogami. I hope we meet again. Until then, young Myobu, be well."

Without disturbing a grain of sand or blade of grass, Kirin walked off the beach and disappeared into the woods.

FIELD FOX

Myobu yawned and stretched, pushing his front paws forward as far as they'd go while sticking his rear end up into the air. He walked in a circle several times before settling back down in his bedding, his mind and body releasing tension. Fire and death had plagued his dreams, as well as a pair of shimmering green eyes that stared maliciously from the darkness.

Those eyes were still peering at him from the depths of the den.

Snapping fully awake, Myobu jumped to his feet. The color of the eyes was green, but they were a much different shade than those that had troubled his sleep. Far less menacing, too, being filled with inquisitiveness and play. He saw they belonged to a pup that couldn't have been more than a few weeks old. Not yet old enough for intelligent thought but not so young it wasn't consumed with curious exploration. It clumsily emerged from its own bed, heading toward him with its sniffing nose up in the air.

The rest of Myobu's senses kicked in. He wasn't in his own bedding. This one was far too fresh and smelled nothing like himself. This den, filled with the scents of three unfamiliar Yokai, was not his. The sound coming from the entrance was not the lapping of waves on the beach but rather the rustling of long, waxy leaves.

Remnants of what he had thought were nightmares fell into place, and he staggered back in realization of his new reality. His parents had been senselessly murdered. Their minds were now expanding throughout the universe, becoming a part of everything they encountered, including himself. He wanted to find that comforting. However, the Yokai believed everything the dead encompassed was no more or less important than anything else. As his parents' consciousnesses grew, his own individuality, his familial importance—his very name—would become lost to them.

Crushing grief fell upon him, and he whimpered. The feeling of emotional torment was not native to the Yokai. They certainly grieved for their dead, but it was more of an acceptance and celebration. The dead were not truly gone, after all. They were all around, even more alive than before. Nothing was more beautiful than that. This other version of grief, this devastating concept of loss, was entirely human.

Myobu was briefly puzzled as to why he knew that, but then the memories Kirin had bequeathed him resurfaced. When the Yokai take the form of other creatures, the transformation can be more than physical. If they choose to do so, they can encompass the mentality of the species, incorporating attitudes, motives, and feelings. Kirin had done this during his time in Gaav, and when his entire family had been taken from him, he had succumbed to the emotional distress.

Shivering despite the warmth of the den, Myobu cried out in sharp barks and pawed at the ground. Now he was grieving not only for his parents, but for Kirin's and the humans Abby and Acro as well. Though he had never known them, he now remembered them clear as day. He felt for them. He loved them.

The thought of Kirin's kin stirred another foreign memory within Myobu: the presence of the demon in Hawte the night Abby and Acro died. It brought forth a renewed desire for vengeance. He found the feeling to be similar to passion. It was consuming, pushing all other thoughts from his mind. One or both of Kirin's parents must have taken the form of a human or other equally emotionally tumultuous creature and then passed the concept to Kirin before they were killed, because vengefulness was certainly not an intrinsic trait of the Yokai.

The younger pup squeaked and tumbled back onto its haunches as the den suddenly grew very warm. Grass roots and bedding burst into flame as ire and enmity toward the murderous green-eyed demon swept over Myobu. The monster had no business being in Urel, swinging a sword and cleaving innocent lives in half. Even worse, it had escaped. It was still alive, free to cause havoc and kill anyone. It had to be stopped— if not to avenge his parents, for those whose lives it had already destroyed or would destroy. Myobu would take it upon himself to kill the creature. It would become his life's purpose. Nothing would—

"Myobu," a new female voice, soft and tranquil, came to him telepathically. He could tell the calmness was forced, as there was an underlying tone of alarm. It was probably the mother of the young pup, concerned for its safety amid the fire.

Giving out an alarmed bark, Myobu realized the small flames had grown into a menacing fire. Smoke was building up in the small enclosure, making it hard to see and breathe. Left unattended, it would suffocate both him and the pup.

"I don't know how to stop it! I can't control it!" he cried out in response. It had been so easy to control the fire last night, to give it life and manipulate it to his will. The skill had seemed so natural then, but now it was being smothered and confused by his new unbridled emotions. A dangerous mixture of love and animosity, feelings so new he couldn't even begin to imagine how to control them, battled for control. They expressed themselves through his power, and the flames grew ever larger.

"Open your mind to me," the soothing voice came again. *"Let me help you."*

Myobu felt the mental tendrils of the voice's owner prodding at his mind. Clearing his head as best he could, he allowed them to slip through his thoughts and deep into the core of who he was. It was an exceptionally personal act, one in which some Yokai didn't even partake with their partners. Sometimes a parent had to do so with offspring if, as in this case, their emotions and power were getting the best of them.

The newcomer's presence drifted through his mind like a cloud, and his thoughts and feelings grew hazy. Memories of the demon, cries for vengeance, and Kirin's tragic history were still there, but their crispness faded and connections to one another fell away. The power inside of him that sought release lost its firm grasp on his emotions and surrounding elements, and the surrounding flames retracted to mere glowing embers. The smoke that had been billowing thinned somewhat. However, it still posed a hazard without ventilation.

"Good," the voice said. *"Now bring me my son."*

Locating the other pup, he wobbled over. Though technically still a pup himself, he was far older and larger and was able to pick up the younger one by the scruff of his neck. Doing so, he made for the entrance of the den.

Bright sunlight dazzled his eyes as he emerged from the burrow. When he blinked several times, the figures of two adult female Yokai came into view. One was irate, glaring at Myobu in a way that made him feel she'd snap his neck with her jaws if the younger pup hadn't been in his. The other had a look of concerned relief, and he was thankful it was she who moved forward to take the youth from him. The pup was coughing, but otherwise seemed unharmed. As the danger had abated, so had the fear.

"I'm so sorry. I just learned of my power. And my parents were killed," Myobu sent out to both adults, mentally choking in grief. *"I got carried away with myself."*

"It was that cursed Kirin," the angry-looking Yokai shouted in response, simultaneously producing a snarl. *"I saw him talking to the boy. Probably passing along all the human oddities he accumulated. Something I'll never do with our offspring! I should have left him there on the beach!"*

"Maroni," chided the other adult with strained patience. *"Myobu is my sister's son. I can smell her on him. Regardless of that fact, you brought him here because he is one of us. One of the Yokai."*

The two females fell into a silent conversation between themselves. It looked odd, the two of them staring at each other, making the occasional facial gesture. Myobu tried to decipher their meanings, but the cloudiness of his thoughts had yet to fully abate. Just after he had sunk to the ground to keep his mind from spinning, the surly one gave a huff, gently picked up the younger pup, and stalked off in the direction of the beach.

"You don't have to forgive Maroni for her rudeness," his mother's sister said, again reaching into his mind to help steady him. *"With what you have taken on from Kirin, I do hope you will at least understand. In her youth, she spent some time across the great ocean with a species called the Ceran. They are a bristly bunch, quick to irritation and anger. Maroni loved and studied them, became one with them, and took on their mindset and emotions. It has stuck with her ever since."*

Myobu nodded, trying hard to look as though he understood exactly what she was saying.

"For all the experience and wisdom Kirin has, perhaps it would have been best if he had stayed in Gaav," the elder Yokai said with a sigh. *"I did not dare explore the memories he transferred to you, but I can feel the ramifications of their presence like the sun's heat reflecting off a large rock. It is clear to me you are not mature enough to handle them. Not in conjunction with such volatile magic at your disposal."*

A bit indignant, he opened his telepathic mouth to retort. As the past several tics replayed in his mind, however, he found no words. Upon awakening, he had been consumed with the human desires of love and retribution, concepts with which he was wholly unfamiliar. The outlet of those feelings had almost killed him. They had almost killed an innocent bystander.

"Is there no other way?" he asked, knowing what his aunt was alluding to.

"I have a family and pup of my own to care for and raise. I cannot stay in your mind and act as a dam against destructive forces until you learn to integrate them with your feelings. Not having taken on the form, emotions, or memories of a human, I would be little help in guiding you even if I choose to do so," she replied simply, though not without kindness. *"You are my sister's son. Much more, you are of*

the Yokai. You matter a great deal. Another may reside here in Urel who would be able to help you, but the best course of action for you would probably be the route of a field fox."

Myobu gulped at the thought. He was familiar with the concept. The Yokai had the innate ability to set aside their conscious thought and power, whether temporarily or permanently, and become nearly indistinguishable from a normal fox. It was an ability rarely used. Few trusted their instinctual impulses and drives over their reasoned thought processes. The practice was not necessarily looked upon with disapproval. Each Yokai was free to live their life as they saw fit, yet if the Yokai were to be disdainful of anything, it would be lives wasted of possibilities.

However, becoming a field fox for a period of time would allow his body and mind to mature without the burden of his and Kirin's memories and emotions. They would be processed in his subconscious where they posed no threat to others. When his sentience reawakened in the future, they should not overwhelm him.

"I am going to join Maroni in teaching our young one to hunt. If you are still present when we return, I will help you find a new home. If not..." She broke off, clearly emotional in her own right. *"If not, may your journey give you the insight and maturity needed to bring you back home. I will eagerly await your return."*

His mother's littermate turned and disappeared into the underbrush. Her presence in his mind faded as her mental tendrils receded.

Death would come to Myobu before seeing another relation.

*

The way Myobu saw it, there truly was no choice in the matter. If he stayed, something he preferred to do for no better reason than not being alone, he'd regularly walk by the spot on the beach where his parents had been mercilessly slain. That normally would not have made a difference to one of the Yokai. With his inherited feelings, however, he'd be drawn to sadness and anger at the loss of those who loved him most. Those emotions would drive his young mind mad, and he would likely succumb to those feelings and hurt others who would only be attempting to help.

No, he would not let that happen. He would not let his or Kirin's past control him or his future. He would take responsibility for himself. If becoming a field fox would grant him control over the negative emotions, then he could later focus more on their intoxicating counterpart: love. From Kirin's memories of being with the humans, he knew how magnificent it felt to be in love. He wanted to feel that for himself, to take on their form and integrate with them.

Becoming a field fox was no great feat. No physical transformation, and it took no practice to achieve. It was purely mental. Just a conscious decision. Once it began, it was like falling asleep, looking deep within oneself, a darkness swallowing one's mind.

Within five tics of being left alone, Myobu had undergone the conversion. By the time his aunt, Maroni, and their pup returned from their morning hunt, he was off in search of his own breakfast.

*

Over the course of the next century, Myobu was driven by the search for food. Usually small rodents were his preference, but he also ate fruit and insects. He would hunt during the mornings and evenings, roam the lands at night, and find suitable shelter for rest during the days. His Yokai blood interfered at times, keeping him from finding a mate or settling down in a den. Instead, he wandered the lands in solitude.

Throughout the sun cycles, Myobu came and went from Gaav, the tribal lands, Kitsunetsuki, and Odom. On more than one occasion, he traveled perilously far into the Wastelands, a region known to be toxic to organic material. Finding no sources of nutrition there, he always turned back before it was too late. He knew to steer clear of wolves, large birds, and other predators, though he did have the occasional run in with an irritated bear or hungry coyote. He survived everything, though. More importantly, through his experiences of being an ordinary animal, he matured.

Toward the end of this time, Myobu occasionally came out of his field fox shell to test his state of mind. He was unprepared the first time and accidentally caused a small brushfire with his magic. It would have destroyed a small human settlement if not for a nearby river. The second time went better, and he remained fully sentient for three days before receding into his mind again. The third and fourth occurrences, each of which lasted up to several weeks, were spent experimenting with his power, controlling and containing it as he cycled through a multitude of emotions. Conversely, he spent an equal amount of time experimenting, controlling, and containing those same emotions. The more he practiced, the more confident he became. During his fifth period of awakening, he attempted his first true transformation, taking on a basic humanoid form. Much like a child's doll, it was genderless and devoid of character. A true human would have fled in terror, mistaking Myobu for a monster.

After testing his powers and feelings in a completely new form, Myobu became a field fox for the last time, spending the next sun cycle living as a carefree vagabond. When he awoke and rose from the ground in full consciousness, he was in perfect human imitation. Without truly meaning to, he had taken on the features of an individual that had remained with him throughout the past century. Thick black hair framed a heart-shaped face defined by high cheekbones and a strong jaw. He was shorter and skinnier than the average human male, but he still exuded an air of strength.

The human form was not a suitable host for Yokai magic, and most of Myobu's power coalesced into a perfectly smooth red ruby—his hoshi no tama. Not having the material or skill to make a ring or chain to bear his stone like Kirin had done, he simply swallowed it.

Now, before he even opened his dark brown eyes, distant sounds of merriment reached his ears. Myobu turned to locate the source, finding that he was standing precipitously close to the edge of a cliff. Still shaky on two legs, he carefully peered over the side. In the valley below was a vast layout of structures and throughways. The buildings, most of which Myobu presumed to be homes, were modest and well-maintained.

All major roads led to the center of the city where a complex of larger but similar structures were nestled.

Despite never consciously having been here, Myobu knew immediately from Kirin's memories that this was the city of Hawte, capital of Gaav. From where he now stood, he could see the fields the older Yokai had helped till and plant, as well as the river he had surreptitiously siphoned water from.

Myobu was ready and more than eager to dive into the culture and lives of humans. He had control over his emotions and power. The desire for vengeance against the demon was still present, but this had been smothered under layers of reason. As he had hoped, the want for acceptance and love burned inside of him, something he suspected defied all reason. Here among the humans, who were so unabashedly passionate, was the place to begin his journey.

Myobu made his way into the city.

WORK LINES

The chirping of songbirds came from outside the open bedroom window, gently pulling Myobu from contented sleep. He looked over at the window and, through sleepy eyes, watched as dust from the nearby fields floated lazily through streams of golden sunlight. The room was still frigid this early in the morning, but he shared his body warmth with the two others in bed with him.

It was the perfect morning.

Treating himself to a good long stretch, Myobu worked his way up to sitting. With his back against the wooden headboard, he looked down at the pair with whom he had spent the night. Ryn and Nikki owned one of the oldest taverns in Hawte, having belonged to Ryn's family for generations. Myobu had met them not long after arriving in the capital nearly three sun cycles ago. Embarrassingly, Nikki had caught him rifling through the tavern's back alley trash for food. They were a friendly and understanding couple, always willing to help the destitute, and had given him food and temporary shelter. After they had gotten to know and trust him, they offered him a job and a permanent room above the tavern. While he agreed to do the odd job for them now and then for coin, he shied away from relying on the couple for his well-being.

Something else had happened as their friendship grew. Late one night, after helping close up the tavern, they had spent a few hours drinking by the hearth. Ryn and Nikki spoke of their first encounter and subsequent marriage, purportedly a scandalous affair. The two met at a festival and, against both of their parents' wishes, saw each other at any opportunity thereafter. They went to shows, walked the markets, and attended jubilees. They explored each other as much as they explored the city—probably more so, considering they had both grown up in Hawte and knew it like the backs of their hands.

Having lived over a century without ever engaging in sexual activity, Myobu had drunkenly bombarded them with endless questions on the subject. The pair looked at one another, a glimmer of humor and desire in their eyes, and answered his queries physically rather than verbally. Taking him by the hand, they led him upstairs to bed.

If Myobu was to forget all but one thing from that night, he'd always recall the extent to which skin was involved in sex. He'd always considered skin to be just a protective barrier that held in the organs of his body. Never had he thought of it as an organ in and of itself with capabilities beyond shielding his innards. Upon closing the bedroom door, the first thing the couple did was peel off their clothing. Myobu had watched in awe as the differences in their skin were revealed. Ryn was a burly man, and there were few areas on his body not covered in hair. He was paler than many of the men in Hawte, his work indoors keeping him out of the sun. Nikki was dark-skinned and appeared free of any blemishes or extraneous hair.

The two had tugged at Myobu's own clothing, which he sluggishly gave up. He wasn't timid or particularly self-conscious, though he had wondered if the human form he had taken was correct in the details. He possessed all the parts of a man, but he lacked the massive tufts of hair Ryn displayed and was almost as smooth as Nikki. Concerned they would figure out he wasn't actually human, he had contemplated adding hair to his body before they removed his shirt.

In the end, the two hadn't given a second thought to his nearly hairless form. They stripped him naked, looked at him appreciatively, and began running their hands over his body. The dual sensations of Ryn's rougher palms and Nikki's smoother fingertips elicited a gasp from Myobu. Goosebumps broke out over his flesh. It heightened his tactile awareness, dulled his sense of time, and deeply aroused him. He tentatively put a hand on each of their bodies, awkward at first, but easily got into it once he realized his touch elicited the same responses from them.

The room grew warmer as their bodies heated up. It wasn't long before their groping explorations became full-fledged embraces and kissing. As they rubbed against each other, Ryn's hair—especially the stubbly growth on his face—scoured Myobu's skin raw. His own skin, now slippery with sweat, slid easily over Nikki's. They had moved to the bed, climbing and crawling on top of and over each other. One of them grabbed hold of his cock, and the explosion of sensation made him moan loudly. He bit down on his lip, thinking he had growled like a canine, but then heard both of them making similar noises.

Nikki had been the one to grab hold of him. She smiled at him with a knowing look, then slipped his cock into her mouth. He squirmed at the new, wet feeling, and his hips naturally moved back and forth. Turning, he sought Ryn's to see what it felt like to be on the giving end of this act. When his lips had found and wrapped themselves around the other's cock, he discovered he loved it.

Much exploration had occurred that night, both physically and conceptually. Myobu found there was no single act that defined sex, and all three of them had climaxed at least twice through different means. While it was a glorious introduction for him, it must have been quite the exploit for the couple, who were plainly experienced veterans. They continued to invite him to share their bed every few weeks, usually after a few rounds of drinks by the fire.

Myobu enjoyed taking part in these activities with Ryn and Nikki, so much so that he explored similar interactions with other folks throughout the city. He knew it wasn't love, at least not the kind he was looking for. Nothing came close to the memory he had of Kirin looking at his wife and son, so full of happiness, warmth, and belonging. Love was so much more than sex, eclipsing it. As Myobu searched for it, though, he would certainly continue to enjoy these dalliances.

A large pebble flew through the open window, jerking Myobu out of his reverie. The stone missed hitting the wood floor by a finger length, coming to rest on a thick rug. A muttered curse followed from outside.

Slipping unnoticed from between Ryn and Nikki, Myobu padded across the rug. After picking up the pebble, he poked his head out the window to look over the back alley.

"Kensie!" Myobu hissed. "I know you're down there. Come out where I can throw this rock back at you!"

Except for the distant sound of horses and wooden wheels on cobbled streets, there was no response. Hefting the large pebble, Myobu threw it down into the backstreet. His aim was true, and it bounced off the side of a garbage bin. A surprised cry reverberated off the alley walls, and a lanky, brown-haired, boyish man jumped out from behind the container.

"Don't hit me!" Kensie cried out, throwing his arms over his freckled face. Strips of raggedy cloth hung from his limbs, a patchwork of discarded clothing.

"When have I ever hit you?" Myobu asked, leaning lazily against the windowsill. "And why are you throwing rocks through windows?"

"I didn't know it was open!"

Myobu rolled his eyes. "You are as dumb as that rock you threw. What do you want at this ungodly hour?"

"It's midmorning!" Kensie exclaimed. "Not all of us partake in sexual marathons."

"I think you mean not all of us are virgins," Myobu teased. He jerked his thumb back behind him. "I was actually planning on waking them soon. Start this morning off right, you know?"

"Myobu," Kensie whined. "The work line is opening in a few tics!"

"Oh," he breathed, eyes opening wide. The night had been so intense, he forgot all about that. "I'll be down in a tic. Wait for me!"

On his hands and knees, Myobu sought his scattered clothing. He smoothed them out as best he could as he found them, thankful he had scrubbed them clean only two days ago. The folks in charge of the work lines appreciated respectable-looking applicants.

Despite the success of the Hawte experiment centuries ago, a significant number of unemployed and homeless individuals lived in the capital of Gaav. To help combat this, city officials created several work line programs. They rarely provided full-time employment but did help participants gain skills and experience they could later use, not to mention coin with which to provide themselves with food and shelter.

When openings were available, work line operators would set up tables on the sides of the roads. Sometimes there would be one or two queues. On rare occasions, there'd be up to a dozen. Even then, the lines would weave down the road and around corners. Tensions could be high among those waiting their turn, especially as the longer queues became a disorganized mess, but fists were rarely made and teeth almost never lost.

Gaav's royal family operated one of these work lines, providing opportunities in construction, food services, and security during times of expansion or visits from foreign diplomats. Wages were usually generous. Because of this, these queues were especially long. Through charm and having built an excellent reputation with the line's operators, Myobu could usually secure a good position. He had built up quite a stockpile of coin, though no one would know by his homeless status.

It was to one of these work lines he and Kensie were now headed. A diplomatic envoy from Kitsunetsuki was due to arrive in four days. Help was needed to prepare, deliver, and clean up after the festivities and functions.

"Tod is already in line holding a place for us," Kensie said as Myobu stepped out into the back alley. Myobu tossed him an apple nicked from the kitchen.

"Then what's the big hurry?" Myobu replied, taking a bite out of his breakfast. He was careful to keep the fruit's juices from dripping onto his shirt.

"He's near the front, and you know they give out particular jobs on a first come, first served basis. All we have to do is meet the requirements. If you want a specific placement, you need to be one of the first in line." Kensie, already halfway down the alley, began walking even faster than his usual jittery, quick pace. He anxiously glanced over his shoulder. "Besides, I really hate the glares other people give when we step in front of them."

"It's not really cheating the queue if Tod is saving our place," Myobu said, attempting to calm Kensie. Inwardly, he appreciated his friend's propensity for not drawing attention to themselves. It was something he strove for while simultaneously experiencing humanity. Humans, he had discovered over the last few sun cycles, loved attention. Good, bad, salacious, or virtuous. It didn't matter so long as it was their name being spoken.

This morning, he was hoping to receive positive attention from the line operators. As Kensie had suggested, there was a specific position he was hoping to get. One that could bring illumination to a question that had been nagging at him.

Myobu picked up his pace to keep stride with his friend.

Kensie and Tod were the first two individuals Myobu had interacted with the night he had walked into Hawte. They had been sitting around a small fire in an alley much less sanitary than the one behind Ryn and Nikki's place. Kensie's pale, freckled face stood out in the light of their fire. Tod, with skin as dark as his friend's was fair, could have slipped unnoticed into the shadows.

As Myobu had stepped into the light, Kensie jumped up in surprise and hid behind the largest pile of garbage. Tod, after a casual glance at the newcomer, said in a rather gruff voice, "There's a blanket here if you'd like to cover up."

It was then Myobu had noticed he was completely naked. He was neither ashamed nor embarrassed by this. Why would he be? He'd spent the entirety of his life without clothing.

As Myobu had wrapped himself in the offered blanket, he had assumed Tod's gruff voice was due to discomfort at the sudden appearance of a naked man. It was soon evident Tod was just a gruff individual. Not that he wasn't friendly in his own right. By the end of that night, he had accepted Myobu as a friend. Tod provided him with a set of clothing—or rather, convinced Kensie to give up one of his own—and introduced him to the work lines the following morning.

Myobu remained close with the two over the sun cycles. Many citizens, whether they were homeless or wealthy, were not trustworthy or had malice in their hearts. Kensie and Tod, much like Ryn and Nikki, were honest and reliable. They would help each other in times of need, providing protection, food, and rumors of potential opportunities for work. Being his first human acquaintances, they meant a lot to him, and he cherished their continued company.

*

"Fucking the tavern folk again, weren't you?" Tod rightfully accused as Myobu and Kensie strode up to him. He sounded as bad-tempered as always, but Myobu saw one of his eyelids lower in what may have been an involuntary wink.

Myobu gave only a sly smile in response, trying to keep a low profile. Despite knowing they hadn't stepped randomly into the queue, others behind them didn't necessarily see it that way. A few angry glances were directed at them, which spiked Kensie's anxious gesticulations.

"Calm yourself," Myobu said tranquilly, allowing a smidgeon of magic into his voice. His friend's fidgeting slowed, but did not abate altogether. He doubted it ever would.

Myobu had refrained from using his powers as much as possible, believing it would interfere with his experiencing humanity. He had spent many a frosty night shivering in the gutters, refusing to perform even the simple task of creating fire. He had somewhat relaxed his self-imposed policy during the past winter when even those with four walls and a roof perished from hypothermia. Reasoning that he couldn't enjoy the humans if they weren't around, he had spent days discreetly starting fires in hearths and trash bins across the capital.

Only occasionally, such as now, would Myobu interfere with the flow of events purely because he wanted something. He knew exactly what he desired today, and he wouldn't let Kensie's fretful behavior or Tod's crass words get him escorted out of the line by city guards.

Moving forward a few steps, Myobu looked up at the tables at the head of each queue. Tod really had gotten a great place in line, and he could already see the operators. He recognized a couple of them and was thankful the woman at the head of his particular queue had always seemed to favor him in the past. He was about to wrestle with the ethical dilemma of using his magic to persuade her to give him the position he wanted, but a conversation in the next queue over caught his attention.

"Do you think it's true," a middle-aged woman asked the person behind her, "that Prince Oni is the head of Kitsunetsuki's diplomatic envoy?"

"Oh, I doubt it," crooned the queue mate, another woman who appeared to be twice the age of the first. "I hear he's to be wed. He'll be too busy honeymooning to bother with foreign relations."

The Kitsunetsuki Kingdom was Gaav's eastern neighbor. Formed nearly a millennium ago, its founding citizens had been so enamored with the Yokai they had created an entire religion around them that eventually spread throughout the lands. Its very name, Kitsunetsuki, was a word that meant *to be inhabited by a fox*. Probably an attempt to draw what they considered to be mystical spirits to them. Their capital and the royal residence, Oinari and Inari Palace respectively, were in fact references to the ideals the Yokai themselves revered and followed.

"You don't think any of their royals will come?" The younger woman did not seem enthused at the notion of Prince Oni being wed. He was widely known for being an extremely handsome man.

"Don't be silly, child," the elder said, causing the other to look briefly abashed. "It's just a renegotiation of trade agreements that've been in effect for two hundred sun cycles. The only diplomats they'll be sending will be old wizened ones about to retire. You won't be breaking up any weddings…though I might be."

Myobu almost chuckled at the elder's innuendo, but the next comment made his breath catch in his throat.

"But Ninko is rumored to be attending, and he obviously doesn't show up for just any old affair."

"Fair point," the older woman conceded. "I've heard those same whisperings. We're just going to have to wait another couple of days for the convoy to arrive and the festivities to begin."

Ninko was one of the king's closest and most mysterious advisors. Strangely, Ninko was not the true name of the man the two women were speaking of. Rather, it referred to the advisory council *position* the man occupied. The office went back centuries, and only a Yokai was supposed to serve in its capacity.

Myobu found the entire practice somewhat ironic. To the Yokai, those who possessed the unique gift of invisibility were referred to as ninkos. Most other species could only perceive such a creature if it took mental control over their mind, essentially possessing them.

Those who held the Ninko title rarely made public appearances, and not all of Gaav's leaders had the position filled. The monarchs who declared themselves atheists refused to give credence to old religions. Others did not have time for the sage, peaceful advice usually offered by Ninko, choosing instead to pursue militaristic border expansion. A king or queen occasionally wished to fill the office, but no one was present that met the qualifications.

The notorious lack of visibility over the ages had naturally led to rumors among the populace that it was all a farce, that perhaps only other humans had been granted the title. Still, the effects of the office had always been felt if someone was there to use it—or possess it.

"If he does attend, do you think he'll display his magic?" the middle-aged woman said.

"No Ninko has ever displayed his or her magic for the people. It's for the eyes of the royals only," the other replied, though there was a hint of hope in her voice.

According to lore, one of the Yokai spirits fell in love with a queen of Gaav. The love was unrequited, but his feelings were so strong he would not leave her court. He protected her from harm and used his magic for her benefit, but it was the advice he gave in nearly all matters that was legendary. Upon her death, his sorrow was so great he took his own life. Due to the success and popularity of her reign, the queen's successor sought a replacement, making it a tradition.

Myobu knew from Kirin's memories that the story did not entirely reflect reality. The office was borne of blood, death, and tragedy, not love. Still, while the Yokai were known for being illusive and private, they could form strong bonds with members of other species like the characters in the myth. Myobu was but another example, living in Hawte in search of a personal connection with another living being.

Whether everyone who had taken the title of Ninko was of the Yokai, he couldn't say. It was his goal, second only to finding love, to determine if the current Ninko was, in fact, a Yokai. It had been so long since he'd conversed with one of his own kind.

"Next!" called the line operator at the head of his queue. Tod, who was technically next in line, was making light of something Kensie had said and waved Myobu forward. The line operator looked tired, and he wished he had brought a cup of coffee with him. Still, her face brightened when she recognized him. "How are you doing, dear?"

"It's too early to be conscious," he replied, giving her a sympathetic smile. "I can't believe they have you out here at this hour."

"Oh, if I wasn't here, I'd still be up doing something," she said, sifting through a pile of parchment on the table.

"Anything available in the kitchens?" he asked, trying to head her off. He had worked that station several times before, having always been commended for his efforts, and didn't think it would be an issue getting placed there again. Security was usually tight while food was being prepared, but it relaxed considerably after meals had been served. His plan was to slip out of the kitchens, find his way to Ninko's residence, somehow quench his curiosity regarding the man's history, and make it back before his absence was noticed.

"Sorry, dear," the woman replied. "You aren't meant for the kitchens this week."

Myobu's heart sank. His entire plan had hinged on that placement.

"Don't you fret," she continued, still searching through her pile of papers. "I've actually got something else entirely for you."

"Huh?" was all he could manage. That was highly unusual. The line operators were forbidden from playing favorites.

The woman leaned toward him and lowered her voice. "This is unrelated to the diplomatic envoy. It is actually a permanent position within the royal court."

Myobu sputtered in protestation. The last thing he wanted was to be tied down.

"Ninko came to me personally," she continued, piquing his interest. He ceased his objections and listened attentively. "He's looking for an assistant. Asked if I knew anyone who was trustworthy, intelligent, and well-connected, yet relatively unknown. I thought of you immediately. Most of the street folk here in Hawte know you. They would be your connections. Yet, we mere line operators are probably the most well-off citizens that know your name."

Myobu decided not to mention Ryn and Nikki or any of the other well-off citizens who not only knew his name, but sometimes screamed it out loud in pleasure. "You thought of me based on that criteria? Surely there are others more qualified."

"I was given other descriptors," the woman replied, sighing with impatience. She finally found the document she was looking for. "The candidate had to be thoughtful and kind. Mostly generic stuff you'd want from any help. The more Ninko spoke, though, the more I believed you'd be perfect for the position. You don't have to accept, but I'd highly encourage you to meet with him. Now take this parchment here and see one of the city guards at either end of the tables."

"Now?" Myobu nearly cried out as she pushed the paper into his hands. He glanced to his right where a group of men and women clad in golden armor stood.

"Now. Tomorrow. I don't care," she said with exasperation, clearly caring. "Just don't make me look bad! Next in line!"

Tod shot him a questioning glance as he stepped up to the table, running a rough hand through unruly black hair. Myobu gestured to a side street, indicating he'd wait there for him and Kensie.

The invitation was simultaneously complimentary and troublesome. He always tried his best to stay on the good side of anyone he encountered, not just the line operators. Such behavior had proven beneficial in the past, and it was also a way of being thankful to the humans as they unwittingly furthered his experience among them. Despite this, it had always been his intention to remain on the fringe. That was why he refused permanent work or settling down in an actual home. If he had to leave Hawte for any reason, he wanted his departure to have little to no impact on anyone. The depth of his immersion into the culture had clearly skewed that intention, however. It dawned upon him now that, best friends and multiple regular lovers aside, he made an impression. This line operator, a woman whose name he didn't even know, had thought him trustworthy, intelligent, and kind. She had thought so highly of him that she recommended him to a respected member of the royal court.

The best course of action would be to ignore the invitation. He did not need to be a permanent fixture in the lives of others, especially anyone so close to the king! Tearing up the parchment would ensure his vagabond nature. She would certainly not risk her own reputation by recommending him again.

Except Myobu couldn't do that. It was in his nature to please others, and he couldn't bear the thought of disappointing his benefactor by not following through. Besides, she herself had said he didn't have to accept. He could simply explain to Ninko that being his assistant—anyone's assistant—would be too much for him to handle. Yes, following through with the invitation would surely be the best avenue to answer his question. He could uncover the man's background, determine if he was truly a Yokai, and then leave.

"What was all that about?" growled Tod as he and a rather elated-looking Kensie came around the corner. "It shouldn't take any more than a tic to get your assignment, and you were clearly exasperating that woman."

"She tried to give me latrine duty," Myobu lied. He hated doing so. It always made him feel horrible. Under the circumstances, he thought it best not to relay the offer of permanent work. Not all the homeless were vagrants by choice. "I hate latrine duty."

"Hey!" Kensie called out defensively. "That's what I got! I don't mind it though. You've no idea how much coin people accidentally lose in a latrine."

"I'm in the kitchens again," Tod put in after throwing Kensie a look of disgust. "Apparently, my lentil soup is known even to the royal family."

"Yeah, that it kills people," Kensie retorted, taking a step back in anticipation of receiving a physical jab. "They must intend to assassinate the envoy!"

"What did you end up getting, Myobu?" Tod said, ignoring his friend.

"A member of the royal court needs some assistance," he replied. "It's preferred I report in today. Probably an elder needing help to prepare for the festivities."

"But it's the end of the week!" Kensie protested, the loose pieces of clothing flying about as he waved his arms in protest.

Despite not having regular work, or perhaps because of it, the week's end was always something to look forward to. Many of those with disposable coin loved to spend it at taverns. Full bellies and mild intoxication tended to make people more generous and wasteful.

"I'm seeing a member of the royal court. I think I'll be fine." Myobu hoped, even after turning down a long-term opportunity, that Ninko would still offer him some kind of recompense for showing up. "Assuming this is only for today, that means I have free rein of the city while you two are slaving away!"

"If you want to get there at a decent hour, you'd better be on your way," Tod growled, pointing to the main street. It was midmorning now, and even those who enjoyed a good sleep in were awake and making their way outdoors. It wouldn't be long before the streets were filled with horses, shoppers, and those making their weekly round of the city taverns.

"Fair point. I'll find you two later," Myobu said, turning toward the street. At the work line, he handed the parchment over to the nearest guard. The metal-clad woman glanced over the paper, looked him up and down quizzically, then indicated he should follow her.

Despite the growing crowds in the streets, it only took a few tics to reach the center of the city. Folks knew to make way for the guards, especially when they appeared to be walking at a brisk pace. Myobu followed along easily, ignoring the questioning looks others threw his way. Anticipation built within him. Not from the crowds, but at how close he was to having his questions answered.

The two passed through a gate into the royal complex. Myobu looked around in interest, but he saw nothing out of the ordinary. For now, other than the usual gardeners putting some extra efforts into the plants they tended, all was quiet. It wouldn't be long before the grounds were alive with activity to prepare for the envoy.

The woman led Myobu down the primary avenue of the compound, passing by several administrative structures. Thinking he'd meet Ninko in his official office, Myobu was mildly surprised when they continued down the road into the residential section. Unlike other kingdoms, whose leaders lived together in giant castles or fortresses, theirs preferred more modest accommodations. They might be the heads of state, but that did not make them better than anyone else.

Myobu preferred leaders who could truly sympathize and live among their subjects.

At the head of the street was the king and queen's home. It was slightly larger and sturdier than the other buildings around it, but it was otherwise indistinguishable. The house to its right was that of Ninko.

Handing the parchment back to Myobu, the guard motioned him to the door. "Just knock."

And knock he did, his heart beating ardently, and he pushed open the door when a muffled voice called for him to enter.

Stepping into the home, Myobu was struck by how open and austere it was. The royals were not known for cluttering their homes and offices with frivolous items. They indulged themselves with larger rooms, taller windows, and colorful draperies, but otherwise preferred to keep it simple—an ode to their previously nomadic generations. This place took the meaning of sparsity a step farther. The windows were large, yes, but there were no drapes or even additional walls that humans usually erected for privacy. It was like a giant, well-lit cavern with only the most basic furnishings. A tidy bed was in one corner, a few chests for storage in another, and a simple table and chairs in the center.

In front of one window stood a figure, presumably Ninko. He was dressed in fine robes of red and black, the colors of high rank, and was leaning on a carved wooden staff. His long, unruly black hair was visibly creased from a headdress that now lay forgotten on the table.

"Are you him?" Myobu said, stepping forward. He knew he was being disrespectful, but his excitement was getting the better of him. "Are you Ninko?"

The man stiffened and dropped the wooden staff in apparent surprise. He turned slowly, revealing a middle-aged man with a well-groomed mustache and goatee. Myobu's jaw dropped when he recognized the man from his distant past.

Ninko was Kirin.

"No, it can't be you. It's not possible," Kirin responded. The look of pain and anguish on his face unsettled Myobu, reminding him of the terrible situation under which the two had met. "My son. My sweet son, Acro."

BECOMING NINKO

Myobu stood frozen in the middle of the room, his mouth agape. For the first time, he considered the form he had taken two sun cycles ago before striding into Hawte. Having never interacted with an actual human, his only frames of reference were the memories Kirin had passed to him. In taking on the guise of someone age appropriate, at least mentally, Myobu must have identified with the recollection of Acro.

"No," Myobu admitted, the excitement and energy at confronting Ninko having drained from his voice. He held up his hands, though he wasn't sure if it was a peaceful or defensive gesture. "No, I am not Acro. I am so sorry, Kirin. I had no idea what I was doing when I took this shape."

The agony partially subsided from Kirin's eyes. Myobu supposed the pain of losing one's entire family might always be present. Raising his head, the older man sniffed the air cautiously. Then, his stiff posture relaxing, he said, "I never thought I would see my son again, and the same goes for you, Myobu."

"I can't imagine how upsetting this must be. It was most disrespectful of me. I will change my form immediately," Myobu offered. This would disrupt his entire existence and livelihood in the capital. Taking on a new persona would require leaving all his current friends and relationships behind and creating new ones. He had his stockpile of coin to help, but it would be hard ignoring his history with Kensie and Tod.

Thankfully, Myobu's future was not meant to be so tumultuous.

"Stay as you are, my young friend," Kirin replied. He bent and picked his staff off the floor. "Kelli sent you from the work line, correct?"

Myobu blinked in brief confusion, having completely forgotten about the reason he'd been sent. He mentally noted the woman's name. "Yes, that is why I am here."

"I gave Kelli a strict set of parameters for the type of person I was looking for. While I did not expect her to find a match for some time, she immediately thought of a single individual who met or exceeded the requirements. If her idea of you is truth, Myobu, you are honoring the memory of my son by taking his form."

Touched, Myobu nodded in appreciation. "You have my gratitude. I hope I continue to do him and you proud."

"I certainly hope so," Kirin said under his breath. He offered Myobu a seat in one of the chairs at the center of the room, sitting down himself.

"How do you mean? And how is it you are again Gaav's Ninko?" Myobu asked. He remembered Kirin promising his services to the king, but that he had left following the tragedy that had befallen his family. He had only the slimmest recollection, the faintest of thoughts, that Kirin meant to return to Gaav after hiding Tsukumogami. Still, that had been over a hundred sun cycles ago.

Kirin saw Myobu had recalled the details. "I hid the sword that slew your parents. As far as I know, I am still one of three souls in the world who knows the location. Kyubi is aware, naturally."

"Kyubi?"

Kirin relaxed in such a way Myobu knew the man had found love again. "Kyubi is one of our kind. Possibly one of the oldest living Yokai in the region, though you did not hear that from me. I spoke of her to you once before, referring to her as the Harbinger. It is a name she has earned, as she has a penchant for answering any question posed to her by visitors. Whether they appreciate the answers is another thing altogether."

Myobu knew as the Yokai grew older, their powers and wisdom increased. This was visibly evident by the number of tails a Yokai had in its natural fox state. The oldest known individuals had nine tails, and they were able to sense and understand everything that occurred around the world.

"I found a kindred spirit in Kyubi," Kirin continued. "We were both broken souls. Deep-rooted cynical outlooks, though each with our own spark of hope for the future. After we concealed Tsukumogami, the two of us spent many a sun cycle together, enjoying each other's company and mending our mental wounds. We tried to produce our own offspring, but it wasn't meant to be at our age. Perhaps that was for the best."

"Is that why you are no longer together?" Myobu asked, trying not to sound insensitive.

"No, of course not," Kirin responded, though his face sagged. "Kyubi told me I had a purpose to fulfill, and that I had to return to Hawte. She would not reveal to me what I was to do or when this purpose was clear, only that I would know when it did. I admit I begged her to let me stay, but she tossed me out of our den and announced I could only return after my destiny had been fulfilled. So I returned to Hawte and have remained here for nearly eighty sun cycles, serving under two queens and the current king. That is not a long time for the Yokai, but it is for anyone with a limited amount of time. I had about given up until you walked through my door."

"Given up?" Myobu shook his head, confused. While Kirin was much older than himself, he was far from elderly. Easily had a couple hundred sun cycles left in him. Then the man's last words struck him. "Wait…you think I am your destiny?"

Kirin held up a hand. "I am not as old or as wise as Kyubi, and I do not put as much stock in purpose or destiny as she does. My love for her is what has kept me here, not a supposed reason for my existence. Still, I would have appreciated seeing things as she does."

Myobu noticed for the first time the staff Kirin clung to was not a theatrical prop of the position he held, but a necessity. He said, "You are dying."

"A result of my brief time carrying Tsukumogami, I'm afraid." Kirin shifted uncomfortably in his seat. "It is a tool truly meant for those few with dual specializations. I was unaware of its effect on those who did not qualify. The effort to keep it hidden is, in the end, quite worth the price. The consequences of it falling back into the demon's hands would have been far worse than my death."

"I am sorry." Myobu couldn't help but feel responsible. It had been he who Kirin saved that morning on the beach.

Kirin dismissed the apology. "It was not you who had the sword there to begin with. If anyone other than the demon is to be blamed, it is Kyubi for sending me to Urel. I would trade none of my encounters with her for anything, however. In fact, I have been preparing to leave Gaav soon to spend my final days with her."

"Giving up on your destiny," Myobu said, realizing now what the other had meant.

"Or so I had thought. My goal with Kelli was to find a potential successor to the Ninko title before I left. I did not really believe I'd find another Yokai to fill the position. Between my stints, the office was often filled by humans with a gift for illusion. But then you…are here."

What Kirin was indicating finally hit Myobu, and he was dumbfounded. The sheer magnitude of the offer was astounding, as were its consequences. He would almost rather change his appearance. It would be less disruptive. "You want me to take your place as Ninko?"

"If it wouldn't be too much of an imposition to you." Kirin gave a wry smile. "At least until *you* would be able to find a proper replacement for yourself."

This was exactly what Myobu did not want—a job that would tie him down, preventing him from finding that ultimate emotional connection with another. Expectations would be placed upon him. People would count on his knowledge and wisdom…as if he had any! With others knowing he was of the Yokai, he would be treated differently, altering the way he enjoyed the human experience.

What would my friends think of me? Myobu thought, nearly panic-stricken.

But how could he say no to the man who saved his life? The one who had given him a purpose and reason to live, to seek and find love? Looking into Kirin's hopeful, lovelorn, and sickly face, Myobu knew his fate had been sealed the moment he had entered the house.

"Perfect!" Kirin exclaimed when Myobu nodded his assent. "Training begins at once."

*

Despite Kirin's enthusiasm, little was accomplished that day before he was called away at the king's request. That was just as well, as Myobu was soon overwhelmed with new information. His life was about to be turned upside down, though not all aspects of it caused him anxiety.

His homeless status was to end, as the sparse home in which he had found Kirin would be turned over to him. Many of his days would be spent sitting through meetings with the king and his council, advising them in areas in which he felt qualified. More specifically, as the Yokai had a keen understanding of the natural world, he was to help direct the country's agricultural advances and budding industries that took advantage of their natural resources.

Initially fearing he would be forced to withdraw from the rest of society, he was pleased when informed otherwise. Ninko had been a mysterious office, shrouded with intrigue, superstition, and lore, but that was because Kirin and others who had taken the mantle preferred it that way. Myobu would be allowed to take it in new directions and initiate new programs if he wished, and he was more than welcome to maintain his relationships. The royal family thought no less of people like Kensie and Tod than they did those like Ryn and Nikki.

While Myobu thought Ryn and Nikki and others like them could go on believing in the character he had created since coming to the capital, he felt coming clean to Tod and Kensie would be the right thing to do. They were the closest semblance to a family he had, and to pretend he was homeless while being Ninko would be next to impossible. He waited patiently at their most recent back alley hideaway for their return from their latest begging endeavors. It must have gone well, aided by the pleasant fall weather, for the two were both in good spirits. They engaged in simple conversation for a few tics before the topic of Myobu's day came up.

"I wasn't entirely honest with you this morning," he admitted. "I was requested by a member of the royal court, but I knew exactly who I was to see."

The two stared at him expectantly from across the flames of the small fire they huddled around. Running his fingers nervously through his thick, dark hair, Myobu took a deep breath and continued.

"Ninko had asked Kelli, the work line operator we saw this morning, to send him a specific kind of person. She thought of me. It was Ninko I met with today."

"Codswallop," Tod grunted, picking grit out of his teeth. He had never subscribed to the religious fascination with the Yokai, and he had often expressed his doubt they actually existed.

"What kind of specific qualifications did Kelli think you met?" Kensie said, taking a bite out of a hunk of cheese he'd scavenged from the trash. With a nervous giggle, he added, "Dirt-covered sexual scoundrel?"

"He was hoping to discover another member of the Yokai race to take over the position for him."

Tod harrumphed, flicking a piece of dislodged gristle from his teeth to the ground, and Kensie gave a high-pitched laugh, as though Myobu's statement was the funniest thing he'd ever heard. When the pair looked back at him, though, their jaws went slack in shock. The bit of cheese Kensie had just bitten off fell out of his mouth, landing next to Tod's gristle.

Where their friend had just been sitting was a reddish-brown fox, draped in Myobu's dirty, ragged clothing.

"Cursed spirits," Tod whispered, his bloodshot eyes as wide as Myobu had ever seen them. "Don't tell me I've been wrong all this time."

Kensie muttered something incomprehensible, shrugging as though rationalizing something to himself.

Myobu transformed himself back into the likeness of Acro just slowly enough that he could fit his arms and legs into his clothes. Once he looked fully human again, he said, "Ninko had hoped for one of the Yokai, and Kelli handed him one without even knowing it."

Tod repeated his curse, though resignedly. He gazed down at his callused hands, looking like he wanted something tangible to appear with which he could focus his attention. Kensie had scrambled back behind a garbage bin, quick as a rat. He peeked his head out tentatively.

"What did he do to Myobu? Did he kill him?" Kensie squealed, looking at Tod. Then, turning to Myobu, "Did you eat him?"

"Sit down, you fool," Tod said, pointing at the log his friend had just vacated. "This is Myobu. He's just...a little different than we imagined. Like when you discovered I had a boil on my ass."

"You got that boil from sitting in the same dirty clothes for too long," Kensie argued. "Myobu...well, he's wearing skin. Human skin!"

For a moment, Myobu thought his friend was saying something profound and metaphorical. Realizing Kensie was being quite literal, he assured him the skin, the shape itself, was all him. He briefly considered explaining how he had come by Acro's likeness, but ultimately decided that would be too confusing.

"You really are of the Yokai?" Kensie said, taking a tentative seat back on his log.

"Of course he's of the Yokai. You think a human looking like him could seduce half the city?" Tod said with a wink. For having his disbelief in the species proven incorrect so suddenly, he was taking the situation quite calmly.

"I want you both to know I've never used my magic to manipulate, steal, or take advantage of you two," Myobu said, relieved his two friends were still with him by the fire. Kensie may have panicked, but he had half expected both of them to go running into the dark with fear. Those who knew of the Yokai, even if just the lore behind the species, knew them to be tricksters. In particular, the yako caused misfortune to others for their own amusement. "I have rarely used my magic at all, preferring to live as you do."

The pair leaned forward, saying in unison, "Magic?"

None of them got any sleep that night. Instead, Myobu patiently and honestly answered all their questions, of which there were an abundance. Where did he come from? What were the Yokai like? Why was he in Hawte? What kind of powers did he have, and why did he not use them?

Several questions could not be answered. Not concretely, at least. He knew what most Yokai were capable of, but there was much he had never performed or practiced to any great degree. For example, he had never created a dreamscape in the mind of another. At most, he had used his ability to control fire to help others on wintry nights.

"Unbelievable!" Kensie said after Myobu demonstrated his specialization by making their makeshift campfire quadruple in size, transform into a sphere, and then return to its previous state. "How many nights have we needlessly shivered through?"

Myobu admitted that, despite the display, he was rather incompetent with his own magic. "Aside from maintaining this human shape, I don't really practice. Imagine it's like a muscle, and I don't flex mine very much."

"With that kind of thinking, either of us could actually be a Yokai," Kensie joked, slapping an unamused Tod on the shoulder. The two could understand what Myobu was getting at, that he wasn't an all-powerful being manipulating the world around him to his will. Any remaining anxiety they harbored disappeared.

"You may not use your magic much, but I can only guess at how you must have helped us out a time or two without our knowing," Tod said, his knuckles cracking as he flexed his fingers. "For that, we thank you. And don't think we will expect any favors from you now that we know the truth."

"Come again?" Kensie said, looking aghast. "We've got to have some kind of benefit from keeping him around. He might convince a lady to lift her skirt for me!"

"Like you'd know what you were looking at!" Myobu retorted.

Tod picked up a small log and tossed it into the fire. Turning serious, he asked, "What are you going to do about Ninko?"

The relief of his friend's acceptance had been so great that Myobu had nearly forgotten all about his new future. In truth, he wished he had clued them in on his abilities ages ago. Now that he had, he wanted nothing more than to continue his vagabond ways. He wouldn't recant on his word to Kirin, though that didn't mean the decision was forever.

"I will become the next Ninko," he conceded, watching his friends' eyes go wide again in wonder. He understood what they were thinking, what they were seeing: a scrawny boy from the streets suddenly attaining one of the most prestigious offices in the kingdom. "I'll take it, though only long enough to find another to take it from me."

"Don't discount yourself or what you will do for Gaav," Tod said, picking his words carefully. "You were always meant to make an impact. I've known that since the day you stumbled naked into our alley. But know this: Ninko or not, magical fox creature or plain old human, we are your friends. And we aren't going anywhere. Besides, you still owe Kensie a set of clothing!"

*

After rubbing the sleep from his eyes early the next morning, Myobu headed to Kirin's home. Surprisingly, he was given immediate and unquestioned admittance to the royal complex. The city guards already knew him by sight. His old friend, who apparently thrived in the morning hours, chipperly demanded he take a bath.

"We are having breakfast with King Yava," Kirin said, handing Myobu a towel. "He may not surround himself with luxuries like other kings in this world, but one does not walk into his home after sleeping in a trash heap."

"I slept *next to* a trash heap, not *in* one," he replied, though he took to the bath graciously. He hadn't cleaned up since before his night with Ryn and Nikko, and that had been a very strenuous encounter.

Next to the bathtub was a set of clothing nicer than anything Myobu had ever worn. It wasn't something a monarch would wear, but the materials were fine enough that most citizens had better things on which to spend their coin. He briefly wondered if they had belonged to Acro, but quickly discounted that idea. Kirin would not have hauled items throughout the region out of sentimentality. Not for over a century, at least.

"Much better," Kirin said when Myobu emerged from the bathroom. The older man moved as though he wanted to ruffle Myobu's dark brown hair, then thought better of it and headed toward the front door. "Let's go see the king."

Kirin led him not to the administrative offices, but across the lawn to the home of the king and queen. Just as the exterior was similar to the surrounding buildings, the interior was laid out in a familiar fashion. Unlike Ninko's home, theirs was filled with furniture, decorations, and mementos. Much of it signified their culture's history, the importance of their family, and the role they took in shaping not just their own kingdom's future, but that of the entire region.

"Good morning, my lord," Kirin said after they were ushered into a private office at the back of the residence. A fireplace was built into the far wall, and tea was brewing over a small flame. The smell of fresh biscuits and honey filled the air. "I wish to introduce you to Myobu. I spoke of him briefly yesterday. He is to be my replacement."

"I remember, of course," King Yava said, downing the remainder of tea in his cup. He stood up quickly, if not a bit shaky, and held his hand out toward Myobu. "I'm old, not senile. It is good to meet you, my boy. Your arrival is most timely."

Though he laughed inwardly at being called 'boy' by a man who was at least two decades younger than himself, Myobu kept quiet. Yava had clearly cut an imposing figure in his younger days. The way he held himself was not a posture of self-importance, but self-assured strength and determination. Much of the muscle those attributes had helped build, however, had wasted away, and not all from growing old.

Kirin was not the only one who was dying.

"Is it necessary that Prince Marauxus attend this meeting?" Kirin asked, looking warily at a fourth individual sitting in the corner.

Myobu recognized the prince immediately, having seen him during numerous social or political functions, though never this close. Like most citizens of Gaav, he had short, dark hair, and he'd inherited his father's physique. Next in line to the throne, he was known for eschewing royal traditions and running away into the wilderness for days at a time. Many thought this childish, but Myobu was intrigued by the behavior. Marauxus was aged mid-twenties, well past his childhood. The man loved being outdoors, appreciated the warmth of the sun and the guidance of starlight, and embraced the legacy of his people.

Now, though, the prince had a somber look on his face.

"I may be king, but that has not kept me from aging. Nor has it exempted me from the ailments and setbacks that come with it," Yava said, confirming Myobu's suspicions. "My son is here because he will take my crown sooner than either of us would like, and he should know what is transpiring here."

Kirin nodded obediently, though Myobu could feel the news had been a blow to him. Ninko was an advisor, but the two had probably developed a friendship over the sun cycles. Each man's deterioration had weighed so heavily upon them they had not noticed the other's.

Leaning forward, Marauxus said, "I believe in the Yokai, Kirin…and my father assures me you are genuinely one of them." He turned his head to Myobu. "However, I don't know you."

Reaching a hand out to the fire, Myobu allowed his own irritation toward the prince to excite the element. Perhaps too much, as flames engulfed the tea pot and licked outward over the table. The prince jumped up, hovering protectively over his father, though the king laughed at the show.

"My apologies," Myobu said, smothering the sarcasm in his voice. "I am a bit out of practice."

"Fire," Marauxus said, nodding in respect. "You could probably control the sun if you wished."

"I expect the succession of the throne to my son will go unchallenged in the usual ritualistic manner," Yava said, picking up another biscuit. "How do you want to handle the transition of your office? How should we inform the people?"

"I will teach Myobu all that can be taught, but his advice to you and Marauxus will be based upon his own life and experiences," Kirin replied, finally taking a seat. Myobu followed suit, trying not to make his grab for a biscuit and honey too obvious. "As for the public… Perhaps it is best not to thrust too many new officials upon them within a brief span of time."

Myobu was busy brushing crumbs off his new clothes when he realized all eyes had turned to him. "You want me to…what, take on your form?"

"You could think of it as a tradition between yourself and members of my family," Kirin said, giving a slight smile. "We wouldn't insist you do so, but it would help ease the minds of the people if one of their most auspicious officials was there to assist a new king."

"But you're so old!" Myobu exclaimed. He gave a nod, though, indicating he agreed with the assessment.

"He's got cheek! I like him already," the king said. Then he grew serious. Even Marauxus, who seemed to have taken affront to the notion he'd require any help when he inherited the throne, leaned forward. "Now, I want to be sure Myobu here is briefed on our eastern concerns."

"Kitsunetsuki?" Myobu asked. Then, thinking of the land on the opposite side of their neighbor, added, "Or Odom?"

"Our relations with both kingdoms are in good standing," Yava said. "Patriarch Kirby has recently taken over duties from his mother, who is unfortunately suffering from dementia. King Gailey of Kitsunetsuki, like me, has enjoyed many sun cycles. A good man, though I am concerned with his son, Oni, who is next in line. His persona is diplomatic, and his people currently hold in him high regard. However, we can't discern his policies; what direction he will take the kingdom once ascending the throne. And our spies have reported some erratic behavior."

"Such as?"

"He'll disappear from their capital, Oinari, taking inexplicable trips throughout the region. Irritates the hell out of Gailey and his wife Veranda. No one knows where he goes. Our own trackers can't keep up with him."

Myobu glanced over at Marauxus, who only stared back as if challenging him to compare the two princes' behavior.

"Also, there are the reports of demon activity," Kirin said. He gave a sudden dry cough. The king poured him a cup of tea, which he accepted graciously.

"It's been nearly two decades since the last attack," Yava said as though dismissing the issue.

"I know. I was in Oinari at the time as part of a diplomatic envoy," Kirin replied. "After examining the victims and the attack site, I confirmed it had been done by a demon. Our demon."

The older Yokai gave Myobu a knowing look. Memories from that night a century ago flooded back to him. The screams tearing through the quiet night, the sand between the pads of his paws as he sprinted down the beach, the angry howls of the dark creature.

"Two decades might seem a considerable length of time to a human," Kirin continued, "but to other life forms, including some demons and the Yokai, it is but a long nap. And that is exactly what the demon may be doing: sleeping, patiently biding its time before it strikes again."

"Of course," Yava conceded, though he clearly cared more about the topic of Prince Oni. "Make sure the boy is acquainted with our network of spies, knows what to look for in the news they bring us, before you leave us."

The two dying men continued to talk, but they had trouble keeping the attention of the younger ones. Marauxus stared out a window at the distant fields, his mind somewhere remote. Myobu's thoughts were also far away, wondering about the reported demon that had terrorized Kitsunetsuki. Had it truly been the same that had murdered his parents? If so, why had it attacked humans in Oinari, and why had it gone silent again?

With a resolve he hadn't felt before, Myobu now looked forward to the responsibilities in his new position. He would use it and the resources it granted him to track down this creature. If it reared its ugly head again, be it soon or centuries from now, he would know about it. Then he would destroy it, blasting it with the flames he could now so readily command.

For he was Ninko.

RISE OF THE SUN

"You're going to be murdered one day," declared a grizzled Tod. He, Kensie, and Myobu were sitting at a corner table in Nikki's tavern. With a colorful paper hat thrust upon his balding head and a slab of cake in front of him, Tod looked immensely displeased. "How did you figure out it was my birthday?"

"I have access to all the city records," Myobu replied.

"There are no records of my birth," growled Tod.

That was, in fact, not true. But as the man had long ago insisted Myobu not reveal any information Hawte administration had on him, preferring to believe in his illusion of anonymity, Myobu kept the tidbit to himself.

Much to Kensie's chagrin, Tod had refrained from most help Myobu's role as Ninko offered. New sets of clothing were occasionally accepted. This always delighted Kensie, who found it hard to find discarded clothing long enough to cover his lanky frame.

"Just eat your cake," Myobu said with a smile. "Unless you'd like me to start singing."

Glaring, Tod cut his cake in half and handed a piece to Kensie, whose eyes bulged in delight. After knowing the pair for nearly a quarter of a century, Myobu knew how to irritate and please his friends. Just as

Kensie had a sweet tooth, Tod hated being the center of attention. The man's bright and festive hat, a token usually bestowed upon children on their birthdays, made him a beacon to anyone who walked through the door.

It had been twenty sun cycles since Myobu had agreed to take on the mantle of Ninko. A mere blink of an eye to him, but he had watched his closest friends nearly double in age. It was intriguing, watching them leave behind their more vibrant and carefree days, becoming more thoughtful and cautious in their actions. Myobu was careful to age his appearance of Acro appropriately, lest he make others suspicious of his secret identity. It was difficult to play a character that was halfway through its life expectancy when he was truly, by comparison, still a young adult.

Even more grim was the certainty that he would one day say goodbye to each of his acquaintances for the last time. Ryn had been the second human Myobu knew who had died, having fallen victim to an illness that had plagued the city four sun cycles ago. Watching Nikki suffer from the loss of her husband had been even more difficult than Ryn's death.

Myobu often wondered if Kirin would have suffered any more or less to have watched his wife and son grow old and pass on.

Following Myobu's introduction to the royal family, Kirin spent seven months transferring his knowledge to his young protégé, training him in the history and ceremony of the Gaav people, and introducing him to those he would work with regularly. For a man that was so rarely seen by the public, Ninko knew and interacted with countless individuals across the entire region.

Part of Myobu's education was an overview of the threats the kingdom faced. An active volcano periodically spewed smoke in the west. Migrating insects from the north destroyed fields of crops. Foreign spies. Domestic spies. And, of course, the demon that had terrorized Oinari. The beast had never reemerged, but Kirin continued to express his concerns. Those included his belief that it was the same creature they had encountered in Urel.

"It was his scent," Kirin had explained on more than one occasion. "It was clearly that of the demonic…but more. Like the indescribable presence I felt when my family perished so long ago. I still don't understand why it was there or its reason for killing in Urel and Kitsunetsuki. Demons are mostly known for inhabiting the minds and bodies of others, forcing them to do their bidding. Even when they were more prevalent in the world, they were rarely violent."

Kirin truly believed it was the same creature that spanned all three events, but his declining health made it so he could do little with the information. Myobu vowed once again to keep a vigilant watch for it and, if the beast did return, hunt it down. He would do this for both his and Kirin's family.

Then, like a canine that knows it is dying, Kirin disappeared one day without a word. Myobu could only hope his friend would make it back to Kyubi before he passed. The man deserved that much out of life. Taking the guise of Kirin's human avatar, Myobu's first official act as Ninko was to inform King Yava of what had transpired.

*

"When is your birthday?" Kensie said.

Myobu blinked, his mind returning to the present. "Pardon?"

"Your birthday! You have made such a fuss about ours over the sun cycles, but you have never let on about your own."

"I don't know the exact day," Myobu mused, sitting back in his wooden chair. "Just that I've been around for about one hundred and twenty-five sun cycles."

Kensie choked on his cake. Tod, as though waiting for the perfect moment to voice a thought, said, "Is that why you always seem so sad?"

That caught Myobu by surprise. He leaned forward again, elbows on the table. "Do I seem sad to you?"

Tod grunted noncommittally. Kensie, who had recovered from the idea that his friend was older than his great grandfather, shoved another large piece of dessert into his mouth and nodded emphatically.

"At first I believed it was because of your position as Ninko. It wasn't something you desired. It was thrust upon you, even though you wanted to remain on the streets. As time passed by, though, I saw you enjoyed your new role. You've made a real difference here, which is something that matters to you. Yet, you always appear as though you are looking for more. A deeper connection. It hangs over you like a cloud."

It was true Myobu had come to appreciate his work. He respected the royal family and believed he had found a place in life by providing them with help, direction, and advice. This in turn profited the people of Gaav, who had shown an outpouring of respect and admiration for Ninko.

The only thing missing was the very thing he had walked into Hawte searching for: the human experience of feeling passionate love. He could still feel how Kirin felt about his family, and Myobu desperately wanted that for himself. Two decades on, though, and there hadn't even been a spark similar to what Kirin had. As Tod had surmised, it weighed heavily on his mind.

"I am very lonely," Myobu admitted to his friends. Kensie looked especially affronted, and he explained, "I haven't made that special connection with someone. The kind that gives your life purpose and meaning. You know, I haven't fallen in love."

"But you've slept with so many people!" Kensie cried out, laughing.

Throwing a utensil at his friend, Myobu said, "Honestly, it hasn't been that many!"

"What about Nikki?" Kensie replied, cocking his head toward the dark-skinned tavern owner behind the bar. His own voice quivered slightly in desire. "It's been a while since Ryn has passed. She may be looking to get married again."

"Ryn took up so much of her heart, I don't think there is room for anyone else," Myobu said. He had been there for her since the death of her husband, continuing to do the odd job when he found the time, but they had never again been intimate with each other. He would have been willing, but he knew a part of her had died along with Ryn. The part that sought adventures new and exotic. "Besides, what would I—as Myobu, not Ninko—have to offer as a man of the streets?"

"That's kind of the problem, isn't it?" Tod pointed out, waving his fork at Myobu. Bits of cake fell off and littered the tabletop. "You always loved being a vagabond, but it isn't often the homeless find love. You will notice Kensie and I are bachelors as well."

"Not on purpose," Kensie muttered.

"It seems you have a choice to make," Tod continued. "Luckily, you have options. You could take a common job as Myobu, make a name for yourself. That would probably cut into your other full-time career as Ninko, though. Alternatively, you could take on an entirely new guise, this time as someone already wealthy. Then you'd have to rely on your charm to win someone over. The last option, as I see it, is the most drastic: Look outside of Hawte."

"I don't think I'd be able to move on from this city. Not for a long time, anyway. Definitely not for seeking something I may never find."

"To us, your lifespan is akin to an eternity. Knowing you'll be around to see my descendants is mind-bending. I simply cannot imagine how strong the craving for companionship has grown and will continue to grow over your lifetime." Tod stopped abruptly, looking as though he had let something slip. With a shrug, he continued, giving the two of them a rare glimpse into his past. "Someone used to love me, and I loved her. It feels like it's been forever since I've had that connection with someone. It's heart-wrenching not to have that anymore, but I wouldn't trade away that time for anything."

Myobu nodded, not sure what to say that wouldn't break Tod's open mood. For once, Kensie didn't let loose with a shallow comment.

"I'm just saying," Tod continued, shoving the rest of his cake at Myobu, "we are your friends. We don't want you to leave, but we will support you and your decisions. We want you to be happy."

*

It was too late to leave Hawte.

As a species, the Yokai distanced themselves from others, preferring solitude and wilderness. That was why so many believed them to be fantastical spirits. If others spotted them, it was usually in periphery. Occasionally, one of the foxlike creatures would become uncharacteristically attached to an individual or group of individuals from another species. Sometimes, it was the species itself that grabbed an obsessive hold of the Yokai's mind. Maroni, the partner of Myobu's aunt, was one such example, having spent a considerable length of time across the ocean with the Ceran. Kirin was another, though his fascination evolved from a desire for retribution into love.

Such connections posed a tenuous danger to both parties. Just as if someone were to come into possession of a Yokai's hoshi no tama, the individual or group that Yokai became enamored with could, depending on the mental fortitude of the Yokai, hold great sway. The amount of control the other side wields—let alone knowledge of the connection itself—was usually unknown to them, the power and magic poorly understood. A variety of disasters had occurred in the past, ranging from explosions of spousal rage to the complete collapse of a kingdom's economy. This was partly the reason the Yokai preferred to isolate themselves.

Though it wasn't known to anyone but himself, Myobu had become uncharacteristically attached to the royal family of Gaav.

King Yava enjoyed and trusted in his new advisor the moment Myobu had alerted him of Kirin's departure. Their working relationship was fruitful and probably would have led to a strong friendship if not for the inevitable outcome of the king's illness. Within a sun cycle, Yava was dead.

The rapport between Myobu and Marauxus was, at first, icy and ceremonial. Little trust and much suspicion existed between the two as the new king took his crown. Myobu considered the young man irreverent and thoughtless, preferring to spend time frivolously outside the city walls. For his part, Marauxus was wary of his advisor's power and motivation, perhaps believing Myobu was attempting to undermine the monarchy.

That had all begun to change one night. Myobu was taking a late walk through the royal complex, stretching his legs after a long day of meetings, when he spotted the new king sneaking off. He took his natural four-legged form and crept after him. What he uncovered over the next several days not only changed his views of Marauxus, but on how Gaav operated as a kingdom.

Gaav's nomadic history was largely a relic of the past. Several large cities had grown and prospered throughout the kingdom, some larger than Hawte. A network of roads and rivers connected them, facilitating travel and trade. Centuries ago, apparently not everyone had been ready to embrace city life, and Myobu had been surprised by the great numbers of people who lived by themselves or in small settlements leagues from any major city or road. They rarely dealt with governmental agencies, most of which were happy enough to leave them be. Very few wanted to waste days riding through the countryside on a horse, trying to collect taxes or pass along new laws and regulations.

Marauxus was one of the few who had not minded such journeys.

Myobu watched through his fox eyes as the young king interacted with several smaller communities across the rural landscape. It was plainly evident these were not chance encounters, that they were all friendly with one another, and the meetings were not completely social. Very often, Marauxus would hand out samples of seed, cured meat, and cloth. He would rarely accept anything in return other than fresh water.

"How hard was it to track me?" the king had asked Myobu during a private meeting not long after the excursion concluded. "No one has ever discovered the nature of my travels."

Myobu was caught off guard, having believed his natural state would keep him hidden, blending into the surrounding environment. "I'm an excellent scent tracker. How did you know?"

"Gaav is known for its dark-haired folk," Marauxus said. Myobu nodded, confused, as his hair was dark as well. "Our native fox population has a white and flaming red coloration. I know yours is a more muted reddish-brown, and you're not as sneaky as you believe you are."

Having successfully snuck fruit from vendors' stands in the past when his stomach demanded it, Myobu respectfully disagreed but kept it to himself. "What exactly were you doing out there?"

"It wasn't obvious?" Marauxus asked. "Those I spoke with aren't really a forgotten people, but certainly an ignored one. After Gaav's resources and populace began focusing on larger settlements, little consideration was given to those that continued to live on the fringes. Their contributions to society were minimal, as were the resources society allotted toward them. Nothing personal. The expense involved would have been taxing, and no one was asking for anything.

"I became aware of these people at a young age. I had run away after throwing a childhood tantrum, escaping into what I thought was uncharted wilderness. Not the case, thankfully, as a frigid night fell upon me. A hunting party found me huddled against some rocks, probably saving my life. Grateful though I was, the blankets that kept me warm were patchy and poorly woven, and the food I was fed the next morning wasn't stored or prepared properly. I can still remember the intestinal cramps! Young though I was, I made it my life's mission to help these people. They may prefer their solitude, but they should still be able to enjoy some of our modern amenities. Over the sun cycles, I have been providing them with food and cloth samples. I've passed along any of my knowledge on farming and curing techniques. Textiles have been difficult, as I have little experience or knowledge of the craft, but they have been able to use the samples I've provided to improve their own techniques."

Marauxus explained his actions weren't purely humanitarian. While he did genuinely care for and sympathize with them, he was also attempting to shore up support for the monarchy. "My father was not a suspicious man by nature, but he always felt there was something off about Oni when he was a prince. As king, his aggressive and warlike nature has given me no reason to alter that frame of mind. Especially now that he has an heir in Prince Kitsune."

"You think he'll march against another kingdom?" Myobu had asked.

"I believe it's only a matter of time. If it ends up being us…well, with the strength of his armies, *all* our people need to be united in purpose to stand a chance."

That conversation had altered Myobu's perception and attitude toward his king, and he now considered him with respect and wisdom. It took longer for the feelings to be reciprocated by Marauxus but was accomplished by an unwavering effort to assist those who lived on the outskirts of civilization and, therefore, solidify their allegiance to the monarchy.

Myobu was able to adopt and expand the king's strategy to help the homeless in all major cities. The efforts made him extremely visible to the public, and the king's subjects looked forward to displays of magic. It wasn't long before Ninko's power earned him a nickname: the King's Sun.

As the young leader's popularity soared, so did his reliance on his closest advisor. Before long, that confidence had turned to friendship, and over many sun cycles, a deep bond grew between the two men. Myobu loved Marauxus. It wasn't the kind of love he was looking for—it was more like being a part of a family, similar to how he felt toward Tod and Kensie. That love expanded when the king married and had a daughter. Myobu found he didn't want to leave them. He couldn't leave them.

Not for very long, at least.

*

"I am hesitant to let you leave for any length of time," King Marauxus said, setting down a cup of tea on the table at which the two men had met so many sun cycles ago. "The menace to the east is preparing for something. I don't need our spies to say so. I can feel it in my bones. Oni is a warmonger, and it has been too long since he has mongered a war!"

Myobu picked up his own beverage. He had grown to love a good cup of tea. It helped quiet his mind so he could think. Since Tod's birthday a few days ago, Myobu had spent much time in thought. "I'm only going north into the tribal lands. It may take me some time to find Kyubi, but I shouldn't be more than a few days' ride. If King Oni was to march toward us, I would know it and return immediately."

"I may be anxious about your sabbatical, my friend, but I would never keep you from pursuing that which is close to your heart," Marauxus said. "After all, you did introduce me to my wife."

Raising an eyebrow, Myobu replied, "You know I have been seeking love?"

"You may be Ninko to the people, a wise man with matters of such importance on his mind that he has little time for personal relations, but you are also my closest friend. I know you, and I can see you are lonely."

Touched by Marauxus' words, which mirrored Tod's, Myobu counted himself lucky to have built a family that clearly cared for him.

"I have heard of this Kyubi," the king continued, turning to the fire in the hearth. "Not just from Kirin, but from those I have visited during my trips. They refer to her as the Harbinger. They seek her out, just like you desire to do, to ask her questions. She turns no one away. Though her age gives her wisdom and insight, she is not commonly described as compassionate or benign."

"I have heard similarly. It is a curious thing Kirin was so enamored with her."

Marauxus grunted. "I ask you to return within a month's time. At least to check in. I fear I rely on you too much. When will you depart?"

"In the morning," Myobu replied. "The sooner I leave, the quicker my return."

"May the spirits guide you," the king said, then he chuckled at his own words.

The two men stared thoughtfully into the fire, finishing their tea. Myobu had to keep from chuckling himself, though not from his friend's words. The impish Yokai part of him was relishing in everyone's misconception. Yes, he was lonely and altogether unhappy he'd failed to find passion in over two decades as a human. His connection and commitment to the royal family overrode that desire, however, and he could no more pursue his own desires outside of Hawte than he could throw himself off a high cliff.

Everyone assumed he was going to ask the Harbinger where he could find the love he so desired. Yet, he had a different question in mind, and its answer would likely keep him from love for a long time.

THE HARBINGER

Myobu had explored much of the tribal lands throughout his life, yet since that time had been spent as a field fox, his memories of it were mercurial at best. His position within the Gaav government gave him access to information, though official reports were surprisingly few. While not as desperately avoided as the Wastelands, which lay to the east, the vast and unexplored wilderness of the tribal lands had given birth to superstition and fantastical stories.

The tribal lands, unsurprisingly, were made up of dozens of small to medium-sized groups of people. No overarching government or law bound them together, and most of the tribes operated independently of one another. Much like how the rest of the world operated, the tribes traded, communicated, and warred among themselves.

Stories of the more brutal populations kept foreigners on the outskirts. Anyone passing through often found it hard to sleep at night, trapped in a perpetual state of anxiety. Still, traveling during the day provided little solace. Dense forests put Gaav's woodlands to shame. The canopy blocked sunlight, and tree trunks the size of boulders provided ample hiding places for ambushers. The darkness of night did little to dispel the notion that each strange sound didn't come from half-naked, green-tinted men standing outside every tent, gripping long blades stained red from countless victims.

The truth, Myobu knew from the reports, was often worse than one's imagination. The tribal lands were not to be trifled with. Luckily, the clans that sought domination over their weaker brethren were not stupid. They were aware of the outside world, the technologies and weapons that existed, and dared not risk their own existence against such odds. As a result, they lived farther north and to the west, leaving the areas closer to Gaav's and Kitsunetsuki's borders for the more peaceful tribes.

Well-worn paths cut through the dense woodlands. They had once been used to trade with the Ruio Territory. Myobu himself had traveled them many times on diplomatic missions. However, King Oni had conquered Ruio nearly two decades ago and closed off the Western Pass. The wilderness had yet to reclaim the trails, and they were used occasionally by random clans, wanderers, or the mislaid traveler.

"Are we lost?" Kensie asked, swatting at a cloud of gnats buzzing about his head. So determined to be rid of the pests, he nearly fell off his horse.

"We are beyond lost," replied Tod in his usual growl. He glanced back at the setting sun, indicating a desire to cease their day's travel and make camp.

"I know exactly where we are!" Myobu defended. "We're a couple days northeast of the border with Gaav, and we'd reach the Wastelands due east in under two days."

"That doesn't mean we're not lost."

Kensie coughed after accidentally inhaling a gnat, though a sharp inhalation afterward gave passage for several more of the tiny insects. "I'm so confused," he wheezed.

"We've been searching for the Harbinger for two weeks now without success. Not even a hint of her location. Just zigzagging through these cursed woods," Tod said. He steered his mount into a small clearing, deciding that this was where they would rest for the night.

"Someone is getting impatient," Myobu said, following suit. "I have another week of leave to continue this search."

"Just not used to all this…nature," Tod grumbled. "I actually miss rifling through the trash behind Nikki's bar."

"Our rations are far better than anything we'd get off the streets, and Nikki's food isn't that bad!" Myobu said. He dismounted his own horse and, after helping Kensie safely to the ground, secured their three beasts where they had access to food and water.

"I'm just saying," Tod said over his shoulder as he set out to find some firewood, "perhaps you should have opted to bring along someone who has actually spoken with the Harbinger."

Myobu had, in fact, underestimated the difficult nature of finding a single individual within a region of land roughly the size of Gaav. Enough of his countrymen had claimed an encounter with the ancient Yokai that he had assumed she'd be easy to track down. Two weeks into their search, though, and they hadn't even come across a single tribe. He knew others were constantly all around, watching the trio with wary eyes. Myobu could smell them. Coupled with the claustrophobic feel of the thick trees, he understood his friends' heightened anxiety.

Had he spent so much time with the humans, attempting to understand and be more like them, that he had forgotten the patterns and habits of those from whom he came? He reminded himself he had spent little time with his kin before his parents were murdered and he journeyed out into the world. Perhaps the Yokai preferred seclusion even more than he remembered, and the Harbinger had secluded herself even deeper into the wilderness or moved on altogether.

"We'll find her," Kensie pressed as he rolled out their sleeping blankets. Myobu placed each of their packs next to their respective bedding, carefully tucking the bow and quiver of arrows he brought along underneath his blankets. "She won't be found until she wants us to find her. Probably knows we're coming, anyway."

Tod eventually piled up enough dry logs to last them through the night, and Myobu set fire to some kindle with his magic just as the sun set. By its light and heat, they cooked some of their food rations for dinner, sat back, and relaxed. With their bellies full, they stared up at the canopy as fireflies took flight and lit up the forest.

"You don't see this in Hawte," Myobu said, appreciating the blinking, golden lights. They appeared in greater concentration as they traveled north. More than he'd ever seen before.

"Yeah, and you don't see Hawte's well-endowed women out here, either," Tod replied. His voice carried less than its usual gruffness.

"Was she pretty, the woman you loved?" Myobu asked, daring to broach the subject of Tod's past. He expected little in the way of an answer, but his friend couldn't run far out here in the tribal lands.

"She was divine," was the surprising response. The man's eyes widened as he gazed into the past, the golden pinpricks of fireflies reflecting off them. "So was our—err, her daughter. I can't rightfully claim fatherhood when I did nothing right past the initial act of creating her. Not that I didn't try, but I was a downright mess back then. She left me. Left Hawte, too, and my heart went with the two of them."

He may have been imagining it, but Myobu was certain he saw a tear find its way down his friend's dark, stubbly cheek.

"Probably would've been found dead in an alley decades ago if it weren't for Kensie here," Tod continued, paying his friend a rare compliment. "He became a surrogate son in a way, even though he's only a few sun cycles younger than me. A stupid son, but they require the most looking after."

"Would you look at that," Kensie said in awe. Myobu thought the man had spotted Tod's rogue tear or was about to ruin the moment's sentimentality with a senseless comment, but the man was staring upward at something behind Myobu. His shaggy brown hair couldn't hide the wonder in his blue eyes. "I ne'er seen anything like it."

The other two looked around, and their own jaws dropped open in amazement at what they saw. Countless fireflies had been landing upon a cluster of nearby trees. The trees' trunks had grown close to one another, and they were taller than all the surrounding plant life. It made them look like an enormous, four-sided tent. Perched upon the branches and leaves, the insects gave the effect of a shimmering, billowing fabric. A conspicuous dark space in the middle of one of the tent's sides looked like an entrance.

"That's one hell of a tree fort," Tod commented, letting out a low whistle.

"Do you think that's her?" said Kensie, shifting uncomfortably. The unnaturally spectral sight was beautiful, but anything unnatural made him uneasy.

"Nah, I think them's just trees," Tod replied, his usual tone of voice returning. "She might be inside, though."

Kensie shot his friend a withering glance.

The more he stared at the tree tent, the more the dark entrance seemed to call to Myobu. It was an invitation from the Harbinger, of that he was certain. She had lit the way for him. He stood up, his blankets falling away from him. "I'm going to investigate."

"N-now?" Kensie stammered. "In the middle of the night? What if she attacks you?"

"Are you coming?"

"Nope," Kensie answered immediately, shaking his head emphatically from side to side.

"You don't have questions of your own for her?" Myobu pressed.

As Kensie muttered to himself about the craziness of their current situation, Tod said, "The two of us are middle-aged men. Old men, by street standards. Our lot in life has been bearable. The clothing you got us for this journey helps. What do we have to ask about? I suppose I could inquire about my offspring, but what if they were not well or in peril? What could I possibly do? What would be the benefit of knowing such things?"

Myobu pondered Tod's words, hoping such wisdom would come to him when he was middle-aged in another couple of hundred sun cycles.

"Besides," Kensie added, apparently wanting Myobu to move on and end the supernatural gathering of insects. "We just came for you. This is your journey."

After briefly debating if he should bring along his bow, Myobu moved away from the fire empty-handed. He was careful not to rustle any leaves or snap brittle twigs, lest he break the magical spell that had befallen the night. He feared that if the fireflies doused their lights, the tent-like structure would disappear along with them.

Only a few tics had passed before he was at the entrance. Despite the bright light illuminating the surrounding forest, he could see very little within. Myobu glanced back nervously, but he could no longer see his friends or their campfire. He hadn't been alone in weeks, and he felt uncomfortably exposed.

"There is no need to be distressed, young one," a voice from within the darkness said. It was a deep, smooth voice, full of power, and did not crack with age like Myobu had imagined it would. "I will reveal nothing you do not ask about, as is my usual practice. I am afraid the answers I have for you are enough to break most minds."

"That is such a comfort," Myobu muttered under his breath. He watched as several fireflies descended from the trees to form a path on the ground. It led to the middle of the tent, where a small fire burst into existence. It illuminated a woman with pale, flawless skin and angular features. Her hair was snow white, pulled back and tied into nine separate sections. Myobu knew this to be an indication of her age and wisdom. Despite this, she barely looked any older than himself.

"My hearing has only improved with the passage of time," the woman quipped. "Would you like a cup of tea, Myobu?"

"Yes, I would love some tea," he answered, walking down the lighted path toward her. "You know who I am?"

"Why wouldn't I? You know who *I* am," she said slyly. She took a kettle off of the fire, poured some hot tea into a cup, and handed it to Myobu as he stepped up. "Have a seat."

"Thank you, Kyubi," he said, nodding to her in respect before sitting. "We have been searching for you for quite some time."

"Two weeks is nothing for those like you and I," the Harbinger responded, taking a sip of her own drink. "Though I would find it a trying period to spend in such proximity to humans. How you do it, just like Kirin did, is quite beyond me."

Myobu found that hard to believe. "Kirin wasn't able to convey the bond he forged with King Yava? With the woman who became his wife and bore his child? Such devotion to another species, though uncommon, is a well-known phenomenon of the Yokai."

"Oh, I understand that well, child," she said. Then she wrinkled her nose. "It's their smell! I can practically taste the two humans you've been traveling with. Your friends may provide a unique blend of entertainment, but I could never get past the assault on my senses."

Smiling to himself, Myobu wrestled with the decision to pass on Kyubi's words to Kensie and Tod. In the end, he decided against it. Nobody wanted to hear how badly they smelled. He changed the subject. "Kirin found his way back to you?"

Kyubi's face softened. "He did. Our reunion was not long lived, even by human standards, but I was uncertain he'd come back at all. His return was one of the happiest moments of my life."

"It must have been difficult to send him away so many sun cycles ago."

"One of my saddest moments." A strange look crossed Kyubi's face, as though she were unaccustomed to speaking about herself. "The parts he played in our story were short but crucial. However, I do not believe you sought me out to ask about your old friend, Kirin."

"No, though the parts of my story he affected—the ones for which you sent him away—assured I would find my way here." Myobu took another sip of tea, relishing its heat. "I am young, Kyubi. Considering the number of sun cycles I've been fully conscious, I'm no older than the friends with whom I traveled. As you no doubt learned from Kirin, the people of Gaav now hold me in high regard as Ninko. Continuing from where he left off, their trust in me endures. King Marauxus, as well as his wife and daughter, hold a special place in my heart. Their devotion to those they lead fascinates me, and I do not wish to leave them."

"There's that bond of which you spoke," Kyubi said kindly. "Those are not questions and, as I see it, no one is asking you to leave."

"No, those with whom I am closest believe that is what I desire. I came to Hawte in search of love. The type of love Kirin shared with his wife." He stopped short, wondering if he was being insensitive. "Not that his love for you was any less powerful. Just less…human."

The Harbinger waved her hand dismissively. "I know what you mean, child."

"Well, I have yet to find that kind of connection, and others have noticed. They think I am going to leave my station for more selfish endeavors, but I am unwilling to do so."

"Misconceptions that can be cleared up with simple conversations," she said, impatience beginning to creep into her voice. "Now, the night is no longer young. What is your question?"

Myobu looked down at his cup. He knew he was rambling, dodging the reason he had traveled all this way. But to say it aloud was akin to officially abandoning his dream. He took a deep breath and said, "How can I best serve King Marauxus and the Kingdom of Gaav?"

"Much like the title you have taken, that is a wise question," Kyubi said. "But does it come from a wise place?"

"What do you mean?"

The Harbinger shrugged, the nine clusters of hair bouncing behind her head. "You could have asked how to keep your current station in life. Even better, how do you hold fast to the meaning you have assigned to your existence? Instead, your question is framed in such a way it appears selfless, that you are doing Gaav a service at a great personal cost. The answer may turn that notion on its head…or reveal another truth."

"Now who is stalling?" he said in jest, pointing at her.

Kyubi's look was stony when she replied, "Death."

"Pardon?"

"Death, Myobu," she repeated. She stood up and held out her hand. A multitude of fireflies descended from the trees and congregated into a sphere above her palm. Their golden light cast strange shadows upon her face. "To best serve Gaav—to best serve the world at large—you must die."

Myobu choked, and his grip on the mug threatened to shatter it. Now he understood what the Harbinger had meant. He knew his desire to stay and help Gaav stemmed from his unnatural connection with the royal family. It was also, as she had insinuated, a selfish act, as it ensured his future and solidified a standing legacy.

Death was something all living beings naturally avoided. Death would sever his connection with Marauxus and his family. With all of Gaav.

"There is more," Kyubi said softly.

"More than dying?" he asked, more loudly than he intended.

She stared fixedly into the golden sphere in her palm. "You are to die by the hand of your love."

Myobu exclaimed, "A member of the royal family, perhaps even King Marauxus himself, must put a sword through my chest for the good of Gaav? I knew you speak in riddles, Kyubi, but this makes no sense!"

"You misunderstand," Kyubi said, shifting her eyes from the sphere to him. "You will die by the *one* you love. You must first fall for someone in the romantic sense."

Myobu barked a laugh. Slamming the mug down, he stood up and began pacing around the fire. "Even better! Attaining the very thing I've desired since I was a pup will literally kill me! Everyone benefits."

"I am serious, My—"

"No, *I* am serious!" he shouted, surprised by the ferocity in his tone. He rarely ever had to raise his voice. "I don't know what you are getting at, but I don't appreciate being made a fool. Kirin was a good man, as much a father to me as anyone else. He loved you, and he suffered at your own request to part himself from you. You do not honor his memory by toying with me."

He turned to leave but froze when the Harbinger snarled in anger. In the corner of his eye, he saw her wave a hand in a single circular motion. He tensed, believing she had performed some magic against him, but then fell to the ground in surprise when the sphere that had been hovering above her palm burst outward, expanding until it occupied the whole of the tree tent. Then it hung there as peaceful as before, hovering above the fire.

"What is this?" Myobu said, slowly getting back on his feet. Even as he asked, however, he saw what the sphere was. It was a representation of the entire world. Looking at it, he thought he recognized the region in which he had lived and explored throughout his life. There was more to creation than Gaav, Kitsunetsuki, Odom, and the lands that surrounded them—he knew that—but he was surprised at exactly how small they were compared to the rest of the world. The realization of how much more was out there was dizzying.

"A dark force exists in our world," the Harbinger said, her voice bellowing out with such force Myobu thought it might knock him down again. "An impetus of such anger and malice that it will destroy everything."

As he watched, the fireflies that made up the giant sphere went out. Kitsunetsuki disappeared, followed by Odom and Gaav. The tribal lands, Urel, and the Wastelands followed shortly, and then the dark blotch spread quickly throughout the rest of the world until the globe had completely disappeared. All the fireflies in the forest had gone dark, leaving only the campfire as a source of light.

"The entire world?" Myobu said incredulously. He stared into Kyubi's eyes. In the darkness, he could only see the firelight reflecting off them. It made her appear more like the Yokai fox she truly was. "You think I can influence events in places I did not know existed?"

"Fire consumes all," the Harbinger replied. "These events were set in motion over a millennium ago. You are but a small cog in the brass machine."

"I…have no idea what you are implying," Myobu said. The impact of the magical display dissipated, especially with her cryptic words. He turned to leave. "If my part in history is so small, then it should not matter what I do."

"The absence of even the most minute gear within a clock would cause the piece to malfunction," she said. When he did not turn back, she spoke again, her voice hinting at desperation. "Kirin played his parts, one of which was to set you down your path. I beg of you not to let his sacrifices be in vain."

Myobu stopped, shaking his head slowly at her tactic. The Harbinger wanted him to give his life for the entire world. And Kirin had dragged him into this, trading his existence for the same cause.

Not for the first or last time, Myobu cursed the beast that slaughtered his parents, robbing him of a proper upbringing. The monster would have killed him, too, if not for Kirin. The man had perhaps only extended his sentence, not really having saved him in the end.

It was for the entire world, though, which included Gaav. Saving his home from this supposed dark malice would be the best way to serve. Conceding to that idea, he turned back. "It's King Oni, isn't it? He's already swallowed up Ruio and Mogo, and my spies tell me he is gearing up for another campaign."

"I know not the details," Kyubi responded coolly. She had returned to a sitting position by the fire and was carefully holding her tea. "Just that we must do all we can to prevent it from happening. Your death by the one you love will not alone be enough to stop it, but it is a necessary step."

"The world is big, much larger than I even knew, and I've been searching for love for quite some time," Myobu said shortly. "Any insight on where I should look for my murderer?"

"I would suggest Rhinecourt."

"Rhinecourt?" Myobu blurted out. "Nobody lives there!"

Kyubi merely took a sip of her drink.

Rhinecourt was a small town on the western border of Odom. It nestled against the Argent Mountain Passageway, or as those in Kitsunetsuki referred to it, the Eastern Gate. A sister city, Onger, was on the other side of the gate. The two had been founded hundreds of sun cycles ago to encourage trade between the two kingdoms. When Prince Oni became convinced Odom spies had murdered his wife, he campaigned for ever-increasing tariffs on imported goods until it made no economic sense for merchants to buy anything from Odom. The gate was eventually closed to traffic. The last Myobu had heard, Rhinecourt was abandoned.

"Am I so repulsive I have to travel great distances to find someone?" he asked with acidic sarcasm.

"You aren't repulsive in the least," she replied, licking her lips in a way that sent shivers down Myobu's spine. "A little small for my taste"

"There you go, calling me small again!"

"But you aren't going to find someone to love you. No, you are going to find someone for you to love. There's a distinct difference."

Myobu shook his head again as he stood there. He wanted nothing more than to leave this place, to flee from the woman he had spent so much time attempting to locate. He needed to find his friends and…what? Bid them farewell? He certainly would not bring them along on a journey that would end in his own demise.

"So…" he eventually said, breaking the silence that had befallen them. "Is there anything else to this? I don't need to pay you or anything?"

"I never charge for the answers I give," Kyubi said with a sniff. "Though watching someone's vanity or greed bring about their own downfall brings me a modicum of pleasure. No, Myobu, I find no joy in the fate that must befall you. I only hope you find the wisdom that is usually so elusive to those as young as yourself to do what is right.

"Now, both the night and I are older than before, and I must rest before the dark gives way to dawn. Until next we meet, child."

The fire extinguished itself. Before darkness wrapped itself around him, Myobu saw the Harbinger transform into her natural form. The nine clusters of hair became nine tails on the back of a sleek, silver fox. As he waited for his eyes to adjust, he heard her pad away, leaving him in disbelief and displeasure at his fate.

*

Tod awoke in the early dawn light. He yawned and stretched so much his back cracked audibly. Kensie snored softly from beneath his sleeping blankets, and Myobu's bedding looked untouched.

The urge to urinate overwhelmed Tod, and he realized this was the first time in some months he had slept through the night. It wasn't the frightening hoots and howls of the vast forest environment they had been traveling through that kept him restless, just like it wasn't the bustling noises of the drunkards or whores back in Hawte. It was age. He was getting old.

As he gifted some underbrush with a warm drink, it occurred to him that his age was likely why he had accompanied Myobu on this foolhardy trip. Sure, he supported his friend, but Myobu had traveled abroad for the king on many occasions, nearly always inviting Tod to come along. Despite that, Tod could count on one dirty, gnarled hand the number of times he had left the city of Hawte throughout his lifetime. He wasn't sure how many more chances he'd get once he returned.

Something was inside of him. Something that didn't belong. It couldn't be seen, but Tod could feel it somewhere in his chest. The first time he had felt it was four months ago, which probably meant it had been there for a while already. It had steadily grown until he always felt it.

He knew it was death.

Tod rarely dwelt on his impending fate. He wasn't angry about the lot. He figured it was a deserved end for how he treated his family so long ago, and as he had pointed out on his birthday, he had lived a long life for a street urchin. No need to tell the others. He wouldn't be able to take all the commotion. All he needed to do was ensure his friends were set up to deal with life after he was gone. Myobu would get along without his sage wisdom, but he worried about Kensie. That man would always be a juvenile at heart…and possibly mind.

Packing his equipment away, he returned to their camp. His stomach growled, and he piled some logs and tinder into the firepit, intending to prepare breakfast for the others. He rifled through his pack for his matchbox, but flames erupted and engulfed the wood without his assistance.

"You would think I'd be used to that by now," Tod grumbled after he jumped back from the sudden heat. He looked up to see Myobu standing at the edge of their camp. Absent was the mischievous expression he usually wore after pulling such a prank with his magic. Instead, he looked strangely still.

"What's the matter, you constipated?" Tod quipped, rummaging through his bag again, looking for a skillet and salt-cured meat.

"No, I am quite regular," was Myobu's response. The words had been playful, but his voice sounded thin. "I must leave now."

"No time for breakfast?" Tod asked.

Myobu shook his head no. A struggle was clearly playing itself out in the man's eyes. He looked as though he wanted to step into the campsite but was forcibly holding himself back. "I'll eat on the road."

"Right. Just give me a tic to wake up Kensie and pack up." He moved to jostle his other friend into consciousness, but Myobu held up a hand.

"Let him rest. The two of you will not be accompanying me any farther." Myobu kept his hand up as if to cut off any objections. "I need you to return to Hawte and apologize to the king on my behalf. Regretfully, I will not return by the time we had discussed."

Tod eyed his friend with suspicion. It did not bode well, being sent back so abruptly. "Anything else you want to add to that?"

"I…I may not return for some time," he said, a strained but resolute expression on his face. "I may not be returning at all."

Tod recognized the look. It was the same brave face he'd donned over the last several months. "What did that woman reveal to you?"

"How best to serve…" Myobu paused for a moment, after which a genuine smile graced his previously troubled face. "How best to serve my friends. The two of you have been my constant companions and teachers. I know more about being human from our time on the streets than any experiences I've had as Ninko. What I must do now is the least I can do for you."

Before Tod could reply, Myobu transformed into a fox. Shaking free of the crumpled clothing, the Yokai turned to leave.

"Myobu," Tod called out. He knew better than to ask his friend to reconsider. Once Myobu made up his mind on a matter, it was difficult to persuade him otherwise. Still, even though Tod woke up each day knowing it could be his last, it was hard to say goodbye.

The Yokai turned his head back. Tod still thought the intelligent look within the animal's eyes was eerie. Thought it so odd this was really his friend.

"We are always with you," Tod said, slapping a hand against his chest. "Just as you are with us. Travel safe. May you find what you are looking for."

AFTER KITSUNE

REBIRTH

Myobu gasped for breath. It was the hardest, most physically taxing exercise he'd ever performed. His chest refused to pull in air, feeling as though it was being crushed by an incredible weight. He opened his eyes—they responded more slowly than he would have appreciated—to identify what was suffocating him.

The only thing above him was a clear blue sky.

Panicking, he rocked back and forth in a slow, lumbering movement until he had enough momentum to roll over onto his stomach. The effort did nothing to improve his breathing. Instead, he inhaled copious amounts of ash that covered the ground. Choking violently, he pushed himself up into a sitting position and then scooted back against the remains of a burned tree.

Despite being outdoors, Myobu felt immensely claustrophobic, as though his body was a small prison. He shook violently from anxiety, overwhelmed with the idea he was forgetting something important. Had he known everything? Yes, but the notion that was dancing about his conscious thought was something very specific.

Dear spirits, he thought, finally breathing in short, shallow gasps of air. *Where am I? Who am I?*

Myobu looked about, trying to ascertain his location. The charred remains of a forest surrounded him. A massive fire had recently swept through the area. Probably within the past few days. That explained the ash he was still coughing out of his lungs. The wind had yet to disperse it.

Something about the skeletal remains of the closest trees struck a chord in his memory. The pattern they had grown in was reminiscent of a large tent. The tallest, healthiest ones were in the center while those farther away looked as though they had fallen and grown along the ground.

He *knew* this place. Had begun something here. Or ended? He couldn't tell the difference.

Sunlight glinted off several pieces of a broken emerald, catching Myobu's attention. They were embedded in the dust by his feet, along with a silver chain. It was an odd find out here in the middle of nowhere.

Beyond the stone and chain was something green. Something simultaneously miniscule and omnipresent. He felt nauseous at that concept and, not wanting to throw up in his lap, fell over onto his side.

Blades of grass were bursting from the soil. Myobu swore they had not been there only a tic before, and he was dumbfounded at the pace at which they were now growing.

That anything was alive, let alone growing, amid this recent devastation was astounding. It was as though the land had been given a second chance at life. It was reborn. At the pace it was reclaiming the environment, it had to have been touched by magic.

Myobu's heart thrummed against his aching chest, and he gasped in surprise and remembrance.

He too had been brought back from death, been touched by the remaining magic of an entity known as the Lady of the Mountain. She had sacrificed herself, her very soul, so he might have life. The power she had used must have bled over into the surrounding area, enabling the plant life to thrive again. As he watched, even the burned tree husks softened and browned, leaves budding from remaining branches.

Just as the forest was healing, Myobu knew his own body was piecing itself back together. He did not know how long it had been lying out here, decaying under the sun. Probably looking a fright, he was thankful no one was around to see him. He willed the tissues in his brain to reconnect faster, straining to remember what had happened.

Who is the Lady of the Mountain, and why did she save me? Myobu asked himself. *What happened here that resulted in my death?*

He looked back to the silver chain and shattered emerald. They sparked a memory in relation to the Lady, but he couldn't quite place it yet. Nearby was a single bloody arrow he had missed earlier. It was quickly disappearing as fresh vegetation overtook it.

Myobu placed a hand against the right side of his abdomen. His heart was beating steadily there now, but he also felt a wound. Looking down, he saw the ragged remains of a hole in his flesh closing itself back up.

That answers one question.

The face of the man who had shot the arrow into his heart bubbled to the surface of his memory. The individual had long blond hair and striking eyes. It was Prince Kitsune, and Myobu jerked at the realization that this man was the key to everything. Kitsune was the son of the Lady, was the man he loved, was the one who had murdered him, and was the reason he had returned. Myobu coughed violently as a rush of fresh memories flooded him. Something caught in his esophagus, and he beat at his chest to free himself of it.

Finding it difficult to breathe, his body writhed and muscles contracted. He pitched forward, catching himself before his face connected with the ground. With a final and particularly extravagant cough, the object was finally dislodged, flying out of Myobu's mouth and rolling across the ground. It was his hoshi no tama, the smooth red ruby he had swallowed some twenty sun cycles ago. It had been glowing brightly then, full of his magic. Now it was dull, matte, barely reflecting the sunlight.

Double checking that he was in human guise, a form in which a majority of his magic was incompatible, he quickly surmised his powers had been stolen. He couldn't recall this happening—it likely occurred while he was absent from his body. Prince Kitsune was the probable culprit, though Myobu would not have believed the man capable of accomplishing such a feat. He wondered if it had been a purposeful or accidental act. It didn't matter—the result had been the same. Myobu had to learn long ago how to control that magic. Anyone who absorbed that power into themselves would have difficulties comprehending it. An explosion of energy could have been a result.

Looking at the regenerating forest around him, he knew his magic had instigated the damage. Just not by his own volition.

Another mystery solved.

Myobu rolled onto his back again, forcing himself to calm down. He could feel his body knitting itself back together. Getting up now and walking would be detrimental to the healing process, so he relaxed, closed his eyes to the bright sun, and let the Lady's magic do its work, reviewing memories as they came to him.

The grounds upon which he now lay were the crisped remains of Kyubi's home. His initial visit with the Harbinger had been a devastating blow to his mentality. He had come to her, consumed with the new purpose of serving King Marauxus and his people. In asking how he could best aid, she had dangled his initial desire to find human love and then ripped both away with the pronouncement of certain death.

Leaving the Harbinger and heading toward Odom had been a hard decision, but he knew it was the right one. It didn't seem fair he should sacrifice himself for everyone after pursuing only love and servitude. Had he gone back to Gaav, he would never have been able to live with whatever fate fell upon the world. Still, leaving his friends there among the trees, Kensie still snoring, had been heart-wrenching. Taking his natural form and heading off into the wilderness alone reminded him too much of his solitary days as a field fox.

It had not been an easy journey, one beset with potent emotions and the pangs of loneliness. On multiple occasions, he lashed out at his surroundings, letting loose spheres of flame about him. His travels supplied him with adventure and mystery, and he wasn't always alone. In fact, the same day he left his friends behind, he had encountered the first tribe since leaving Hawte.

Taking the form of Arco once more, Myobu had tentatively walked into a small village. The natives were friendly and, despite a communication barrier, he identified the clan as the Purple People, a welcoming group with green-tinged skin and mostly brown hair. They were known by some scholars because they watched over the nearby ruins of a pyramid, although the ancient building had been searched numerous times and no treasure or artifacts of importance had ever been found. What exactly the Purple People were watching for was a mystery, as was why they were referred to as being purple.

They had offered Myobu clothing, food, and shelter for the night. He felt terrible leaving the next morning with nothing to give them in return.

As he traveled due east, the dense woods of the tribal lands gave way to the Wastelands. It had once been home to a thriving, technologically advanced civilization, although it was now barren and inhospitable. The civilization may have disappeared, but it had left a lasting footprint. A smattering of buildings attributed to them could be found throughout the entire region. Gray, smooth-walled, and boxy in design, the simple structures still appeared to be in pristine condition. At least, they appeared so from the outside. No known person had gained entrance in a millennium.

No person. The Yokai, however, were another matter.

The Yokai had a deep understanding and appreciation of nature. Their ancient civilization held an uncharacteristic respect for the environment, the cataclysm that destroyed them and poisoned the air notwithstanding. They had actively sought the Yokai as they expanded, expressing a desire to build and live in harmony with their surroundings.

When constructing the large, gray boxes within the borders of other kingdoms, they used technologies that would recognize a Yokai. While no living humans knew how to access them, the walls could still recognize a Yokai and open a doorway.

Myobu had come across one of these strange buildings on the far east side of the Wastelands. He had padded around the building twice before he walked close enough to its hidden door. It activated, allowing him access. He spent the night in the structure, if only to satisfy his curiosity. Completely by accident, he figured out how to activate a controlled light source. The interior of the building proved to be just as intact as the outside, though it did not furnish any hints as to why it existed.

A rickety bridge provided an austere entrance into the Odom Empire. Myobu remained in fox form as he traveled south, as it was easier to move unnoticed and hunt for food. As the Argent Mountains grew taller, his anxiety increased. He struggled to keep his emotions under control, not wanting his magic to express itself. The last thing he needed was to attract attention to himself here in Odom.

Anxiety was difficult to suppress, especially after he finally arrived in Rhinecourt several days later. It was, as he had expected, an abandoned village. Dilapidated homes and storefronts, each lined with moss and vines, lined streets cracked by fledgling grasses and trees. A faint odor of wood decay hung over the town, reminding Myobu of some of the ancient forests he'd trotted through in the past. It would have been a quaint, peaceful place to spend some time if it hadn't been for the fact he was there to fall in love with someone…and there was absolutely no one there with whom to fall in love.

He had tried to be patient, and he explored the village and its surroundings over the next several days. Uncovered some appropriate clothing, a bow, and a quiver of arrows to replace those he had left behind in the tribal lands. Without the luxury of distraction, his mind focused more on his fate. The anger he had felt at traveling all this way to meet the individual who would bring an end to his life, and then having to wait so long for that person to actually show up, was infuriating. Thinking about it highlighted the absurdity of the situation, which made him even angrier.

His emotional state finally broke late one night. Seeking release, his magic had again exploded outward in a fiery fury. He refused to withdraw or temper it after the initial outburst this time, instead letting his power spread throughout Rhinecourt. The plant life—foreign invaders slowly breaking the village apart—were the first to shrivel and blacken. Then the wooden buildings, which had stood solidly for hundreds of sun cycles, succumbed to his wrath.

Odom had no other nearby cities. It was not a seafaring nation, so no one witnessed the village's destruction from the ocean to the south. Inhabitants of Onger on the other side of the Argent Mountain Passageway surely noticed, though they sent no one to investigate. Not one building stood by the time dawn broke on the horizon. All that remained were smoking embers, huge piles of ash, and Myobu.

Emotionally spent, Myobu wandered aimlessly away from Rhinecourt. He looked back only once at its smoldering remains, wondering briefly if he was the dark force that was to set the entire world ablaze. It was surely possible, but then the Harbinger could have just killed him herself or advised him to jump headfirst from a tall cliff.

*

Green lightning skewered the evening sky, breaking Myobu's sullen mood. He had been walking about in a stupor for three days, coming close to reverting into a field fox, when a tremendous thunderclap knocked him off his feet. Rain suddenly fell from billowing clouds above, and human voices could be heard from just over a mound where the lightning had struck. He clamored to the top of the hill to investigate.

Four men played out a dramatic scene worthy of a stage play. Two were on the ground. One of these was dressed as a soldier and the other was in fine but dirty clothing. They both looked in a sad state, though the soldier appeared to be seriously injured. The other two men were advancing, malice in their expressions. One was shorter and thinner, while the other was large all around. The bigger one said something about magic and bore down on the one dressed in plainclothes. Shockingly, the soldier leaped up defensively, pushing the large man to the ground.

A cracking sound came as the attacker's head connected with a rock. The group was down to three.

Enraged, the thin man pulled a sword, advanced several steps, and thrust the weapon into the soldier's chest. Before collapsing dead to the ground, the soldier looked apologetically at his companion.

Now only two.

Sword still in hand, the man turned to the remaining opponent. The way in which he moved made his intentions clear. He meant to be the last man alive.

Without even thinking, Myobu pulled and nocked an arrow into his bow. He took only a heartbeat to aim. When he loosed the projectile, it flew true into the thin man's chest. Blood blossomed around the wound as the man stared down at it. Myobu nocked a second arrow.

Why am I interfering? For all he knew, the man he'd just shot was good and honest, and the well-dressed one on the ground had murdered his entire family in cold blood.

Something about the scene seemed wrong. Perhaps it was his Yokai intuition, but he *knew* the sword-wielding man was evil. Not a bad guy who swindled money from others while chuckling under his breath, but one who cut their throats and laughed maniacally while watching their blood soak the earth.

And something about the man on the ground struck a chord within Myobu.

He sent off the second projectile, watching as the armed man fell to the ground.

The remaining individual, feverish and malnourished, had fallen unconscious. Over the next few days, Myobu used his magic to raise the other's temperature when it dipped too low. If it crept up too high, he submerged the man in nearby creeks. Eventually, he found a small, abandoned castle in which to take refuge.

Before the man had regained consciousness, Myobu had stripped him of his dirty clothing, bathed him, and tucked him into a makeshift bed. He tried his best to be practical and clinical about it, but there were a couple of fine details he could not help but notice. The man's hair, for one, was mesmerizing. Long locks of fine, blond hair floated in water or splayed out across bedding. It was unlike any color or style seen in Gaav, and Myobu was fascinated by it. He found himself running his hands through the strands on multiple occasions.

Several clues pointed to the survivor's identity. His clothes had seen better days, but they were of an expensive cut. The man either belonged to a wealthy family, had close ties with the palace, or was a member of the royal family. The self-sacrificing soldier had belonged to Kitsunetsuki's military and may have been acting as an armed guard, so Myobu guessed the latter.

In his feverish state, the unconscious man had a tendency to mumble aloud. More often than not, he seemed to speak of or refer to Kitsunetsuki's monarch. He used the words "king" and "father" interchangeably, leading Myobu to the conclusion he was in the presence of Prince Kitsune.

Myobu had encountered Prince Kitsune nearly two decades ago during his first diplomatic visit to the Kitsunetsuki capital. The prince had been but a child then, bravely sneaking into a function and staring at all the guests from behind a curtain. Again, the oddity of human aging struck Myobu, especially as he stroked the man's hair with an admittedly increased desire.

Also curious was Myobu's guise of Acro. After carefully aging his appearance over the sun cycles, he had subconsciously reverted the form back to its original younger visage.

It did not escape Myobu that, if Kitsune was the person he was to fall in love with, the eventual murder could have wide-ranging consequences. King Marauxus might declare war in retaliation, bringing an end to this business of a fiery scourge upon the world. The more

Myobu considered this, the more at peace he felt about the entire thing. It made sense. It was orderly. It was a sacrifice worth making.

With this new frame of mind, Myobu's anger and anxiety slipped away. This did not lessen the frequency of his fiery outbursts, however. As he came to realize, the flames of his magic could be easily associated with so many emotions. Anger, betrayal, lust, and love could easily stoke the fire that burned within all beings.

The unconscious man wore an emerald hoshi no tama around his neck. The stone, set into a silver chain, pulsed bright green with magic. It wasn't the prince's magic, Myobu knew, and this gave him cause for concern. It was a terrible thing to steal the magic of a Yokai, a nearly unforgiveable sin. He postponed judgement, as a story behind it had yet to be revealed. All reports on Prince Kitsune claimed him to be a good and honest man, if not overly earnest.

Furthermore, the prince was a magical creature himself. Myobu could smell both human and Yokai blood running through his veins.

*

Myobu had been lighting a fire in one of the abandoned castle's fireplaces when his sleepy companion finally awoke. Starting the fire had been an effortless task. Too easy, actually. His thoughts had drifted back to the man's silky blond hair just as he was releasing some of his magic. The resultant blast kicked up sun cycles' worth of soot. He backed out of the hearth, rubbing grime from his eyes, and found the man was out of bed, a look of concern on his face.

Myobu had thought the prince attractive before. A little too thin, maybe. He preferred those of Ryn's stature. Not anything he'd turn down, however. Now that the man was finally awake, Myobu could not help but stare. Kitsune was utterly naked, and lean muscles moved under taut skin. While the prince may have lacked an imposing stature, Myobu saw a spry and agile body; the look in his eyes conveyed an equal helping of intelligence.

And that hair! Long strands of straight blond hair hung down around his face and neck, mesmerizing Myobu.

Suddenly realizing he was grinning broadly, Myobu tried to think up something witty to say. "Good afternoon!" That really wasn't very witty, so he pointed to the hearth and said, "I, uh, got the fire started."

You're an idiot, he thought. At least his voice had sounded cool and even.

The rest of the conversation went better. He introduced himself, discreetly commented on the man's nakedness—was saddened when he covered up with a sleeping blanket—and caught him up on the previous days.

Later, after eating, the man confirmed what Myobu already suspected, though he filled in some of the narrative blanks. He was Prince Kitsune of the Asher lineage. He had been banished from his homeland, his birthright stripped from him, but he was seeking King Marauxus' son to help him find a way back in. Laughing, Myobu explained Kitsune was looking for the King's Sun, not Marauxus' son.

*

The next several days were spent traveling northward. Myobu spoke freely about his life under the guise of Acro but kept his identities as a Yokai and the King's Sun to himself. He may have been attracted to the prince, but he had been likewise attracted to many others. Attraction and desire did not equal love. To bide time to see where his feelings would lead, he proposed a trip to see the Harbinger, who would surely point Kitsune in the right direction.

Kitsune seemed to be open and honest about his life, though it became obvious over time he was hiding something. The prince talked about his upbringing within Inari Palace, his strange relationship with his father, and his plans for Kitsunetsuki. It was plain to see how learned the man was. However, his naivety about the world at large and how it operated was equally transparent. Kitsune would speak about leading his people into more prosperous times, appearing to be knowledgeable about the forces that drove economies. But he also spoke about leading armies into glorious battles, expressing little guilt or even acknowledging the loss of life such actions would cause.

Myobu recognized that logical disconnect as the Yokai blood that flowed through the man's veins. Kitsune was unaware of it or unwilling to divulge that information. Despite what many humans thought, the Yokai had powerful emotions. They just didn't express them or their reasoning in the same ways and quantities as humans.

As Myobu stared at the other man more and more, he had known his own emotions were running on overdrive. His attraction grew into lust and infatuation. He often daydreamed Kitsune was still unconscious, which would give him an excuse to touch his skin and hair again. It was a miracle he was able to pull off such a calm demeanor, for he felt he would burst into flames at any moment.

At times, it seemed Kitsune was flirting, but Myobu often attributed it to the prince's naïve personality. Surely, he was well versed in making his desires known. The man was a prince and had even admitted to bedding a fair share of men and women back in Oinari.

Late one evening, Kitsune finally admitted he had magic, and when he requested help and guidance with meditating on the subject, Myobu was all too willing to oblige. It had been a cool evening with a bright, moonlit sky. Perfect for bold actions. Unable to contain his own desires any longer, Myobu had snuck up on him while his eyes were squeezed tight in concentration and kissed him.

It had paid off. Prince Kitsune returned his kiss with equal amounts of desire and passion. It wasn't an obligatory kiss, but something the other had been holding in as well. They had eventually stopped to catch their breaths, and Kitsune was about to say something, but distant screams of terror interrupted that magical moment.

The calls for help were from youths Allison and Joseph, whose camp had come under attack from a couple of bandits. After their rescue, the children claimed to be travelers on their way to Sandya. As the city lay along their intended path, Myobu and Kitsune did not hesitate to escort them to their destination.

Sandya held many revelations. The children had not been common travelers, but were the offspring of Patriarch Kirby, ruler of Odom. The leader graciously welcomed Kitsune and Myobu, introducing the prince to a stately-looking woman. Kitsune quickly realized she was his grandmother, mother to King Oni. He had previously believed her deceased and was shaken by the truth. More shocking were the revelations she had regarding Oni. Her son had been the one to murder Kitsune's mother, claiming afterward the woman had died giving birth to Kitsune. Believing her own life to be in jeopardy, Veranda had escaped Kitsunetsuki. The death of her husband—the king at that time—reached her ears shortly thereafter.

Kitsune wasn't the only one to receive major revelations in Sandya. Myobu had had his first bite of ham, the taste of which was heavenly. How had he gone so many sun cycles without it? More importantly, though, was Kitsune's admittance of his true intentions.

Late into the night, Myobu had snuck into Kitsune's bed, aiming to continue what they had started the previous evening. Kitsune put a quick but reluctant stop to it. He revealed that, though it was his father who had banished him, the king had also given him a directive. All Kitsune had to do to find favor with Oni was kill the King's Sun.

Whether it was Kitsune's naivety or Yokai blood, his unquestioning desire to follow through with his father's demands contradicted his otherwise good-natured and heroic persona. It was enough to spin even Myobu's head. For his part, Myobu's growing feelings for the man had clouded his knowledge of what was to come. He had hoped that perhaps there was another way to save the world, that he could avoid death and the two of them could always be together.

With the truth now having fully reasserted itself, Myobu left the prince's room in silent anger. He stalked about Sandya, asking himself why he had ever wanted to find love in the first place. Love was a messy, hurtful business, keeping humans from making sane, grounded decisions. All worked up and self-righteous, he fled the city, hoping to escape both destiny and the trappings of humanity.

Destiny and love were excellent trackers, however, and they caught up with him in short measure. Still angry, Myobu kept his distance from his partner, choosing instead to follow from afar for a couple of days as Kitsune traveled to the northernmost region of Odom. Then, purely by chance, they reunited as the prince was escaping a massive storm.

The gargantuan tornado, larger than any natural formation Myobu had ever seen, chased the pair into the Wastelands. Barely escaping with their lives, they found shelter from the storm in the same gray building Myobu had encountered on his previous journey. Once they had calmed down in the dark of the room, Myobu stripped the man of his shirt.

"Your heart beats here," he said, placing his hand against the prince's chest. Then he moved it to the right side of his abdomen. "Ninko's heart beats here. Unlike yours, it is not protected by a cage of bone. It is, however, the quickest and surest way to kill him. I want to be with you. I will travel with you on your journey, and I will help you find the King's Sun. I cannot assist in attacking, so when you loose your arrow or stab with your sword, it is here that you must aim."

Continuing to keep Kitsune from the whole truth made Myobu feel awful, especially now that Kitsune had come clean about his intentions. To keep himself from breaking down and making another mistake, Myobu relieved the prince of the rest of his clothing under the pretense of checking him for injuries. There were plenty of abrasions, and he discreetly used his magic to heal and sterilize the dozens of cuts Kitsune had sustained from flying debris.

Despite the seriousness of what they had escaped together, Myobu's medicinal labors had aroused them both. Going with his instincts, Myobu grabbed hold of the prince's cock. Starting off as an inspection for splinters, the appendage eventually ended up deep in his mouth. They both enjoyed themselves immensely. Myobu could still remember the howls Kitsune let loose as he grabbed hold of Myobu's head and thrust it into his groin.

The emotions, excitement, and physical touch had been so intense Myobu's magic almost boiled over into release. Only barely did he keep flames from engulfing the entire room and its machinery as he climaxed.

Kitsune had been too consumed in the experience to notice his companion's eyes were glowing orange.

Their reunion confirmed what Myobu both wanted and dreaded. They each had feelings for the other. They were together. Myobu was truly in love, which meant Kitsune would kill him.

He wondered how Kyubi's prophecy would come to pass. Did he have any say in the matter? He continued their trek toward the Harbinger. She'd probably find it humorous.

Succumbing to their base desires had made for a satisfying evening, but it would be some time before they would be able to explore each other even further. Pushing deeper into the Wastelands the next morning, they were greeted by frigid nights and winds strong enough to kick up sand and dirt.

"I'm not sure who would be pained more if I stuck it in you," Kitsune said one evening, trying in vain to brush sharp granules of earth from his private areas. "Spirits, it hurts me just by being there!"

"Please, sand or not, don't ever just *stick* it in me," Myobu had replied in a rare moment of irritation. Aside from the sand, the howling wind made it hard to speak with one another. While they traveled side by side, their relative silence made it seem as though they were walking in solitude.

Their trip through the Wastelands, though miserable, was uneventful. Kitsune had spent much of the trip reading through a journal purchased in Odom. Its author was an intelligent but unbalanced woman who was likely the cause of the catastrophic event that created the Wastelands. She wrote of a tumultuous relationship with a man named Damian and of her work researching energy. Damian had left her without explanation, leaving her in a poor mental state. Her last entries spoke of depression, anger, and a belief that her research project would yield disastrous results for everyone involved. Despite the warnings, she had intended to proceed.

When Myobu and Kitsune reached the green trees, fresh air, and clean water of the tribal lands, their spirits were immediately lifted.

Myobu led them to the Purple People, who welcomed the pair with open arms and a private hut. With the dirt washed away from their clothes and bodies, bellies full of delicious stew, and minds cleared of the depressions of the Wastelands, they enjoyed each other's bodies again.

Kitsune verbally expressed his love for Myobu, then proved it physically. It had been a blissful time, and it would be the last night they'd spend together before Myobu's death.

The next evening, Kitsune killed him.

The events unfolded more or less how Myobu had imagined. They found Kyubi's tree home as the sun was setting. The day's travel, walking step by step toward the end of his journey, had been emotionally toiling for Myobu. He was wracked with guilt, knowing Kitsune would suffer after the act was done.

"I love you, my pretty prince," he had uttered with tears in his eyes. He hoped Kitsune would carry those words with him afterward and believe them.

Kitsune returned the sentiment, confessing how much Myobu had changed his life in the little time they had spent together. "There are so many things I want to do now. Changing my father's mind about…about people…is just one of those goals."

"But you still want to kill Ninko, don't you?" Myobu couldn't help but hope there was another way. The Harbinger couldn't possibly see every path. An option must exist where the world was saved and he and the prince were together. Kitsune's answer took him by surprise.

"I don't know. I mean…I don't want to kill him."

The words, while opening the avenue he had hoped for, filled him with dread. He could try to convince Kitsune not to proceed with murder, but the potential consequences for the rest of the world were simply too dire to ignore. For the sake of all life, he had to proceed as planned.

Kyubi played her part well. She was charming, engaging, and completely unhinged. Recognizing the conflict that broiled within the prince, she goaded him into taking the necessary action, prodding at his torn mental state, conversing in a confusing manner, and insulting his father.

"Just tell me where he is," Kitsune finally begged, referring to the King's Sun. "Tell me so I can do what is necessary."

"Dear spirits," she whispered, giving Myobu an imperceptible glance. He had been drinking what he imagined would be his last bit of tea while the two verbally sparred. This was his cue. With a heavy heart, he shapeshifted into the guise of Ninko. For effect, he projected the images of the clothing he usually wore while carrying out his duties. "He's right behind you."

Kitsune turned about swiftly, wide-eyed and feverish, nocking an arrow into his bow. The look frightened Myobu, but he held to his resolve.

"Are you him?" the prince asked. "Are you Ninko? The King's Sun?"

Myobu took a deep breath, then raised his arms and shouted out threateningly. His keen ears told him when Kitsune's fingers were letting the arrow fly. At that point, he transformed back into Acro's form. That was the form in which he wanted to die, not that of Ninko.

Then there was a sharp pain in his abdomen. Right where his heart was. The impact of the arrow forced him back a step, after which he looked down at his stomach. The projectile was there, embedded into his flesh, jerking slightly to his last beats of life.

Myobu had collapsed into Kitsune's arms. The prince was shaking his head and talking, clearly distressed, but Myobu couldn't understand him. He reached out a small hand, grateful when Kitsune took it, and said, "Ky…Kyubi saw this ending…before you and I had even begun. You truly have been the one for me."

And then the darkness swallowed him.

*

Death was but the beginning of the next phase of existence. That's what the Yokai believed, and it had been instilled in him when he was but a pup. He could now verify that as truth. The afterlife was an ever-expanding consciousness. His mind engulfed the entire world and all the souls it held, then expanded outward into space. He was still growing into the galaxy when he encountered the Lady of the Mountain, Kitsune's mother. What was left of her earthly consciousness had been in the hoshi no tama hanging from the prince's neck. She had fully embraced death just as her son had taken Myobu's life. She had sensed Kitsune would need his love, that the world needed them to be together.

As one of the Yokai, the Lady's special power had been to breathe life back into lifeless things. In death, she could use that magic one more time. It was an all-consuming act, striking her from existence altogether, but it was a sacrifice she was willing to make.

"Everything will burn," she said, referring to what Kitsune would do with all his magic and power now that he had no emotional anchor. "Mountains will be blasted into dust…rivers and oceans will dry up…entire cities will be decimated. Mostly, though, everything will burn. My beautiful son will be remembered as a monster if anyone were to survive his wrath."

So the Lady had sent Myobu back, cramming his consciousness back into his small body.

*

Myobu squirmed as he lay on the ground. The tissues in his head had completed their healing, and all of his memories had come back to him. He knew who he was, who Kitsune was, and why a pass at death had been awarded unto him.

Kyubi had said his passing alone would not stop the blight that threatened to consume the world. It was imperative he find his love. For Kitsune's sake. For the sake of the entire world.

Though his mind was now intact, his body was still piecing itself back together. If he got up, he could do more damage. He could literally fall apart as he walked through the trees. It was best to let the Lady's magic run its course before beginning his search.

With a great sigh of impatience, Myobu lay still, staring up into the blue sky, and waited.

THE PURPLE PEOPLE

"Mother! They're back, Mother!" Clas shouted in the tongue of the Purple People. He ran as fast as his little legs could propel him, weaving between campfires back to his family's hut.

At the sound of his voice, Clas' mother turned away from a group of people. They had been laughing, and she continued to smile as she squinted into the darkness at her son. Their own fire, burning just outside the entrance of their home, illuminated little of the surroundings.

"I saw him, Mother! They're back," Clas continued as he skidded to a halt within the circle of their firelight. Clouds of dirt and soot followed him.

Kneeling, Clas' mother gently pressed two green-tinged fingers against his lips. She said, "It is late, my son. Others are in bed, and your voice carries."

Despite the reprimand, she looked at him adoringly. Clas thought his mother was the most beautiful person in the world, and he always did everything he could so she smiled at him that way. Lowering his voice, he said again, "They're back. Should we tell the elders?"

She tilted her head toward the next campfire. Two older men and a tough old woman were chatting amicably with another family. The three were the village's oldest living members and were sought for advice and policy. Clas made to sprint toward them, but his mother put a staying hand on his shoulder. "They'll be around shortly. Who is it you are speaking of?"

"The two outsiders! The ones that were here a few nights ago," he said, barely taking a moment to breathe. He struggled to keep his voice from rising again. "They stayed in the home at the edge of the village, remember? Made a lot of noise like you and—"

His mother pressed her fingers against his lips again, this time laughing out loud. "You have just given yourself away, my son! You should have been fast asleep in bed by that time."

Standing up, she scanned the area, paying close attention to the clusters of trees and bushes that the fires' light could not penetrate. She bore a questioning look, and Clas knew she was thinking the same thing he was: Why had the two men not entered the village? The dark-haired man had walked right in the first time he came through, unashamed by his nakedness. And on the second visit, he did not hesitate to present his companion, whom Clas found trustful despite the fact they didn't speak the same language. Plenty of adults were awake and walking about this evening. It would have been no inconvenience to announce themselves. Surely, they didn't want to sleep out in the woods!

"Where did you see them, Clas?" his mother asked. Her smile had disappeared.

Pointing toward a clearing at the edge of the village, he replied, "I saw one of them there. He was just standing still, looking at us."

The clearing was empty now. There was no sign of either man.

"You just saw the one? Not both?"

"Just the one. I assumed the other one was close by. Maybe hiding their belongings." Clas shrugged. He knew outsiders would sometimes hide their belongings in the woods, thinking the Purple People might steal them. Outsiders were fascinating, but quite odd.

"Perhaps you are right. We should go tell the elders," Clas' mother said gently, though there was now concern in her voice. Taking him by the hand, she started walking to their neighbor's campfire. "Which one did you see, my son?"

"The blond one," he replied. "With the long hair."

*

To the man with the long blond hair, few things in the world were as grating as laughter. Especially the mirth of children. The young should be in bed at this time of the day, not running gleefully about campfires, playing games with one another. It was dangerous, and the adults should have put an end to it hours ago.

He should put an end to it for them now.

A rustling in nearby underbrush caught the blond man's attention. Instinctually, he reached for his sword, but then he realized his long, slender fingers were already around its hilt and had pulled the blade halfway out of its sheath. He stood motionless for a full tic, blinking in confusion. He had reached for the weapon before the rustling. What was he going to do? Threaten the village's children?

Cut them down?

Prince Kitsune watched as a rabbit bounded from its hiding place and disappeared into the woods. Forcing the sword all the way back into its scabbard, he looked back at the village. These were a peaceful people. They had been kind to him, and he had wished not long ago that they would survive the more aggressive tribes. He did *not* want to hurt any of them.

Adjusting his pack, relatively light with the weight of a single book and fruit he had deemed edible, Kitsune turned away from the view. He respected the Purple People and held them in high regard, but they were also a source of great pain for him. Near the edge of the village, Kitsune had spotted the very hut he and Myobu had stayed in several nights before.

Myobu, or was it the King's Sun? Possibly Ninko?

To you, he is called betrayer, came a hurt voice from within. A pained grimace marred his thin face, and salty tears threatened to wet his cheeks.

After long and weary travels, Kitsune had confessed his love to the other man in that hut. They had made love afterward, or at least he had thought they had. Perhaps it had just been sex to Myobu. A way to pass the time, or to make his duplicity the next day that much harder to bear.

Myobu's deception had not been the fault of the Purple People, and the prince bore them no ill will. They didn't know the man. Didn't speak the same language.

Why, then, were you just considering showing their children the pointy end of that sword you carry? said the pained voice, the part of his conscience that demanded retribution.

Kitsune shook his head, clearing his mind of that horrific thought. And of Myobu. Over the past three days since leaving the remains of the Western Pass, Kitsune found he had to block out thoughts of the other man. They kept creeping back into his head, playing like the films mentioned in the odd journal he had rescued from a street vendor in Odom. The memories caused his head to hurt and eyes to shed tears, an emotional turmoil he had never experienced.

Looking ahead, he focused his attention on his destination.

The tribal lands were known for its fabled pyramids, massive structures built from large, chiseled stone. Apparently, the farther one traveled into the tribal lands, the bigger and more intricate the structures became. Some of them were supposed to be as large as Inari Palace, the base of which covered a hundred acres. Just like Kitsune's home, such buildings would appear like small mountains jutting out of the forest's canopy.

Having never left Oinari before, Kitsune wasn't certain the pyramids of legend existed. He didn't doubt it, though. Not anymore. Mere weeks ago, he questioned the existence of the Yokai, magic, and love. He had been proven wrong on all counts, though he was still skeptical of the wisdom and usefulness of the latter.

A short distance away from the village of the Purple People was a pyramid, decrepit and overgrown with plant life. Hardly the inspiration of legends, it stood abandoned and largely ignored. The peak of the structure barely crested the forest canopy.

He had first seen the relic of a building a few days ago when gazing out at the village from the hut he had shared with Myobu. His companion told him that their tribal friends looked over the ancient structure, which itself housed a valuable artifact. It had not dawned on him at the time what that artifact was. No one could know. But it had revealed itself to him after the fact. Showed him where it was. If he could recover the item, he could use it in his fight for his father.

Against your father, the angry, bitter voice reminded him. *You are against him now.*

King Oni, monarch of the Kitsunetsuki Kingdom, had banished Kitsune, his only offspring and heir to the throne. The act had been done under the pretense of enacting new laws and a moral code Kitsune did not fit into. In particular, it was Kitsune's choice of bedmates that had been so offensive. The king had offered a course of action that would grant Kitsune access to his homeland and future: kill the son of Marauxus, king of Gaav.

The king's son turned out to be the King's Sun, a respected advisor to Marauxus, and the King's Sun had actually been Myobu. Even though Kitsune had fallen in love with the man and decided not to follow through with his father's wishes, the Harbinger had cajoled him into killing the other.

In retrospect, Oni's offer made little sense. How did murdering another man wipe away the sins of his sexuality? It didn't. The act had been a ploy to start a war. If hired mercenaries had killed Kitsune in Odom, the kingdom into which he had been banished, Odom would have been the unfortunate target. If the prince succeeded in killing the King's Sun, Marauxus would have had to retaliate or risk looking weak. Kitsune had been so focused on pleasing his father, on finding his way back to what he thought his destiny was, that he had fallen for the trick.

You will not be fooled again.

Pushing away thick vines that hung from massive tree limbs, Kitsune found himself at the base of the pyramid. He looked up at its ruined façade. Weather and looters had cracked away what had once been a smooth exterior. Plant life had taken hold within those nooks, widening them. The entire place now looked like an enormous pile of blocks. Ironically, it appeared as though the vines and other plant life that had hastened its dilapidation were all that held it together.

Kitsune saw an entrance to the structure on the opposite end of the wall from where he stood and made his way over. It surely had not been the original entrance. He couldn't imagine an architect would spend so much time and energy to create a structure so perfectly symmetrical and then stick its door to one side. Then he reminded himself they were tombs or vaults, not meant to be reentered once they were sealed. Whether this was the original entrance, its current form had been made by thieves, explorers, or scientists.

Whatever or whomever the building had been built to protect had been forgotten, either being pilfered long ago or still hidden away within the myriad hallways and rooms. Throughout the entire region, unsubstantiated rumors claimed many of the colossal structures had been repurposed over time to house new and fantastic objects or treasure. The stories said roaming tribes had been conscripted and tasked with overseeing them. They had been simple fables meant to entertain children.

Except Kitsune knew the story was true. At least with this pyramid. The artifact that resided within it had been calling out to him. Beckoning him. And like a hungry man drawn to the scent of food, he had answered its call.

Back at the Western Pass, shortly after he had realized his father had betrayed him, he had used his fury to focus his powers. As a result, the passageway collapsed. Half the mount had been shorn away and dumped into the Rout River. The prince was about to continue his tirade, perhaps block the river from flowing altogether, but had come to his senses before acting. That was when the clanking brass machine had appeared through the mist of reality. It was all around him. It always had been, always would be. Hidden behind the fabric of reality. For just a moment, while he laid eyes upon the monstrous wonder, Kitsune knew everything there was to know.

That was how he had learned of the artifact within the pyramid. Or how it had learned of him. During the heartbeat that he had gazed upon the brass machine, the artifact's voices—for it had many—called out to him. When the mysterious, noisy pipes disappeared once more, some of those voices stayed with him. He knew whatever object from which they came would help him conquer his father.

Staring into the dark, yawning hole in the wall, Kitsune wondered exactly what function the Purple People provided. It certainly wasn't to protect or guard the artifact. Here he was, about to enter the structure through an obvious entrance. Other than overgrown plants, there had been no deterrents. No traps. No warriors.

The haphazard entrance itself would probably have been enough to scare off most, but Kitsune felt no fear about what lay within. He had felt no fear in days. Immense sadness because of betrayal and loss, and plenty of anger. He could use those to his advantage now.

Holding out his hand, he tapped into the anger and conjured up a ball of fire above his palm. The flames burned bright and hot, licking his skin without burning. Their light easily illuminated his path.

Kitsune dropped his pack and stepped through the entrance. He immediately felt the temperature drop. Sounds of dripping water echoed down long corridors, and the cool air felt damp against his skin. Massive roots hung from the ceiling. They hampered his progress at first, as he had to brush them aside to keep from lighting them on fire.

While traveling back to the village, Kitsune had wondered how long it would take him to find the artifact. If so many others had pillaged the pyramid before him without uncovering it, how quickly did he think he'd be able to? Occasionally, the thought crossed his mind that the stress and turmoil he'd endured was causing a bout of insanity. He was hearing voices in his head, after all.

Then the sensation would come again. The pulling of the object on his mind and soul. He knew it was real. It would lead him to it.

After a hundred footfalls down the first hall, the prince took a left. It was the third offshoot corridor he had come across, but he knew this was the only one that would lead to his destination.

The fire in his palm guided the way. It dazzled his senses, as he was still not used to wielding the power. It was a pleasant distraction, as it was eerily quiet. No sounds other than the padding of his feet upon the stone floor. Not even the scuffling of expected rodents.

Several long tics passed as he traversed the dark corridors, listening for the voices of the artifact. He took a right, went up a flight of stone steps, then made two more lefts. The structure was a puzzle of paths, and he hoped he'd be able to find his way back out. It would be too easy to get lost in the maze of halls and rooms.

He ascended to another level. The passageways were becoming shorter and narrower as he neared the structure's apex. A feeling of claustrophobia was descending upon him, as did the terrible thought that this was a trap. Perhaps his father, who had his own magic, was so intent on silencing him that he laid out a snare in this dark labyrinth. But no, the pull of the prize was so strong. It was so close now. Just one more turn.

Kitsune stepped into yet another hall made of unadorned stone. It was a short pathway, and his fire showed how confined the space was. The ceiling was a palm's length above his head, and he could easily touch both walls without spreading his arms out fully. The flames also revealed a dead end with nothing else to be seen.

Others might have been discouraged and given up at this point. The prince may have, too, not so long ago. He'd seen the tricks and hidden nature of others and now knew to always look beyond what was apparent. Walking down the quiet corridor, he ran his free hand along the rough walls. He completed his first pass in just over a tic and, upon reaching the dead end, turned around. Cocking his head, he strained with all his senses, trying to locate the artifact. On a whim, he closed his outstretched hand into a fist, dousing the fire and plunging him into darkness.

The darkness did not match the dead silence. A soft light emanated from behind the wall to his left.

"There you are," Kitsune said aloud, jumping as the sound of his voice reverberated off the walls. He strode forward to examine the finding. The light was coming from behind the wall, pulsing brilliantly enough to shine through the mortar for a few moments before going dark again. It gave the wall a haunted mood.

Cursing himself for not carrying a dagger and wishing he had a crowbar, Kitsune set to work chiseling away at the mortar with his sword. If Oinari's royal sword smith knew what he was doing, saw how he was blunting the tip of the trusty weapon, Kitsune would never again receive a new blade. Nevertheless, he continued, knowing what lay behind the wall would ultimately take the place of his sword.

For nearly half an hour, he carved with the unsuitable tool, blew out dust and crumbling mortar from the crevices, and pulled on the heavy stones. Kitsune knew he could probably use one or more of his powers to blast away the wall, but he didn't want to risk damaging the hidden artifact or causing the structure to collapse on top of him.

At last, with a final heave, the prince lured the first stone from its place in the wall. He jumped back to keep his feet from being crushed. A wave of purple light spilled out of the gap and into the narrow hall. His eyes hurt after being in near darkness for so long, and it took several heartbeats for them to adjust. Once acclimated, he peered inside the hole.

It's here! It's real! Kitsune thought, his eyes tearing up as much from emotion as from the light. He had tried to keep the hope of its reality at arm's length just to keep from being sorely disappointed, but here it was in front of him.

Behind the wall was another layer of stone, but a shelf had been hollowed out in it. Resting neatly upon it was a massive, sheathed sword. It was longer than Kitsune was used to handling, but he didn't worry about it being unwieldy. The weapon was straight and its hilt well-crafted.

The scabbard appeared rather plain, lacking the ornamentation many associated with ancient relics. Only two features made this object immediately stand out from all others: it was wreathed in purple flames, and the fire's light made the lettering stitched into the scabbard clearly legible.

"Tsukumogami," Kitsune whispered.

No sooner had he uttered the sword's name than the flames flickered out. Although unable to see, Kitsune still managed to pull another stone free from its home, hearing it crack in half as it hit the floor. The opening in the wall was now large enough to liberate Tsukumogami, and he blindly reached in toward its hilt.

"What in the blazing hell do you think you are doing?" came a voice from the darkness to Kitsune's right. He whirled about, reaching for his sword, but stopped when he felt the touch of cold, sharp metal under his chin.

"I, err, was going to follow up on my inclination to take that blazing sword," he replied, straining to see the individual who had expertly snuck up on him. As he stopped speaking, the weapon burst into flames again, lighting up the corridor in a purple hue.

"Well, you can't take it," said the woman who had him at sword-point.

"But it's calling to me!" Kitsune asserted. He was taken aback by the look of his new acquaintance. Her skin was an exquisite shade of dark brown. Her hair was medium length, jet black, and straight, and it stuck out away from her round face at odd angles. The clothing she wore was the oddest bit about her. Patches of colorful, shimmery cloth had been stitched together to form a thigh-length jacket and trousers. It was like nothing he'd ever expect to find a person wearing in a deserted pyramid in the middle of nowhere. Somehow, though, it fit her.

It also made him acutely aware of his own shabby clothing and filthy state. He hadn't had a bath or change of clothes in some time, unless wading through a river counted.

"Hmm," the woman said to herself. "And the pretty man is also a bit crazed."

A flash of anger pulsed through Kitsune. He jumped back, her sword shallowly cutting him as it grazed his chin. Able to draw his own weapon, he brought it up defensively. Growling through his teeth, he said, "Do not call me pretty."

"Struck a nerve, have I?" she replied, unaffected by his actions. She didn't even appear to take his defensive stance seriously. "If you don't want to be called pretty, why do you look it?"

"Huh?" Kitsune puzzled, knowing he was covered in threadbare clothing and a week's worth of grime. Then he decided he had no time for this. He had not come all this way to be delayed by taunting words. Especially those calling him *pretty*. Not again. Jabbing forward with his sword, he made to stab her. Not kill her—he wasn't that angry—but maybe injure her sword-bearing arm. Take away her threat and teach her for being so mouthy.

But the colorfully dressed woman knocked his sword away with her own. It was an ungainly motion for her, but he wouldn't have known that by looking at her facial expression. For all she gave away, she might have been swiping away an irritating mosquito.

She's not even taking my offensive seriously! Kitsune cursed in his head. He brought up his weapon again, slashing it at her horizontally. This time, he didn't care if he truly hurt her. He didn't think of what might come afterward, what the consequences might be.

Not that it mattered. She stepped fluidly out of the range of his weapon, smiling down at the blade as it passed harmlessly by her chest. Then, just as Kitsune rushed her, the purple flames of Tsukumogami went out, plunging the hall back into darkness.

The sword found purchase, but it was not in the chest of his opponent. Instead, it ground against the rocky wall of the hallway. A girlish laughter rang in his ears as sparks flew off the blade. He grabbed a hold of the bits of fire with his mind and, spinning about, threw out a roaring ring of flame. His rage fed the magic, and he had days of pent-up wrath. The fire moved across the walls, ceiling, and floor like water in a riverbed, and columns of fire connected the ceiling and floor. Everything outside of a two-footfall radius of his body was consumed by the deadly, heated air.

The woman had either expected his actions or was incredibly lucky. Inside the safe area about his person, she stood directly in front of him, the flames outlining her figure. Their two noses were only a finger's width apart as she stared into his face.

"Don't want to know my name before you stab me?" She moved forward, opening her mouth. Kitsune thought she was going to bite into his cheek, but she instead stuck out her tongue and licked it. Leaving behind a trail of saliva, she whispered into his ear, "I want to know yours."

Kitsune shuddered in revulsion, and the surrounding flames winked out. He would have backed up if it weren't for the wall behind him, so he pushed her away.

"Spirits, who *are* you?" he said, wiping at the spit with his sleeve.

"Oh, good, we are going to play!" Still holding her blade, she gave a formal bow. "My name is Mai."

"I am," Kitsune replied, then hesitated a moment. He decided that, for once, he should wise up and not reveal his identity immediately. He reached for a name from recent memory. "Joseph. My name is Joseph."

"Pleased to meet you, Joey," she said.

Kitsune took a better look at the young woman. Her flashy clothes were well cut and clean, two descriptors rarely heard in the tribal lands. The colors of her skin and hair indicated she wasn't one of the Purple People. "What are you doing here, Mai? In the woods? In this pyramid?"

"Oh, I'm with my father," she responded, nodding her head energetically. Then, a little darkly, she added, "He's around here somewhere. Another pyramid, maybe."

"Well?" Kitsune pressed, uncomfortable with the thought that there might be other frenetic individuals like her around. His temper had cooled, but he still wasn't convinced he shouldn't have stabbed her. "What are the both of you doing out here?"

"My father is an anthropologist! We're from Gaav, you see, but we've been up here studying these ancient things. Trying to make heads or tails of 'em. Well, at least my father has. I've been studying *him*."

Mai stopped short but smiled broadly at Kitsune, revealing a set of perfect white teeth. He wanted to ask her more about her father's studies, but he couldn't find a reason to pursue it outside of intellectual curiosity. That, and he couldn't get past how her presence unnerved him.

Instead, he chose a different path that he hoped would extricate him from the conversation. "Why did you say I can't take the sword?"

"Because it's a valuable artifact! My father will want to study it," she exclaimed. "Besides, this is Tsukumogami, a blade with power only the Yokai can wield. And while you, my new and very pretty friend, obviously maintain some control over magic, you are not of the Yokai."

Kitsune ground his teeth. "What makes you think I'm not?"

"Because they're spirits," Mai said matter-of-factly, as though she had rehearsed it. Raising her sword, she prodded him in the chest—not enough to even cut the fabric of his shirt, but with enough force to prove her point. "And you are quite solid."

"Oh, the Yokai are much more than ghostly beings," Kitsune assured her. "And they can bleed."

"That sounds like the beginning of a very personal story, and I'm not interested," she said, finally sheathing her blade. Apparently, she no longer considered him a threat. "Anyway, to you and I and most of the Yokai, Tsukumogami is just a regular sword. No benefits come from carrying it, unless you plan on selling it. Is that what you're thinking of doing? No? Good. You'd more than likely be killed for it before you could find a buyer."

"I am already familiar with the legendary history of the blade," Kitsune said. He recounted stories he and other children all throughout the region grew up sharing with one another. Stories of Inari, her dual gifts, and of the sword she forged in secret. Upon her death, the weapon would only accept individuals with more than one magical gift, and it consumed their souls and power when they passed. "Did I miss anything important?"

Mai shrugged. "How do I know? They are just stories. It could be noted that just because the thing contains magic and souls, the two don't necessarily align."

"How do you mean?"

"The sword takes the magic of its wielders upon their deaths. Adds the power to that which it already has. Helps make the next holder stronger. New souls are also added to a collective consciousness and made available to the user, offering advice, wisdom, and history, but that consciousness can no longer use magic, nor does it have any true say in how it's used."

Kitsune stood there for several heartbeats, nodding at what she said. Then he reached through the breach in the wall, going for the sword. He heard Mai sigh and say, "I already told you—"

But as his fingers closed around the hilt, coming into contact with the leather wrapping, Tsukumogami burst into purple flames. They wrapped around his arm, working their way toward his head. Too transfixed to react, Kitsune could only watch and feel the flames as they consumed his body.

You found us, came the multitude of voices Kitsune had been hearing intermittently for days, only now it was stronger and more choral. A sea of voices. *We felt you, called for you, and you found us. It has been so long.*

The flames swirled about him, lighting up the hallway, blowing away the remnants of his previous fires conjured by magic. They did not burn him or Mai. Instead, they felt cool and soothing against his skin. As he watched, the flames separated into a multitude of ghostly apparitions. Yokai, either in their natural form or in the guise of other species, filled the corridor. Some appeared to be warriors. Others were explorers. One in particular caught Kitsune's attention. It appeared in the back of the crowd toward the end of the hall. It had a brooding, malignant look about it. The prince tried to get a better look, but the voices continued.

Who are you? he thought. All his senses tingled. *What are you doing?*

We are Tsukumogami. We found you, one of the gifted, was the reply. *You answered our call, and we are now binding you to us. One day, you will be us.*

That made Kitsune hesitate. He'd forgotten that point from the stories, that the souls of its handlers lived in the sword for all eternity. Like many of the fantastical things he had only recently discovered were real, he had never given it a second thought. Thinking it might be wise to carefully think his actions through, he made to let go of the sword.

Before he could, the dark figure at the end of the hall raised its head high, and the chorus of voices asked him, *Why did you seek us out?*

To help remove my father from his throne. He has done terrible things as king and will continue to do so if left unchecked, Kitsune replied automatically. As his father's betrayal washed over him again, his grip on Tsukumogami tightened. *I have access to a great well of incredible power, but my father has an unknown source of magic as well. That and sun cycles of experience. I need you as an advantage over him. I need you to save my people from his tyranny.*

The flames intensified, his senses tingling again, almost to the point of pain. Then the energy withdrew into the metal.

It is finished. We are bound, Tsukumogami whispered to him. Then it fell quiet.

Kitsune stood motionless in the dark, wondering if he had just found a gift or brought a curse upon himself. What would death be like? An eternity spent inhabiting cold steel, sharing his mind with countless other souls, did not sound appealing.

Conjuring up a flame to bring light back to the hall, he turned to face Mai, expecting her to make some snide comment or perhaps ask to lick the weapon. He was surprised to find a stricken look on her round face.

"How did you…what did it…" she stuttered. Despite her apparent unease, Kitsune was pleased she was flappable. It meant she was human, after all. "But you're not one of the Yokai. I would know it if you were."

"I am not one of them," he admitted. "but I come from them. Their blood runs through my veins. It must be enough for the blade, for it has bound with me."

Pointing to his flame, she said, "What is your second power?"

Before he could answer, the distant, muted sound of a horn found its way through the cracks in the pyramid's walls. It sounded to Kitsune like a call for war or a warning of impending battle. He looked inquisitively at Mai. If possible, she looked even more aghast than she had before.

"It's the Purple People," she said, confirming his assumption. "They are under attack!"

The clan was friendly and peaceful, and they had many talents and specializations. Battle was not among them, or at least that is what Myobu had told the prince. Other clans inhabited the lands, and many thrived on war. The traveling and trading of more advanced civilizations had kept them away from the Purple People for decades, but now that most of that had ceased, it was only a matter of time before they sought to claim more land.

"I must help them," Kitsune said. He dropped his dinged sword to the ground and tied Tsukumogami's scabbard to his waist.

"I'm coming with you," Mai said. Having recovered from her shock, her voice sounded far more confident.

"You most certainly are not!"

"I most certainly am," she countered, pointing at his new sword. "I said you couldn't take that. Since you were so determined to do so you bound your bloody soul to it, the least I can do is accompany it and you. Anyway, I can help you learn how to use it."

He paused, squinting at her in the dim light. "You know how to use it?"

"I'm the daughter of an anthropologist," she replied with a shrug. "I don't know how to actually use its powers per se, but I know a great deal about it. Might be able to lessen its learning curve."

That would be advantageous, especially since he didn't have the time to properly train with it. King Oni had to be stopped, and the quicker he unfolded his plans, the better. However, the voices within the blade seemed more than capable of passing along its knowledge. And he didn't think he could stand a companion right now. He wouldn't be able to trust them.

He was about to tell her this—was prepared to pull the sword on her if she refused to stay behind—but the horn sounded again. It was closer now, and its vibrations shook loose granules of mortar from the walls and ceiling.

Waving away dust from his eyes, Kitsune remembered how well she had initially disarmed him. Mai might not be the greatest swordswoman, but she could obviously use a weapon. She would perhaps be beneficial against what they were about to face.

"Come along, then," he said, waving her on as they retraced his steps out of the pyramid.

FIRE AND LIGHTNING

The night was no longer young, and a damp chill emphasized how otherworldly the woods could be in the dark. Clas should have been in bed. Most of the adults had gone to sleep by now. If he had been smart, he'd be right there along with them, dreaming of something pleasant. Instead, he was sprinting through the trees as quickly as possible.

Why had he not listened to his mother as he should have done, as he had always done? Disobedience was not in his nature. He was adventurous, sure, but not rebellious. He loved his parents, knew his place within the family, and sought their approval. What had possessed him to think wandering off alone into the woods at this hour was a wise choice?

It had been the blond man, of course. Clas couldn't get the image of the foreigner out of his mind, standing all alone in tattered clothing at the edge of the village. The more he'd thought about it, the more certain he was the outsider had been alone. The dark-haired man was far away. Gone. The blond one was by himself, lost, and was looking for something.

When Clas' mother had told the elders of what he had seen, they had spoken at some length with one another. More adults had joined them while others went out into the forest to confer with their sentries.

His mother, eventually realizing he was still hanging around, shooed him off to bed.

What were they concerned about? he had thought while pulling wool blankets over his body. *Are we in danger? Is he in danger?*

Clas' mind refused to settle after that last question posed itself. Eventually, as tired as he was from a full day of chores and play, he had the bright idea to go out, find the blond man, and warn him. Nevermind they didn't speak the same language, or that Clas didn't know what danger they faced, if indeed there was one.

Stupid, he thought now as he skirted around a tree, racing back to the village. *What did you think you were going to do?*

The blond man was not to be found, but Clas had nearly stumbled into a group of fellow tribesmen. He kept himself hidden, standing behind a tree as he listened in on them. They spoke softly, and he was only barely able to make out that they had spotted multiple outsiders creeping about in the woods. The group disagreed on how to proceed: alert the others or wait and see if the strangers would pass on. It was possible—more than likely, actually—that they meant no harm.

A volley of arrows had proven that sentiment incorrect. Clas watched as the entire party fell within a heartbeat. One was dead before he hit the ground, but the other two shouted out in alarm before they were silenced by another spread of projectiles.

That was when the horn first sounded, and Clas ran back toward home. Back to his mother.

He had just reached the edge of the village—exactly where he had seen the blond man standing earlier—when a searing pain seized his back under his right shoulder blade. A razor-sharp arrow had found purchase there, and its force drove him to the ground. Clas screamed at the sudden agony. He looked up. The adults were awake again, and he recognized many of the faces now looking his way in concern. One of them was his mother. His eyes went watery with tears, but the last thing he saw before his vision left him was her abject terror. He hated that he had caused that.

She screamed, but he did not hear. The pain had become too much for him to bear, and his mind fell into darkness.

*

Large leaves slapped at Kitsune as he tore through the forest. Mai grunted behind him as the branches he shoved away snapped back and hit her. The horn had sounded a third time when they exited the pyramid, its source definitely being the nearby village. It had yet to sound a fourth time.

The two came across three prone bodies in a small clearing. Kitsune did not recognize them but knew they were Purple People by their clothing. Two were dead, the third was gasping her last breaths of life. She gurgled unintelligible words at the prince before closing her eyes for the last time.

"There!" Mai exclaimed, pointing as a large fire erupted less than a hundred footfalls away. Panicked screams echoed in the air.

"Let's go!" Kitsune replied, knowing the tribe's homes were partially constructed of flammable timber and leaves. He drew Tsukumogami from its sheath. It was lighter than it looked, and he held it deftly.

As moonlight glinted off his new blade, the anger he felt toward those who would attack a peaceful and defenseless people exploded throughout his body. The emotions fueled his magic. He could feel the fire that now raged from within the village, and he saw the storm clouds that blotted out the skies above. Both fire and weather contained an energy that awaited his call.

Use us, he thought he heard from the sword. It was a calmer sound, contradictory to how he felt. *Together, we shall defeat the enemy.*

As they traversed the distance, Kitsune recalled from his first visit that he had estimated the tribe numbered around 150 individuals. While the Purple People were wise enough to have sentries patrolling the woods, they were certainly not equipped or trained to handle even a small incursion. If the alarm had not been sounded, the enemy could have slipped unnoticed from hut to hut, silencing each sleeping family they came across without opposition.

They will fail.

Without bothering to take stock of the situation from the tree line, Kitsune burst into the outskirts of the village. Mai hung back, taking a more cautious approach, but he hoped to immediately distract the offenders. He quickly scanned the grounds, estimating the enemy numbers to be around thirty—more than enough to overpower and enslave the unsuspecting village.

An abrupt rustling sounded directly behind him, followed by the clashing of metal. Kitsune spun around to see Mai leap from the shadows in time to stop a silent enemy from slashing at him. The man, nearly a footfall taller than him, looked bewildered at the bundle of shiny, metallic colors coming at him from the side. With a flick of his own wrist, Kitsune used Tsukumogami to knock the man's sword from his hands. The blade went flying off into the brush. Mai swiveled and finished off the startled man by stabbing him through the chest.

"Do I have to take all of them on myself?" Mai said as four others emerged to take the fallen man's place.

Refraining from pointing out that her swiveling flourish before the kill was unnecessary—the move an amateur would make—Kitsune stood back to back with her as they faced their new foes. Mai laughed as she clashed with two of them, and time seemed to slow for the prince as he faced the others. Given the opportunity to study these rival tribesmen, he saw they had the same physical characteristics of the Purple People: skin with a green tinge and dark brown hair. Perhaps their home was much farther north, as they wore their hair longer and were clothed in fitted black furs. Streaks of dark red paint crossed their faces and arms, meant to intimidate.

It was obvious by the way the newcomers held their blades—as though the swords were natural extensions of their own bodies—that they had trained for many sun cycles. Trained, honed, and used those skills. They moved fluidly, perfectly balanced, not letting their gestures betray their next act.

Unfortunately for them, Kitsune had also trained in combat for nearly all his life. He, too, had killed. Undoubtedly, his kills were far fewer than theirs, but he had something to fight for. Something good.

And he had Tsukumogami, legendary sword of Inari.

These two have not fought together, Kitsune thought as they advanced. *They are both attacking from above.*

With a slight step forward, the prince brought up his blade and parried both of their downward swings. A loud ringing sounded as the weapons met, and while he felt nothing, the impact must have been jarring to the others. They both cried out in surprise, and one nearly dropped his sword. They could all see the tribesmen's blades had been compromised by the engagement.

Kitsune brought his sword back and, his face twisting with effort, swung it laterally at his opponents. As the blade sliced through the air, it gave off a bright violet hue. It struck the first man's weapon, which responded by shattering into a dozen shards. The broken pieces flew back into the faces and necks of Kitsune's opponents, finding purchase in soft tissue. It took the second enemy several heartbeats to realize he had been dealt a lethal blow, and he stared in horror as his companion fell to his knees, blood spilling down the front of his body. Then the second man's energy gave out. Dropping his own weapon, he fell to the ground alongside his fellow warrior.

Without pausing to admire his handiwork, he turned to help Mai finish off her half of their foes. To his surprise, she had already bested them.

"What took you so long?" she asked, leaning against her sword as though it were a walking stick.

"You may just prove yourself useful," he replied, throwing a bit of her jaunty attitude back at her. Looking down, he saw the two Mai had slain looked sickly and weak. "How were they even able to fight?"

"Useful to *you*?" she said, ignoring his question. Stepping closer to him, she ran a hand across his chest. "I'm only here to keep an eye on Tsukumogami. Besides, I can be so much more than—"

Mai's hand fell away from his chest, and her flippant look evaporated into disbelief. Thunder roiled above them as greenish clouds grew heavy with rain. The prince followed her disconcerting gaze, at first seeing nothing but trees, grass, and a few rocks. One rock shuddered, though, and he saw it was actually the huddled form of a small child. An arrow protruded from his back.

Kitsune's head swam as the arrow twitched. The sight didn't make him squeamish, but it brought back the vivid memory of loosing an arrow of his own, one that had embedded itself into Myobu's abdomen. That projectile had shuddered along with the heart it pierced…until the heart had stopped beating altogether.

He tricked you, Kitsune thought. Or was it the voices of Tsukumogami? *He had taken on his guise of Ninko and acted as though he was about to attack. He wanted you to shoot him.*

But why? was the question he kept asking himself. He wanted a reason, but the answers were gone. It saddened him just as much as it angered him.

Mai rushed to the boy's side, but Kitsune hardly noticed. His emotions boiled inside of him just as the thunder rolled in the clouds above. He and the clouds were connected, the prince knew. He had used devastating weather before. As he searched for a responsible party, someone who had the gall to shoot a child, he knew he was going to use it again.

Near the center of the village, the enemy gathered the surviving Purple People like a flock of sheep. They were corralled into a compact crowd, kept in a tight huddle by the points of arrows and swords. Ten or so red-striped men walked around the perimeter of the captives, forcing individuals to their knees. The frightened and helpless villagers discreetly moved the youth into the center, hoping to protect them from whatever horrors were to come next.

Kitsune stalked toward that group, his feet treading across well-worn grass. Still gripping his sword in his right hand, he raised his other up into the sky. He felt for the raw energy above him, understood it, *was* it. At that point, he could do with it as he wished.

A few of the enemy party glanced up as Kitsune approached. They didn't give him much thought, and he was sure he looked an odd sight. With long blond hair and a slender body that hid his physical strength, he had rarely been described as menacing. Even while fighting hand-to-hand or with a sword, he was more often said to be birdlike and agile. Such a slight creature wielding a long, deadly blade was bound to raise a few eyebrows.

Then, sensing that something was wrong, the trespassers stopped. The metal in their weapons and ornamentation glowed violet and emit a high-pitched ringing sound. Some of them dropped their swords and worked feverishly to remove rings or chains from around their necks. Others looked skyward, their faces full of resignation.

Decisively, Kitsune brought his fist back down to his side.

A bolt of green lightning streaked down from the storm clouds. It looked as though it would strike the huddled group of prisoners, and most of them shrieked. About twenty footfalls above them, the bolt split into a dozen branches, splaying out in all directions. Each member of the advancing party was struck square in the torso, throwing them off their feet. All their hair was singed away and their clothing shredded. Intricate, fernlike burn marks raked across each person's skin before the enemy hit the ground.

Even as their smoking, ember-ridden bodies were falling, the vacuum created by the green bolt collapsed, creating a thunderous roar. The survivors cried out again, cupping their ears. Nearby trees swayed in response, dried branches cracking off and crashing to the ground. Even Kitsune was thrown onto his back.

Some bodies of his victims twitched in convulsions, but none of them were breathing.

Use us, Tsukumogami whispered again in Kitsune's mind. He stood up and surveyed the group of Purple People. Frightened faces, dazed expressions, and a few bloody ears, but they looked otherwise unharmed. He turned, searching for other enemies.

I thought I was using you, the prince thought as he tried to differentiate between friend and foe. Acrid black smoke from the fires hindered his visibility. Screams came from all directions—some from the blast of lightning and resulting thunderclap, most at the horrors unfolding around them.

We have done nothing but help focus your feelings, the sword whispered. *Now let us assist you in directing them.*

Kitsune identified another ten of the enemy spread throughout the village. Some were forcing captives forward with the point of their weapons, while others chased down new victims. Those who fought back or proved otherwise troublesome were cut down without hesitation.

The heat from a nearby hut that had been set ablaze caressed Kitsune's skin. Just like the energy from above, he joined with its fiery source. Tsukumogami erupted into purple flames, casting a colorful hue about the village. He stretched the sword out toward the hut, extending—directing—his anger along with it, and seized control of the orange fire. It twisted and crackled, grew brighter and hotter, and climbed into the air.

As he swung the sword away from the structure, the fire followed his motion and direction, flowing off the flammable materials like water from a leaf. Using his new power, Kitsune reached out to the other buildings being consumed, pulling the fire away from them and pooling them into the first blaze. One by one, the huts went dark, night reclaiming much of the village.

No one seemed to notice at first, but then one attacker stopped pursuing his prey as a ball of flame the size of a horse floated lazily just above his head. The man's jaw dropped as his gaze followed the phenomenon. His eyes bulged in terror when he saw the much larger ball of flame into which it melded. It was like the sun had descended from the sky and, now being the only source of light, commanded attention.

The village grew silent. No one suspected the blond-haired man was behind the magical acts. Just like the citizens of Kitsunetsuki, most had never seen a display of such power and therefore did not understand it. The villagers were grateful for the distraction, but they were still terrified of the harm it could still cause. The rival tribe seemed to deduce it was a reaction to their attack. However, they hadn't a clue how to counter it.

One of them loosed an arrow.

With a crackling sizzle, the wooden projectile disappeared into the swirling flames. For a heartbeat, it appeared nothing would happen. Then, like the lightning that preceded it, the star exploded outward in a dazzling display, creating twelve smaller spheres of flame. Like falling meteorites, these smaller versions seared across the night sky at incredible speeds. Unlike the natural phenomenon, these did not move in straight, predictable paths. They zigzagged and circled around huts, made hairpin turns around trees, and even disappeared underground before popping back up at unpredictable points.

Kitsune reveled at how he was now able to control fire with ease. Only an hour ago, he had impressed himself by creating a small flame in the palm of his hand by which to see, and now he was lighting up the entire village. It came so easily to him, unlike the drudgery of unsuccessful training and meditation he had forced himself to endure in the preceding weeks to control and use his power over the weather. With Tsukumogami, he could probably do incredible things with lightning, winds, and rain.

The prince looked at the sword with admiration, noticing a curious detail in the purple flame that encompassed it. While it had extended toward him welcomingly—invasively—back in the pyramid, it was now stretching away. At first, he thought it part of the outward flow of magic, but somehow it looked as though it was attempting to escape.

Is it afraid of me? Kitsune wondered. He looked harder into the light, trying to spot the individual souls of which it was comprised.

The prince was hit with two distinct memories. One was of a massive tornado, which had descended from the sky above like a predator, inadvertently created by his lustful desires for Myobu and sadness at the man's absence. Kitsune was certain its destructive rage had decimated a nearby Odom outpost. He had been wracked with guilt over the likely fate of that community.

The other memory had also been a cyclone, though this one had consisted of fire. After having shot Myobu in the heart, Kitsune had pulled at what he thought was the spark of life in the other's body. He had been mistaken, and what he had thought was life had actually been Myobu's magic. After pulling at it with his mind, he had somehow transferred it into himself. Unable to comprehend this new power, his body had expelled a rush of swirling flames up into the atmosphere, incinerating a grove of trees.

"No!" Kitsune shouted, rejecting the shame and guilt he associated with those memories. The ghosts of those who had wielded this sword would not trick him into any kind of submission.

What are you afraid of, anyway? he asked as he pushed the protesting voices away—all but one. He remembered what Mai had said about them: that while both the souls and magic had been absorbed, they were no longer in control over it. *I am using your powers to save people!*

Seething, he pushed away the awful memories, focused on his anger, and guided the spheres of flame to their intended targets.

The first two men were caught off guard. They had been staring up at the spectacle when spheres struck them from the side, engulfing their bodies in flame. Instantly falling to the ground, they writhed about in agony. Attempts to shriek only invited the superheated air into their lungs.

By the time a third individual was lit up—the fire had erupted from the ground as she ran—the enemy realized they were the only ones being attacked. The Purple People, now ducking for cover inside huts or behind trees, were not being targeted. The foreign tribesmen abandoned their attack altogether, dropped their weapons, and fled. Running did them no good, as the fire circled them, corralled them, and eventually settled down on each of their bodies. Their fur clothing was eaten away within a heartbeat, and their skin crisped and curled as they fell to the earth in agony.

As the last man was engulfed in flame, Tsukumogami's purple light extinguished itself, appearing almost relieved as it flickered into oblivion. Ignoring their pitiful cries, Kitsune instead stared out across the village at the numerous tiny bonfires rolling about in the dirt. As the pained wails died down and the bodies stilled, he felt a sense of immense satisfaction.

Do I feel that way, or does the blade? he asked himself. The carnage he had unleashed was not something that would normally please him. Nor did Tsukumogami's disembodied voices seem to crave wanton violence. Most of them, at least.

"There are still survivors!" Mai called to him from behind. Kitsune turned to see the injured child in her lap. He vaguely registered the boy's open, wild eyes. A woman, presumably the child's mother, skidded up to them. She crouched down and tentatively took the youth from Mai's embrace. "We should go after them!"

"I would like nothing more than to end them all. They were a group of warriors, however, not an entire tribe. If none return, they will send more. If some come back with tales of horror, they will hesitate to attack again."

Taking a final scan of the village to verify no more of the enemy remained, Kitsune slid Tsukumogami into its sheath. As he took his hand off the hilt, the energy that had driven him through the battle disappeared, replaced with a sudden exhaustion. The prince stumbled and nearly fell to the ground beside the charred remains of one of the enemy warriors.

Mai was there in a heartbeat, taking him by the arm and leading him away from the turmoil. He resisted at first—they needed to assist in the immediate aftermath of the attack. She led him back to the same clearing he had been standing in earlier in the night, refusing to hear it. He had not the strength to fight her.

Instead of helping him to the ground as he expected, Mai thrust him against the shadowed side of a tree, out of sight of prying eyes. The colored patterns of her jacket and pants appeared to go dark, and Kitsune had just enough time to see an animalistic hunger in her eyes before she moved forward and kissed him. Her lips pressed against his, full of desire. To his own surprise, he responded with the same longing. They had just survived something together and, despite his fatigue, he was urged to celebrate their continued life.

With a sudden burst of energy, Kitsune spun Mai about, taking his turn at pinning her against the tree. She squealed in delight as he ran his fingers through her black hair. He pondered at just how inappropriate this was while others were suffering close by, but then they were again kissing. He pressed up against her. They both moaned with desire.

Mai reached down and grabbed him, smiling in satisfaction at what she felt. Should he ask if she wanted to go further? He realized this kiss was not like the first one he and Myobu had shared: tentative, sweet, explorative. This kiss was much more like their second and third rounds, which had led to other indulgences. This kiss wasn't the kind that led to further things…it was *already* further. The only thing standing in their way was their clothing.

A sense of betrayal washed over Kitsune, and he took an unsteady step back from Mai. The moment their contact ceased, fatigue returned with a vengeance. He leaned against the trunk of a tree, panting.

"I can't," he said, trying to hide tears. The face of Myobu floated about in his vision, his soulful brown eyes full of forgiveness. "I just can't."

Mai thrust out her lower lip, pouting. She took a provocative step forward, but stopped short when Kitsune gave her a stony look.

"Go help the villagers," he told her. The woman's eyes glanced downward. He thought at first she was going to make another move on him, but he realized she was looking at his weapon. "Do not worry. I am not going anywhere. The sword is safe."

*

It was noon of the following day before Kitsune emerged from his resting place in the woods. After Mai had left him, he had wanted only to follow and help the Purple People in their greatest hour of need. Much had to be done: a headcount, disposition of bodies both friendly and not, and sweeping the nearby woodlands to verify there were no more enemy stragglers. In the wake of using so much power and magic, exhaustion overtook the prince.

At some point during the night, the villagers had realized his location and urged him to rest in one of their huts. He feared his fragile emotions would get the better of him—his last time spent in the hut was the final night he had spent with Myobu—so he opted to instead sleep under his cloak in an isolated clearing nearby. Having experienced fitful nights of rest since leaving the Western Pass, he was pleasantly surprised to have slept through the morning.

"Spirits, you look like death," Mai said upon spotting him. She detached herself from a group and bounded over to him, shoving a plate of food in his face. "Did you sleep with a sounder of swine?"

"Thanks," Kitsune replied, refusing to be goaded into a verbal sparring match so soon after awakening. He took the plate, realizing he hadn't had a prepared meal since his previous visit here. "How is Clas?"

Stealing back a slice of meat, Mai pointed to a group of children making a game out of collecting the most ash from the damaged huts. It was a dirty endeavor, and one they reveled in. Kitsune spotted Clas among them, a bright smile on his soot-covered face. He moved slower than the rest of the children, and he held his right arm closer to his body, acting as though it were sore, but he otherwise looked in perfect health.

"Amazing," Kitsune said. "He looked to be at death's door when we first spotted him last night. You'd never know he had been struck in the back with an arrow."

"Barely a flesh wound," Mai responded, rolling her eyes. "He's got a future as an actor, though. He knew his best chance at survival was to fall down and pretend to be dead."

As she and her father, who Kitsune had yet to meet, had spent so much time in the area, Mai was able to communicate with the villagers. With her as his interpreter, Kitsune could help continue repairs throughout the afternoon. Even though their adversaries had attacked with murderous intent, the Purple People wished to give them proper burials. With nearly half of the dead burned to ashes, that left just over a dozen holes to dig for them. Surprisingly, the Purple People lost only six during the attack: the three bodies he and Mai had come across running toward the village, and three other individuals who had put up a brave fight defending the young.

The damage to the huts had looked worse the night before. Raging fires had that effect. The villagers had purposefully built the structures far enough apart for just such happenings, and it would not take much to return the living spaces to their previous conditions.

Aside from digging graves, there was little Kitsune could do. His language kept him from comforting those who had lost a friend or family member, and he felt strangely deficient. He was, after all, still suffering his own loss.

As dusk fell once again, Kitsune sat by one of several campfires, exhausted. Someone had brought him a bowl of soup. His hands were sore and callused from all the digging, and he gingerly spooned the hot liquid to his mouth. He had barely finished half his meal when the village grew quiet and he heard footfalls approaching. He looked up, expecting another tragedy had befallen his friends.

Ten men and women stood on the other side of the fire. Their expressions were tired, but their eyes conveyed determination. They were dressed in heavier, sturdier versions of their usual clothing, leather bags slung over their shoulders.

Kitsune glanced over at Mai, who had been napping close by. "What are they doing? It looks like they are about to travel."

"That's exactly what they intend to do," she responded, sitting up slowly. "They are the Purple People. Their tribe has been charged with looking after Tsukumogami since it was hidden in the pyramid. It's probable they believe it's been waiting here for you, but to let it slip from their sight would be a dereliction of their duty."

"They can't follow me!" Kitsune cried out. He was horrified at what could become of them, knowing what the next steps in his plan were. "I don't even want *you* to come along!"

Mai stuck her tongue out at him, clearly not giving a fig what he wanted.

Through her, Kitsune expressed his sorrow and condolences for those they had lost. He did not expect to be returning to the tribal lands soon, he explained, and other enemy tribes could strike at any time. "The Purple People cannot afford to lose any additional members. Not when they need to comfort one another. Not when preparations and training need to be done to counter any future offense. I am truly grateful for all you have done for me, but I will not lessen your numbers when you are already deprived.

"Besides," he continued, jerking a finger toward Mai. "She won't let me out of her sight. Tsukumogami is safe with us, and I promise to return the sword when I have finished using it."

Kitsune's unbidden companion gave him an odd look but passed along the words. The group looked relieved and thankful. As he expected, they had volunteered because they felt it was their duty, not their desire. He understood that all too well, having undertaken his father's mission to kill the King's Sun. Though he had believed at the time he should never question his king, he had not wanted to commit murder—not at the end, at least.

Yet, he still had.

As the men and women withdrew back to their families, Kitsune felt tears streaming from his eyes. Before Mai could see and say anything, he grabbed the remains of his dinner and slipped back into the forest. He needed his rest before they started the next leg of his journey.

Tomorrow they were headed toward the Wastelands.

THE PRISONER

An abrupt sound drew the filthy, unkempt Captain Pan out of his already erratic sleep. His tired eyes greedily scanned the dirty floor of his prison, hoping the noise had been a biscuit dropping in from the tiny window near the ceiling. The guards would do that for him. Some of them, anyway. Most taunted and jabbed at him with their swords through the window or the thin food slot. Each wall was about three footfalls in width and height, nearly a perfect cube, giving him just enough room to dodge their sharp blades.

Recognizing the sound that had awoken him as the growling of his own stomach, Pan sat back against one of the cold stone walls. He was mildly surprised he still noticed the aching pit in his belly, as the hunger pains had been his constant companion now for sixteen—no, seventeen—days. Food rations had been meager at best, and half of what he ate came from the few soldiers who risked their own freedom by sneaking him their leftovers.

While it was a comfort to know others were thinking of him, that he was still remembered outside of this cramped cell, Pan stopped short of considering them potential allies. If he did—if he dwelled on that and the possibilities of escape—the enemy would know. King Oni had the power to read minds. Oni was always in his head. He knew this for a fact.

The man therefore incessantly mulled over trivial matters. For instance, as he rested his foot against the opposite wall, Pan tried to recall his last inspection of this facility before his incarceration. He didn't think the prison cells had been this tiny when originally constructed. So small that even his gaunt frame, which even in a healthy state was a far cry from most of the other soldiers' builds, felt claustrophobic in the space.

An image of a cell box, a mobile prison constructed out of wooden planks and used by the Kitsunetsuki military, popped into Pan's head. The boxes were only big enough to allow for one person sitting cross-legged and hunched over. Small holes in the sides allowed for air, but the chamber became maddeningly stuffy within tics. Pan had once imprisoned a drunken lieutenant in a cell box. The man's belligerent anger had quickly turned to frantic repentance and eventually compliant silence. The officer had only spent two days in the box, but he had sweated out several pounds by the time he was released.

Considering the alternatives, Pan was quite thankful for the roominess of his current living situation.

Just two and a half weeks ago, Pan had been a free man, an officer in the military. His rank of captain had been a recent promotion given by Major Saxma, who himself had just vacated the position. Saxma's rise in the ranks had been a reward from the king for doing him a favor. Saxma and a contingent of his men, Pan included, had escorted Oni's son, Prince Kitsune, to the border and banished him into Odom. Before doing so, Saxma was supposed to secretly send in men disguised as commoners, armed with coin. They were meant to find and bribe mercenaries or thugs to capture the prince and hang him outside of Huem, their capital city.

The deeds were done, the promotions awarded, and the new major was given an important assignment. Saxma, Pan, and five hundred of their soldiers marched north almost immediately to oversee the construction of the northern wall, what many considered to be King Oni's pet project. Saxma and Pan, who had traditionally not thought well of each other, had struck up an unlikely alliance on the journey. They had observed in both themselves and the soldiers a general acceptance of what their monarch proclaimed: that Ruio and Mogo, once two kingdoms that had been annexed into Kitsunetsuki by force, had been a backward people in dire need of civilization and enlightenment. That their previous neighbors' pagan rituals had ferreted their way back into the very core of their proud kingdom. That even though new laws and codes of ethics were being put into place to keep those vulgar behaviors and rites from spreading, the heir to the throne had been found guilty of one of the most heinous of them. For taking members of both sexes to his bed, he had been stripped of his titles and rights and banned from the kingdom.

It had made perfect sense at the time. No one questioned it—not even Pan, who had studied both kingdoms extensively in university, or Saxma, who had traveled to Mogo as a child. They knew their previous neighbors had been culturally and scientifically equal to Kitsunetsuki, that the only reason they had been so easily subdued was military numbers. They also knew Prince Kitsune's behavior, though not meant for everyone, was perfectly acceptable in the known world.

Only as they marched north did the strange acceptance of Oni's words wear off. Saxma hadn't cared for being a pawn in a game intended to harm people he had sworn to protect, and he had enlisted Pan, who was more educated than himself, to help him ponder the discrepancies. Together, they had come to the uneasy conclusion that King Oni either possessed magic or wielded control over magic, and that the man was using this power to influence the minds of others. Saxma, having once seen a mysterious golden light spilling out of the king's throne room, surmised that an object or objects housed said magical properties. They further guessed the monarch had stored some of that substance in a locked tower here at the northern base as a way of extending his power and keeping a constant eye on his subjects. Such towers were being built throughout the kingdom.

Saxma and Pan had argued endlessly over their various theories. A common sticking point was their own ability to think freely and subversively. How could they do so if Oni was able to influence people's thinking, especially with a tower nearby that amplified his powers?

Pan posited that the leader's magic had certain limits. Perhaps he couldn't exert his will on everyone at all times. Why would he bother with the men and women who had already pledged their allegiance to him? No, he would instead use it against the Ruio citizens they had enlisted to build the wall.

Enlisted—or rather enslaved, as they had been pulled from their homes and families and forced to live in tents. Despite their conditions, the workers usually had blank, docile looks on their faces, as if they went about their work with little or no objection.

One of Major Saxma's spies, a man by the name of Jasper, had appeared one day out of the shadows. He alerted his employer to Prince Kitsune's survival and proximity. Saxma had sent both Pan and Jasper on a mission to find the banished man and gage his interest in overthrowing the king. Unbeknownst to Jasper, Pan was given a secondary mission.

Using Jasper's knowledge of the landscape, the two men had found the prince and his new companion. After laying out the facts, prostrating himself on the ground, and asking Kitsune to take action for the sake of his people, the royal ordered Pan to continue his investigations into Oni and plans for a coup. Before he could contribute or lead an army, he had to complete his current path. After Jasper had assisted them with finding a westward path, Pan executed his secondary mission and beheaded the spy.

It was the captain's first kill. It didn't excite him as it did some of the other soldiers, but he did not feel ashamed by the act. He attributed this to Saxma's lessons and training since being promoted, and he was thankful for it.

The trip back to base was short but lonely. He would have appreciated the company. Not long after his return, he would have preferred solitary travel to the prison cell he found himself in.

"Did you find the prince?" Saxma had asked as Pan walked through the gap in the wall that was to become the Northern Gate. The major was standing tall among a pile of rubble, looking as though he had been waiting there for quite some time. A tight grin stretched his lips, and it looked odd upon the man's face. The captain couldn't recall ever seeing his superior officer smile.

"Yes, sir," Pan responded, keeping his voice considerably lower than Saxma's. The mission was supposed to be a secret, just like their conversations regarding Oni and his son. Pan had not thought too much of the other man's indiscretion at the time. He'd been busy surveying the debris—a storm had been bearing down on the base before he had left. Pan had missed the majority of it, skirting around its edge, but it had apparently hit the base full force. Roofs were torn off buildings, all the tents swept away, and numerous injuries sustained. Luckily, it looked like nearly everyone survived and was busy cleaning up the storm's mess.

Impatience had shown across the major's face, clearly unsatisfied with Pan's vague response. "And what was his response?"

"He refused to return with me," Pan said, choosing his words carefully in the presence of others. "He said he had other matters to attend to. Are you sure you don't want to speak of this in your office, sir?"

"I am quite certain. Do not concern yourself over listening ears. The men will do as I say, when I say." Saxma walked along the perimeter of the base, his hands clasped behind his back. The captain trotted alongside him, uneasily noting two other soldiers falling into step behind them. "It is good the prince is continuing westward. Did he reveal his intentions after his mission was completed?"

"Nothing specific," Pan replied slowly. He was distracted from the conversation. Something was wrong here. More than the damage caused by the storm. The captain felt strangely isolated among the bustling people, like he was walking through enemy territory. Feeling lonely wasn't unfamiliar to him. Usually being the most educated person amid other soldiers, he often felt out of place. Of late, he had felt most comfortable talking to Saxma. They alone were uncovering a mystery that affected the entire kingdom. The entire region, probably. It made him feel like he was actually making a difference. He didn't sense that connection to the other man now. "He did request we continue on with our orders here."

"Very good. The prince continues to be loyal to a fault." A particular look appeared in the man's eyes. It was just a glimmer, but Pan could not decide if it was cunning or madness. Either way, it did not belong there. It made him uncomfortable, and he looked about nervously for something else to focus on.

Near the center of camp was the tower they postulated held material that extended Oni's influence. It was the tallest structure around, situated on top of a small hill. His eyes were easily drawn to it. The tower had not escaped the storm's wrath unscathed. Parts of the lower wall had fallen away, and the door—

"Sir, the tower!" he exclaimed.

The strange grin that had remained plastered on Saxma's face grew broader, revealing beer-stained teeth, and the gleam in his eyes brightened. The major turned his head toward him at an awkward angle. "Yes?"

It was in that moment Pan knew what had happened, and a bolt of fear made his spine go rigid. He had been speaking to Saxma's face, but he had not been speaking to Saxma. His speech, his gait, and his queer smile indicated another person entirely.

It could only be King Oni.

"I should, uh, have some men secure the building," Pan said, fishing for something to say. He knew he had to get out of there immediately. Escape to the north. Follow Kitsune's trail. "We don't want any curious minds entering, hoping to find the king's gold or something of the like."

"The tower is well secured, I assure you," the thing inside Saxma's body said. "The same cannot be said for you, however."

Before Pan could make a move, dash back toward the break in the northern wall, the two soldiers grabbed his arms with rough hands. He looked up in disbelief, about to protest, but stopped when he looked into each of their faces. They were blank and emotionless, with no conscious thought behind them.

"I have been rooting around in your head since the moment you stepped into camp," Saxma's body voiced, looking smug as the soldiers forced Pan to face him. "You said the prince asked you to continue your work here, but he also agreed with your proposal to amass a large force. When he completes his task in the west, he is going to travel here and, with your men, march to Oinari.

"We both know you are aware of who is really speaking, Captain." King Oni's dialect was now perfectly identifiable behind Saxma's voice. "The traitor Saxma is gone. However, I have full access to both his and your memories. There is enough evidence and justification to convict you of high treason. Seeing as I already have this body to carry out orders and business here, I have no further use for you."

*

Death was expected. Treasonous acts had been rare during Pan's lifetime. The few traitors that had been uncovered were all court-martialed, found guilty, and hanged. With the king so involved in Captain Pan's case, he did not really expect the luxury of a trial. He was, after all, truly guilty of conspiring against the monarchy.

After being thrown into the tiny prison cell, Pan had waited for his execution to be announced. Days passed, and then weeks. As his slight frame diminished even more, he wondered why he was being kept alive. There had to be a reason. Eventually, Pan decided Oni had either lied about not having a use for him or had found one in the meantime.

Though Pan could not see much outside his room, he had spent a good portion of time listening to activities through either the window above or the food slot in his door. He had been in the military for two sun cycles and had gotten used to the noises of camps both large and small. The base had a noticeably and unnervingly quiet atmosphere. The sounds of soldiers walking around, going about their duties, reminded him of the way the Ruio civilians acted while constructing the wall:

mechanical and placid. It was as though Oni had doubled his focus here, ensuring there were no other traitors in the midst.

That had lessened to a degree over the past two weeks. Either Oni had become more and more satisfied that mutinous thoughts were limited and was loosening his grip on the minds of the soldiers…or those men and women were somehow fighting back, reclaiming their mental faculties. He suspected it was more of the former but had an idea that an increasing number of individuals were catching on, questioning their thoughts, actions, and beliefs. Pan thought that was the reason some risked their own careers and lives to sneak him food. They hadn't particularly cared for him as their commanding officer, but they might see the king and his actions as immoral and unjust.

Through the food slot, Pan heard a door open down the hall. He straightened, his back flat against the wall. It was a little early for a change in guard, but a new shift meant another chance for food. Chances were greater the new guard was more hostile than friendly and would poke at him through the door or demand he perform humiliating acts, but he could usually avoid being jabbed and, at this point, was willing to oblige them with their demands. All he could do was hope for food.

The newcomer said nothing at first, but then Pan heard the current watch scramble to her feet, saying something contrite. In return, there was an admonishment and dismissal. The captain shrank back at the tone of that voice. It sounded like Saxma's, though somehow different. Sick, maybe. Dying.

Pan was well aware of how quickly a corpse decayed under natural conditions, and he wondered how Oni's magic would affect that process. Stop it entirely? By the sound of Saxma's raspy voice, no. Probably just slowed it down. Oni had not visited Pan since he had been arrested, and the captain was not eager to lay eyes on him again.

The woman who had been assigned guard duty left the building. A long silence settled, one that left Pan anxiously scratching at the walls of his cell. Then heavy footsteps began making their way down the hall. They were long and drawn out, yet still found their way to his door more quickly than Pan would have imagined. He hoped it was his imagination or hunger-induced delirium, but the footfalls sounded *wet*.

The boots are holding his rotting feet together, Pan deduced. For the first time since he had found himself in his place, he was without hunger.

The lock clicked, and the door swung to the side. Only a few torches lit the hall, but it was still more light than the window provided at this hour. Pan squinted, looking up at the man who had put him in this position. Laying eyes on him, he sincerely hoped Saxma's consciousness was dead, that it was not locked up in a corner of his mind. To return to a vessel in such a shape would be truly horrifying. The man's skin sagged under the weight of unused muscle, splotchy with blood or water. What remained of his hair was a damp mess, lying flat against his skull. His clothing, which did not look as though it had been changed since Pan had last seen him, was dirty and dank, bulging in the lower extremities where fluids collected.

The major's lower eyelids drooped, giving him a spooked look. Despite that, the cunning gleam Pan had seen before still shined brightly.

This body is failing him, Pan thought. It was followed by something even more terrifying. *That's why he's keeping me alive. As the next ranking officer, one who has a friendly relationship with the prince, he plans to sweep me from my own body and take it over.*

Pan shuddered at the thought of someone else wearing his skin. Where was Kitsune, and how long would it take him to return?

"That is why I am here," Oni said. Saxma's voice was sickening, full of rasping air and phlegm. Some of the major's teeth had fallen out. "To ask about my son."

"I don't know where he was going or what he was planning to do," the captain replied, surprised by the strength of his voice. A month or two ago, he would have been a cowering mess.

"I know perfectly well his destination and goal," Oni said with a dismissive gesture. "I gave him a task to accomplish, to kill the man I thought was Marauxus' son. My spies failed to alert me to the fact the king's son was actually the King's Sun, a nickname given to one of

Marauxus' advisors. Regardless, Kitsune uncovered this on his own and disposed of the individual for me."

"Why?" Pan asked, feeling his own body involuntarily inch farther into the cell, away from the monstrous sight. "Why would you do that?"

"To start a war, of course." Oni said this as though it should have been obvious to the officer. "With a Kitsunetsuki royal murdering one of Gaav's princes, Marauxus would have no choice but to retaliate. The King's Sun, while not family, was highly regarded, his death a significant loss to their kingdom. It should serve the same purpose."

"Don't you have enough land, or do you simply want to rule everything?"

"It's not about ruling," Oni said, his voice hardening. "It's about control. Now, I know my son was planning to return here after completing his task. Furthermore, I am aware he attempted to cross into Kitsunetsuki through the Western Pass. The tower I had under construction there was not yet complete, and I had no way of overseeing or influencing what transpired. Needless to say, the encounter was botched by an incompetent gatekeeper."

Oni took a deep breath, as though he was attempting to calm frayed nerves. The wet sucking noises it made in Saxma's throat made Pan's skin crawl. The captain took the opportunity to ask, "Botched? You mean the prince made it in?"

"No," the king said, shaking his head slowly. "I have issued a standing order to kill my son on sight. The gatekeeper, as well as the soldiers stationed there, received the communications but ignored it for a night of imbibing. They failed to take him out of play, and Kitsune…destroyed the Western Pass."

"He's already raised an army?"

"No," the king said again, his voice flat. "As you and this body's previous occupant suspected, the boy has powerful abilities. They had remained dormant until his banishment. Even I remained unsure if he had them at all, but it seems the emotional ramifications of all he has endured brought them to the surface."

Despite his best efforts to keep his thoughts and feelings locked away, Pan could not help but feel a surge of hope at this news. Oni's supernatural ability to influence other people had cast doubts on the wisdom of marching an army into Oinari. If the prince had powers to match or counter the king's, it was possible to move forward. Kitsune would still think it to be in his best interest to travel here for the latest news, planning, and procuring an army.

"I thought the same thing," Oni said, again displaying the ease with which he could read Pan's mind. "Which is why I've kept such a firm grip on this base. I don't want him suspecting anything is amiss. He should have arrived by now, and yet none of my spies can locate him. What do you think his next steps would have been if he'd arrived here safely…or what do you think he'd do if he knew I was in control here?"

Pan knew what the monarch was doing. While he obviously didn't have the answers to the prince's whereabouts in his head for Oni to pluck out, he had had sufficient contact with Kitsune to make an educated guess concerning his actions. The king was posing questions to ascertain his son's motives.

Resigned, the captain spilled out his thoughts as they came to him. "Prince Kitsune will need an army before he can march to Oinari. More soldiers than we have here. He could make a plea to King Marauxus, but I doubt he'd get much help after murdering his advisor. Or he could make a case with Patriarch Kirby."

"Yes, Kirby. They've spoken once before. Could have made some type of agreement," Oni said. Saxma's face looked like he was trying to display concern or worry, but the muscles failed and the skin only sagged further. "I don't like that idea at all."

Pan only shrugged from within his small room.

"Do you know anything about the brass machine?" Oni said.

Brow furrowing, Pan replied, "The brass machine? I don't think I've ever heard of it. What is it? A weapon?"

The king made to close the door, but Pan slid forward, pushing against it with his foot. Anger surged through him suddenly. He was tired of being used by his superiors, friendly or otherwise, because he was smarter and could think. He didn't want to be bullied or cajoled into giving up any more information. Starved and slight as he was, he wanted to be the one to strike fear into the other's heart.

"I really don't know what he's going to do, which means you—his own father—are completely in the dark. With all the energy you are expending to find him, it is clear you are afraid. You fear the very thing you set loose into the world!"

"That is quite enough out of you," Oni said gruffly, phlegm flying from Saxma's mouth. He pushed on the door. As decrepit as Saxma's body was looking, it had not yet lost its strength. Pan pulled back his foot before it was injured.

The cell door slammed shut, plunging the prisoner into near darkness. Despite that, he found satisfaction in the king's apparent discomfort. On the other side of the door, Oni turned the lock and walked away, his feet again making the sloshing sounds. Pan pressed his mouth against the food slot and called out, "You've unleashed your own doom, sir!"

"Don't go anywhere," the raspy voice returned from down the hall. "I'm going to have need of you soon."

THE WHITE HORSE

A rarely used dirt path meandered through the trees. Its winding path made it difficult to see, though everything was dim and hazy in the moonlight. Nothing was visible beyond the trees lining each side of the trail. Nothing except blackness. That blackness oozed from between the tree trunks, encroaching on the road. The rhythmic thrumming of cicadas heightened Myobu's sense of unease.

Turning about, Myobu found himself upon a white horse. He was quite unsure of how he had gotten himself on the path or where he had acquired the equine, which was an exceptionally fine specimen.

Together, he and the beast were slowly making their way down the trail. Thick tree branches, swaying in a noiseless wind, overlapped one another above his head. It gave the impression he was riding through a living tunnel. He looked back and then forward again, but there was no sign of where he had come from or where the white horse was taking him. The haze that hung over everything blurred away all fine details. Not even squinting his eyes helped him see better.

The droning sounds emanating from behind the tree line were no longer those of cicadas. They were now the soft sobs of someone crying.

"Hello?" he called out, looking for the source. The blurry trees and dirt road behind him all appeared the same, but when he looked forward again, an angry, churning cloud blocked his path. Somehow, he knew the forest abruptly ended and what lay beyond was a swirling whirlwind of dust and sand. The sounds of tears and sniffling were coming from within the stormy winds. "Are you okay?"

Other than more rhythmic sobs, no answer came.

Myobu recognized he was in a dream. In the waking world, the surreal nature of his surroundings would disturb and baffle him, and the unseen crier would spark serious concern. Now, even though everything looked and felt off, it was also natural, and he took it all in stride. If anything was amiss, it was a feeling of moroseness, as if the soft sobbing was pulling down his own emotions.

Dreamscapes were a concept with which Myobu was familiar. Imaginary realms the Yokai could create at will either within their own minds or the minds of others, dreamscapes were so much more than normal dreams. While they could be completely fantastical constructs, they could also mimic true life. If their creator so desired, what occurred within them could also resonate out into the waking world.

Though he had never experienced a dreamscape as a creator or participant, Myobu was certain this was not one. Neither fantastical nor realistic, it bore all the hallmarks of a normal reverie, albeit more eerie. Granted, it was plausible to create a dreamscape to mimic the other, but Myobu could not fathom why anyone would want to do this.

Still, this felt different, like something in between the two. It was as if he had been pulled unwittingly into someone else's dream.

Unguided, the white horse plodded through the gusting, dirty winds, leaving the dark trail behind them. He felt the sand upon his skin and, though he knew it couldn't actually hurt him, shielded his eyes against it. As the wind swept over him, pushing gritty earth underneath his clothing, a memory of the Wastelands stirred within his mind. They were neither good nor bad memories—they were both. That desolate region was a terrible place to traverse, even the outer edge, but he had been with Kitsune during his last pass through.

The swirling winds were suddenly those of a massive tornado, reminding Myobu of yet another petrifying experience he and his love had shared. Breaking free of the ferocious outer section, the horse stepped into the relatively calm eye of the storm.

Kitsune sat on the ground by a fire that was completely unaffected by the raging winds surrounding them. Naked and alone, the prince looked absolutely wretched. His nudity was not sensual, but stressed the man's vulnerability. The long blond hair Myobu had once washed clean was now matted with tears, sand, and dust. Dirt caked the prince's face, and muddy patterns ran down his cheeks, neck, and torso.

Looking up from the fire, Kitsune's eyes fell upon Myobu. Their gazes locked, and the prince's mouth fell open. For several long heartbeats, he appeared shocked and at a loss for words. The sobbing had ceased, but the new silence made Myobu anxious. Then Kitsune seemed to find himself and, moving his lips slowly, breathed out the word, "Why?"

Myobu made to respond, to beg for Kitsune's forgiveness for misleading him. To explain everything. He thought to himself, *The fate of the entire world was in my hands, small as they are. How could I deviate from the path laid before me with so many lives at stake?*

But just like how in some nightmares he couldn't call for help, Myobu was unable to find his voice. He just sat on the white horse, dumbly looking down at the naked prince.

"I loved you, Myobu," Kitsune said, leaning forward desperately. Positioned just above the fire, his face looked gaunt and haunted, and his hair singed as the strands caressed the flames. "I know you loved me, too. I felt it. I saw it in your memories."

Myobu puzzled at that, wondering how the man would ever have had access to his memories.

"There was love between us, amid the charade," Kitsune continued, looking up at him piteously. "You come to me now how I secretly imagined: heroically, romantically, here to save me. But I must know why. Why was I not enough to keep you from your lofty goals? You let the Harbinger dictate your actions."

He doesn't know, Myobu reminded himself. *He thinks I did this because of my attachment to Gaav and King Marauxus. He doesn't know I had to sacrifice my life to spare all others.*

Try as he might, he could not express a thing.

"Look what you have done to me," Kitsune said in an angry whisper. Loathing was in his eyes as he crawled through dirt and ashes toward the horse. Then, suddenly, his entire demeanor changed, and a fresh wail escaped his mouth. "What have I done to us? What have I lost? I killed you, Myobu! I killed the one I loved. Why? Fear? For my father? Anger?"

It was intensely disturbing to see the man like this. In their weeks together, Myobu had seen him display wonder, curiosity, and awe as he discovered magic and the world outside of Kitsunetsuki. The prince was confident in his abilities and proud of his intellect. Confusion and sulkiness had cropped up as Kitsune internally dealt with his feelings and family issues, but only at the very end when Kyubi was purposefully confounding him did Kitsune outright express anger. It was an emotion so raw it caused him to act without thinking, loosing a particularly well-aimed arrow.

But this…this was a side of his love Myobu had never seen, and it made him want to jump down off the mount and embrace the man. If it was possible, he'd never leave Kitsune's side again, forever protecting him. Myobu would help build the man back up. Love him the way he deserved to be.

This dream he was stuck in kept him glued to the top of the white horse. The only thing he could do was watch Kitsune crawl upon the ground like—

"A dog! I'm nothing but a feral dog." Kitsune's voice wavered between hysteria and fury. "You saw that, and you fled from me. Even my mother ran from me!"

A dog? Myobu thought the words sounded familiar. *Something about foaming at the mouth. Dear spirits, is he mimicking the woman from the journal?*

Then the words the Lady of the Mountain had left him with before sending him back into life: *Everything will burn. Mountains will be blasted into dust, rivers and oceans will dry up, and entire cities will be decimated. Mostly, though, everything will burn.*

Kitsune was reacting to Myobu's departure as the journal's author had responded to her lover's withdrawal from the relationship. Both persons were ill-equipped to deal with their feelings, and an emotional being with untrained access to magic was a dangerous creature indeed.

"I don't care who you are—Ninko or Myobu or both! I can't live without you. I don't want to live without you," Kitsune said, using the horse's legs to draw himself up to his knees. "I've been wishing for your return with all of my heart, and now here you are on a horse. Oh, Myobu, I love you so much. WHY DID YOU LEAVE ME?"

With the last sentence, Kitsune had brought himself up to his feet and, locking crazed eyes with Myobu once again, blasted the horse and rider with a wall of flame. Myobu opened his mouth to scream, but still no sound came out. The horse toppled, and he fell along with it. Falling, falling, falling right out of the other man's dream.

*

Many leagues away, somewhere along the southern border of the Wastelands, Kitsune lay by an actual fire. He was not naked, as being so would have been neither practical in the current environment nor appropriate with Mai sleeping nearby.

Tears were streaming down his face, and he was extremely vulnerable. Even though he was sleeping, dreaming of Myobu, he was curled up, shivering in emotional agony. The new clothing and sleeping blankets provided by the Purple People did little to protect him from that kind of coldness.

One of Kitsune's hands reached out from under his blankets. The dwindling firelight made his long, slender fingers appear even more elongated. The hand made broad, sweeping gestures across the ground, seeking something, and found the scabbard of Tsukumogami. His fingers walked up the sword's sheath until it found the metal hilt, which he grasped tightly.

Gradually, Kitsune's tears dried, and his face hardened. His dreams turned to other subjects, like storming Inari Palace and deposing King Oni.

Kitsune slept through the night, sword in hand.

*

Myobu jerked awake. He tried to sit upright. The sensation of falling had followed him out of the dream, and he could only roll over onto this side. Cold air chilled the tears on his cheeks, and he wiped his face clean with the palms of his hands.

It was the middle of the night. The moon was near full, and it cast long shadows over the clearing in which he lay. The same field in which he died. How many days had it been since the Lady brought him back? Was he finally fit to travel?

"Don't do that again."

The voice came from just behind him. Myobu bolted upright and spun around. "Spirits, Kyubi, don't *do* that! I didn't return from death just so you can scare me back into the afterlife."

The Harbinger, in her human form, sat cross-legged on the ground, moonlight highlighting the rather stern look that defined her current mood. The nine bundles of hair on the back of her head moved only slightly as she said again, "Do not do that again."

"What, die?" he said, settling back down. "You were the one who told me I had to leave this plane of existence."

"Do not let yourself be drawn into his dreams," Kyubi said with an exaggerated sigh.

"Oh," Myobu responded. He couldn't bring himself to say anything else for several heartbeats. He had hoped the dream had been his own. That what he had seen and felt was not rooted in reality. "Is he really so far gone?"

"Prince Kitsune is in a…fragile state of mind. He sees the revelation of your being the King's Sun, of being one of the Yokai, as a betrayal of the feelings you shared," she said, showing little emotion. "It is tearing his soul asunder. Encountering you in his dreams may tip him over the edge into total madness. With his magic, that could have disastrous effects."

"He could become the very dark force we are trying to prevent from overrunning the world," Myobu murmured.

"Precisely. I have said before that love can be a destructive force in this world."

"You said my death by his hands was a step in preventing that from happening entirely," he said. "I'm afraid to ask what the next step is. The next sacrifice."

"Nothing you can't handle, I'm sure." Kyubi reached forward, putting a hand on one of his. It was a familial gesture, quite unlike her. "I am glad your death didn't stick. I wasn't sure if you still had more story left in you. Even if you hadn't, Kirin would be proud."

Despite the kind words, Myobu grew cold. The morning air was making him shiver, a sensation he was not used to feeling. He reached out to a nearby bush and attempted to light it afire with his magic.

Nothing happened.

He reached out again, focusing on the dead, dry wood. No magic flowed through him, however. Realizing he was clutching his hoshi no tama in one hand, he remembered he had previously thought Kitsune had taken his powers from him.

Panic rose within Myobu as he clutched at the dull red stone. Part of him—a piece of his very soul, what made him…him—was gone. The Yokai were not known to be prideful of their magic, but they were reverent and respecting, acknowledging that it helped define them as a species.

Getting to his feet, Myobu paced the clearing. "Kitsune took my power?"

"Yes, Kitsune stripped you of your magic. It's in him now."

A new shiver ran throughout his body as he gripped his empty stone, this one caused by revulsion. It was taboo to touch another's power without their express permission, and to take it away entirely was virtually unheard of. Such a thing was a defilement, an egregious violation against Yokai both living and dead.

"I saw it," the Harbinger continued. Her calm demeanor cracked as she remembered, and there were hints of longing desperation in her voice. "Even as I was running away, I saw it. He was trying to save you. Didn't know if he could. He just tried. The power in your hoshi no tama must have felt like life within your body to him, and he pulled at it, trying to bring it forth. It responded to his pull."

Knowing the deed had not been purposeful or malicious made Myobu feel slightly better. That his magic still existed, and that he might somehow retrieve it, helped tremendously. His fidgety pacing slowed, and Myobu looked down at Kyubi. "How could he even do that?"

"His father, King Oni, exhibits a similar power, so it is conceivable that it's an inherited gift. Where Oni got it is a mystery. Both of his parents appeared to be nothing more than human."

"Weather, fire, and now this," Myobu whispered, incredulous. "Three special powers."

"I rather suspect he harbors four."

"*Four?*" Myobu was aghast, and his jaw fell open. He found a new respect for the prince. As shattered and pathetic a creature as he appeared to be in the dream, he was at least still in one piece.

The Harbinger glanced around at the clearing. Myobu noticed again the charred remains of trees and other plant life. He said, "This was your home, wasn't it?"

Shrugging, Kyubi responded, "It was time for a change. I have been here far too long. Made myself more comfortable and stationary than I care to admit."

Though his first instinct was to provide support and offer assistance, he ultimately refrained. The Harbinger would have seen them as meager platitudes. In truth, they would have been. All he could truly give her was a place to stay in Hawte, and he knew her well enough to know she would not take residence amid stinky humans. Instead, he got to the point.

"What do I need to do, wise one? For Kitsune and Gaav. For the world. I beg of you to be forthcoming and plain with me and not layer your answer in mysteries."

She sat still on the ground for many tics. Her eyes were open but vacant, and Myobu guessed she was using her magic to look out into the world, see what there was to see, and analyze what results those happenings could have.

Just as Myobu was about to nod off, Kyubi shook her head slowly. With a resigned look, she said, "I do not know."

"That's a little more forthcoming and plain than I wanted, actually," Myobu said, blinking.

"More and more, I have noticed our world's present activities and potential futures are hidden from my sight. At first, I thought this was the work of dark forces like King Oni keeping their plans protected by magic. To some degree, I still believe this to be true." She looked up into Myobu's face, and he saw she looked different—only minutely, and it took him a heartbeat to identify what it was. When he did, he knew what she was going to say next, and it saddened him. "I am an ancient creature, Myobu. Old even by our standards. For all my power and wisdom, I did not see time was taking its toll on me. It has slowly…*insidiously*…stripped me of strength and magic."

Myobu did offer platitudes at this, saying he was sorry to hear her words.

Kyubi stood up. After a moment's hesitation, she took hold of one of his hands. "I do not know if King Oni is the one who will spread darkness. Perhaps what I feel is to befall the world will be Kitsune's doing. Both men, maybe, or neither of them. What I do know is my part in this story is coming to a close and I will soon be with Kirin again."

The Harbinger turned north and stepped forward. Myobu wanted to say more but knew the desire to do so was a human attribute gained from his time in Hawte. The Yokai did not make a big fuss.

Before he lost sight of her among the husks of trees, she turned back to him and, her voice carrying over the burned remains of her home, said, "Do not go through the orange door, Myobu. It will deliver you to death from which there is no return."

With that, she changed into a silver fox and disappeared.

*

Myobu walked in the opposite direction of Kyubi, into the rising sun, following the same path he and Kitsune had traveled after their journey through the Wastelands. The intention was to retrace their steps back through the cursed land. If the prince's dream had any hints of reality, it showed he had already ventured back into the east.

Not that dreams could ever be counted on to reflect reality.

When Myobu had been forced back into life, his galaxy-spanning consciousness stuffed back into his physical head, he had noticed Kitsune wandering around the outskirts of the Purple People's village. The stealthy way with which he was going about his business had concerned Myobu. It didn't make sense, as it didn't seem to move him forward toward his father. While Myobu didn't particularly want to go running into the Wastelands again, at least his love was back on a logical path.

So long as the rest of the day's traveling went undisturbed, Myobu would make it to the natives' village by nightfall. Maybe there he could get an explanation for Kitsune's skulking about in their vicinity.

Technically, it would be quicker to follow the path he was on farther southward from where he and Kitsune had come across it—where he himself had left it on an earlier journey west. It would eventually lead to Kitsunetsuki's Western Pass. Security was tight and passage was generally banned. Under normal circumstances, Myobu would not have been concerned. With his magic, he'd have been able to take the visage of one of their soldiers or Ninko. Or he could have crept into their minds and coerced them into opening the doors to him.

As it was, he had very little power left. He could no more control fire than he could keep himself from breathing. Some magical remnants were left within him, which explained how he was able to find his way into Kitsune's dream. Experimenting, he found he could perform simpler tasks native to all Yokai, but could only sustain them for a few short heartbeats. He didn't have the power to maintain illusions or mind control. Certainly not long enough to get through the Western Pass.

Which meant he was stuck in the form of Acro. This suited him just fine.

The sudden clattering of a horse's hooves interrupted Myobu's thoughts. He looked up just in time to see a wild-looking steed whip around a bend in the road and bear down on him. He leaped to the side of the path to avoid being trampled, feeling warm spittle from the horse's frothy mouth splatter on his skin.

Once the equine had passed, Myobu spun around. A middle-aged man was on the horse's back, leaning over the mount's neck as though he were trying to keep from being seen. At first, it seemed the man would not stop to apologize. Perhaps the rider, with his field of vision so limited by the horse's head, had not even noticed the slight man as he came around the corner. But the horseman pulled back on the reigns, bringing his mount to a quick halt, and looked hesitantly back at Myobu.

Whereas the horse, loaded with paper-filled bags in addition to its rider, appeared relieved at the reprieve, the man looked agitated and spooked. Wide eyes were set in deep sockets, and his jaw was clenched so firmly Myobu thought he could hear teeth cracking. Myobu felt if he made the slightest move, the man would tear off again down the path.

"Where are you headed?" said the rider, his voice surprisingly shrill.

"To the village of the Purple People," Myobu answered. He noticed the man looked rather sickly, like he had not eaten well in many weeks. His clothing, which had seen better days, hung loosely on his frame.

"No! No, you mustn't go there!" It didn't seem possible, but the man's eyes widened even further. He turned the horse around and trotted toward Myobu, who recognized this as a strong statement. "If you value your life, you will not go to that place."

"How do you mean?" Myobu wondered if the man's malnutrition had caused his head to go funny. "I was there twelve or so days ago. The villagers are friendly. They have been nothing but kind to me."

"Yes, but twelve days ago, she was occupied. Would have posed no danger to you," he said. "But I escaped her clutches two—no, three days ago. Probably ensnared the new one by now. Still not worth chancing your own life if she hasn't, though."

"Wait, what?" Myobu said, holding his hands out to cut the man off. He took a step forward, but the movement immediately made the rider nervous, so he stilled. "I have no idea what you are talking about? Who is 'she,' and why did you have to escape her?"

The man lowered his voice to a whisper. "She is Mai, and she is one of those blasted Yokai!"

Myobu was only just able to keep his face from contorting into a look of distaste over the insult. He already had an idea what the man was getting at. If this Mai individual was, in fact, of the Yokai, she may be one of the infamous and ill-reputed yako. Their mischievousness was known to get the better of them, and their torment of other creatures could go beyond mere amusement. All the Yokai had the potential to become obsessed with others, but the yako could take the obsession a step too far.

"Would you like some water?" Myobu asked after introducing himself. "Your horse certainly would. Looks like he's dry as a bone. I can hear a creek just over this way."

The man looked at Myobu suspiciously. Myobu continued, "You've got nothing I want, judging by your scroll-filled bags, and it's clear just by looking at you that you haven't any food. Besides, I know a thing or two about the Yokai. I doubt this Mai woman is pursuing you, but if she is, I know how to get rid of her for good."

The rider dismounted the horse, but he kept a respectable distance from Myobu as they left the road for the nearby creek. After swallowing several handfuls of water and washing days' worth of grime from his face, he said in a slightly less shrill voice, "The name is Jorin, and you will accept my apologies for the rudeness. I came out this way from Gaav—must've been two sun cycles ago—to study the tribal lands. I was curious about the natives' origins. I'm an anthropologist, you know."

"I did not," Myobu replied, but nodded in acknowledgement. He vaguely recalled an official report of a missing researcher.

"Well, I was poking around one of the many pyramids scattered about this land, and I came upon this young woman. She looked a bit out of place out in the woods, all dressed up in colors, and she had a unique way about her. I let her camp with me that night. Nothing funny, mind you, but the next morning she starts calling me father!"

"That's quite odd," Myobu said, taking a drink of water for himself. He wondered briefly if this was the same creek he and Kitsune had bathed in after leaving the Wastelands. "You're not actually her father, though, right?"

"Absolutely not!" Jorin said, his face flushing. "I would know if I had offspring! Besides, she wasn't young enough to be my child. I tried explaining that to her at first, thinking perhaps she had something wrong in the head. She *did* end up getting into my head, however. Made me believe things that weren't true, see things that weren't there… Forced me to stay in the tribal lands well past my intended three months. At least…at least I was able to continue my work."

Jorin pointed to the saddlebags hanging off the sides of the horse, stuffed full of used parchment.

"How did you escape her?" Myobu asked. Speaking of the ordeal clearly distressed Jorin, and Myobu thought it best not to dwell on whatever else the man was forced to do under Mai's control.

"Found something else that caught her attention," Jorin answered, looking relieved. "Probably someone more to her liking. I could feel it the moment it happened. Her presence in my head slipped away. I made to get out of there as quick as anything. Wasn't going to wait around in case she changed her mind and came back for me."

"Did you see her new fascination?" Myobu said, wondering if it was a native.

"Only from a distance. Small guy, like yourself. Long blond hair like I've never seen before."

Myobu's head snapped up. *Kitsune?* "When did you say you escaped? Three days ago?"

The man nodded, looking uncertain at Myobu's anxiety.

It must be him, Myobu thought. *The timing is right. Judging from the dream, this yako isn't in his head yet, not like this simple fool's. Kitsune is too consumed with me at the moment, but that will fade with time. That bitch is trying to steal him from me!*

Standing up straight, Myobu began making his way back to the road. "I must leave now. Have to cross the border into Kitsunetsuki, and it's a long walk to the pass."

The Western Pass was the quickest route to intercept Prince Kitsune and Mai. Never mind the fact it was heavily guarded. He'd find a way through, even if he had to fight every man to the death.

"You can't go there!" Jorin called after him, confused.

"Don't worry. I'll skirt around the Purple People in case Mai is still there. But I must get to the pass."

"You can't," the man repeated, following him back to the road. The horse watched them go, hesitant to leave the refreshing water source behind. "The pass is no longer there."

Myobu stopped in the middle of the path, stunned. "What?"

"That is why it's taken me so long to get this far from the village. In my panic to get away, I headed south. Came to the pass that leads into Kitsunetsuki. Except it's no longer there! The tunnel has been collapsed, and it looks as though a giant tore away the top half of the mount it had been carved into. Several fires had burned through the area. The military presence has increased, too. Soldiers marching around every which way.

I spoke to a couple of 'em. Funnily enough, they say it was their own Prince Kitsune that caused the damage!"

Myobu forced himself to stand still and think. It was logical Kitsune would find his way to the Western Pass. After completing the mission his father had given him, his next course of action would have been an attempt to enter his home kingdom. King Oni was probably never going to honor his promise, though, and the gatekeeper would have denied the prince entrance. Consumed with emotions and magic, the prince would have lashed out.

The fire made sense. It could have been caused by lightning strikes or by Myobu's stolen power. Collapsing the tunnel, though? Or tearing down a small mountain? That wasn't within the man's power.

Or was it? The Lady of the Mountain had said mountains would be blasted into dust because of her son. Myobu got an inkling as to what Kitsune's fourth power, yet unknown even to Kyubi, was.

Even more worrisome was the increased military presence. It forced him to think as Ninko. To act like the highly regarded official. If King Oni was planning to attack Gaav, then he had an obligation to warn King Marauxus and his people immediately.

And as long as Kitsune could keep out of Mai's clutches, it could be the best course of action for him, too.

Looking over at Jorin, Myobu said, "Get your horse. We need to ride to Hawte as quickly as we can."

THE NORTHERN GATE

"After all your talk, Joey, I was expecting something…bigger," Mai admitted, tilting her head. She pursed her lips in obvious disappointment.

"It's because of your vantage point. You're looking at it all wrong," Kitsune replied with a sigh. He realized he was forcefully massaging one of his temples. A headache had been brewing over the last several days. The pressure against his skull threatened to become debilitating, especially as they looked down at the construction efforts on the northern wall. It was hard to tell, but he was sure the barrier had to be a few footfalls higher. "The northern wall is a massive undertaking for King Oni. Believe me, it is truly impressive."

"Eh," she said, giving a shrug. "I've seen bigger."

The two of them stood on a crest overlooking the northern edge of Kitsune's homeland. They were near to where Captain Pan and his associate Jasper had intercepted him and Myobu, pleading for the prince to lead a revolt against their monarch. While he had encouraged them to continue making preparations for such an attack, he had foolishly declined to assist. The belief that he could reach his father, persuade him to change his mind, had pushed him into the Wastelands.

A foul stench wafted by. Kitsune stifled a gag, but his head throbbed in pain. He wondered if the smell was Jasper's corpse. Pan had decapitated the scruffy-looking man at the end of their last meeting. The prince had been disgusted by the violence at the time. Now he appreciated Pan's ability to act swiftly—to do what was necessary.

"I suppose that would be our way in," Mai said, pointing at a large base in the distance. Several camps for the laborers had been established along the wall, but this one had several permanent fixtures, including an odd tower and a break in the wall that would become a fixed gate. "What's our next move?"

Kitsune gave an internal sigh, but he simultaneously chastised his own irritation. As a leader, a prince, and a hopeful successor to the Kitsunetsuki throne, he should expect others to look to him for guidance and direction. Yet Mai hailed from Gaav, and he certainly had not asked her to leave her father behind and fight by his side.

In this moment, he was exhausted and wanted nothing more than to lie down, curl up, and sleep. The emotions he'd been made to bear, the intense sadness that permeated his very being, wore him down. He hated that the betrayals by his father and Myobu affected him to this degree, that they caused his headaches. His stomach, too, was having fits.

But no one wanted to hear such things from a leader.

"How are you feeling?" Kitsune asked, equally ignoring her question and the thoughts in his head. It was only midday, and while he didn't expect trouble in seeking Pan and Saxma, he wanted to be rested and alert when they entered the base.

"Me? Aww, I'm fine," Mai replied in a mockingly cute tone. "I've survived the tribal lands, you know."

"With your father."

"Yes, with my father," she retorted, exasperated. "Who has always been too busy with his studies to even realize I've left on another explorative adventure."

"I still question the wisdom of your leaving without informing him," Kitsune said, a subject he had tried to discuss several times over the course of their journey through the Wastelands. "This is not an explorative adventure. It's dangerous and could take quite some time."

"I left word with the Purple People," Mai replied, dismissing the topic once again. "If he ever comes back. Besides, you made the trip here incredibly easy."

The prince's first time through the Wastelands with Myobu had been miserable. Coarse sand, blown by strong winds, ate away at his skin and forced itself into every nook and cranny of his body. This second trip had also been miserable, mostly due to a conversational dance with Mai during which nothing was ever said. They each tried to pry personal information out of the other, but both resisted. Mai's evasiveness made Kitsune even more reluctant to offer any details about his life or true identity. Not that he wanted to talk about any of it, as they put him in a mood.

The winds had been just as ferocious as the previous trip, but Kitsune had used his power over weather to manipulate air patterns throughout their journey. He pushed back against the sand-filled winds and blasted away impediments that stood in their way.

The increased use of magic had helped him become more confident in his abilities. This was bolstered by Tsukumogami. Only seldom did he hear the souls' voices since leaving the tribal lands, but he could feel their constant presence rooting around in his thoughts. Every time he held the enormous blade, even merely gripping its hilt as it hung at his side, he felt surer about himself. It drove away the sadness that consumed him.

Tsukumogami never left his sight. As they traveled, Kitsune found he craved unsheathing the sword. He desired to use it more and more. To enhance his power. To win battles. To escape the constant pain that beset him.

"Joey?" Mai said with an air of impatience. "What's the plan?"

"We'll head down midafternoon. Should arrive around the time the laborers head back in for the evening. Blend in and make it through the gate," he answered. "We may have to ask around, but it shouldn't be difficult to find the ones in charge."

*

The shadows on Pan's cell walls provided most his entertainment. The monotony of his days afforded him ample time to study the line separating the shadows from sunlight. By its movement, he could tell when the guards' shift change was to occur, when the laborers were heading out to or coming in from work, and when meals were served. The latter was of particular interest, as it was likely to be followed by a defiant individual dropping food in through the window.

Despite King Oni claiming he was keeping a tight lid on the base, the occurrences of food drops had been more frequent and regular. It strengthened Pan's suspicion that others were waking up from the monarch's influence over their minds. Not only were the soldiers thinking for themselves again, but they were actively working against the military order. Prisoners were not to be coddled, much less traitors like Pan.

The prisoner hoped his previous subordinates were doing more to defy their king. Perhaps someone had taken his and Saxma's place in planning a coup. Even if that wasn't the case, the fact they considered him at all had kept his spirits—his hope—from disappearing altogether.

Pan realized that, even with a modicum of cheer, it was likely he was losing his mind—if he hadn't lost it already. Who wouldn't after seeing the decaying, animated face of their superior officer?

Just as well I go insane, he had thought more than once. Saxma's body had been in grotesque condition over a week ago. He could only imagine how it looked now. *Either way, Oni will eventually force me out of my mind.*

Cocking his head to the side, Pan looked again at the shadow on the wall. By its position, he could tell the day's hours of hard labor were at an end. Food was ready to be doled out in the mess halls. The air smelled of cooked meat, so he knew meals had been prepared. There should have been a stampede of people transitioning from work to rest. Soldiers, too, either eating or barking out orders for others to fall in line or behave.

The air was soundless, though. All the noises that a busy military base made had ceased. No shouting or running about. Not even the chirping of a bird. Just an eerie, dead silence.

Pan lifted his head, peering out of the small window. The absence of sound was foreboding. Something was about to happen. Everything was going to change.

*

The northern wall cast long shadows in the late afternoon light, making it look more daunting than it had from above. It was tall enough now Kitsune would have to stand on Mai's shoulders to look over it. Doing so would be a surefire way of attracting unwanted attention. As it was, the two of them were draped in long cloaks with their hoods drawn. It had been a challenge to cover up Mai's clothing. Even though she had swapped her jacket and trousers of colored patches for black ones with threads of silver, they still caught his eye.

"Our goal is simple," he said as they walked among the multitude of laborers. Their backs were arched, weary with work, and they dragged their tools as they headed to the gate. Their downcast looks were exaggerated by gathering clouds, created by the prince in case he needed to call upon lightning. "Get through the gate alongside everyone else. Once we're inside, we'll find someone in charge."

"Why are we sneaking about?" Mai asked. "Why go through all the trouble of being stealthy when we're hoping to find their leadership?"

Kitsune paused. He had gotten used to her calling him Joey, but had mostly forgotten she didn't know his true identity. She had no idea he was a banished prince. That a misstep here could end in his execution.

"Mai, there's something you should know," Kitsune started, intending to confess everything. She'd catch on once they found Saxma or Pan. However, she was no longer by his side.

Looking about, he saw Mai had stepped behind two tired-looking men with a pickaxe and a chisel. He hurried to catch up, wincing as his steps worsened the aching in his head. His respite earlier in the afternoon had not lessened the pain that had been plaguing him. If anything, it was more distracting than ever.

Two guards were on duty at the gate. They lazily scanned the crowd, waving small groups through the opening. He pulled his hood down over his eyes as they neared the checkpoint, looking at the ground and turning away from the fading sunlight. He imitated the tired march of the others, missing only a workman's tool to perfect the masquerade.

Not knowing how Mai would react to his true name—to his lie—he decided to delay revealing it until they were safely on the other side of the barrier.

The two laborers they were following eventually walked through the gate unhindered. The guards gave Mai a quick once-over before their bored eyes moved back to the incoming crowd. Just as she was passing through the gate, one soldier grabbed hold of her arm.

"Hold on there," the man said in a calm manner. Friendly, even. "These cloaks are not standard issue. Where'd you pick 'em up?"

"They're the latest thing!" Mai responded before Kitsune could even think of a reply. The way she said it, cloaks with hoods may well have been a novel idea. As though remembering the situation, she lowered her voice and continued, "I made this myself."

No way that's true, Kitsune thought. *The garment isn't gaudy enough for her!*

The guard nodded and let go of Mai's arm. He had apparently only been interested in the garment, not the goings-on of its wearer. She again made to enter the base, but didn't make it another step before the other guard had a look at Kitsune's figure.

"Hold up. He's wearing the same style cloak she is."

"Like I said, it's catching on," Mai interjected, giving a hopeful shrug.

"All right, I want everyone to queue up. No one gets in until they've been thoroughly searched," called out the first soldier, grabbing for a nearby torch. To his companion, he said much quieter, "Since when did these backward folk care about style? We'll sort this out."

The crowd had grown thick around the gate, with many natives peering above the heads of others to find out what the holdup was. At the announcement, a collective groan let out. They were all tired and hungry, and they had nothing to look forward to but a meager meal, a cold bed, and another day of toiling.

"We mean you no trouble," Kitsune said, finally speaking up. His voice sounded confident, but he felt a bead of nervous sweat on his temple. While he reached out to the clouds above, preparing to call upon them for defense, he put a hand on the man's shoulder in what he hoped would be interpreted as a friendly gesture. "We are friends of Major Saxma and Captain Pan. We need to speak with them."

The soldier didn't answer at first. He was staring at Kitsune's feet, where Tsukumogami was poking out from the bottom of his cloak.

"If you're friends of Saxma and Pan, then you are no friends of ours," growled the other guard, reaching for his sword. "I said line up!"

As the man drew his weapon, Kitsune withdrew his hand, pulled back his hood, and rested his palm on the pommel of his own weapon. He drew courage and strength from it, his anxiety melting away. Even his headache, which had been pounding at his skull in an exquisite fashion, dissipated. "I can't speak for the laborers you have enslaved here, soldier, but my friend and I won't be lining up."

The two men stared slack-jawed at Kitsune. The prince did not recognize them, but that didn't necessarily hold true for them.

"Kindly relinquish your weapons," Kitsune said, shocking even himself with the bold demand. It was two on two at the moment, and the odds would only get worse if they called for reinforcements.

Both soldiers complied with his order immediately, clumsily unbuckling their sword belts and allowing them to drop to the ground.

Reaching forward, Kitsune plucked the torch from the man's grasp. "And what did you mean about Saxma and Pan?"

They did not answer his question and continued to stare dumbly at the prince, their mouths agape. Frowning, Kitsune moved the torch closer to their faces. They did not flinch, and their eyes appeared vacant.

No, that wasn't quite right. Something was in there looking back at him, but it wasn't the guards.

"It's not their best look," Mai said, collecting their blades and tossing them into nearby brush. "What did you do to them?"

"I didn't do anything," he replied, leaning in closer to one of the men's faces. He peered into the nearly empty eyes, trying to identify what it was he found so disarming.

The crowd of natives, whose dissatisfied mutters had died down, pushed forward again. Giving up on the soldiers, Kitsune and Mai moved along with them.

Finally passing through the gate, the first thing the prince noticed was the stone tower. The base itself felt large. He had seen from above it was composed of several permanent barracks, mess halls, and administrative buildings. Acres of open space surrounded the installation, filled with rows of flimsy tents. The tower, however, effortlessly commanded attention, as though it was the true reason for everyone's presence. Constructed at the heart of the base, Kitsune could not decipher its purpose. Its foundation was too small and narrow to house ammunition, and no arrow slits had been built into its side for defense. Not even a window at the top to look out over the wall for enemies.

The second thing the prince observed was the base's silence. He had expected the usual bustle that accompanied mealtime, maybe the raucous noise of entertainment. Hundreds of soldiers and workers could be seen on the grounds, but they all appeared to be standing stationary in small groups. No one was talking. No one was looking.

Kitsune thought again of the blank stares of the guards at the gate.

"I'm inexplicably drawn to it," Mai said, saddling up next to him as she appraised the tower. She raised her eyebrows at him. "I kind of want to lick it."

Grunting, Kitsune unsheathed Tsukumogami while throwing his cloak behind his shoulders. He didn't like the feel of this place. Something was wrong.

"Oh, come now," Mai continued, casually throwing off her own cloak. The silver in her clothing reflected the fading light, as though it'd been threaded with precious gems. "You know I'd lick you again if you let—"

A sharp noise exploded, and a nearby soldier was thrown off her feet. Landing on her back, she looked about wildly, as though confused by her whereabouts. She clutched at her chest, and Kitsune saw blood pooling quickly.

The horrible smell of rotting flesh assaulted his nose. For a moment, he thought it was coming from the fallen soldier, but then he realized a breeze had delivered it to him. Looking up, he saw a man had stepped away from a small group. Or at least he thought it was a man. Nearby campfires cast odd shadows over the figure's skin, which was gray, cracked, and sagging. The skin on the form's head—which had no hair—had split, revealing the skull underneath.

It looked like a walking corpse.

Despite the visage, Kitsune could still recognize the figure as Major Saxma. A persuader was in the man's hand, his stiff, swollen fingers finding purchase around its trigger. The weapon was unique in design from the model Saxma had once shot the prince with in Inari Palace.

Saxma gave a wide, droopy smile that revealed a mouth mostly devoid of teeth. In a raspy, sickening voice, he said, "Prince Kitsune."

"What have you done, Saxma?" Kitsune bellowed. "You're shooting your own troops?"

"Do you like my new weapon? An enhanced persuader, modified with an explosive charge," Saxma said. The words came slowly, and he had to draw in large amounts of air for every few words. "Much deadlier, as you can see, though its accuracy leaves something to be desired. I was aiming for you."

"I came here in peace, responding to the olive branch you sent through Pan!" Kitsune hesitated, not sure how much he should reveal about Saxma's supposed preparations to march against King Oni. He opened his mouth to say more, but he stopped. The words of the gate guard returned to him: "If you're friends of Saxma or Pan, then you are no friends of ours."

The glimmer Kitsune had seen behind the men's stares—the notion that someone else entirely was staring back—had not only been familiar, but familial. Even though he was a hundred footfalls from his old nemesis, he could recognize the same spark in the man's eyes. It wasn't hidden behind a blank look, but was bursting out like rays of light.

"You're not Major Saxma," Kitsune said.

"No, my son. I killed him long ago." The decrepit-looking man lifted the modified persuader again. "Now I am going to kill you."

"Run!" Kitsune shouted, leaping to his left as another explosive sound followed a second projectile. It missed him, but it hit another Kitsunetsuki soldier in the side, spinning him around. Reaching out to the dark clouds overhead, the prince brought down his own explosive weapon. A single streak of white-hot lightning lit up the entire base, illuminating the stone tower as it came down upon the body his father was now governing.

Through whatever power King Oni was using to control the corpse of Saxma, he raised its arms defensively. The bolt of electricity ricocheted off and exploded into the side of a nearby building.

"What is it you hope to accomplish?" Oni asked, looking down at what remained of Saxma's left arm. Once strong and commanding, it was now a charred, smoking stump. "You will never be able to defeat me."

*

Pan could barely hear a thing.

That wasn't true. He hadn't heard anything a few heartbeats ago. Then there had been some shouting. An explosion. Now there was a ringing in his ears that drowned out anything else that might be worth hearing.

Stars danced in his vision, the result of a blinding flash of light just before the explosion. He blinked rapidly, trying to make the brilliant afterimage dissipate. Even as the pinpricks of light went away, he still saw white. After nearly a tic of waiting for that to fade as well, he realized he was looking into a thick cloud of dust, illuminated by the setting sun—but the position of the windows in relation to the sun would not have allowed this much light into his cell.

A breeze made its way through the small room, the first such sensation Pan had felt in weeks. It carried away enough of the dusty air for him to see the explosion had ripped a hole into the exterior wall of the prison—a wall that included his cell. Through the crevice, he could see the tower. It looked intact, the damage the structure had sustained during the storm completely repaired. The magic contained within was again secure.

Of course that would be the first thing I see, Pan thought. *The bloody thing dominates everything here.*

More concerning was the congregation of people spread about the grounds of the infernal tower. They must have been the source of the voices he'd heard before the explosion. Others populated the surrounding area, but they all stood as still as statues.

Pan clamored toward the break in the wall. His arms and legs protested, weak from disuse, but he ignored them as best he could. If his suspicions were correct… Yes, one of the men was Saxma, or King Oni in Saxma's body. Even from this vantage point, Pan knew it could only be him. He had been right: the walking corpse had not fared well since they had last met.

The other man—Pan squinted his eyes, then gasped—was Prince Kitsune! The royal looked little worse for wear. A little older. A lot angrier. The look was enhanced by the new sword he brandished. With an air of determination, the prince was marching toward Saxma.

"No, wait," Pan croaked, but his voice was barely above a whisper. He was through the wall now, a free man. He had to warn Kitsune. Had to let him know the only way he could win this battle.

And he had to do it before the prince struck down Saxma. He had to do it before Oni's consciousness took over his own body.

*

"You should retreat," Kitsune said to Mai. After the abomination had deflected his lightning, he didn't want to take his eyes off of it. "I will meet you back on the bluff."

"Haven't you been paying attention?" was her response. She sounded slightly indignant. "Even if I wanted to run off with my tail between my legs, I doubt I would make it out of here alive."

"What do you mean?" The prince reluctantly looked away from Saxma, who now appeared to be testing the abilities of his remaining limbs. Mai stood with her sword drawn, her posture far more guarded than her tone of voice. The weapon was pointed toward the major, but her gaze was now behind them.

Glancing back, he saw a sea of glassy, blank stares. The two gate guards, soldiers, and the Ruio natives. Hundreds of pairs of vacant eyes looking at the pair of them, blocking off their path to the gate. They were surrounded.

"You're all alone, my son," Oni said. "Lay down your weapon and die. Do that, and I will spare the life of your friend."

"Absolutely not," Kitsune responded. Raising Tsukumogami up, he marched toward his opponent. None of the blankly staring bystanders moved to stop him as he closed the gap between the two.

Saxma's face did not seem capable of conveying emotions anymore, but Kitsune thought he saw the edges of his mouth flicker in an attempt to smile. The persuader was tossed unceremoniously aside, and a sword was drawn. It was brought up just in time to block the prince's attack.

"You cannot win," Oni said, every syllable a taxing strain on the failing body. "You will not escape this place."

Rays of the setting sun reflected off their blades. Saxma's head cocked to the side, the vertebrae in his neck popping, and looked at Kitsune's sword. When he spoke next, his raspy voice did not sound so certain. "You found Tsukumogami?"

Moving swiftly, Kitsune stepped out of their deadlock and then brought the flat side of the sword up underneath Saxma's arm. Even through layers of clothing, he heard skin split and the humerus snap.

Saxma's remaining fingers went limp, and his sword clattered to the ground.

The prince brought Tsukumogami up above his head for a powerful downward stroke. Rage filled him as the blade cut through the air. Anger at his father, but also toward Saxma. The man had drugged and raped him, paraded him naked through the streets of Oinari, and seen him out of the kingdom. The need to avenge himself surged through his veins, even though Saxma had later extended a flag of truce. Even though Saxma's consciousness had already been extinguished.

With a satisfying *thwack*, his sword embedded itself into Saxma's exposed skull. Kitsune wrenched Tsukumogami free and stepped back, watching as the corpse fell to its knees. He had apparently damaged the head enough that Oni could no longer control it.

As he observed the remaining light dim from its eyes, he said, "I am coming for you, Father. I will burn you out of your palace."

The body collapsed sideways to the ground. Major Saxma was now truly gone.

Silence hung over the camp. Kitsune had expected the others to snap out of Oni's hold, for life to come back to all those glassy eyes. But everyone remained still.

No, not everyone. There was movement near the building into which his bolt of lightning had exploded. Mai, hustling up beside him, noticed the activity, too.

"Is that a tiny man?" she said, pointing with her sword.

The figure fell to the ground in a heap but, after a struggle, found its way back to its feet. Something was familiar about it.

The figure called out. The words were unintelligible, but the voice was recognizable. Pitiably weak, but identifiable.

"That's Captain Pan!" Kitsune exclaimed. He made to hurry over, but Mai put a staying hand on his arm.

"Not yet," she said in a singsong voice.

Pan called out again, and this time Kitsune was able to make out two words: "The *tower.*"

Then Pan's eyes rolled back into his head, and his body collapsed.

*

The icy tendrils of another consciousness forced its way into Pan's mind. It was unlike anything he'd ever experienced. If he hadn't known better, he would have thought he had finally snapped. As it was, he knew his end was near. Nevertheless, he did all he could to stall, to buy enough time for Kitsune to act.

"Why would you keep me locked away in a cell if you were planning to take over my body?" Pan asked, directing the question at the invader. His vision suddenly failed him, and he felt his body hit the ground again.

"You think a simple door can contain me?" was the monotone, distracted response. The icy fingers forced their way further into Pan's head. He vaguely realized he was screaming in pain, turning about on the ground. It was only a matter of time.

"The men don't like me. They've never respected me," Pan argued. *"They know I've been arrested and stripped of my commission. They'll never follow my orders!"*

"I inhabit bodies such as yours to conduct my affairs in person, so to speak," Oni replied, his voice chiding. *"But you know I sway the minds of anyone within my reach. The soldiers will do as I say."*

"What is the reason for all this? Why conquer your neighbors, or build this wall, or conspire against your own son? Why kill Saxma and me?"

The foreign entity within his head had surrounded Pan's consciousness, and he was now in total darkness. Total emptiness. He felt, heard, and saw nothing, existing as thought on a small island surrounded by only the king's voice, and that patch was dwindling by the heartbeat.

"To stop her," King Oni said. This time, there was a hint of emotion in his voice.

"This is about a woman?" Pan shouted, though his voice was growing smaller with each passing moment.

The little island stopped shrinking. Only enough room remained for him to be self-aware. It reminded him so much of the cell in which he'd spent the past couple of weeks. He couldn't believe this was how he was going to die. As a pawn in someone else's game.

"You're not dying, Captain," Oni said, catching him by surprise. *"Well, at least not now. I did not foresee the deterioration of Major Saxma's body. Apparently, the body cannot survive this type of invasion without its original occupant. I will keep you alive. For your continued lack of cooperation and respect, I will even let you see what I do through your own form."*

A narrow shaft of light pierced through the ocean of thought surrounding Pan's consciousness. It was like looking through a telescope, the image slightly distorted. He recognized he was witnessing what was again happening through his own eyes.

With the invader pulling the strings, Pan's body rose off the ground. The movement was a little unsteady at first, but Oni quickly became more comfortable with his new appendages. The head lifted, and Pan saw Prince Kitsune and a strangely dressed woman looking his way with concern and hesitation. Kitsune broke away from the woman's grasp and began walking toward him.

"Watch as I end your source of hope."

*

"Are you daft?" Mai said, reaching out to grab his arm again. "Would you listen to me?"

"Pan is a good man," Kitsune said, wrenching himself free. He turned back to his friend, a man who had believed in him while others, including the prince himself, thought he had done something criminal. The captain had stood, lifting his head so their eyes met.

The look in the other man's eyes was not that of Pan. It was King Oni, staring back at him once more.

Kitsune came to a quick stop. His confidence wavered, and he muttered, "How?"

"I told you so!" Mai called out from behind him.

Without looking away from the pair of them, Pan's frail-looking body marched over to a nearby group of soldiers and withdrew one of their swords from its scabbard. Then, with a patient smile, Oni moved to close the distance between them. "You were warned. You cannot stop me."

Still thrown off by this turn of events, Kitsune did not know how best to proceed. He knew he could defeat his father's new avatar, but what was to stop the monarch from taking over yet another body? With thousands of other vessels for him to inhabit, Kitsune would certainly fall at some point, if only from exhaustion. He could burn the lot of them with a wall of fire, but he had come here to take command of an army, not destroy one.

He looked about, hoping to find a clue that would explain how his father was accomplishing this feat. Despite what the prince was now capable of, he was still new to the world of magic. The amount of control the king was exercising from such a great distance was surely not possible. Not without the aid of something onsite.

The formidable tower came back into his view. It was the only structure that didn't make sense. Kitsune had never seen anything quite like it, but knew it had to serve a purpose. Then he recalled Pan's last words, understanding now they had been a warning. A directive. A plea.

"Get back!" he shouted at Mai. He retreated several steps, trying to distance himself from Pan's approach.

"How are you endangering our lives now?" Mai responded, though she complied with his request.

Torrents of purple flames spewed from Tsukumogami as Kitsune's grip on the weapon tightened. He pulled from its power, experience, and knowledge, fueling his own magic. Through his new senses, he felt the ground beneath their feet, learning its physical makeup and weaknesses. As he reached with his mind, the earth shook.

Giving a startled cry, Mai lost her footing as the ground rippled beneath them. The sound of breaking glass and objects smashing to the ground reached Kitsune's ears, but he knew it wouldn't be enough. The tower could be destroyed if given enough time, but Pan's body was bearing down on him, murderous intent written all over his face.

Flames writhed about the blade's metal. They were a slightly darker shade than usual.

You are the most powerful entity in the world, but you only show weakness, came the sword's voices. No, it was only one voice this time. Kitsune couldn't be certain, but he suspected they belonged to the dark, ghostly figure he'd seen at the end of the hall in the pyramid.

Own your anger. Tap into it. Channel our power and make it even stronger.

A hesitant pause, and then, *Here, take mine!*

Anger broiled up Kitsune's sword-bearing arm like a bolt of lightning and exploded in his head. He roared, a monstrous sound that swept over the base. It wasn't from pain but a righteous fury that had to be expressed. He had been used by his father, the king, and Myobu, his love, in their own separate and selfish agendas. He had been raped, coerced into murder, and abandoned in a foreign wilderness. Even his own mother, the most pure and good thing in his life, had turned tail. It left him feeling hollow and cold toward the entire world.

Those that had wronged him would suffer his wrath.

Raising Tsukumogami above his head, he gripped its handle with both hands and drove it into the ground before him. As the flames disappeared beneath the grass, he poured every ounce of himself into that connection with the earth below. The rolling quakes became volatile, the cracking and screeching of the rock bed beneath them audible.

And then the ground split open in front of Kitsune. A small, jagged line at first, but it quickly spread between him and the tower, widening at a frightening rate. Heat rose as flames gushed from the new crevice and cascaded over the field.

Kitsune looked up in time to see Pan's body skid to a halt just footfalls away from him. Another step or two and the man would have fallen into the crack. The orange flames lit up the man's face, and the prince saw something he'd never witnessed: His father was afraid.

The sound of tumbling rocks rose above the shifting ground and roaring fires. Kitsune looked up in time to see one side of the tower fall away like flowing water. The crevice in the ground widened further, finally reaching the structure. The building visibly tilted to the right as its foundation disintegrated. Cracks formed along its remaining shaft like a growing tree, bits of mortar showering down. The top half of the tower eventually became unsupportable, and it careened forward onto the ground, crushing a group of soldiers. The bottom half disappeared into the underground furnace.

Kitsune, Mai, and Oni stared as the bulbous top portion of the tower collapsed in upon itself and then, surprisingly, expanded outward. A number of brilliant golden spheres pushed their way out of the rubble and floated upward and away. Kitsune recognized them immediately, recalling similar orbs circling the Boleyn Room at the center of Inari Palace. Seeing them before had been his first taste of magic. Now he knew—he could feel—they were pure fountains of power.

They are yours for the taking, said the voice of Tsukumogami's dark soul. For a moment, Kitsune considered taking the power for himself. He could do it, just as he had taken Myobu's magic. He lifted his hand, knowing he could become unstoppable.

No! the rest of the voices shouted together, crashing into his head and overpowering the dark one. *This magic was stolen from countless souls. It was a terrible sin to do so then. To continue doing so now would prove you no better.*

Through Pan's eyes, Oni must have seen the decision Kitsune made. He rushed around the crack in the ground and, hand outreached, leaped toward his son. Eyes wide with fear and anger, he shouted, "You can't!"

Bringing his hand down, Kitsune released a strike of lightning from the sky above. It branched out like the roots of a tree, piercing the sides of each floating sphere. The imprisoned magic exploded with a blinding light and a thunderous concussion that overtook the lightning itself.

Hundreds of bodies were thrown to the ground by the thunder. A tic later, Kitsune was blinking the stars from his eyes and rubbing his ears. He saw Pan's form slumped over just a footfall away, his hand still curled in a death grip, but he knew his father was no longer there.

"You lied to me," Mai said nonchalantly, looking down at him. He hadn't heard her walk up beside him. "You're not a Joey. You are a Kitsune."

He stared back at her. Even though he could barely make out her shape through his compromised vision, the bright silver lines of her clothing still shone through. "Clearly, I'm not the only one lying about who they are."

TRIBAL ORIGINS

Few buildings in Hawte were over three stories. The capital was unlike Kitsunetsuki's Oinari or Odom's Huem, where palaces and fortresses could be spotted from leagues away. Still, Myobu's keen eyes spotted his home's skyline while he and Jorin were still half a day's journey away. They could not have reached it soon enough. Myobu's patience, usually overflowing with abundance, was wearing thin.

As they had crossed the border and ventured further into civilization, Jorin had become more relaxed. The anthropologist forgot his fear of Mai following them, and he became exponentially more confident in himself. Myobu recognized the man's intellect and understood why the royal family had backed his research expedition into the tribal lands. However, even intellectuals were prone to the same sins as others, and Myobu also recognized bigotry and xenophobia in the man.

"Imagine my surprise when discovering Mai's abilities," Jorin had said at one point. "Not only were the legendary Yokai real, but I was under the spell of one. The creatures would have been wise to have kept hidden forever. I fully intend to recommend an expeditionary force to root them out and rid the world of them."

Myobu was inclined to be forgiving of Jorin's behavior at first. The stressful and prolonged experience of being under another's complete control would warp anyone's perception for a tic. However, as they traveled, it became apparent the man was disdainful toward many other cultures and races. All citizens of Kitsunetsuki were warmongers and had to be stopped. Odom deserved their economic hardship after hording wealth for so long.

It was a tiresome thread of conversations, and Myobu considered the man lucky he no longer had his magic.

Initially, Myobu was baffled as to why Jorin was interested in the peoples of the tribal lands—why he had even become an anthropologist to begin with—if he was so intolerant of others. The reasons became apparent as he spoke of his research, a subject Myobu found fascinating. Jorin wasn't so much concerned with the tribal lands' current occupants. As he had stated when they first encountered one another, he was curious about their origins.

"Like any child, I was fascinated by the mysterious pyramids of the tribal lands. Huge, ancient structures that protected many a secret," Jorin said during their second day of travel. "As I grew older, a far greater conundrum presented itself. There is a disconnect between the clans and the technical prowess needed to construct such grand monuments. To complete even one of their pyramids would be a significant accomplishment for today's societies!"

"So you believe that in the past, a highly evolved civilization must have inhabited the area?" Myobu guessed. Remembering parts of the journal Kitsune had summarized, he knew its author had not only lived among the clans but had performed some highly advanced research alongside them. She herself had admitted the people were far more intellectual and sophisticated than most realized. Myobu hadn't given it a second thought. He knew civilizations rose and fell over centuries.

"Just as the people of the Wastelands disappeared, something happened to those in the tribal lands. Perhaps it resulted from the same catastrophic event. A lot more is missing than the region's intellect. I believe the pyramids once held treasure. Not the kind we've fantasized about, but a technological trove. The types of knowledge that would appear like magic to you and me."

Myobu thought of the gray buildings and Kitsune's reactions to the one they entered together. The prince had been fascinated, thinking the portal entrance and light sources were surely magic at work.

"I theorize the great people that used to inhabit the tribal lands," Jorin continued, "were a relation of, if not a direct offshoot of, those of the Wastelands. If true, that would make the current clans—"

"The only surviving ancestors," Myobu completed. Now he understood the man's anthropological interest in the tribal lands. He didn't care a lick about the current societies, but he idealized the once-powerful and knowledgeable people they may have descended from.

The theory did intrigue Myobu. However, his new companion did not offer any hypotheses as to what caused a technologically advanced culture to devolve into what amounted to a rather backward collection of societies. Jorin segued the conversation into a running diatribe against the clans, claiming their ancestors would be ashamed of what had become of their accomplishments. Myobu had nothing to add to either conversation.

*

When Myobu had first entered Hawte so many sun cycles ago, there had been little to no security. No guards or soldiers were present to stop and question a naked young man. Getting into the city still wasn't difficult, but Gaav had been adopting some of Kitsunetsuki's security methods. Passage into and out of the city was limited to specified roads, and city guards were always on duty at those posts.

One of those sentries would have questioned Jorin and Myobu as they entered the city, but the older man marched up to the closest one and made first contact.

"I demand to see...to see someone!" Jorin said to a rather bewildered guard. "I've been missing for well over a sun cycle. Surely there have been questions concerning my absence. Search parties are probably out looking for me now! They must be recalled immediately, lest they fall victim to Yokai invaders. We must prepare for war!"

The young sentry appeared at a loss for words. He looked as though he were about to turn the older man around and send him away from Hawte like he would any raving lunatic. Then he saw Myobu standing quietly behind Jorin. Doing a double take, he asked, "Ninko? Is that you?"

Even in the younger form of Acro, it did not surprise Myobu that he'd been recognized. While most of the city's inhabitants were unaware of his multiple personas, it was a well-known secret among the extended royal family, council, and city guard. It helped him move about more easily, and it had helped Kensie and Tod stay out of trouble with authorities while he was around.

After Myobu nodded, the guard bowed in respect and continued, "We were not expecting your presence today, Ninko. The city has missed you in your absence. Would you like an escort home?"

Jorin turned around to stare at the man he had been traveling with. The look of terror on his face, as though he thought Myobu would strike him down in retribution, almost made the pains of listening to his racist rants worth it. Myobu wished he still had the power to transform into his visage of Ninko just to push Jorin over the edge.

Being gleeful at another's humiliation, even if the embarrassment was well deserved, was not Myobu's way, however. "I have no need of an escort," he said. Being surrounded by city guards would draw unwanted attention to the young Acro form. Pointing to Jorin, he continued, "This gentleman here may still have a home and family to whom he would like to return. Kindly ensure his swift arrival."

Once inside the city, Myobu made his quickly to the royal complex. He thought about rooting out his friends first, but decided that would be indulgent. With soldiers at the kingdom's door that could be given orders to march onward and attack, he had to stick with priorities.

As he walked the streets and side roads, taking every shortcut he could remember, he couldn't help but feel Hawte had changed. Colors were brighter. Buildings appeared taller. Passersby had happier, broader smiles. It was as though he had been gone for decades and was returning to a whole new generation of citizens who had brought a different feel to the city.

In truth, he had only been gone for two months. Still, something had changed.

It's me, he thought. *The city is the same, but I have changed. How I view the world and my place in it has altered. Even more so now that I have been separated from Kitsune. That's what finding love does to a person.*

Expecting to find King Marauxus at his home this late in the afternoon, Myobu was surprised when the monarch called out his name from one of the administrative buildings. Turning, he saw Marauxus practically leaping down the front stairs in delight.

"Working so late in the d—" Myobu nearly inquired before the king squeezed all the air from his lungs in a firm embrace.

"I don't think I ever fully realized all the responsibilities you have taken on over the sun cycles," Marauxus answered nonetheless. "You are never allowed to leave city limits again, let alone the kingdom's borders!"

"I'm afraid I am going to be forced to disobey your request for once," Myobu replied in a low voice so the servants who had followed the jubilant man down the stairs couldn't hear. "May we go to your office? We have much to discuss."

*

Other monarchs had throne rooms or lavish halls in which to meet their subjects or councilors. Just as the royal family of Gaav did not live in a palace, they conducted their duties in offices like any other public administrative officer. Granted, Marauxus' suite of offices was the largest in the building. Much like his home, though, it was modestly decorated with items that reminded him and visitors of their ancestral past as well as souvenirs from other lands.

One such reminder was a ceremonial mask designed to emulate a fox or Yokai. When used by grooms in Kitsunetsuki wedding ceremonies, such masks were covered in red felt or fur and had prominent black ears and noses. Marauxus' hung on a stand at the small conference table where he and Myobu now sat. It wasn't so much a memento as it was a constant reminder of the eastern threat.

"After your friends returned with your message, we didn't expect you back for quite some time, if at all," Marauxus said as an aide put down a tray with a kettle of tea and two cups. The servant looked distastefully at Myobu, who was grimy and unkempt. "Reports of your demise at the hands of Prince Kitsune have thrown the council into an uproar."

"Have I been replaced already?" Myobu asked with a chuckle as the king poured tea into both cups. The monarch did not even crack a smile at the attempt at humor. "What has taken place since then?"

"We had been using your secretaries to run messages in your name even before the return of your companions, and we've kept news of your death from becoming common knowledge among the people. Rumors are spreading, as they are wont to do. It would do them good to see your face. Well, err, the face of Ninko." Marauxus looked uneasy, as though he knew he was about to receive unpleasant news. "I haven't seen this youthful face on you in many sun cycles, my friend. Why are you wearing it now?"

"Would you mind if I started at the beginning?" Myobu said, looking at the cup of tea in his hands. He remembered thinking just days ago he might never enjoy such a luxury again. "I feel it would be unfair to answer your question without background. In any case, it includes information you must be made aware of."

"The council had just left before news of your return came to me. It will take some time for them to reassemble." Marauxus nodded. "Please, tell your story."

Between sips, Myobu relayed what had ensued since he had left Hawte. He stuck to the main points: Kyubi's warning of a malevolent force, his part in keeping that entity from destroying the world, saving and falling in love with Prince Kitsune, and eventually being killed by one of the prince's arrows.

"In an attempt to save my life, Kitsune accidentally took my powers," he said, explaining his current form. "Unless I can retrieve them—something I am not entirely certain is possible—I am stuck like this."

"So Kitsunetsuki's prince murdered you, an idea put into his head by King Oni as part of a plot to start a new war. You basically led the prince to the act at the request of the Harbinger to keep the world from being consumed by fire. The boy's mother, a Yokai spirit, found you in the afterlife and sent you back," Marauxus summarized. "Do you realize how insane that sounds?"

"I wouldn't bother explaining that to all your advisors," Myobu said with a shrug, again trying to lighten the conversation. "They may attempt to oust you from power."

"The council and I have been holding day-long meetings to discuss the ramifications of your murder at the hands of Prince Kitsune," the monarch continued, talking mostly to himself as he thought things out. "Now that we know Ninko is still alive—that *you* are still alive—we no longer have to respond to Oni."

"Wrong," Myobu interrupted. He got up from his seat to circle the room. The king looked startled, not used to being declared incorrect even by his closest advisor. "Even without my magic inside him, Kitsune poses a significant threat to this world. In his susceptible state of mind, he could be the destructive force Kyubi warned me about. Or it could still be Oni, who is amassing troops at the Western Pass. Possibly even farther south along our border. That is why I am here now instead of pursuing the prince. We must mobilize our forces for defense. To launch an attack of our own, if necessary."

"I thought your death stopped the path of destruction?" Marauxus said, his brow furrowed.

Shaking his head, Myobu replied, "No, it was only one necessary step in the process. I must push forward. We both must, if we are to save everything we hold dear."

The king glanced up from his cup, a sad look in his eyes. "You want me to call on the rural folk."

"You spent your entire life reaching out to them, gaining their trust, support, and respect," Myobu said, looking his friend straight in the eyes. "Now is the time to reap the benefits of your work. Gaav has an able and competent military, but we are no match for Kitsunetsuki's strength and experience. Unlike Odom, our borders are far more open with theirs, with few natural barriers. We need more people."

"It's like sending your own family into battle," Marauxus murmured. Then, as if realizing he had said those words aloud, he drew himself up. "But this is one reason we have made continued overtures. Dark force or not, we have perceived King Oni as a threat for decades. I will send word to the rural folk that we need every able person to arm."

"Immediately," Myobu pushed. "The enemy is already at our door."

Marauxus moved to his desk. Gathering parchment and ink, he prepared to write the necessary letters to be sent. "You said you would not be staying in Hawte for long. What exactly will you be doing while we prepare for war?"

Between Jorin's bouts of conversation, Myobu had given thought to his subsequent actions. More than anything, he wanted to head east and find Prince Kitsune. This drive was instinctual, but only on an emotional level. Logically, he knew he could never catch up with his love before something terrible happened. The darkness may have already spread.

"I wish I could seek Kitsune," he said, sitting down again to finish his drink. It would probably be yet another stretch of time before he'd enjoy another. "But I believe I must help him in another way. Hopefully, if I am lucky, the path I must follow will lead me to him. I might save his heart and mind. Ultimately, I hope to save us all."

*

Myobu walked down the steps of the administrative building. He had hoped by including Marauxus, the Gaav military, and the rural folk on what was happening, he would feel less pressure to stop whatever storm was brewing. The weight of the world still hung on his shoulders, however, and he wasn't sure what to do next. He wanted to sleep, but he felt hunting down his friends should take precedence.

Thankfully, the latter decided for him.

Their scent reached his nose even before he heard their footsteps on the road. As Kensie and Tod sidled up next to him, Tod said in his gruff voice, "Did you find what you were looking for?"

"I did. I really did," Myobu replied. He gave Kensie a hug. When he turned to greet his other friend, he was struck by how pale and thin Tod looked. He knew in that instant the man was sick. He could *smell* the sickness wafting off him.

How did I not notice this before? Myobu asked himself. *Was I really that self-centered?*

Eyes wide with shock, he opened his mouth to say something. Tod shook his head ever so slightly, and Myobu could read into what that meant. Kensie was apparently still oblivious, and the other did not want to break the news yet.

"I fear the work the Harbinger has put before me is only half done, and I cannot stay for long," Myobu continued without pause. "Thank you for delivering my message to the royal family."

"You had a lot of nerve asking us to do anything!" Kensie exclaimed with an exaggerated sulk. "I can't believe you left without saying goodbye to me."

"I didn't want to…oh, what is it they say…wake a sleeping baby!" Myobu replied, jabbing at his friend. "Have you been taking care of yourself while I've been away? Keeping an eye on Nikki?"

"Of course!"

"Not too close an eye," Tod interjected with a wink.

The trio walked in no particular direction as they caught up, but they eventually ended up in front of Ninko's home. Myobu wondered if he had led the others here out of habit, having walked the path hundreds of times before, but it was his friends who had directed him. As they had never accompanied him inside the royal compound, he wondered how they knew to venture in this direction.

"Don't be too upset with us," Tod said as they walked up to the door, though there was little apology in his voice.

Myobu looked at the pair questioningly, but the answers became apparent after stepping into the house. "Spirits, what in the blazes happened here?"

"After we delivered your message to King Marauxus, he asked us to shack up here for a time." Tod spread his arms, grandly presenting the room, which was now a dirty, cluttered mess. Clothes were strewn about, dishes were stacked precariously upon the few pieces of furniture, and it looked like someone had perhaps urinated in one corner. "We found it sparse, so we made it feel a bit more like home."

"It looks like a back alley!" Myobu proclaimed. He wondered how long it would take to return his home to the austere condition in which he had left it.

"Yeah, that's what I said." Tod rolled his eyes, closing the door behind them.

"So, yeah, the king damn near demanded we stayed here," Kensie interjected nervously, picking up clothes off the floor. "He would speak to us occasionally, asking what we thought your opinion would be on various matters."

"Asked us what our opinions were on matters," Tod said with a shrug that Myobu interpreted as respect. "Decided to take advantage of the opportunity and rest up from our journey before returning to the usual routine again."

"This guy has been getting old and slow," Kensie said, casually tossing the clothing into the corner of the room, covering up the questionable stain. His voice was jovial and mocking, but a sudden watery look in his eyes made Myobu believe his friend knew more than he let on.

Ignoring the jab, Tod asked, "So where is the second half of the Harbinger's work taking you? Back into the tribal lands of boredom?"

Myobu shook his head. "All the more exciting events of late have occurred in the tribal lands. We were just in the wrong places at the wrong times. But that's not where I'm headed. The first leg of this venture will take me south, then east. No idea where it'll end up. Sure to be a more perilous endeavor. Like before, I may not return."

"Sounds harrowing. When do we leave?" Tod said. He reached for the pack he had traveled with through the tribal lands. It didn't look like it had been touched since he had returned. Myobu watched as the man sniffed at the contents, grimaced, then shrugged as though he were convinced the bag's contents wouldn't kill him or his companions.

Despite the pack's odiferous contents, Myobu put a hand on it as if to stay his friend. Softly, he said, "I'm not asking you to come this time."

"I know you're not asking," Tod answered, pulling his bag out of Myobu's reach. "We're not asking to join you. We just are."

"We are?" Kensie said with a gulp. "I mean, did you catch the part where he may not be returning?"

"Even if he comes back, who is to say we'll both still be around?" Tod said with more volume and gruffness than usual. Then, more lightly, he added, "I mean, the man will basically live forever. The entire city could be dust by the time he returns."

"I could use the company. Much has happened on which I would appreciate your thoughts and advice. But you must be sure," Myobu said, trying to phrase his words tactfully. He didn't want his friend to insist on coming, only to prove to himself that he was healthy enough for it. "Are you sure you've recovered from your previous trip? This will be a fast, taxing journey."

Tod waved at Myobu's and Kensie's worried looks. "I'll be fine, and I know you'll push forward without us if forced. I must do this, though. The three of us sought the Harbinger to find someone you could fall in love with. You left abruptly, saying she had revealed to you the best way to serve your friends. I'd wager she told you a lot more, especially after some conversations we've had with King Marauxus. Now let me do the same thing. Serve my friends to the best of my limited abilities. Serve the family I should have looked after all these sun cycles."

Even if Tod had been on his deathbed, Myobu would have been hard pressed to deny him that wish. That he knew the effects his actions had on his family of the past, was willing to take ownership of it and work toward restitution, showed great maturity. Myobu always thought the man wise, albeit in a coarse way. This reinforced his opinion.

Plus, the man had never said so much at one time!

"Just when I was getting used to all this luxury, you want to change up my life again," Kensie said, sulkily gathering up a few shirts of his own. Then he swaggered a bit. "I suppose Nikki is just going to have to wait until I return to get a piece of this action!"

DEVASTATION

Kitsune felt like he was experiencing one of the Lady of the Mountain's dreamscapes. After walking through the dirt-saturated winds of northern Odom for hours, his foot had struck the solid street—a dusty, barren road—jarring him from his wandering thoughts. No buildings lined the path, and the fifty-footfall stretch appeared from and disappeared into mounds of sandy ground.

It was an otherworldly sight, much like the many worlds his mother had dreamed up. Kitsune knew exactly where he was, however. It was a real place. Rather, it had been.

Before being chased into the Wastelands by a tornado, Kitsune had first visited the northernmost settlement of Odom. It was initially a trading outpost, founded as a waypoint to and from Ruio and Gaav when King Oni had effectively barred access to Kitsunetsuki through the Eastern Gate. Even before it could become a fully established city—the prince wasn't certain it ever had a proper name—Oni had annexed Ruio into his kingdom, effectively cutting off safe passage to the west.

Even at its height, the outpost had been a dirty, ramshackle place on the edge of Odom's civilization. Still, it had been home for some who had eked out a living. Kitsune had purchased the ancient journal from a wizened old street merchant. That had been moments before hastily departing into the Wastelands, pursued by the unnaturally violent storm.

The tornado had been unwittingly created by Kitsune, an expression of his emotions through magic. His infatuation with Myobu had grown stronger each day since they met. Those feelings were accompanied by a sense of immense loss, as the other man had departed a few days earlier after Kitsune had revealed his true intentions for the King's Sun.

The prince had barely survived the storm, and he had guiltily worried afterward over the fate of the outpost. The rickety wooden buildings would never stand up against the winds. He had hoped the deadly twister hadn't touched ground until after passing over the settlement.

Now, as he stood on the lonely stretch of road, he knew that hoping had accomplished nothing. If he stared hard into the dusty, swirling winds, he could make out a few wooden beams sticking out of the ground, remnants of what might have been buildings. Otherwise, nothing remained. No homes, barracks, or stores. Certainly not the merchant who had sold him the journal.

The entire outpost was now a trail of debris.

I caused this, Kitsune thought, wondering if any had survived. It pained him that he'd spent so little time training with and understanding his newfound powers. His lack of control over magic and emotions gave birth to the monstrosity, and he would never be able to forgive himself. *Surely, though, this was not my fault!*

He had been a conduit for the actions of others. His father had banished him into Odom, leaving him confused and miserable. Myobu had found him, saved his life, and encouraged him into a doomed relationship. Kitsune had been used and manipulated, and others had suffered and died because of it.

They treated you like a pathetic dog, he thought, tears stinging his eyes. *You should be the one who is dead. Not these people. Not Mamori. Not even Jasper.*

Tsukumogami thrummed at his side, and he drew strength from it as he breathed in air.

No, I should not be dead, he corrected himself. *And this was not my fault. But I will bring the ones who are responsible to justice.*

Turning about, Kitsune faced the horde of people standing idly behind him. He could not see the line of men and women stretching back into the horizon, but knew over three thousand soldiers—an entire regiment of King Oni's military—was sandwiched between just as many former Ruio slaves. All had sworn allegiance to him, had answered his call to fight against the tyranny of the king, but he placed a bit more of his trust in the former citizens of Ruio.

As soon as Kitsune had freed the magic from its spherical prisons, the minds of the soldiers and natives had been freed. Confusion and disorientation had overwhelmed everyone. They were not used to thinking for themselves. As the ranking officer, Captain Pan had attempted to take command of the situation, but the man was weak from his ordeal. His voice was thin, and no one aside from the prince would listen to him. Pan quickly relayed all that had developed since their last meeting.

"This confirms our suspicion that King Oni has a massive amount of magic at his disposal," the man said as Mai tended to his condition. She had kneeled by his side after learning his wasted physique had been the result of time in a tiny prison cell. A few freshly pulled muscles from Oni's abuse of his body didn't help, either. "Not only does he know how to use it, but he has the will to do so."

Kitsune had raised his voice to capture everyone's attention. The volume and authority he projected surprised even himself. "You are all confused and scared. I understand why and sympathize with your situation. You have been under the control of King Oni. He violated your minds and assumed control of your bodies.

"The kingdom and right to rule is his, and some of you may willingly answer to the monarchy. As soldiers, you may have sworn allegiance to him. But he does not own you, and he has no right to influence your thoughts in such a manner or force you from your own minds. In doing so, he has overstepped the boundaries of his duties."

The sentiments were vaguely reminiscent of words spoken by Mamori, a soldier who had accompanied Kitsune as he was forced into Odom. Unfortunately, he had not survived the journey, but the prince thought the man would be proud of how his worldviews had changed. "Oni will answer for these crimes!"

The prince asked Pan to order the base perimeter watched for any soldiers that might attempt to flee in the middle of the night. Once the captain gained some strength, he also sent out trusted messengers to nearby camps. As the wall project spanned the northern border nearly as far as the Western Pass, several smaller camps had been established. It wasn't possible to bring all of them under Kitsune's control by morning, but the messengers were sent to the closest ones with orders to pick up immediately and march through the night.

The next morning, Kitsune stood before thousands of men and women, dressed in a conglomeration of clothing. A commanding officer's uniform with the rank insignia stripped off. The hooded cape provided by the Purple People. The sword belt he had found with Tsukumogami. A new traveling pack gifted by one of the Ruio natives. While still maintaining a sense of individuality and rebellion, he wanted to appeal to everyone. Especially as he gave them all an ultimatum: join him in his venture to dethrone the king or be destroyed.

Murmurs spread throughout the crowd as people turned and spoke among themselves. They didn't know if the exiled royal was serious. The prince they knew would never do something so drastic. Did he even stand a chance against his father? Did he actually have authority over them?

A man at the front of the crowd stepped forward and called out, "We may not agree with what King Oni did to us or even you, but he is still our king! We are bound to him by oath. Knowing what he did to you, now you want us to make traitors out of ourselves?"

Kitsune's grip on Tsukumogami tightened. It took all his self-control and common sense not to engulf the man in flames. Instead, he replied, "Yes, I am asking you to revoke your oath to my father. It is my sincere hope in doing so that you will not be a traitor to your own conscience."

More quietly, so only the other man could hear, Kitsune added, "Everyone is coming with me. Whether that is willingly or in a cell box is up to you."

No one else raised any objections. Everyone fell in line. Half of the Ruio natives marched at the front of the group, as Kitsune felt safer within their vicinity. The other half marched behind the Kitsunetsuki soldiers, keeping a lookout for those who might otherwise conspire against him.

With the bridge connecting Odom and the Wastelands over a canyon destroyed by the tornado, they had marched east through a hidden pass in the northern portion of the Argent Mountains. Stealing into Odom, Kitsune reached the remains of the outpost by midafternoon of the following day.

Now, as he looked out over the pool of miserable-looking people behind him, he wondered if he had done the right thing by forcing everyone along. The man who had balked hadn't been wrong, and he hadn't been against Kitsune. The rest of these people, especially the Ruio natives, looked unsure of the situation. They were certainly grateful to be freed from their labor, but had they simply been forced into another form of servitude? Perhaps he should have simply asked for volunteers in his crusade against the king.

No, you chose the correct course of action, came the voice of the dark soul. *Left unchecked, that man would have sowed discontent among the others. More would have stayed behind. Questioned your leadership. Alerted your enemies.*

Kitsune waited for the chorus of other voices to disagree. They did so more and more. No opposition came this time, though, and he felt the matter settled.

"What was this place?" Mai asked, interrupting his internal conversation. She looked down the barren street. "This may be the only road in the world that truly goes nowhere! Does it mean something to you?"

"A settlement stood on this spot just days ago. I traveled through on my way to find the Harbinger. You might know her as Kyubi," he said, turning toward her. Looking through the fine strands of his hair, he wanted to gauge her reaction. "Seeing you are both Yokai."

"That is a very generalizing assumption," Mai replied, her dark eyebrows furrowing in disappointment. "Despite you and the anthropologist both being human, I would be downright stunned if the two of you knew one another."

A long pause fell between the two. When Kitsune did not speak again, she asked in a demure voice, "How did you know?"

"Aside from your utterly bizarre personality?" he replied, sidestepping a punch to his arm. "You now know who my father is. What you probably haven't heard is he banished me from my kingdom several weeks ago. I'm certain there are many reasons behind his actions, but I surmise one of them is because he can't control me as he can other humans.

"You said when we met you could tell I was not one of the Yokai. That is true, but my mother was. Her blood is the only thing I can think of that keeps me safe from my father's mental influence. Before I destroyed the tower, you were the only other person unaffected by his magic. If I'm correct, you are of the Yokai or one of them."

"One of them," Mai confirmed. She twirled about as though shyly proud. Her garish clothes, now a gray cloth with heavy splotches of glittering gold, shone despite the dusty air, reminding the prince she was anything but shy.

"Who are you really? What were you doing in that pyramid?"

"The only truth I passed on to you was my name," she admitted, flashing a wide grin. "I am Yokai, and proudly consider myself a yako.

Despite my earlier comments, I do in fact know the Harbinger. Kyubi is my mother."

Kitsune's jaw clenched at that revelation, and his hand twitched toward his sword. What he would give to make that wretched old woman feel the pain she had caused him. He did not draw his weapon. Mai may have been a loud nuisance, but she had more than proven herself useful to have around. She was not his enemy. Not yet, anyway. Myobu had been beneficial, too.

"My mother is a bitch," Mai continued unabashedly. "I left her den long ago and, despite our relative proximity, have rarely seen her since. Our last encounter was about a century ago. She and one of her many partners—a malleable man named Kirin—found me. Using her deep wells of magic, the two of them bound my life force to Tsukumogami. My soul doesn't reside within it like its past owners. However, if I stray too far from it, my life force weakens. I will die if separated from it for too long.

"They hid the sword away in the pyramid. I was directed to watch over the place and tend to the Purple People, who had also been tasked with observing the area."

Mai sighed, scuffing some of the sand on the road back and forth with a foot. "They were attempting to resurrect the idea of the Inari's disciples. I'm not a follower, and my disposition does not lend well to living for a singular purpose in a singular location. I bore easily. To pass the time, I have captured the attention of the random traveler or tribesman. Never one of the Purple People—that would have gone against Kirin's directive. One of their enemies, though, or someone they traded with who was handsome or pretty. They would keep me company for as long as they could."

"You enslaved them," Kitsune corrected. "Until you drove them mad."

"That's an awfully harsh way to word it," she said with a wicked smile. "But nonetheless true."

"And your father, the anthropologist? Did he not exist?"

"I don't know who my father is, but there actually is an anthropologist." Mai's face brightened. "Hey! That's two things I told you that were true!"

Rolling his eyes, Kitsune said, "He was just another innocent victim? What happened?"

"Like so many others before him, he came in search of answers. He wasn't particularly interesting or striking. In fact, he was a bigoted ass. An easily confounded bigoted ass, which made him fun to play with. At least until someone else caught my attention."

"Let me guess: me."

"Yes, I had intended to enslave you like those before," she said slyly. "It's not as horrible an experience as you might believe. Some have even found it a pleasurable period in their lives. But then you *found* the sword, and what was I—"

Taking a quick step forward, Kitsune reached toward Mai's face. The movement caught her by surprise, and she reached for her weapon on instinct. As his slender fingers caressed the soft skin of her cheek, her sly look turned to befuddlement. "Huh?"

Brushing thick strands of her black hair aside, he leaned forward and kissed her. It was not a hesitant gesture—he was rarely hesitant with anyone—but it was tender. Mai's body stiffened in surprise, but she relaxed as she fell into the kiss. Placing a hand on his chest, she countered his tongue with her own, his lips with hers. Gradually, she turned more aggressive, pulling Kitsune forward by his tunic and clamping down on his lower lip with her teeth.

The nearby Ruio natives stared at the two of them. A few even gave encouraging whistles. It had to have been a strange sight, the two of them groping one another on a road that led nowhere.

An image of the dark-haired man flitted across the prince's mind, followed by a powerful wave of guilt. He extricated himself from the embrace with Mai. "Not here. Not in front of everyone."

"Well, you started it," she retorted, looking at him curiously. "What was that for, anyway?"

"It wasn't for anything. I did it because I wanted to and because I could. The kiss was my choice…a mutual choice. Like it was before my father disowned me. Like it will always be from now on. I will never be enslaved by anyone again. Especially one of the Yokai."

Mai stepped back, pursed her lips, and looked him over from top to bottom. Finally, she said, "Good for you. You've nothing to fear from me. Despite my link to Tsukumogami, I cannot touch it. And you're proving too exciting an individual just the way you are."

Kitsune turned away, signaling for Captain Pan. The man had been standing a respectful distance away from them, appearing quite uncomfortable. As the officer approached, Kitsune turned back to Mai. "If you lie to me again, I will not hesitate to kill you."

Flashing a wide smile that was unsettling, she responded, "I knew I liked you!"

Despite being holed up in a cramped prison for weeks, Pan had displayed a remarkable recovery since his escape. Gaunt, disheveled, and weak, he had barely the strength to stand on his feet. Color had returned to his skin, light to his eyes, and he marched alongside everyone else all day. Like Kitsune, he did not appear as though he wanted to stop marching.

"The people are tired. Especially those we called in from other camps," Pan admitted. "Still, I doubt anyone would want to make camp in this misbegotten landscape. It is demoralizing and depressing, not to mention spooky."

"Then we move south. The air and landscape will become more favorable before the day's end," Kitsune said. After walking through the Wastelands, he was looking forward to green trees and mountain views. "We should arrive at a city called Sandya in another couple of days."

Pan signaled for some messengers, ordering them to pass their new directive along. Watching them disappear into the dust clouds, he said, "I've heard of Sandya. Few haven't, I would wager. Supposed to be a massive fortress built right into the side of a mountain. What do you expect to find there?"

"The political and economic states of Odom are tumultuous. Patriarch Kirby and his family have relocated to Sandya from their home in Huem. The fortress is their newest and most secure stronghold." When the captain gave Kitsune a quizzical look, he explained, "I was their guest for a night as I traveled through their land. I met with Kirby personally. He is as concerned with King Oni as we are, and he offered me his support."

"He proposed an alliance?" Pan asked, looking surprised. Kitsune couldn't blame the man. If word got out Kirby had sided with the prince, it would have been akin to declaring war on King Oni.

"Of a sort," Kitsune answered. "He offered to place much of his own military under my command."

"They'd be able to learn a thing or two from our own soldiers, but their numbers are nothing to balk at," Pan said, giving an impressed whistle. Then he scanned the desolate landscape surrounding them, the lonely road leading to nowhere. "Such devastation as this can only increase the political turmoil he faces. What happens if Kirby refuses you his men? What if he needs them to hold Odom together?"

Without hesitation, Kitsune replied, "I would tear down the mountain stronghold."

Then he started the second half of the day's journey, walking southward.

RAISING AN ARMY

Finding peace and quiet in the dead of night, surrounded by thousands of people, was difficult. The more Kitsune tried to ignore the sounds of snores and rustling sleeping blankets, the more it bored into his ears.

Then there were those who had not fallen asleep. The Ruio natives had been under Oni's spell of complacency for so long, and many of the soldiers had never felt free to express themselves. Both groups did so now with one another. The prince gritted his teeth as the sounds of moaning and thrusting traveled unhindered through the open air.

It had been so long since he'd been with anyone. Back in Inari Palace, rarely a day went by that he wasn't intimate with a man or woman. He'd thought little of it at the time. Like good food and wine, it was a luxury one didn't truly appreciate until it was gone.

Kissing Mai had been an attempt to appease the physical desire growing within him. Her odd sense of style and individuality were attractive, and he knew she would lie with him if he asked. However, the kiss had been revolting. The more Kitsune thought about it, the more he wanted to throw up. The fault wasn't Mai's. And while he wanted to blame Myobu, who continued to be a curse on his soul, he knew the problem was in his own mind.

Guilt had consumed the prince when he had touched Mai. Myobu's face appeared before him, looking hurt. To kiss her—to kiss anyone—was a disgraceful action against their relationship.

He's dead! Kitsune shouted at himself, clamping his hands over his ears as a fresh wave of congregational ecstasy overtook him. *Even if it had been a genuine relationship, he's dead! I've done nothing wrong. And it wasn't real. I am well within my right to do anything with anyone I please.*

It didn't help that Myobu kept visiting his dreams. Most of them were just brief glances at memories. The touch of his hands on his skin. Their bodies nestled next to each other at night. Myobu's soft lips over his—

Kitsune shook his head, turning over indignantly in his own sleeping blankets.

Twice now had his dreams involving the other man been vivid and memorable. If he hadn't known better, he'd have thought he was within a magical dreamscape. The first had occurred shortly after entering the Wastelands. He was glad it had only been a dream, as his appearance and behavior were embarrassing. Both had been much improved during the second go-around, the one from which he had awoken several tics ago.

In the dream, Kitsune had been onboard a ship and was surrounded by the ocean. Or at least he thought it was a ship. The expected planks of worn wood were under his feet. A mast skewered the sky above, supporting billowing sails. Rudimentary railings lined the deck. Doors and stairs led to other compartments, presumably quarters and storage.

But then the visage of the ship faded slightly, and Kitsune got the impression he was standing on warm, wet leather. Instead of a ship bobbing in the ocean waves, he saw a giant creature was swimming along the surface of the water.

Was the ship alive, or was the appearance of a boat merely an illusion on top of something else, something his brain could interpret or understand?

This is a dream, he told himself. *It doesn't have to make sense.*

Kitsune turned about, looking out across the waters. He was awed by its sheer expansiveness and uniformity. It appeared so still, yet it had the power to make him feel small, unimportant, and lonely.

Except he wasn't alone. As he rotated, Myobu came into view. He looked whole and perfect, exactly the same as the last time they were together. The man looked at home on the deck of the ship but appeared concerned at Kitsune's presence.

"I shouldn't be here," Myobu said. At least, he mouthed the words. His voice rolled across the ocean like thunder.

Hearing the dead man's voice—so crystal clear and exact—stunned Kitsune. Kitsune opened his mouth, intending to make a snide comment, but found he couldn't speak. *No, you shouldn't be here. You're dead!* Nothing but puffs of air came out. He contented himself to glare at the apparition standing across the deck from him.

"I'm so sorry, my pretty prince," Myobu continued. "I'm sorry for what I did to you, for not revealing the full truth. You must believe me when I say it was for the greater good."

The greater good is subjective, Kitsune mouthed, growing angrier that he couldn't verbally combat the dream. In lieu of words, he gave the dark-haired man a rude gesture and turned away. The problem was, Myobu's form followed him, standing wherever the prince looked.

"I understand you are angry with me," Myobu continued, his voice booming over them. "Before you and I met, the Harbinger warned me of a blight that would burn through the world. She said I could stop it, Kitsune, but I would have to fall in love. And I did, my prince. I fell in love with you."

Though he could make no sound, Kitsune screamed a mental *No!* at the torturous apparition. As though reacting to him, the air about the ship crackled with energy. He unsheathed his sword, the metal sounding out over the deck, and pointed it at the other man. *Leave me alone! Stay out of my dreams!*

"Tsukumogami," Myobu whispered, his eyes growing wide. "So, Kirin hid it in the pyramid near the Purple People. With your multiple powers, it called out to you. That's why I saw you there. I should have known."

Kitsune frowned at that. He understood less than half, but the mention of Kirin was enough to convince him this was all nothing more than an elaborate dream. Nothing more than his mind stitching together the old and new.

The vision faded, and Kitsune felt the familiar sensation of regaining consciousness. Myobu had stepped forward, shouting, "Kitsune, I love you!"

Brandishing his blade to ward off the visage, Kitsune turned and stepped back into wakefulness.

*

A tear slipped from an eye as Kitsune recalled the desperate look on Myobu's face. Despite the unfettered anger he felt, the need to avenge himself, the willingness to do anything to achieve his goals, he could not deny the simple fact he wanted Myobu back. His idea of Myobu, anyway. The quietly confident dark-haired man. The one who nurtured him, kept him safe, opened his eyes to the wider world, and made him want to be a better person.

Turning over again in his blankets, the prince reached out for Tsukumogami, which was always close at hand. The cold metal was real and comforting in its own way, as it banished the nostalgic thoughts from his head. Myobu was dead. Kitsune had killed the man himself. He could not let himself fall victim to these distractions, not when he was getting closer to his father with each passing day.

As cool anger flooded through his body, replacing sentimental memories of Myobu, Kitsune pondered Tsukumogami. He was not blind to what was happening around him, within him. The sword was malfunctioning in some fundamental way. It was damaged, likely the mechanisms of the dark soul residing within it. That morbid voice, however, influenced him more than all the others combined. It swayed his thoughts, plans, and whims. Had he not recognized that fact, known the darkness wanted something from him, he would have been making the same mistakes all over again. Never again would he fall victim to the inspirations and ideals of others.

He wanted this, though. Welcomed it. The righteous anger offered by the blade provided more than clarity and strength. It gave him a singular will.

Keeping the sword close kept his depressive headaches at bay, and it prevented him from regressing into the sniveling, pathetic version of himself. The one that mourned Myobu. Missed him. That version dreamed of him at night, awaking with tears pouring from his eyes. That version was angry, too, but it was untamed, confused, embroiled with emotion.

Never again, Kitsune said to himself, pulling the blankets tight over his slight frame. He squeezed his eyes shut and concentrated on clearing his mind.

Never again.

*

"Absolutely not!"

"Sir, you know weapons are not allowed within the city walls."

The captain stood fixedly in Kitsune's path, her arms folded across her chest. She was the same woman he'd encountered the last time he came to Sandya. She had intercepted him and Myobu at the main entrance, accompanied them to Patriarch Kirby, and she had allowed in none of their weapons then either.

Those armaments had been mere metal and wood. Tsukumogami had become an extension of his self. Sometimes he felt as though a part of his soul lived within the blade, congregating with the others—especially the one.

"I don't care who you are, how fancy your sword is, or how attached you are to it," the woman reiterated. "You are not entering the city with it by your side."

Kitsune felt the sudden urge to take her up on the challenge, but knew she was only performing her duty. Drawing upon the patience and advice of Tsukumogami's other souls, the ones he listened to less and less, he calmed his temper and mood.

"Fine," he conceded, unbuckling his sword belt. Looking around, he spotted the same youth who had taken his weapons the previous time. "Guard this with your life. Lose it, and you'll lose something precious to you."

The young man's face turned red. Kitsune might have been satisfied with the reaction, but he felt his strength and confidence suddenly slip away as his fingers lost contact with the blade. In their absence, his headache reemerged, accompanied by a wave of emotions. They weighed heavy in his chest, but not all the feelings were negative.

Looking up at the rocky walls of the mountain fortress, the prince realized he missed more than just Myobu. Yes, it was here in Sandya their relationship came to a critical juncture. After Kitsune confessed his true intentions for the King's Sun, Myobu had left him alone with his thoughts and tears. The prince had been unsure if he'd ever see the other again.

The immense city had also been a source of immense joy, for it was here he found family in his paternal grandmother, Veranda. Sun cycles ago, upon suspecting her son Oni had murdered his new bride, she had escaped Kitsunetsuki and sought refuge with the royal family of Odom. Not long afterward, her husband died, leaving the throne open for her son.

The treachery of Oni gave them something in common.

"Follow me," the captain said tersely, though Kitsune detected a hint of relief. Perhaps she had sensed his want to challenge her.

Glancing back, Kitsune saw the sea of people that, whether out of faith, fear, or obligation, had uprooted their lives and followed him. Much like the mountain range along which they traveled, the caravan stretched as far as the eye could see. He imagined they had caused quite a fright from a distance, instigating Sandya's city guard to hurriedly prepare for battle. Messengers had been sent back and forth, however, declaring peaceful and friendly intentions.

"Are we going to Kirby's office?" Kitsune asked as he watched Mai surrender the last of her myriad weapons. Many of the colorful, glittering shapes upon her clothing were apparently meant as cover for hidden pockets.

"Patriarch Kirby is currently with Lady Veranda in her quarters," the captain replied, leading the pair through the entrance into the city.

Just as before, he marveled at the differences between one side of the wall and the other. From the outside, the fortress was quiet and nearly invisible against the jagged Argent Mountains. It could have been abandoned, a relic of a forgotten city. Inside, the streets bustled with life and energy. An ingenious system of mirrors hung about the walls of the narrow alleyways, providing light from above. Sheets of colored tapestries dampened the noises of the crowds filling the streets.

The sense of stress and extreme tension that had permeated the market during his previous visit, making citizens look like they were constantly ready for an attack, had somehow intensified. Tired, reddened eyes looked back at him as he searched the crowds, watching him and Mai warily as they walked the streets. Hands were kept shoved in pockets as though close to something sharp, ready to jump the two newcomers if they made the wrong move.

In her usual fashion, Mai voiced what he had only been thinking. "Is it just me or is the paranoia quite palpable?"

"Quiet now. The sound of your voice might set them off," Kitsune replied, drawing a small smile from her.

"Odom may be politically and economically cut off from the rest of the region, but news still travels fast," the captain said. "Rumors spread even faster. Word of your actions against Ninko of Gaav reached us days ago, as have reports of Kitsunetsuki's military movements toward the Western Pass."

Kitsune nodded, satisfied his father was continuing forward with his plans. In doing so, the king was inadvertently helping the prince with his own strategy. With luck, nothing had changed since the two had battled each other at the northern wall. "If Oni is marching away from Odom, why the tension?"

Glancing over her shoulder, the captain stated, "If Gaav falls—*when* it falls—we know Odom is next."

The trio walked in relative silence for several tics, zigzagging through the maze of streets. Mai looked ill at ease, probably uncomfortably claustrophobic. Eventually, unable to take the quiet, she elbowed Kitsune in the ribs and quipped, "The patriarch is with Lady Veranda, eh? Maybe she's doing something very unladylike with him!"

Kitsune glared at her angrily, but asked, "Why is the patriarch in my grandmother's quarters?"

The captain paused for a moment, looking back at them. "Lady Veranda isn't well."

"What ails her?" Kitsune said in a whisper, stepping closer to their guide. He was unable to stand the thought of her suffering, that she might pass before he could see her again.

"I can't say, sir," the captain responded. "She was not young when she came to us, and I wouldn't think the last couple of decades have been easy for her."

They continued traversing the city, though Kitsune's increased pace urged them on. The path to their destination was no less confusing than the last time. It was frustrating to think the woman's job was to confuse them so they'd never be able to make their way about the city without assistance. If that truly was the case, she was succeeding.

The rougher streets and stone walls gradually gave way to finer, more luxurious materials and craftsmanship. The section of the fortress in which they found themselves was reminiscent of where Patriarch Kirby's office was located, though it felt slightly more relaxed and lived-in. Apartment entrances lined wide hallways, reminding the prince of his own rooms in Inari Palace.

The captain came to a stop in front of a set of wooden doors, then gestured for the two of them to enter. She crossed her arms and stood sentry. Her head moved slowly back and forth, her eyes daring any passerby to make a move at her.

Inside the apartment, Kitsune and Mai found a grand entryway and a sitting room. The only window was on the far side of the cavernous living space, but it was large enough to light the room. Black oak trees, potted in giant urns, dominated the corners, though they were sickly compared to those that grew in nature. Branches reached up to the high ceilings, their tips pointing out the detailed ornate stonework. Large paintings hung on the walls. They looked familiar to Kitsune, and it took him a tic to realize they depicted views from the various balconies of Inari Palace.

"You are here to see Lady Veranda?" came a soft voice from behind Kitsune and Mai. They turned to find a short young man with a mop of dark hair. Emerging from the shadows, he had momentarily looked like Myobu. The prince choked and, unable to speak, simply nodded. The man, likely a servant, continued, "You are aware of her condition?"

"She's old, frail, and likely nonresponsive," Mai answered, tactful as always.

The servant eyed her, but it wasn't the reproachful look Kitsune was expecting, the look he himself was probably wearing. Noting their clothing, the cleanest out of a dirty lot of travelers, he asked, "And you know Patriarch Kirby is with her?"

At their assurances they'd been properly briefed, the slender man nodded genially and opened a door off the side of the sitting room.

Kitsune had anticipated entering a dark and stuffy bedroom, dank with the smell of sick. In defiance of his expectations, the room's curtains had been drawn open, allowing the afternoon sunlight to filter in. A fire was burning in the hearth, but the window had also been cracked, allowing for a pleasant flow of air.

A large bed was set up against the far wall in which a frailer-looking version of his grandmother lay sleeping. However, attention was drawn to a circular table in the middle of the room where a young woman and an even younger boy were sitting. They were chatting animatedly over books and toy models. Upon noticing the newcomers, they called out the prince's name and rushed to him.

"Mai, these are Allison and Joseph," Kitsune announced after being inundated with hugs.

"Joseph, eh?" Mai responded, raising an eyebrow at him.

A rustling sound caught their attention, and Kitsune turned toward the bed in time to see a large, bald man hoist himself out of a chair. Though still overweight, Patriarch Kirby looked visibly diminished since their last encounter. His braided goatee, the longest Kitsune had ever seen, was frayed, and the man's joviality now seemed forced. Still, as they greeted each other and shook hands, it was good to see the man again.

"It is lovely to make your acquaintance," Kirby said to Mai, who was playing coy by giggling and curtsying. "To the other room with you, children! Give your aunt a kiss."

They watched as Allison and Joseph packed up a few of their books, gave the sleeping Veranda a peck on the cheek, and headed out to the sitting room. Kitsune was touched Kirby thought so highly of his grandmother that he made her an honorary family member. It made him happy she had others to look to after she had lost so much.

"Did you ever see your friend Myobu again?" Kirby asked once the door had closed behind his offspring. "He seemed like such a pleasant fellow. Very odd how he disappeared overnight."

"No, I never saw him again," Kitsune replied, not wishing to revisit the truth.

Mai glanced over at him, clearly detecting the lie. Despite her frequent inquiries for details of his life, she knew very little of his deeds before they had met. Less even of Myobu. Still, with his increasingly violent mood swings, she had to have theorized something tragic had transpired recently.

"How is Veranda?" the prince said, redirecting the conversation to the grand, four-poster bed in which his grandmother slept.

"She's not doing well," Kirby replied, leading the pair over. "She has defied the crippling effects of time for many sun cycles, but no one escapes them forever. The physicians tell me her organs are shutting down. It is only a matter of time before the inevitable occurs, Kitsune. Days, if I had to guess. Maybe even hours. I am glad you arrived when you did, so you can say your goodbyes."

"I only just met her," the prince whispered, slowly getting to his knees beside the bed. He grasped one of her weathered, vein-ridden hands in both of his, surprised by the lack of warmth. Veranda's face looked tired, shrunken, but her stately, handsome features Oni had inherited were still recognizable. "I thought for sure we'd have more time. A chance to talk again."

"She's held on for so long, worrying for you day in and day out. Her greatest regret was leaving you behind in Kitsunetsuki, and her greatest concern was always your being at the mercy of King Oni. I think that seeing you alive and well put a piece of her mind and heart at ease."

"Only a piece," Kitsune said. He tucked her chilly hand under the blankets, then smoothed out a few stray strands of her long, white hair. "She was still troubled by how I felt about my father."

"Your belief in your father gave her pause. She thought it could be the source of your eventual undoing." The patriarch walked back to the round table, falling back into a chair. It groaned in protest at the sudden weight. "Veranda wasn't too keen on your seeking the Harbinger, either. Did you ever come across her?"

"I did," Kitsune said, taking the seat next to Kirby. Mai stayed behind, sitting on the bed next to Veranda, probably not wishing to hear about her wicked mother.

"What did she say?"

"I put little stock into what the Harbinger said. However, I came away from the journey with a very different perspective and opinion of my father." He raised the volume of his voice slightly, just in case Veranda was listening to them. "No one need worry that I still believe him to be a worthy leader for Kitsunetsuki. I've realized he is a tyrant and must be removed."

Kirby trailed a finger along the grain of the table for several heartbeats, then said, "If the reports are to be believed, you return from your journey with blood on your hands, as well."

"An act of self-defense. One I am told has been beneficial to Odom."

"It has bought us some time." Kirby met Kitsune's gaze, and the prince saw a man just shy of resignation. Only the slightest spark of hope shone in the back of the leader's eyes. "Now I must ask for the reason of your return to Sandya."

"During our previous encounter, you hinted that, under your direction, Odom's armies would follow me," Kitsune answered, getting to the point as quickly as possible. "If that offer still stands, I would like to enlist your help in unseating my father, releasing the entire region from his influence."

"Consider them yours to command," Kirby said gravely, giving a curt nod. The words surprised the prince, who had expected demands for strategies and promises of future alliances. Contracts and treaties. Reasonable requests when handing over the reins of a sizeable destructive force.

Kirby continued, "I do this at significant risk to my control over Odom. I fear the military is all that stands between my family and a horde of unhappy subjects. I'm not just speaking of the increasing number of bandits and thieves—groups with which you have had the misfortune to cross paths—but also the poor and the destitute. At this point, there is not much hope I can offer them."

"I appreciate your faith in me," Kitsune responded. He didn't know what else to say. Looking at the man, he felt the awful truth of what Oni had done to Odom, reducing the kingdom from a proud people taking part in the wider world to a land practically overrun by anarchy. With that feeling came an increased responsibility to right that wrong. "Know that once my father has been removed from power, I intend to help you secure your seat here in Odom. That includes opening the border and commencing trade immediately. I see a great friendship in our future."

Just as before, Kitsune purposefully failed to mention his Yokai heritage, any of the powers he wielded, or the magic-ridden sword of lore. Kirby would probably have accepted them as insurance for his soldiers, but the leader had once spoken somewhat negatively of the Yokai. Nothing terribly off-putting, but also nothing encouraging. If Kirby had not been informed of such things through his own network of spies, Kitsune would not risk a coalition by enlightening him.

"I have a thousand soldiers on site that can march out with you, and I will send word to the capital and have another three thousand meet you at Rhinecourt," Kirby said. "I assume that is where you are headed?"

Kitsune nodded in agreement and appreciation, then watched as the man reached into his robes and withdrew a sheathed dagger. Several colored jewels dotted its hilt, which was otherwise inlaid with gold and silver. The letter K, centered in a circle, was carved into the middle of the handle. The prince had seen Allison with a similar dagger.

"Take this with you and show it to the general at Rhinecourt. It will verify your leadership at my behest," Kirby explained, handing over the small blade. He made to get up from his chair. It was a slow movement. Kitsune couldn't tell if it was because the man was tired, old, or both. "Spend some time with Veranda. Some guest rooms are on the other side of the apartment. Will you and your lovely companion be bedding together?"

"Absolutely not," Kitsune said, perhaps a little too quickly. He could practically feel Mai roll her eyes.

"Very well. I'll have the servant put down fresh linens in both rooms. Dinner should arrive in the early evening, when Veranda usually prefers to eat, and hot baths can be drawn if you'd like. Will you be leaving in the morning?"

Kitsune nodded. "At first light. The sooner I can arrive at Rhinecourt, the less time my father has to arrange his armies to bar my entrance."

And fewer people will have to be removed from my path, cut down by my hand, Kitsune thought to himself. His heart ached at the thought of slaying those he had trained alongside with, practiced with, and possibly taken to his own bedchamber. *I will get into Kitsunetsuki, though. I will take Inari Palace. No matter the cost.*

*

The next several hours passed by in relative boredom. Such a state of being, Kitsune realized, was a luxury. One in which, despite all the training and education he had undergone throughout his life, he had basked. After having been totally devoid of boredom for well over a month, it was now a luxury he would willingly give up. Without Tsukumogami at hand to shroud his mind and heart, he was open to attack by his own emotions.

As promised, food arrived just as the sun was disappearing behind the tall peaks of the Argent Mountains. It was probably delicious, but Kitsune could taste nothing. He kept thinking of how Myobu had unabashedly wolfed down plates of food the last time they had been here. What wouldn't he give to share another meal with the man?

Likewise, the hot bath that had been carefully drawn for him should have been soothing. Kitsune couldn't help but imagine sharing the experience with his love, to feel their wet, naked skin glide smoothly against each other. They would splash about, rub soapy bubbles from their faces, and laugh openly.

Instead, Kitsune stared blankly at the high, stone ceiling as dripping water punctuated what was otherwise a deafening silence.

With its silky sheets and soft blankets, the bed that had been made up looked like the epitome of indulgence. The prince stood beside it for several long tics, willing his body to crawl in between the fabrics. It had been so long since he'd slept in a proper bed, and Myobu was supposed to have been there with him. Despite its tempting comforts, this one seemed sad and lonely. What was more, Kitsune did not feel he was worthy of reveling in its comfort. After all he had done, the best he deserved was a threadbare carpet on a cold stone floor.

Tired of the internal debates, Kitsune left his room. He stood by Mai's door for a few heartbeats, considering knocking, but then he heard the muffled sounds of passion. It took him a moment to recognize who she had taken to bed. The soft-spoken, slender servant actually had quite a pair of lungs in him!

Kitsune's heart ached with jealousy. He considered joining them—and would have if the situation had occurred a few months ago. Like everything else, he did not feel he deserved such niceties. Such joy. Such happiness.

He padded across the foyer back to Veranda's room, sighing. When he closed that door to the sounds of lovemaking, he was surprised to find his grandmother sitting up in bed. Color had returned to her skin, and her eyes were clear and focused as she read through papers strewn about her bed.

"Grandmother!" he exclaimed, running to her bedside. "You're awake!"

"Of course, my child," she replied matter-of-factly, welcoming his embrace. Her long white hair had been brushed smooth over her shoulders, making her appear even stronger. "Death has yet to claim me, though I feel better than I have in many days. I've just been catching up on current events."

She waved a shaky hand at the various parchments, and Kitsune saw they were a mixture of public articles and high-level military reports. As an advisor to Patriarch Kirby, she had access to such material.

"Have you gotten to the parts about me?" he asked, taking a seat.

"I read enough to know you should have heeded my words and stayed with me here in Sandya." She patted his hand in good humor. "I am sorry your first foray into the wider world has been so challenging, my child. With my failure to save you from your father, I fear I am to blame. At my age, I cannot live in regret but can only help prepare you for the future."

"You don't need to worry about Oni. I'm heading back to Oinari to meet him head on," Kitsune assured. "He'll pay for what he did to us. To my mother and Gailey."

Veranda nodded, pointing at the papers again. "I see you were given command over much of Odom's forces."

"They will help, no doubt," Kitsune said, carefully picking his words. "But I know I will have to face him myself. That only I can remove him. Short of running him through with a sword, I haven't really come up with a strategy. I know you haven't seen him in many sun cycles, but I've come to realize I barely know the man myself. Is there anything you can tell me about him that might give me direction?"

His grandmother's eyes took on a faraway look as she remembered the distant past. "Oni was a very bright child. Outgoing and sociable— he was always a pleasure to have around. When he was four or five, there was a spree of gruesome murders in Oinari. It was a dark time in the capital, and I fear it affected the formation of his persona. Outwardly, he remained the same, but a secretive side to him came about, a dark well within him no one could access. Gailey and I first believed it was adolescence, simply a symptom of growing up. But even as Oni happily met and married his wife, we could tell something malevolent was inside of him. When he returned from his honeymoon early and alone, my husband was wise to send me away.

"I can tell you he was cunning and remembered everything he learned, but I can't say what his favorite color is or what he likes to eat. His pleasures in life elude me. I believed for the longest time it was my failing as a mother, that I was too busy with my duties as queen. Now I know, even if I wasn't the perfect mother, he didn't *have* those kinds of traits. Or, if he did, he kept them hidden from the rest of the world. No one knew who he truly was."

"I know how you feel," Kitsune said. "I grew up a stone's throw from my father, but I rarely ever saw him. Our last conversation, the one where he ostracized and disowned me, was also our longest."

Veranda shook her head sadly, then brought it up in sudden remembrance. "When Gailey sent me away, he had me bring along a lot of art he deemed culturally significant. Paintings, mostly. In their haste, the servants packed up Oni's personal collection. I have stared at them for many hours over the sun cycles, trying to ascertain their significance to him. I admit I'm not the most creative person to walk this world, and their meanings have escaped me. The paintings just look like people in different scenes. I encourage you to look at them yourself, though. You might glean something I couldn't see. They are in a gallery downstairs. I would take you there myself, but I fear my legs will not yet support me. If I'm not mistaken, there will be a sentry or two outside the quarters who will show you the way."

"They won't let me out of their sight!" Kitsune said with a laugh. He leaned forward, kissing her gently on the forehead, and said goodnight.

PIPES IN THE GALLERY

As Veranda had predicted, two armed guards were posted in the hallway outside her apartment. Kitsune half expected the captain to still be there, but she had returned to more important duties or retired for the night.

"This way, sir," one soldier, a large man whose muscles strained the limits of his uniform, said respectfully. The two sentries had shared a puzzled look at his request to visit the gallery. Kitsune supposed it was an odd petition at this hour.

The trip was brief, giving the prince a small window of time to discreetly admire his guide's physique. Only a flight of stairs down and a brisk walk along a hallway, and the muscled man opened a heavy door. Before ducking through the doorframe, he said, "I'll light the candles so you can see."

A breeze swept across Kitsune's face, kicking up a few strands of his blond hair. As he stepped over the threshold, he saw he wasn't entering another room, but a passageway that was open to the elements on his righthand side. Over a waist-high stone balustrade, he could see the city streets below, which were far quieter than they were hours before. Scents of savory food wafted upward, though he could not find any evidence of cook fires—further evidence of the thought and ingenuity that went into building Sandya to be a hidden city.

A high ceiling jutted outward into open space, protecting the walkway from precipitous weather, and the rocky wall to the prince's left stretched up into shadows. A series of shallow alcoves drew his attention, and he stepped nearer to the closest one. Something was on display within it, but when Kitsune reached out to touch it, his hand was blocked by an invisible force. Smooth, hard, and cool, it was like a pane of glass that did not reflect light from the stars, moon, or illuminations from below.

"Here you go, sir," the soldier said softly, lighting up a candelabra that was built into the banister. He moved down the balcony to the next collection of candles. Kitsune could not see how far this strange gallery went.

The painting in the alcove before him was an excellent example of still life art, displaying a bowl of fruit. It was set on a wooden table spanning the width of the frame and had an edge painted in gold. Nodding, he moved on to the next two alcoves, built one on top of the other. These, too, held paintings, though they portrayed scenes of nature. Tall, majestic trees whose superior height was only rivaled by distant, snowcapped mountains. In one, sunlight glinted off the surface of a lake. The scenes were unremarkable. Indeed, the paintings were not unlike the multitude lining the halls and rooms of his home. Looking down the long hall, he saw it was lined with countless recesses, many carved into the wall up near the ceiling. He wondered if they all held similar art.

What did Veranda think I could glean from these?

The next set of pictures was a departure in both subject and style. The lines weren't as crisp, the images more abstract. An enormous field was littered with neat rows of cut rock. In the foreground were several dark figures looking down into a fresh hole in the ground. It was daytime, evidenced by the curved, golden surface of the sun in one corner. It looked out of place, as rain was also falling on the scene.

It's death, Kitsune thought, shivering. *The whole thing is permeated with it.*

Each of the surrounding pictures had a similar feel. One was obviously a funeral procession. A few glimpsed the interiors of a home with sofas, beds, and bookcases. Most were devoid of people, and the rare human subjects were all turned away, looking elsewhere.

Kitsune was no art critic. He appreciated beautiful things, but he preferred them to be alive and in the flesh. Still, if the artist who created these was expressing his or her own feelings or experiences, the individual was experiencing more than grief.

Loneliness, the prince knew. *It's overwhelming. The artist had lost someone very close to their heart, and everyone else is just a backdrop to what is now a very bleak reality.*

"All the candelabras are lit, sir," the soldier said, striding up to him. "Would you like for me to attend to the chandeliers?"

Looking upward, he saw the hall was lined with several fixtures that could be lowered by rope and illuminated. They were meant to light the recesses located nearer the ceiling.

"I don't think that will be necessary," Kitsune replied with a sigh. "I won't be too long."

"Okay. I'll be just over here by the door then, sir," the soldier concluded.

Moving away from the sad series, Kitsune was surprised by what he found next. A beautiful woman stared back at him. The lines and fine details were not as crisp as the bowl of fruit, but obvious care had been taken in her depiction. The woman was standing in front of a gold cross, but her gorgeous mane of long brown hair blotted most of that detail out. Her skin was pale and free of blemishes. Unless she was one of the Yokai, like Kitsune's mother, the woman seemed to have spent most of her days indoors.

Though obviously young, the woman's face was lined with stress and sadness. A hint of madness was in her eyes, which looked out at him in silent desperation.

Kitsune couldn't say how, but he thought he had seen the depiction before. The cut and style of her clothing was unfamiliar, but there was something about it that tickled his memory. He glanced around at the surrounding pictures, hoping to garner further clues.

Outdoor adventures. Tours of old buildings. Lazy days spent in bed. All featured the woman, who smiled broadly in each of them, madness morphing into a fanatical desire and infatuation. It was clear the painter could *see* the subject, was acutely aware of her thoughts and desires. Her neurosis.

It was also clear the artist cared deeply for her. The canvas appeared to tell the truth, showing someone who was broken by her past and in need of love and acceptance, but it did not exemplify that trait or cast it in a negative light.

In the next painting, the woman sat staring from across a small table, cradling in her hands what appeared to be a steaming cup of coffee. The setting was public—others were sitting in the background. What looked like the long counter of a bar appeared on the left-hand side. Some chairs were shoved up against it, but a crowd of people were standing in line. Strange mechanical devices were on the other side of the bar. Bright signs advertising drinks and prices hung above it, just under a gold-painted beam.

Kitsune stared uncomprehendingly at the scene—then he blinked in sudden realization. The signage was written in an ancient language, the same one used for the civilization that once inhabited the Wastelands.

Kitsune squinted at the piece, placing his hand against the cool protective glass, certain he could identify none of the mechanical devices shown. He retraced his steps, analyzing the previous pictures. Sure enough, upon closer inspection, many of them had elements he could not make sense of. Small things, like objects placed on tables or walls, that clearly had a function he could not understand.

Are these actually over a thousand sun cycles old? he asked himself in wonder. *Who made these?*

In the painting of the funeral, the prince found a capital *D* inscribed in the lower left-hand corner. Moving back to the bowl of fruit at the beginning and then to where he'd left off, he saw the same initial on each canvas.

Who is D, and why did my father have so much of the artist's work?

And then it hit him. A painting of the same woman D featured so heavily was hung in the Boleyn Room, his father's secluded throne room. Historically, no one but the monarch entered that space. For a reason Kitsune had yet to grasp, he had been summoned there before being banished. He had noted the portrait as the only decoration within the room, but that morsel of knowledge into his father's life had been dwarfed by the floating, golden orbs that thrust the reality of magic into his mind.

She meant something to my father, he realized, but he couldn't imagine what. If she was a member of the long-dead culture, then she had preceded him in life by centuries. *Perhaps the answer is with the artist. With D.*

Kitsune moved on, but he was filled with growing hesitance and dread. He was eager to discover the answer, excited now he was catching on to Veranda's meaning, but was somehow convinced the elucidation would catch him off guard. That it was so horrible he might regret unearthing the secret.

The next set of paintings was a return to the previous, more abstract style, and with it came the sadness. The woman was still the primary subject. She was smaller now, diminished. Her hair appeared frayed, her skin more taut. The maniacal look in her eyes was more obvious.

Thankfully, her face could not be seen in most of the paintings. She hid behind pillows or under the blankets of her bed. Tissues had amassed beside her and piled up on the floor. Eventually, the series focused less on the anguished woman, and more on the same empty, lonely scenes that had proceeded the funeral. Only one depicted a public place, as if D had been forced out of his or her own stupor.

A new woman was shown in this one. It was clear she, too, was significant. Her look was more familial, though, or perhaps reminiscent of friendly concern. She was trying to get the painter to move on with life. Move past the sad loneliness that was all-consuming.

Kitsune moved on to the next alcove.

And froze.

"No," he muttered as his blood turned to ice.

When traveling through the Wastelands, he had seen distant, skeletal remains of buildings so tall they might have skewered the clouds. In the latest paintings, he saw grand, sprawling cities as seen from a similar distance, and their height was indeed stunning.

But they were on fire, burning and collapsing. The result of a massive explosion.

As though they were written in script below the set of paintings, the prince recalled some of the last words the journal writer had put down: *I cannot live with myself knowing that I truly am the thing I've run from for so long. The emotional depth necessary to care about the fate of others has disappeared as well. At least, it has for all but one person, and I have made arrangements for him to be far, far away from this place today.*

D was for Damian, the man who had broken the poor woman's heart!

Kitsune sprinted back to the beginning of the hall once again, earning a raised eyebrow from the soldier standing by.

Using what he remembered from the journal, the prince pieced together a narrative. The first couple of pieces—the fruit and trees— were early examples of Damian's artistic talent, a precursor to his more personalized and reflective work. The man had maintained a close relationship with his mother until she had died unexpectedly. Short on money, possibly a result of his chosen profession, he had moved into his mother's former residence.

Kitsune knew what it was like to live a lonely life, but Damian had a rich and fulfilling one, strengthened by a bond with his mother. To be suddenly thrust into abysmal isolation like the man had been could only have been confusing, throwing his life into a tailspin. Other family members and friends must have been around, evidenced by the funeral and burial depictions, but they were clearly poor relational substitutes. If shown, they were painted as shadowy outlines, often looking away. Peripheral characters. There appeared to be no way out of the dismal shroud of depression.

Until Damian had met the journal writer.

From the diary, the prince recalled she had eyes for Damian for several sun cycles before having a mutual friend set them up under the pretense of business. The two had become instantly enamored with one another, and their initial meeting lasted several days.

By her own admission, the woman had quickly fallen in love. Even Kitsune could tell she was not the most mentally stable individual, craving the sense of importance and belonging Damian offered. The artist had realized it, too. He had included it in his depictions of her. The detailed attention he gave her showed the love was mutual.

Quite suddenly, however, the relationship had ended.

Kitsune stood between two series of paintings. On the left were the ones showing their budding relationship. On the right, the woman had sunk into the type of depression with which he was now all too familiar. In the blink of an eye, Damian had withdrawn from her. In the wake of that action, she had felt subhuman and miserable.

But why? Kitsune asked the long-dead artist, looking at the blank divide between the two sets. *Why did you leave her? What stayed your heart?*

He doubted the man had had access to her living conditions after they separated. Kitsune surmised the scenes showing her gradual descent into madness were assumptions. Having read her personal accounts, they were incredibly accurate guesswork.

Why would you leave her if you loved her so? he thought angrily, aware that tears were running down his cheeks.

He was also aware he was truly asking the question of Myobu, not Damian.

The woman had been a scientist, part of a team that discovered a way to share and distribute unlimited energy with the rest of the world. She realized their designs were flawed. Moving forward with the project would obliterate her land and people. In her solitude, in her anger toward others for putting her in a position of helplessness, she did nothing to prevent it.

Well, she did one thing, Kitsune thought, coming to the paintings of explosions and cities ravaged by fire. *She made sure Damian was at a safe distance. She ensured his survival.*

The prince moved on to the next series, wondering what the man had done after his civilization vanished. It was the largest set of paintings, and it was also the last. The images were perplexing to look upon, and Kitsune wiped the remaining tears from his eyes.

A mixture of bare human skin and black, red-tinged fur dominated dozens of paintings. He moved as close as he could to those at eye level, pressing his face against the dividing glass. At first, he feared he was looking at something grotesquely sexual—then he came to see it was a fight. A struggle to survive. Not just for the human, but also for the beast to which the black fur belonged.

Backing up—Kitsune almost toppled over the balustrade—he looked up at more of the paintings. They climbed higher toward the ceiling like a pyramid. In them, he saw an uneven mixture of eyes, nails, teeth, and claws. Yes, both subjects were fighting to survive. Both were failing.

"Guard!" Kitsune called out, then waited impatiently as the soldier hurried over. The prince pointed up to the uppermost canvas, the pinnacle of the set. Cast in shadow, he was unable to make out its content. "Would you be able to illuminate just that area?"

"Yes, sir," the man said. Kitsune watched as the muscled soldier lowered a chandelier.

As a dozen freshly lit candles were hoisted back into the air, the hair on the back of Kitsune's neck stood on end. It was clear even before the painting was properly illuminated that it was unlike all the others hanging below. It was not a muddled mess of skin and fur. Instead, it contained only a single entity.

"What is that?" Kitsune whispered as the chandelier leveled out. A beast stared out from the canvas. Vibrant green eyes relayed intelligence, pain, and pure hate. Horns protruded from the sides of its head, and long fangs framed a hideous snarl.

"Must be some kind of demon," the soldier replied. He, too, spoke in a low voice, as though to speak any louder would invite the creature to leap out from its painting, breaking through the glass and descending upon them.

A slash of gold had been painted behind the fearsome being, the only bright color other than its green eyes. It looked out of place against an otherwise murky background. Kitsune mused aloud about it.

"Couldn't say," the soldier said, turning his head askew. Like Kitsune, he was apparently not an art critic. Had probably never seen the beastly portrait before. Then, much to the prince's surprise, he continued with: "But it appears in nearly every painting."

Brows furrowed, Kitsune backed up again, mindful of the railing this time. Looking over the pieces one by one, he saw his companion was correct. Each of them had a slash of gold. Usually in the background and overshadowed by the subject in the foreground.

"It looks like it's connecting all the paintings together," the man said, and the prince gawked at him in disbelief.

Sure enough, the streak of gold from the top portrait lined up with the one below. In many cases, the line branched, connecting multiple other canvases at once. Retracing his steps yet again, Kitsune saw the line of gold ran through each series. The beam above the bright signs in the bar. The cross of gold behind the woman. What he had thought was the sun in the corner of the graveyard scene. Even the first painting with the fruit, with its table edged with gold.

"Maybe it's a ribbon?" guessed the muscled guard. With a smirk, he added, "Meant to tie it all together."

Kitsune rewarded the man with a weak smile, but said, "No, I don't think so, and I don't think it's gold."

The man stepped back with a shrug, acknowledging he was wholly out of his depth. Kitsune didn't notice, however. He was fighting off a sudden wave of vertigo, as though everything around him was moving while he stood still. It made him nauseous, and he resisted the urge to heave over the banister.

"It's not gold," he repeated. "It's brass. And they're not ribbons, but pipes. Part of the brass machine."

Now that he knew what he was looking at, the network of brass piping stood out from the paintings. The soldier had been right in thinking the purpose was to tie each piece together. Everything was a part of the brass machine. It *was* everything.

In his mind's eye, Kitsune saw what had not been painted: cogs, wheels, levers, and steam. Mountains of material and gas that contained all knowledge. The machine had revealed itself to the prince for a moment, shared that knowledge, and then receded back into the shimmering folds of space, leaving the prince as alone and in the dark as ever.

Kitsune knew the journal writer had seen the brass machine, too. It had shown her the fatal flaw that would destroy her civilization. By the looks of it, Damian had been granted a visit, too, or at least was keenly aware of the construct.

Had King Oni seen the brass machine? If so, what had he learned from it?

*

"Kitsune? Why are you on the floor?"

The prince looked up into Mai's dark, round face. No sarcastic wit gleamed from her eyes—only genuine concern. But was it concern for his well-being or for something else entirely?

"Was he good in bed?" he said to her. "The servant boy?"

"Why? Are you jealous of him?" The mischievous light returned to her eyes. She offered her hand, pulling him to his feet. With a forced gasp, she continued, "Or are you jealous of me? You know I'm Yokai. I can take whatever form you find pleasing."

Kitsune pretended to wretch in response, but the act nearly made him lose the contents of his stomach.

"Have you been drinking?"

"I may have come across some wine." He looked down at the floor, where an empty chalice lay on its side. It had been full when he returned to Veranda's rooms. The details were hazy, but he couldn't remember walking in any farther than the front doors. Instead, he thought he had simply backed up against the smooth wood and slid down to the floor.

"Tell me what ails you," she said, helping him to his room. He could tell she was sincere. She hadn't even snickered at her own joke.

The prince stopped short at his bed, resisting her guidance to get in. The feeling of unworthiness, of being less than human, had only compounded since he'd left earlier. He wanted to cry again, didn't even care if she witnessed it. But there were no more tears left within him.

"Everything is connected. The brass machine reaches through space and time," he said. His statement elicited no response from her, and he watched as she crawled into his bed. "Your mother was alive when the Wastelands came to exist, and my father had a collection of paintings by a man indirectly responsible for its demise. Everything is connected, and it is harder and harder to make sense of that fact. You know who else knew your mother? Myobu!"

Without even knowing how it began, Kitsune found himself curled up on the bed, telling Mai everything. It was a hard story to orate, and not only because his breathing was labored and his body shuddered from nervous chills. Everything came out. About his father, Saxma, and Mamori. The mercenaries Jimmy and Benjamin. Saving Kirby's children. Discovering his magical abilities and creating a massive tornado. The trek through the Wastelands, meeting the Purple People, and, finally, the encounter with the Harbinger. Mostly, though, he spoke of Myobu.

He almost ended with his experience at the Western Pass. Destroying the tunnel and shearing the mount in half. Seeing the brass machine. After a brief hesitation, he revealed his suspicions on the nature of Tsukumogami. How one of its many souls had a corrupting nature. And how Kitsune may have been willingly succumbing to that force.

"We have been traveling together for some time," Mai said once he had quieted. She had stretched out next to him, pressing her body against his, letting her heat soothe his chills. "Why are you telling me all this now?"

"I want to die."

Mai's touch remained soft and calm, but her voice hardened. "I can't let you die. You wouldn't be any fun to me dead."

"I will not kill myself," Kitsune said, trying to sound reassuring. He wasn't sure who he was trying to soothe. "I've been betrayed and abandoned by everyone I've ever loved or put faith in. It's left me feeling…broken and…and lost. There's an emptiness in me, and it has eaten away at all I've cared about. Including my will to surge forward in life. It's hard to know what I'd be moving toward."

He was again reminded of the journal's author. After the sadness and desperation evaporated, she had felt devoid of emotion. He wasn't there yet, but he could feel the wells in his brain running dry. Her confession of numb detachment was documented in her penultimate journal entry. That had been several months before her final writing, just before everything ended.

"You need to focus on the things you still care about, like freeing your people from your father's rule," Mai suggested. "What can be done to help with that endeavor?"

"Tsukumogami," Kitsune murmured. "You're not the only one that has been tied to it. The blade is the only thing keeping me feeling strong, and I've been relying on it more and more since we left the tribal lands. Being separated from it has been harder than I expected."

He felt Mai move closer against his back, putting an arm around him in a tight embrace. "You'll be reunited with Tsukumogami within a few hours. You won't have to part with it again, and it will help destroy your adversaries."

"I think I could defeat my father on my own, but the blade emboldens and focuses my will to do so." His voice hardened, suddenly cold. "Holding it, I want to live forever just so I can watch my enemies fall. So I can see the entire world burn at my feet."

Mai ran her hand up and down his chest a few times, then said, "All right."

Turning on to his back so he faced her, Kitsune asked, "You won't try to stop me?"

"I will if I must," she replied lightly. Then, with more than a hint of pride, "But I am a yako, and I enjoy watching things burn."

The prince couldn't help but smile, and Mai returned the look with a devious one of her own. Throwing the blankets over them both, she said, "Now let me see if I can fill up that void within you until the morning arrives!"

THE DARK IMPETUS

Kitsune slipped from Mai's embrace and the warm sheets just before dawn. Sleep had been difficult to attain, and her continued presence had filled him with shame. After what they had done, he felt like he had betrayed Myobu. It was a ridiculous notion. It was not possible to be unfaithful to someone who wasn't there, who wasn't alive, someone whose own truth was a lie.

Attempting to escape his feelings of regret, the prince padded across the apartment and peeked in on his grandmother. He was surprised to find her bedroom brightly lit. Veranda was awake and sitting at the table in the middle of the room. Having bathed and clothed herself in a long dress of heavy, dark red fabric, she looked even healthier than she had the night before.

"Come in and sit, my child," she said without looking toward the door. Her voice was strong and crisp. "I have fresh coffee."

"How are you feeling, grandmother?" Kitsune asked, taking a seat next to her. "You look wonderful!"

"You look conflicted," she responded, which was probably a nice way of saying he looked tired. She poured him a cup of coffee. No sugar was on the table, a commodity to which Odom probably no longer had access. "Strength continues to return to my body. I never thought I would again have the energy to leave my bed. Still, I admit this is about as far as I plan on exerting myself for the day."

"But it's so early!" the prince exclaimed, inhaling the rich aroma of his drink, letting the vapors awaken his mind.

Veranda gave him a reproachful look. "Child, the day does not begin with sunrise. You will learn this when you ascend the throne."

"Do you believe I can succeed?"

"As my grandson, my only desire for you is success. That your dreams come true and happiness rules over your life. Do I believe you will attain your rightful place in Kitsunetsuki? I wouldn't let you leave Sandya again if I didn't think you had a chance."

For a moment, Veranda gazed through Kitsune, and he knew she was looking at a distant place in her mind. "Admittedly, my desire for your victory is partially selfish. Despite my renewed vigor over the past day, I know I am not long for this world. I would prefer to see Oinari one more time, to see the splendor of the terrace vistas from the palace with my own eyes before I close them for the last time."

"For that reason, then, I will strive even harder for triumph."

They raised their cups to one another, toasting health and success. Their words skirted around the fact that good fortune for them meant the defeat of his father—her own son. A discussion of the gallery was the closest they came to that subject. Unfortunately, she had little to add to what Kitsune had discovered. Neither the brass machine nor the Wastelands held any significance to her. She didn't even know where Oni had come across the art or why he was such a devotee of Damian.

The first rays of sunlight were splaying out from the eastern horizon when she eventually shooed him from her room. Giving him a prolonged farewell embrace, she said, "The patriarch—yes, he's awake, too—is undoubtedly at the city entrance now, addressing the troops. Lead them well, my child, and may the spirits lead you."

*

Autumn was descending upon the region. Kitsune could see his breath condensing as he and Mai were led toward the main entrance, but he did not feel the biting cold in his lungs when he inhaled. He didn't feel much at all, physically or mentally. He found it hard to care. Leaving Veranda's presence was like cutting out the last vestiges of hope and goodness from his soul.

They had best return Tsukumogami to me with haste, he thought. *Otherwise, I'm liable to just lie down here and give up.*

Mai, on the other hand, did not favor the rapidly changing weather and didn't hesitate to share her displeasure. Despite having grown up in nature, she was visibly shivering underneath her layers of colored clothing. A string of vulgar comments crossed her lips. Most were mumbled and inaudible, but Kitsune thought he heard her say something regarding human tits not being properly adapted for this climate.

Their guide deposited them at the fortified gate. The doors were immediately opened as if the city itself had been eagerly waiting to purge itself of the pair.

"Spirits," Kitsune whispered as they stepped out into the open, leaving behind the dark, claustrophobic alleyways of Sandya. He had thought the army he left outside the fortress walls the previous day was massive. The combined numbers of the Kitsunetsuki soldiers he had stolen from the north and the Ruio natives had appeared formidable. Now, joined by another thousand from Odom's army, it appeared invincible.

Where all the new men and women had come from, Kitsune did not know. A barracks could have been built into the fortress, a series of rooms that would take sun cycles for him to find within the maze of a city. Or they could have been stationed within strategic distance, ready to defend their patriarch at a moment's notice.

Either way, the prince's respect for their ability to camouflage and disappear into the environment grew. It was clear that, despite everything Odom suffered, its military infrastructure was not under-funded. With their uniforms, an individual or small group could easily disappear into the landscape. This was unlike the garments and armor of Kitsunetsuki's military, which were colored red and meant to impress and intimidate.

With Odom soldiers working to outfit the Ruio natives with proper armor and weapons, Kitsune knew there was no hiding a force of this magnitude. Seven thousand soldiers, a number greater than the population of Oinari, now dotted the landscape.

Seven thousand people who were about to follow him.

In a way, that fact made the endeavor seem bleak. That there had to be a battle—a war—was a notion that awed and terrified him. And for what? So he could forge his own fate and retake his rightful place within the monarchy? It seemed so self-serving. So selfish and petty.

No, he thought to himself, remembering what Mai had told him the night before. *I'm doing this for the people of Kitsunetsuki. For all those my father has wronged.*

"It is no secret our great kingdom is on the verge of collapse. Of being overrun. Not only by outsiders, but from those within our borders who have lost all hope," Patriarch Kirby was saying from a small, raised platform. Kitsune understood why others respected him. The man's deep, booming voice rolled over the countryside, giving warmth to an otherwise icy morning. "But I still have hope. Hope that better days are ahead of us. That we, as a kingdom and people, will be respected not for what we were but for what we are! Strong, proud, and a force to be reckoned with! My hope lies in you!"

Odom's leader held his arms out. Not just to the thousand soldiers belonging to him, but to everyone in attendance. The cheers and whoops of thousands grew steadily louder, reverberating off the mountains. Kirby turned to Kitsune, and the prince knew the man believed every word he had spoken.

"I give you Prince Kitsune, renowned throughout the region for his legendary strength and prowess. He will lead you into the lion's den. He will lead you to victory!"

Kitsune expected resistance. He was the son of the lion, the source of Odom's suffering. The three thousand Kitsunetsuki soldiers had basically been conscripted into his service, threatened with punishment if they did not fall in line.

Everyone cheered, however. Everyone was hopeful. Their noise dwarfed the previous ovation, and there was no way anyone could still be asleep within Sandya.

As the applause and whistling continued, Kitsune watched as a stableman walked two saddled horses up to him and Mai. One quadruped was mottled dark gray and white. The other was pure black, reminding him of the horse he had been forced to ride upon from Oinari to the border. The journey had begun in the most embarrassing fashion: him bound naked atop the beast. Despite that, he had grown fond of the animal and was dispirited when he wasn't allowed to take it with him into his banishment.

"We're not known for our horses, but these are two of my very best," Kirby was saying, proud of his gifts. Kitsune hardly heard him. He had stepped forward, rubbing the equine's nose and looking into its eyes. They were trusting, but fiery, unlike the two nags he and Myobu had inherited from the mercenaries Benjamin and Jimmy. Kitsune liked him immediately and quickly found himself sitting on its saddle.

"I've never ridden upon such a creature," Mai said. "Do they always stink this badly?"

As he turned to tell her off, Kitsune found his words caught in his throat—her horse's reins were in one hand, and her sword was in the other. He whipped his head back around, turned his mount in a circle, and nearly trampled the young soldier he had entrusted Tsukumogami with.

"It never left my sight, sir," the man said, raising the weapon up to him. Kitsune took it back greedily, barely noticing the soldier looked slightly more peakish than he had yesterday.

The moment Kitsune took hold of Tsukumogami, the self-pity and emotions fell away. His mind cleared, his focus sharpened, and his resolve strengthened. A moan of desire escaped his lips. It wasn't one of his moans, though. He knew those well. The sound of ecstasy belonged to the dark soul inhabiting the blade.

No more delays, said the voice in the prince's head. It was a declaration, not a request. *We ride to our destiny. To battle.*

Yes, Kitsune replied, unsheathing the blade. *We are unstoppable.*

There will be death. We will strike down our enemies, the voice growled.

Breathing in the crisp morning air, Kitsune felt more awake and energized than he had ever been. *We will lay waste to them all. They will burn before us.*

The prince raised the sword upward and, with his magic, skewered the sky with a bolt of lightning. The hot band of electricity contacted the ground far to the south, the direction in which they were headed.

As the thousands of soldiers continued to shout and cheer their support, Kitsune led the march.

*

When Kitsune had been unceremoniously tossed out of his kingdom, ten days passed before he came to Sandya. Much of that time had been spent in a drugged stupor after being captured by mercenaries and, subsequently, being nursed back to health and consciousness by Myobu. On his own, the prince probably could have made the trip back to Rhinecourt in well under half that time, especially now that he had a horse. He was leading an army now and he had quickly learned they were large, lethargic entities.

Five long days of travel had passed before they finally arrived at the remains of Rhinecourt. It was high noon and the sky was clear, but Kitsune barely recognized what he saw. Granted, it had been dark the last time he was present. What had been the smoldering wreckage of buildings, caused by a fire the prince now knew was set by Myobu, was now piles of charred wood whose previous purpose was unrecognizable. The hot embers and ash Mamori and the prince had slogged through had long since cooled and been dispersed by the wind. Thankfully, the settlement had been abandoned long before it was destroyed.

Overshadowing the ruined settlement was the Eastern Gate, otherwise known as the Argent Mountain Passageway. Standing fifty footfalls high and spanning a distance of a thousand footfalls between the base of two mountains, it was a colossal feat of engineering. Constructed of wood, stone, and metal, it not only blocked the road linking the two kingdoms, but also sat atop the Rout River. Metal bars had been driven into the riverbed, spaced far enough apart to allow the rushing waters to pass from Kitsunetsuki into Odom.

The mountain positioned at the southern end of the gate was legendary. Castle Verde, an ancient structure, once stood upon it. Just like Inari Palace, it was believed to be a focal point for the magical abilities of the Yokai. Prince Oni had stripped his new bride of her powers within its halls, and she had exploded in a brilliant display of light and energy. The castle had been completely leveled, and in its place formed the rocky silhouette of a woman's face, hair, shoulders, and chest.

The Lady of the Mountain, as she had been referred to afterward, appeared to be sleeping peacefully. Kitsune suspected his father used his powers of persuasion to convince citizens and travelers the geographical oddity had been there for millennia. That Castle Verde had always been a fantasy.

No need to convince anyone of such deception now. The famed silhouette had disappeared, in its place a monstrous hole. Kitsune had seen the Lady dislodge herself from the mountainside in his first dreamscape, raining boulders upon the ground. With no evidence of freshly strewn and broken rocks littering the countryside, he surmised her figure—her essence—had simply disappeared into the hoshi no tama he had been wearing around his neck.

Looking up at the ruined slope, Kitsune realized this was where he had been born. He was fortunate he hadn't been obliterated when his mother's being shattered. He was equally lucky his father opted to return home with him.

It would have looked a desolate scene if not for the three thousand soldiers waiting to be absorbed into Kitsune's force. By the looks of it, they had arrived a day or so earlier. Tents had been set up and cook fires started. Three massive wooden trebuchets were being constructed while soldiers were sparring, sharpening their skills.

"Very good," said the general of the adjunct force after Kitsune showed her the jeweled dagger gifted by Patriarch Kirby. "Follow me inside."

The prince followed the general, a squat, older woman who introduced herself as Ryon, into a large command tent set up at the rear of the encampment. The heavy fabric walls cut out the chill of the air, and the inside was further heated by many individuals poring over documents and maps. He recognized the maps immediately as those of his own kingdom.

"Strategizing?" he asked, picking up a document. It listed military numbers, the size of troop regiments and where they had last been stationed, horses, and stores of food.

"Been doing just that for many sun cycles," Ryon said. She may have winked, but her eyelids never opened more than a sliver, so Kitsune couldn't tell. "Now we have to decide which plans to execute. Have to breach the wall first and take Onger. Trouble is, Rhinecourt is dangerous ground."

"Why's that?" Kitsune said, glancing over a map that laid out siege plans on Oinari.

"Traps have been set, sir," Ryon said, her eyes somehow narrowing even further. "It's as though they tamed fire and buried it just below the ground. We lost a couple of scouts walking over them, causing an explosion."

Kitsune frowned, wondering if these hidden weapons were built off the same incendiary technology used to create the new persuaders. "How do you propose we proceed?"

"The catapults should be completed within the next couple of hours. We can use them to rain devastation down upon Onger. Catch them by surprise. Then we can bring down the gate itself, clear a path through Rhinecourt, and enter your homeland."

"It's a good plan, but it will fail for one reason," Kitsune replied, choosing his words tactfully. "There is a tower on the other side of that gate. It contains a significant source of magic. Through it, King Oni controls soldiers stationed there and monitors what transpires in the surrounding area. He already knows we are here."

Also, with much of the king's military engaged in the west, most of the lives they'd take would be civilian or support staff. He didn't want to sacrifice innocents.

"A magical tower," Ryon commented, her voice teetering on disbelief. Her eyes looked down at the dagger on Kitsune's belt, then she continued, "What is the range of Oni's control? Could he be in our heads as we speak?"

Kitsune couldn't answer the woman's questions with any certainty, and he said as much. The truth was, he had been concerned Oni would seize control of the adjunct army as it approached, and he had sent scouts ahead of him to check for any suspicious behavior. They couldn't discern any, but the prince knew his father would have a plan, even if it was a desperate one.

Placing a finger on the closest map, Kitsune continued, "To the best of my recollection, the tower stands here. We should aim the catapults there. I will bring down the gate myself, triggering any remaining underground explosives. Once the tower's location is visually verified, we can take it out, neutering Oni's power."

*

The plan had sounded simple enough as it came from Kitsune's mouth. Maneuvering ten thousand disparate men and women to prepare for a large-scale attack within a few hours made for a hectic period while they awaited the completion of the catapults. General Ryon, despite her experience, senior position within the military, and rather grumpy-looking face, was amicable enough to go along with the prince's strategy.

The clear skies became overcast, the clouds matching the somber mood that settled over the encampment. Sitting atop his black horse, Kitsune was located a few hundred footfalls east of what had been Rhinecourt. Mai was to his right, and the general, despite warnings she would be vulnerable to King Oni's power, was on his left.

Three trebuchets were stationed behind the trio, having been positioned and aimed at exactly the point Kitsune had indicated on the map. Each had a team of large, muscular men. Some loaded and released the mechanisms' payload, large chunks of rock hauled up from the base of the mountains. Others were present in case the large constructs needed to be readjusted once the wall came down—in case Kitsune was off with his estimation of where the tower was.

To the south were Odom's four thousand soldiers. The other six thousand were positioned to the north, led by Captain Pan. Swordsmen stood at the front of each force, ready to rush forward into Onger once the gate came down. Behind them were archers, prepared to darken the already cloudy sky with their arrows.

It is time, came the voice in the prince's head. *These swords and arrows are nothing but trinkets next to our power, but they will strike fear in the heart of our enemies. Now let us claim what is ours!*

Yes, the prince agreed. He kept his face hard and stoic, but anger burned in his heart. *Enough waiting.*

Kitsune glanced at General Ryon, who nodded her readiness. Then he looked over at Mai. She winked in return, a crooked smile on her face.

Unsheathing Tsukumogami, he then looked to the Eastern Gate, the ugly monstrosity that had cut him off from his home. For a moment—the timing had to have been just right with ten thousand people in the vicinity and the ocean in the background—everything went quiet. No wind. No whispering. No waves.

Just Kitsune and the gate.

Reaching out with his sword hand, Kitsune pointed the blade at the ground before them and brought an end to the silence. With his mind, he felt for what lay beneath the ground: lines of tectonic plates slowly crushing against one another, creating the Argent Mountains above. A low rumbling filled the air like distant thunder. Loose earth and rocks skittered down the nearby mountainsides, telltale signs that a dramatic shift was occurring.

And then, like a whale breaching the surface of the ocean, a huge slab of rock burst from the earth at the edge of Rhinecourt, jutting so high into the air it cast a shadow over half the army. To their credit, the startled militia did not cry out. Or perhaps they did, but Kitsune could not hear them over the earsplitting screeches of giant pieces of rock grinding against one another.

The slab's ascent slowed and then stopped. It stood there, higher than either Inari Palace or Sandya. It was like a monument, godlike in its presence. Everyone stared at it in awe.

Kitsune did not believe in gods, however. He didn't believe in anything he couldn't destroy. Grinding his teeth, he clenched his left fist and hissed, "Fall."

As though he had wrapped his hand around the giant rock itself, its entire midsection crumbled. Like the tower the prince had felled in the north, the slab drifted westward to the ground, appearing to fold in on itself. The upper portion remained fixedly solid, though the lower half continued to break up into smaller and finer pieces.

The ground beneath their feet groaned and shook as the rocks crashed back to earth. Those on horses struggled to maintain control over their mounts. Everyone else watched as the remnants of Rhinecourt disappeared under heaps of crumbling rock. The impact set off several explosions, the ones Ryon's earlier scouts had not accidentally triggered. Plumes of fire, rock, and smoke blasted upward.

Behind the rising dust and smoke, Kitsune could just barely see the top of the monolithic slab come down upon the Eastern Gate. The wrenching sounds of twisting metal and ripping planks of wood sounded out. Pulling away from its mountain moorings, it collapsed into a heap, kicking up new plumes of dirt. Though it couldn't be seen, the Rout roared in protest, wetly slapping against its new impediments, finding alternative paths.

Shouts and cheers began working their way through the men and women, and it took Kitsune several moments to realize he too was hollering. Mai's eyes twinkled as mischievously as ever, and while Ryon's eyes were barely visible, she appeared slightly less grumpy as she nodded her head in approval.

As the dust was settling, a series of high-pitched whistling noises sounded. It was difficult to pin down where they originated, but their source was clearly skyward. Kitsune looked up just as an explosion of green and orange bits of light burst across the darkening sky, accompanied by a deep, concussive boom. Some soldiers gasped and even cheered as more of the blasts went off, painting the clouds above them with red and blue, believing they were more magical demonstrations by their leader.

Kitsune wasn't responsible for them, but he immediately guessed their purpose. Confusion and distraction.

"Keep alert," he said to Ryon and Mai, guiding his horse into a southward trot. He did not want to be a stationary target. Mai was already inadvertently drawing attention to them. Even he was momentarily mesmerized at how the flashing, sparkling lights above played off of the Yokai's colored clothing.

Another series of whistling noises signaled more detonations of light in the sky, but they were accompanied by sharper, more staccato sounds Kitsune recognized immediately. They belonged to persuaders.

Thousands continued to cheer, still believing this was a display of magic. Then those standing on the front lines fell, thrown back by the sudden impact of tiny, deadly pellets.

A gust of wind—a manifestation of the sudden anxiety welling up within Kitsune—swept across the plain and between the two mountains. The remaining dust in the air blew away…revealing a battalion of soldiers standing along the streets of Onger. At the front, mere footfalls from the gate's wreckage and seated on a black horse of his own, was a man the prince recognized as Nasuno. The soldier had been one of four men, including Mamori and Pan, who had been kind to him as he was escorted out of Kitsunetsuki.

Bringing his horse to a halt, Kitsune squinted across the crushed remains of Rhinecourt. Even at this distance, he could discern the look upon Nasuno's face. Grim, stony determination. His eyes were familiar. Too familiar.

Nasuno wasn't Nasuno anymore.

"It seems they knew we were coming," Ryon said while Kitsune scanned the terrain. "A thousand men at—"

"Fire the catapults!" Kitsune shouted, seeing the location of the tower was exactly where he had remembered. "Do it no—"

Quick bursts of light flickered across the slopes of the mountains that had flanked the decimated gate. Deep, concussive booms followed them. Kitsune had only a heartbeat to wonder what the purpose of those were before one catapult behind him was destroyed in a shower of splintering wood. Soldiers from both north and south cried out in pain.

The prince turned his black horse and galloped toward the two remaining catapults. Pointing Tsukumogami at their crews threateningly, he shouted, "Fire the damn things!"

Purple flames momentarily spewed from Tsukumogami, and the men, who were keen to vacate what were obvious targets, quickly returned to their duty. Kitsune watched as the trebuchets' slings were released, the arms pivoting up into the air, and their payloads sent.

Another hushed silence fell over the area as both sides of the conflict craned their necks upward, watching the two massive rocks arc through the air. It took only a few heartbeats for them to sail over Rhinecourt and into Onger, but it felt like hours. Thousands watched as the projectiles drifted closer to one another, meeting just as they pulverized the base of the stone tower.

Kitsune observed as the phallic-like structure came apart and crumbled to the ground. Pride swelled up in his chest, and he prepared to again shout out in victory with the others.

No cheers were issued, however. No recognition of triumph.

Something else was amiss, and it took Kitsune a few heartbeats to pinpoint it. The tower had fallen, its bulbous head now a pile of rubble, but no golden spheres of magic had been released. Looking across the battlefield at Nasuno, the prince still saw the malevolent glint of his father in the soldier's eyes. The corners of his mouth even twitched upward into a mocking smile.

You've been misled, the dark voice said. *You've been betrayed.*

"No," Kitsune replied aloud, "but he knew we were coming and stored his magic away elsewhere."

Looking back to where he left Ryon and Mai, he shouted, "His source of power has been hidden in another location. It is imperative our forces retreat until I root it out."

Mai looked back questioningly, but Ryon didn't budge.

"General!"

The woman's body jerked as if having been jolted awake. Her back went stiff, and her head swiveled slowly back and forth. When she looked at Kitsune—*through* Kitsune—the prince saw only blankness.

"No…*NO!*" Kitsune cried, kicking his horse into action. "Mai, get out of there!"

Confused, Mai continued to look back at him. To her side, just beyond her vision, Ryon sidled her horse next to the Yokai's, drew her blade, and drove it into Mai's side. Eyes widening in pained shock, Mai's mouth opened and closed several times. Her face went gray as blood seeped from the wound, and she slid slowly from the horse to the ground.

"NO!" Kitsune screamed again, finally reaching them. He jumped from his mount and kneeled next to the woman. The dazzling cloth she was dressed in seemed to fade, and her eyelids were flickering as though she struggled to stay awake.

The sky went from gray to nearly black, and the temperature dropped. Kitsune didn't notice. His hands were shaking as he held Mai's face, willing her eyes to open. For her tongue to let loose a scathing comment. For a hidden knife in the folds of her clothing to be flung at the general.

But her face only stilled, and her eyes ceased fluttering.

Behind you, came the voice in his head. The prince spun around, bringing Tsukumogami across Ryon's midsection just as the woman was about to cut him down. The woman's eyes cleared as her innards spilled out, her mind vacated by Oni. She looked at Kitsune, her face filled with pain, confusion, and betrayal.

"What…why?" Ryon whispered, gurgling blood, before falling next to Mai.

Another round of whistling filled the air. It was unlike those that lit up the sky with bright colors, more brilliant now that the heavy storm clouds blotted out the sun. Kitsune was familiar with this new sound.

Arrows.

The prince knew better than to hope Captain Pan and the other commanders had taken the initiative and released a volley on the enemy. No, Oni had stolen the free will of the north and south armies. Suggested to each that the other was their enemy. Persuaded them into action.

And Kitsune was right in the middle.

Stop being so weak, Tsukumogami's dark soul said, letting loose an impatience the prince suspected had been long simmering. *These things are nothing compared to our might. Sweep them aside so we may lay waste to our enemies.*

A thunderous roar bellowed out across the battleground as hundreds of arrows crisscrossed above. Kitsune thought it was the swordsmen on both fronts, now running full tilt toward each other, weapons raised. Then he realized it was him, screaming, face up to the sky.

Let our powers combine, the voice growled. *Let me show you what we are truly capable of.*

Tsukumogami erupted into flames again as Kitsune thrust it into the air. He felt the power and knowledge of the dark soul. He let it into his mind. Touched it. Joined with it.

The dark, greenish clouds above flashed with internal lightning. Swirling about, a massive funnel formed, moaning as though being awakened from a deep slumber. It had yet to reach out for the ground, but the prince knew this creation would dwarf the tornado he had accidentally created in the north.

"Your time is over, my father. You are old and weak, and your power will not protect you from me," Kitsune said. He mouthed the words, but his voice projected from the widening funnel. Father and son looked up as the latest explosions of colored light went off. The prince seized hold of the fire, expanded it, and drew it into the storm. Flames of red, blue, and green spun around the tornado, encompassing its entire outer surface as it lowered to the ground like a creeping predator. Before it came between him and Nasuno, Kitsune saw anger, consternation, and maybe even fear on his face.

"You and your men are kindling for my fire. Everything will burn, and your ashes will fall from the sky!"

Still under the control and direction of King Oni, the two sides of Kitsune's army continued to rush each other despite the swirling inferno between them. Most were picked up and thrown backward by the heavy winds. Swaths of colorful flame would spew outward, as well, setting any nearby men and women ablaze. Oni apparently released their minds at that point, because they howled in anguish and confusion.

In his own anger, Kitsune didn't care about any of them. It didn't matter if they were his soldiers or his father's.

Yes, the voice said. *Pour out your anger. Make them taste it!*

Kitsune did just that, watching as the base of the tornado swelled and expanded. Hundreds of individuals disappeared within it, their own cries of pain drowned out by the howling of the fiery winds. It didn't matter. They were in his way. Obstacles to his destination and ascent. They would have turned on him eventually, anyway.

In the end, everyone betrayed him.

A shrill ringing sang out across the battlefield, and a purplish hue bloomed over groups of people clad in metal. Giant bolts of lightning seared the air, striking the ground with such ferocity that dozens of individuals were tossed back like rag dolls. Fist-sized hail pelted the soldiers, cracking skulls and breaking bones. Drenching sheets of rain overflowed the Rout.

The tornado spun, burning ever brighter.

Climbing back onto his horse, which had remained calm and still despite the commotion, Kitsune moved forward. With his mind, he pushed the storm forward toward Onger. As he did, the very mountains that had flanked the gate crumbled and fell away. Rock slides spilled down and out into the plain, crushing anyone and anything in its path, including much of Onger and its army.

More, the voice droned. *We can do so much more.*

He could, too, and he knew it. The scene before him was unrecognizable, changing by the heartbeat. He could reshape it to his liking. He could reshape everything. Including…

Staring at the monstrously dark funnel, Kitsune looked into it. Saw through it. The chaotic nature of all the intertwined magic was producing the tiniest of cracks in the fabric of space and—

Thrusting Tsukumogami forward, a line of purple light shot forth into the swirling cloud. Into one of those tiny cracks. And forced it open.

A vertical gash opened up along the side of the cyclone, golden light peeking out of it. The aperture did not appear to affect the rotating tornado itself. Clouds and dirt and fire would disappear on one side of the bright gash and then reappear on the other side. The tear wasn't changing the veil of reality. It was letting Kitsune see through it.

More.

The prince widened the opening even more, the golden light spilling across the plain. Except it wasn't quite golden. It was brassy.

More.

He was looking into another reality. Another universe. Focusing, he could see innumerable pipes. Leagues of pipes. Entire mountains of them in various widths. Countless interlocking cogs turned, some quickly, while others slower. All were enveloped in thick, billowing steam. The heated air poured out of the widening tear and onto the battlefield.

It was the brass machine, and it was a larger, more complex mechanism than he had thought before.

More.

The sudden onset of knowledge and understanding that had accompanied his last sighting of this behemoth did not recur. Kitsune guessed this was because he had forced the door between worlds open, whereas it had happened of its own accord previously.

No matter. With Tsukumogami, he would make the machine reveal its secrets again. He would keep them this time and use them to destroy everything.

MORE!

With an earsplitting screech and an eruption of fresh steam so hot, Kitsune could feel the heat from his side of the tear, the brass machine began to rotate and bend. Watching something so bulky move about with grace and nimbleness was disorienting, and Kitsune was hit with the urge to vomit.

But that was nothing compared to the sudden realization that the machine was alive. A living entity that did not simply contain knowledge, but was knowledge. It was everything. And with an alien, spiderlike sight, it was looking right at him.

The center of the universe, reality itself, had its sights set on him.

Despite his fear and nausea, Kitsune was certain that, with Tsukumogami, he could control the brass machine. Bend it to his will. Force it to do as he desired. He was about to thrust his will and power out through the blade and into the rift, but something new entered the cacophony of noise.

Beyond the southern army came the shrill yapping of canines. There had to be hundreds of them barking in unison to be heard amid the storm and battle. The prince looked toward the ocean and started at what he saw. Hundreds of foxes were emerging from the dark waters. Each would shake itself dry, look out over what was unfolding, and then take off running at full speed toward Onger, yapping wildly all the while.

"Kitsune!"

Hearing his name, the prince fumbled in hesitation. Apart from his father and possibly the machine, he had thought himself the only conscious entity here. The voice had been faint, impossible to locate or identify.

"Kitsune!"

He scanned the horizon, trying to find the source. It sounded so familiar. But a sea of people was out there. No way to find any one individual.

The foxes do not pose a threat to you, the soul growled. *Focus on the machine!*

Just as he was about to turn back, one of the brassy beams of light from beyond the rift illuminated a small mound. Upon it was a bright white horse with cunning, intelligent eyes.

And sitting on the animal was a dark-haired man with a heart-shaped face.

His own prince. His savior. His knight on a white horse, just like from his dream.

It's not real. Myobu is dead.

"It's me, Kitsune!" the man shouted out, seeing he had the prince's attention. He threw up a hand. It was a small hand. "It's truly me!"

Joy bloomed in Kitsune's heart. A new energy and excitement, borne of love, spread through his body, dispelling the hate and anger that had filled him. It was Myobu. He didn't know how or why, but he felt in the core of his being this was no trick. Inexplicable though it was, this was his love.

Suddenly, Tsukumogami was forcibly ripped from Kitsune's grasp. He looked back in time to see a tendril had emerged from the gash in the tornado. No, not a tendril, but a living pipe. The blade flew through the air and, with a resounding clang, lodged itself into the side of the conduit.

"No!" Kitsune screamed as the pipe withdrew back into its own realm. He didn't know exactly what he was screaming at. The machine. The sword. Myobu. Himself. He screamed, nonetheless, over and over again, "No!"

Once the pipe had fully retracted, the rift collapsed. The brass machine vanished from sight, the tear in the universe's fabric sewn up. The tornado was just a tornado.

Or at least it was before it exploded outward in a deadly, fiery wave.

HOME

Coughing up copious amounts of water, Myobu climbed out of the ocean. Dozens of Yokai streamed by him, fluidly transitioning from various aquatic creatures into their natural fox form. Still stuck in the guise of Acro, he wanted to roll over on his back, gasp for air, and not move for hours. Magical energy reverberated throughout the air like electricity, making even his wet hair stand on end. Looking up from the sandy beach, what he saw before him was both awe-inspiring and horrific.

The entire landscape had changed. Mountains had been leveled, the river rerouted, and giant swaths of land had been overturned. The black sky above had given birth to a giant of a storm. It was unlike the last tornado he'd survived, most notably because it was aflame.

With *his* fire.

"Are we too late?" Tod asked, hauling Myobu to his feet. The gesture required a strength and energy the man could not afford. Myobu could see traveling had not been kind to his friend's physical state. Tod wore a determined look, but his face was sickly pale.

Kensie appeared from behind Tod, looking like a frightened animal with no place to hide. He kept glancing between the dark, choppy waters and the otherworldly sight farther inland. "What do we do now?"

Below the crumbling mountains and gargantuan cyclone, thousands of soldiers were locked in lethal battle. Lit up sporadically by bolts of lightning, Myobu could see with his keen eyes these men and women were supposed to be joined under a common banner. They were not acting of their own accord, but were instead being controlled by another. As charming and persuasive as Prince Kitsune was, he did not have the power to force an army to fight among itself.

That magic resided with King Oni.

"Our enemy is here," Myobu said as hundreds of Yokai—his brethren—gathered about him. It was a strange feeling. As Ninko, he had directed and influenced Gaav's policies and laws for decades. Now he was being looked to for direction from his own kind. By creatures centuries older than himself.

Myobu pointed to the broken remains of a gate. Beyond it was Onger and a much smaller army appearing to be patiently standing by. "King Oni is feeding off a source of power from within that village. It is imperative we find it. The magic must be destroyed or released."

"It shall be dealt with," Maroni replied with a resounding telepathic wave. Myobu had barely remembered the irate Yokai whose offspring he had nearly killed so long ago, but she had been the first to meet him when he and his friends arrived in Urel seeking help. Both Maroni and her son had helped to convince much of the population to follow Myobu.

Giving out a series of yips and barks, Maroni led the ever-growing group of Yokai westward along the beach toward the flattened remains of a mountain.

"You're not going with them," Kensie cried out, seemingly unsure himself if it was a question or demand.

"No," Tod answered for him as all but one of the Yokai foxes scurried away. "He's looking for Prince Kitsune."

"I know he's here, but there are so many of the humans," Myobu said, his sharp eyes sweeping the terrain. "So many smells, and I can only cover so much ground on two legs."

"Then let us help you," Tod offered, ignoring Kensie as the man suppressed a gasp. "We can split up and cover more ground."

"No!" Myobu exclaimed. A little too quickly, perhaps, and he regretted the hurt look on his friend's face. "Not speaking ill of your abilities, but I don't want either of you to fall victim to King Oni's persuasion. I don't know how far his reach is or what he would do with you."

I can be your legs, said the remaining Yokai. Myobu recognized the voice as his mother's sister, Maroni's partner. He looked down at his aunt but saw only long, slender legs. Glancing back up, he saw she had transformed into a magnificent white horse.

"You would do that for me?" he asked. It was generally taboo for a Yokai to let others ride upon any form they took, even others of their kind. There had been quite the commotion when Myobu had announced he, Tod, and Kensie would need transportation over the water.

You convinced Maroni to leave Urel, no small feat. This is the least I can do, she replied in a mixture of morose and familial tones. *Quickly now. Before I change my mind.*

"Thank you," he said, resisting the urge to pat her flank before climbing onto her back. Then, to his bemused friends, "Stay here! I will return shortly."

Into the melee they charged. Surrounded by the thunderous noise of sweaty, stampeding soldiers, the clash of steel on steel, and the roaring winds of unnatural elements, it took all the courage both of them could muster and share with one another to move forward. Difficult though it was to navigate through the sea of chaos, they soon rode its waves, moving along with the throngs of bodies.

"Kitsune!" Myobu called out, knowing his voice would be lost in the fray. The drenching rain made it difficult to see. "Kitsune!"

Maroni is the warrior, not me, his blood relative whispered into his mind. *You must have more insight into the human mind. Where do their leaders stand during battle?*

"Human military tactics are as varied as anything else in the world," Myobu said in frustration. Then he brightened. "But I know Kitsune. He'd want to be at the front, leading the charge!"

After that insight, it took only a few more heartbeats to locate Kitsune. As they came to a stop on a grassy knoll, Myobu gasped at how different the prince looked. Toughened. Hardened. Angry. The determined fury burning in his eyes was palpable. It was such a marked difference to the broken, crying man he had seen in his dream.

Lightning struck near Kitsune. The man didn't flinch, but the white light reflected off his blade, illuminating the letters etched into it. Even at a distance, Myobu could recognize the sword that had been used to cut down his parents over a century ago.

"So it's true. He found Tsukumogami," Myobu whispered in awe and disgust. Bile rose in his throat at the thought of all the blood that stained the blade.

The Sword of Inari? his aunt asked. *Surely not.*

Myobu ignored her question, remembering his old mentor Kirin had thought the weapon best lost to history. Seeing the surreal carnage unfolding about him, he concurred. Kitsune was powerful. Possibly one of the most powerful creatures to tread upon this world, but this display of magic could not be accomplished without help. It required all the minds and magic and knowledge Tsukumogami had absorbed.

One in particular, he thought to himself.

"Kitsune!" he shouted again. He willed his voice louder, to cut through the masses. "Kitsune!"

Miraculously, the prince heard him, evidenced by a crack in his furious concentration. He looked about the battleground, his long, wet hair clinging to his skin.

Lightning hit the ground nearby, splitting Myobu's vision. His ride reared up on her hind legs, blinded by the light as well. He clung to her neck, trying to comfort her while not toppling off.

As the dazzling lights in his eyes dispelled, he saw Kitsune had spotted him. Recognition crossed the prince's face. So did doubt.

"It's me, Kitsune!" Myobu called out. He gave a wave, then felt stupid doing so. As though any gesture would make an impact amid all that was happening around them. "It's truly me!"

It was enough. The anger, hate, and malice that had defined the man's face melted away. A joyous smile brightened his features. As realization set in that Myobu was not an apparition, love shone through.

Kitsune's body suddenly jerked, and Myobu watched as Tsukumogami flew from the prince's grip. With a resounding ring that cut the air as sharply as any lightning bolt, it flew straight into the brightly lit tornado and disappeared.

"No!" the prince screamed, his voice emanating not from his mouth but from the stormy skies above. He looked about, his joy overtaken by crazed panic. As the heartbeats slipped by, Myobu recognized the man from his dream. The broken prince. "No! NO!"

Their eyes met again. The look of love and exultation returned, but only for a moment. Those emotions slipped away, too, replaced with horror and shame. The prince's mouth dropped open as he looked out over the landscape, as though he was just now realizing what he had done. What he had unleashed upon the world.

Without warning, the fiery tornado exploded outward. Heated winds threw soldiers to the ground, incinerating those who were unfortunate enough to be in proximity. A concussive force hit Kitsune and the black horse, tossing both creatures back like parchment. The expanding wall of flame followed close behind, but Kitsune didn't appear to react as they descended upon him. He did nothing at all. His face had relaxed into the dull look of depression.

Spirits, he's going to get himself killed, Myobu thought. *And he knows it!*

"Kitsune!" Myobu screamed, reaching out with one of his hands. Another useless gesture, he knew, but it was the only act he could—

*

Kitsune lay still on the hardened ground. The wind had been knocked from his lungs, but he had not the desire to draw in fresh air. He waited for the crushing force of the horse to fall upon him, knowing it would kill him. When the pain didn't come, he thought perhaps he'd already suffered his inevitable injury, and his body had yet to register it.

Then he realized there wasn't only an absence of pain, but also of most sound. No fiery storm. No clashing of swords or cries of the dying. No explosions of light or lightning. Only a slight, whistling breeze.

A blistering, whistling breeze. It burned at his skin like the sun on a hot, dry day.

Opening his eyes, Kitsune saw the black clouds he had created still hovered above. They no longer had the look of fresh clouds, and their reach now extended well beyond the horizon. Lightning was no longer leaping between sky and earth, but he could hear the distant rumbling of thunder.

Sitting up, he noted the land itself was completely charred. No plant life remained. No life at all aside from himself. Just blackened, hard earth. Veins of heated rock crisscrossed over the landscape like blood vessels under the skin, providing the only illumination.

"What is this?" he said. The lack of moisture in the air made his voice raspy and weak.

"It's what might have been," came a reply from behind. Despite the intense heat, Kitsune shivered at the voice of the man he thought never to hear again. "It is what may still come to pass."

"Because of me?" he said. Tears stung his eyes, and he did not fight to keep them from streaming down his dirty face. He thought of all the things over which he could be crying. The devastation he could have caused. The destruction he already had. Hundreds, perhaps thousands of soldiers had perished over the course of a few tics because of him, and all he could think of was how he had abandoned Myobu, believing he was dead.

He was dead! the prince thought, and he was hit by great, racking sobs.

"Possibly," Myobu answered. Kitsune felt the man's small hand rest upon his shoulder. It was a comforting gesture he did not deserve. "You or your father."

"It—it's the most horrific thing I-I've ever seen," Kitsune stammered, motioning shakily at their surroundings. He knew it was a dreamscape. That it came from Myobu's imagination, or perhaps even his own. As he soaked in the desolation, he knew it could have been worse.

The dark soul had certainly imagined worse.

"Is this why…" Kitsune asked, trailing off. He didn't know how to finish the question. Why Myobu had lied to him? Misled him? Coerced him into murder? It all seemed too awful to put into words.

"This is the only reason." Myobu kneeled behind him, snaking an arm around his chest. Kitsune hung loosely, his head down, not sure how to physically react. "I was shown this was the probable fate of our world if I did not act. I know it wasn't fair to you, to us, but I couldn't let my feelings for you keep me from saving everyone."

"You should have told me!" Kitsune shouted. He hated how childish he sounded. "My father betrayed me. You pretended to be dead. My mother even abandoned me!"

"No," Myobu replied, his voice soft and sorrowful. "No, I really was dead. My consciousness left my body, crossed over, and expanded throughout the universe. And your mother didn't abandon you, Kitsune. She loved you too much to do that. She had some insight into the future, however. Following me into death, she used her magic to send me back to my body. She brought me back to life."

"Th-that was her specialty. Bringing to life that wh-which was lifeless," Kitsune remembered. A fresh wave of tears came as he asked the next question, afraid he already knew the answer. "What of her now? Where is my mother?"

Myobu took several heartbeats before answering, solidifying Kitsune's fear. "Your mother loved you and believed in you so much. She made the greatest sacrifice a mother—anyone—could make for that belief. She is…no longer."

For a moment, Kitsune thought the other had stopped midsentence, but then he realized the meaning of the open-ended statement. His mother was no longer *anything* or *anywhere*. She was truly and irrevocably gone. His heart ached fiercely at that knowledge. At his loss. Her sacrifice. How he had assumed the worst in her for leaving him. How doing so revealed the worst in himself.

"No," the prince said in defiance. He clutched at his chest, his hand over his hurting heart. "No, she will never be gone. She's right here. With me. Always will be. The pain proves that."

He fell back into Myobu's arms. "I'm such an awful person, Myobu. Spirits, I *killed* you! Then I found a sword that helped me to kill and destroy more. Even now, I am filled with such rage toward you. A part of me blames you for everything that has happened, even events in which you had no part. It makes me miserable and so tired because, despite all of it, I have a desperate need for you."

"You are not an awful person," Myobu assured him. "Granted, some might see you that way, a burden all leaders must face. Did you handle the situation well? Perhaps not...but I don't blame you. Magic and emotions are so tightly intertwined, and you were so ill-prepared to handle either. The sword you found, an ancient Yokai artifact meant to amplify the powers of the one who holds it, could not have helped matters. Especially after the one who previously wielded it.

"No, I am the terrible one," he continued. "For not thinking there could be another way. For not believing in your strength...in the power of our relationship."

Several tics went by in silence, Kitsune remaining wrapped up in Myobu's embrace. It was a kindness he didn't deserve but would take advantage of as long as it was offered to him.

The darkness was receding. The underground veins of smoldering fire were cooling, and the searing heat had diminished.

"Would you still take me back?" he said eventually, his voice barely a hoarse whisper. "Now that you know, that you've seen what I've done... With Tsukumogami gone, I feel...less. Like part of me disappeared along with it. Even without it to amplify my powers, I know

I could still be the dark impetus that overtakes the world. Do you still want me?"

"I came back for you, did I not?" Myobu replied. "I would rather let the world be swallowed whole than let you slip away from me again."

The clouds overhead broke up, and sunlight shined through. It was both beautiful and grotesque. The life-giving rays of golden light illuminated how far gone the earth was.

"I misled you, Kitsune, and for that I am truly sorry," Myobu apologized. "We've both misled each other in the names of our own causes. You for your father. Me for King Marauxus and, well, everyone else."

Despite himself, Kitsune gave a short bark of laughter.

"No more deceptions or hiding. Now we can rely on each other, help heal each other, and build a new bond between us. A stronger one, built on truth."

"What happens now? Do you think we could just slip away?" Kitsune said, watching as the crisped ground slowly overturned into rich soil. Bright green blades of grass emerged. "I have killed so many in my anger. Surely, no one will follow me to Oinari."

Myobu forced him into a sitting position. Feeling he was now strong enough, Kitsune turned and looked into the other man's dark brown eyes. They were so full of passion and incredulous wonder that he still felt short of breath.

"Do you really not know what is happening out there?" Myobu said, shaking his head in disbelief. "What you witnessed in this dreamscape is not something that would suddenly befall the world. No, it is already happening. The region has been a dark and decaying place for many sun cycles, or at least it has outside of Kitsunetsuki. Think of what happened to Odom—to the Wastelands!

"Everyone who is on that battlefield, human or Yokai, is here because of you, Kitsune. Even in your anger, you have given them hope. They share your feelings for King Oni. No one expects to survive. They all know what they are up against. But they will fight for good. For what is right.

"If we win this battle, if we defeat Oni, there will be many who cannot forgive you. Much of what you have done with your powers and with Tsukumogami was wrong, but like any general, prince, or king, you must be able to move forward and fight alongside the rest of them."

The sky was now blue, and Kitsune could feel the warmth of the sun. Trees had taken root, and animals were foraging for food.

"Even if I do surge forward, how am I to fight alongside forces that are no longer my own?" Kitsune asked, desperate. "My father has exerted his influence over the entire army. Made everyone fight among themselves. At this point, they are basically all our enemies."

Myobu looked at him mischievously.

"What?" Kitsune said, exasperated. As he saw it, the situation was hopeless. Even without Tsukumogami, he could probably destroy everything and everyone in the vicinity. To get out alive, to give those who had followed him all this way the most honorable end, might be the only thing he could do. "What are you not telling me?"

"Why do you think your father banished you to begin with?" Myobu asked. He would rather avoid taking such action. "Why is it you are acting now of your own free will?"

Thinking for only a heartbeat, Kitsune replied, "Because he cannot control me."

"Exactly, and he can't see into your mind for the same reason he can't see into mine."

"Because you are Yokai and I have Yokai blood. We're immune to his power. I know this already," the prince said. Then he remembered the great number of foxes he had seen running along the shoreline, and realization came to him in a flash. They hadn't been foxes. They were a whole new kind of army.

Raising his head up in renewed excitement, he said, "How many did you bring with you?"

"Enough to do the job," Myobu answered. "I sent most of them into Onger. They should be able to sniff out the source of Oni's power."

Kitsune felt a surge of energy. The hope others must have seen in him, he now felt in Myobu and the Yokai. The battle was not yet lost. Putting aside his remaining personal feelings, he focused on doing what was good and right.

Standing in what was now a field of flourishing life, he said, "Let us end this. The storm must pass on."

"No, not yet," Myobu said, surprising the prince. Climbing to his feet, he continued, "I heard you encountered another Yokai. A yako, to be exact."

"Mai," Kitsune replied, ashamed he had not thought of her. "Yes, she was cut down before you arrived."

Then the memory of their night together in Sandya came back to him, and he gasped. Looking into Myobu's eyes in shame and horror, he said, "Spirits, forgive me! Myobu, I had no idea!"

Myobu shook his head, continuing to surprise him. "I'm not concerned about that, though I will admit jealousy may have hastened my journey. No, I just needed to know if she *had* you. Your mind, not your body."

"No," Kitsune said, his face still hot. "She did want me. Was biding her time as I broke down bit by bit. The one time we were…together…was a result of her patience. Still, as snakelike as she was, I still considered her a friend. I think I will miss her."

Myobu nodded, pensive. Then he said, "Before we go, I'm going to need my magic back."

"I did not mean to take it from you. I thought it was remnants of life within you, and tried to pull it forth," Kitsune said apologetically. He shivered at the recollection. In the form of flames, magic had burst from Myobu's mouth and eyes and poured into the prince. They had burned and blinded him, bringing him memories of the other man's life. "What do we do? Will it hurt?"

"I cannot say. I believe you inherited the ability to transfer one's power from your father. It's probably how he has amassed vast quantities of magic over the sun cycles," Myobu said, and Kitsune remembered his mother telling of how her husband had ripped her magic away. "I don't know if it will hurt, but I suppose we could always start with something that doesn't."

Kitsune looked up just in time to see one of Myobu's hands reaching for him. The prince leaned into it, relishing in the warmth and feel of soft skin against his cheek.

"I've missed your touch," he said. Looking into Myobu's brown eyes, he took a tentative step forward. He wanted to take hold of the man's hands, never let them go, stay in the dreamscape forever, but crushing self-doubt and shame left him feeling impotent. He hung his head. "I don't know how far I can go…what I'll be able to do. My emotions…"

Myobu's other hand came to rest on the back of his head, snaking its way through his long, blond hair. It wasn't an aggressive move, but a comforting one. "You are my pretty prince, Kitsune, and I will always love you. I cannot fix you, but I will always be right here by your side. I don't need—"

Closing the remaining distance between them, Kitsune pressed his lips against the other man's. The kiss was instantly returned with a giddy zeal. Myobu's fingers moved across his face and scalp, brushing against his ears and tugging at his hair. The prince couldn't help but moan at the touch. He snaked his own arms around Myobu, pulling him even closer.

A warmth slowly enveloped the two of them. It wasn't the type of heat born from arousal, though that was certainly occurring as well. No, the sensation came from the magic that rightfully belonged to Myobu. It emanated from Kitsune's body like a fever, flowed from him like blood leaving his veins, and was ravenously absorbed into Myobu's.

Kitsune wanted the power gone, for it to live in its rightful owner, but he had expected a void in its place. It had been a part of him, after all. They had done great and terrible things. But he did not feel empty. As the magic left him, it was replaced with something else.

As the two continued to embrace, to kiss, the warmth enveloping them grew hotter. For Myobu, it was the return of his power and identity. For Kitsune, it was love. It was acceptance. It was happiness.

He was home.

THE KING'S FEAR

Kitsune opened his eyes, awakening from the dreamscape only a heartbeat after the scorching tornado had exploded outward toward him. For the briefest moment, he was certain he was a dead man and that his reconciliation with Myobu was the timeliest of settlements.

But just as the fire began licking his skin, they diverted. Like a river, the flames flowed to his left toward Myobu and his horse. The prince hit the ground hard. He was unscathed by heat and the falling bulk of his horse, which had also been knocked down by the blast. Ignoring his body's protests, Kitsune sat up, watching as the fire stream reached Myobu. The white horse's eyes went wild with fear, but it stood perfectly still as the flames entered Myobu. The man swallowed up the element as though it was a delicious cup of tea.

As Myobu's eyes glowed red in delight, Kitsune remembered there was a battle to win. He reached upward with his mind, dispelling the remnants of the shattered tornado. Storm clouds were still raging, rain and hail and lightning pummeling the ground. With Tsukumogami gone, it felt like parts of his body, mind, and soul were missing. He found it harder to concentrate and focus his magic. It would take much more of himself to either calm the storm's anger or direct it onto his enemy.

But who is my enemy? Kitsune thought. The soldiers surrounding him had ceased battling each other. Instead, they had turned their attention to the Yokai making their way to Onger. While swordsmen sprinted to intercept, archers nocked and loosed volleys of arrows. Moving targets were harder to hit, but the sheer number of Yokai made it inevitable some would fall victim to projectiles. Even hundreds of footfalls away, Kitsune could hear the occasional yelp of pain.

Surely I can't attack all the soldiers. Their actions are not their own. They are still innocents. The prince's eyes fell upon Nasuno. Through the man, his father was glaring back at him with a mixture of dismay and anger.

His black horse was uninjured. He climbed back into its saddle and grabbed the reins. Together, they zigzagged through the throngs of soldiers, attempting to get to his father.

Oni is to blame. I will destroy his vessels as many times as I must until the Yokai have located and freed the magic he has bound here.

Myobu galloped up next to him on his white mount. The prince noticed the animal was not fitted with a saddle or reins, and he wondered if it was a horse at all. "It shouldn't take long for us to find where King Oni has stored the magic. We must survive until then. Where are you heading?"

Kitsune jerked his horse to the right, avoiding a clash of swords. He tilted his head toward Onger, just beyond the ruined gates. "That man in front is my father!"

Using fire to blast a path in front of them, Myobu scanned the soldiers who stood like statues. "I've seen King Oni before, and I don't see him now."

"My father can do so much more than influence armies," Kitsune said, remembering that the last update Myobu received on Oni's likely abilities was back when they had encountered Pan and Jasper. "He can influence entire armies, as you can obviously see. But he can also inhabit the mind of any individual. Speak or act directly through them."

"He can be *anyone?*" Myobu gasped.

"Yes, and he's taken the body of that man in front. His name is Nasuno." The two of them were halfway through what used to be Rhinecourt. Kitsune could see his old friend was pale. Bags under his eyes showed the man hadn't slept in several days, likely since Oni had seized control of his mind.

To their left, the Yokai wave began making their way into Onger either by swimming against the Rout's current or running along its bank. Only then did Oni's men move to action, brandishing steel. Kitsune watched in amazement as some of the magical creatures used their power to defend themselves, displaying powerful feats he had never imagined. Men turned to stone. Blades melted in the hands of their owners. Trees became animated, swiping at or falling upon victims. It would have been a wonder if it hadn't meant members on both sides were dying.

Through it all, Nasuno remained still and implacable.

*

Myobu felt as though he had drunk all the tea in the world. His body sang with magic, his senses tingling and alive. It was as if he had awoken from a refreshing nap. All that had occurred since his death seemed a muted dream.

Pulling his hoshi no tama from a pocket, Myobu was relieved to see that the red ruby was again glowing brightly with his magic. He felt light and giddy, especially now he had found Kitsune. Their relationship had been reset and was headed in the right direction. The prince wasn't about to lay waste to the world.

What he had sought for so long was finally his.

Marred only by the fact the two of them were facing down one of the most powerful, deadly creatures in the world.

They were close enough to Nasuno to see rain splashing off his waterlogged uniform. The monarch's avatar stood stock still, staring unblinkingly at his son as they approached. Progress was excruciatingly slow. Despite Myobu's efforts to create a path with his magic, their opponent simply willed more soldiers into the narrowing chasm between them.

It wouldn't matter in the end. The Yokai would win this battle. He had directed them to spare as many lives as possible, but they would only suffer so many casualties before turning their powers on the humans. The one life he wished they could track down wasn't even truly here.

What is taking them so long to locate the magic? Myobu thought impatiently. He could feel the great stores of power thrumming from within Onger. Knowing that in altercations like these, mere heartbeats could feel like tics, he chided himself.

Nasuno's head suddenly twitched, then tilted upward. His nose flared as though he were sniffing the air. Myobu wondered what he could be smelling in the muck other than rain, blood, and death. The look of interest, of deep thought, on the man's face was disconcerting.

Then the king broke eye contact with the prince, just now giving notice to the dark-haired companion riding on a white horse alongside his son. A flicker of recognition crossed Nasuno's face as their gazes met. It was a look Myobu did not understand. The only time he had seen Oni, he had been dressed as Ninko and the royal had been but a babe. Surely, he could not recognize him now in Acro's form.

The certainty was plain on Nasuno's haggard-looking face. As was the rage and loathing that quickly distorted it. Shadows lengthened and darkened upon his face and the ground on which he stood. Nasuno's mouth opened, and while it formed a single word, the voice came from all around them. All the men and women under Oni's control spoke out in a menacing growl.

"You…"

With that, the sea of soldiers ceased their momentum toward the Yokai. They stood as still as Oni's avatar. The storm was expending the last of the magic Kitsune had poured into it, and the pounding rain lessened to a soft drizzle. The silence over the battlefield was eerie.

Bringing their mounts to a halt a hundred footfalls from the border, Kitsune glanced at him questioningly. All Myobu could do was shrug. "I have not seen your father since he was a small child."

"Spirits, how old are you?"

"*Now* is the time you want to discuss my age?"

Emphasizing his point, all the soldiers turned toward the pair in unnerving unison. Then came the unmistakable sounds of blades being unsheathed and arrows being nocked.

"Kitsune," Myobu warned, raising his hands defensively. If they were to survive the onslaught of thousands of people, they would have to act fast and use their power. They could not hold back or hesitate. To do so would be fatal.

His love understood and held out his own hands toward the ground. It would probably take too long to reinvigorate the forces of weather, and he was opting instead to use one of his other gifts.

Fire burst into existence around Myobu's hands, and the ground beneath their horses' hooves shook.

And then a flash of red caught his eye. A red fox, one of the Yokai, had made its way through the throngs of people. It was limping, clearly injured, but was still darting with exceptional speed toward the man who embodied Oni. When it cleared the mass of soldiers, it leaped into the air, its jaws expanding horrifically, and sunk its pointed teeth into Nasuno's vulnerable neck.

Oni had been too busy glowering at Myobu to notice the stealthy Yokai. He staggered back under the impact and, looking down, appeared surprised to find a fox hanging from his throat. He swatted at the creature ineffectually with his hands. Opening his mouth to scream in rage, he only succeeded in gurgling out something incomprehensible. Blood poured from the man's neck and mouth, drenching the fox in a deeper shade of red. It took only a few moments for the two to fall together to the ground.

The entire army had ceased their movements as Oni busied himself with defending Nasuno's body. Myobu and Kitsune took advantage of the opportunity to get closer to their target. They were only twenty footfalls away when Nasuno stopped moving.

Sensing their approach, the Yokai released its prey from its jaws, turned toward them, and morphed into a human woman.

*

Nearly every militant man and woman on each side of the destroyed wall had stopped moving. As though their minds had been muted, they stared dully into the void. Kitsune barely noticed this fortune. All he could do was stare at the woman who had taken shape over Nasuno's corpse. Though her choppy, black hair was matted with the man's blood, he recognized the crooked grin on her face.

"Mai," Kitsune gasped. Looking at Myobu, he repeated, "It's Mai!"

Myobu looked both thankful for the woman's actions and less than pleased she was alive.

"Keep your wits about you," Mai called out as they rode up next to her. She wiped blood from her lips with her forearm. "It's only a matter of time before he finds a new host."

"I thought you were dead! How did you survive?" Kitsune said, dismounting. The wound on her side was red and angry-looking, but blood no longer seeped from it. He removed his cloak and threw it around her shoulders, covering her naked body.

Mai covered the wound with her new garment so he could not examine it further. "I turned at the last moment. It isn't as bad as it looks."

"Myobu!" came a strangled shriek from behind them.

All three of them swung around in time to see a lanky man with brown hair collapse to the ground. Kitsune did not recognize him, and his clothing was not a style with which he was familiar. The man had the nervous look of someone who lived in a constant state of anxiety, but that might have resulted from the blade protruding from his chest.

"Kensie!" Myobu gasped in shock. Then, "Tod?"

That was when Kitsune noticed the other man. He had been still, which made him disappear into the background of statuesque bodies. Grizzled-looking with dark hair, he would have fit in well with the soldiers if not for his clothing, which was like that of the one dying on the ground.

Jumping down off his white horse, Myobu ran toward the two newcomers. "Why didn't you stay on the shore? Tod, what happened?"

Kitsune watched as Tod reached down, grabbed the hilt of the blade sticking out of Kensie's chest, and yank it free. The sword made a wet, sucking sound as it was separated from the body. Kensie gave a faint yelp before his head fell back.

Brandishing the sword, Tod looked up so the prince again saw the angry, crazed look of his father staring back at him. The new puppet moved to close the short distance between him and Myobu.

Kitsune reached for his sword, remembering with a pang that Tsukumogami had been pulled into the tornado by the brass machine. His hands automatically reached for the bow that hadn't been with him since his time in the tribal lands. The last arrow he had shot had pierced Myobu's heart.

Desperate for anything, he considered sprinting forward. Time wouldn't allow for it, however. His father was nearly to where he could swing his own weapon, and Myobu had done nothing to protect himself.

*

"Tod, no," Myobu whispered, panic and grief rising in his chest. He didn't know what to do or say. "I told you to stay at the shore."

As Tod raised the sword up, Kensie's blood flicking off its edges, Myobu remembered these two individuals were not like him. They were purely human, just like the thousands of others around him. They had fallen victim to Oni's control, been forced to seek him out. Too dumbfounded by the sight of Kensie's bleeding body, he had failed to realize this had been a trap.

Guilt swept over Myobu. This was his fault. He had allowed the two to accompany him over the ocean waters to Odom. Partially for Tod, who would have soon died of illness, but mostly because he needed the companionship. He desired their friendship. He couldn't stand to be alone any longer.

Tod deserved a better end than this, but now it was too late for—

Something small and metallic flew by Myobu's left ear so close he could feel the air being displaced. He looked away instinctually, only hearing the object embed itself into soft skin.

With a garbled yelp of pain, Tod's hands flew up to his throat. The jeweled hilt of a dagger—one with the letter *K* carved into it—was stuck there. Myobu saw a flash of green vacate his friend's eyes, leaving behind a confused and pained Tod.

"What?" Tod rasped. It was clear he could feel the object in his neck, saw the blood on his hands, and knew something was terribly wrong. The man swiveled slowly about, looking for the friend who accompanied him most anywhere. Seeing Kensie on the ground, he let out a grieving, wet moan.

Myobu leaped forward as his friend's knees buckled and gave out. Tears fell from both their eyes at a furious pace, the salty water mixing with the blood.

"You can't go, my friends. Not when I've just brought you to him. The one I have been searching so long for," he whispered, distraught. A cacophony of light and noise arose nearby. Something profound had just occurred, but Myobu had no attention for it. "If I had known it would come to this…had I known the love we shared as a family was enough. Spirits, you can't die on me now!"

Soft steps came from behind him. In a voice that was apologetic but firm, Kitsune said, "They will not die today."

*

In his desperate search for a weapon, Kitsune's slender fingers had grazed the fancy hilt of the dagger Patriarch Kirby had gifted him. The piece was ornamental, but he knew the small blade fastened to it was as sharp and deadly as any knife.

Without thinking, without hesitating, Kitsune pulled the dagger from its sheath around his waist and threw it at the grizzled old man his father now inhabited. For a horrifying moment, he thought the dagger was going to strike Myobu in the back of the neck. The prince's eyes bulged in panic, but then his body flooded with energetic relief as the weapon sailed just left of his love's head, finding its true target.

Kitsune stood motionless, his arm still outstretched. The attacker, Tod, muttered something, and Myobu rushed forward to catch the man as he fell.

The prince walked softly toward the trio. He heard Myobu crying and the laborious breaths of the two dying men. He wanted to help, to save them, but that kind of power and magic did not live within him. All he had was words, and he knew they would not suffice.

A sudden explosion rocked the ground, and Kitsune saw a plume of earth spray into the air within the village of Onger. For a few heartbeats, it looked like sunlight was emanating from the airborne dirt. As it cleared, he saw a multitude of golden orbs rising. The Yokai had found Oni's store of magic.

Reaching into the air, Kitsune prepared to gather some clouds and bring down lightning to tear open the orbs and free the trapped magic. This quickly proved unnecessary. Dozens of Yokai used their individual powers to do just that. Shards of ice formed in midair, large chunks of splintered wood levitated off the ground, and thrashing waters from the Rout were but a few of the fantastical displays the prince saw. Together, they broke the spheres apart and, in a vivid display of light, the magic inside them expanded outward and disappeared.

Thousands of soldiers began coming to their senses. They milled around, confused about where they were and what had transpired. Kitsune watched them all, recognizing the multitude who would never rise again. He realized how much chaos and death he had caused with so little effort.

Some leader I turned out to be, he scoffed. *Dark impetus, indeed. I am done killing people.*

The men and women around him were looking all about, seeking a superior officer for answers or direction. He knew he should offer such things. He was their leader, after all. But he couldn't jump back into that broad position quite yet.

I'm done watching people die.

Turning about, Kitsune came face to face with Mai. She was still standing over Nasuno's body like a carnivore protecting its kill. He motioned for her to join him and turned to walk to Myobu. As they neared, he heard his love exclaim through tears that his friends couldn't die on him now.

Kitsune said softly, "They will not die today."

Myobu looked back at him over his shoulder, his brown eyes wet and pleading. "You can heal?"

"No, I've only demonstrated a knack for destruction," Kitsune conceded dryly. He nodded at Mai as she came up next to him. Looking at him questioningly, she appeared completely unperturbed by the state of her attire. "She can, however."

Pursing her lips, Mai glared at him and said, "Why would you think I can heal?"

Kitsune brushed aside her cloak to expose her bare abdomen. The cut was even fainter than it had been a few tics before. "I saw what Ryon did, and she did not miss. I also know my grandmother was only hours away from death's door. You sat with her for some time, and she was awake, aware, and lively shortly thereafter. Captain Pan and the child in the tribal lands, too. Both were gravely injured. You spent time with each of them, and both were up and about the next day as though nothing had happened."

"I wasn't about to let Clas die," Mai replied, clearly uncomfortable with the insinuation she might be kind or selfless. "The others were important to keep you motivated and moving forward. These two," she said, gesturing down at the bleeding, dying Kensie and Tod, "smell like they sleep in the garbage. They have very little to offer me."

Kitsune stepped closer to her. Putting a hand on her shoulder, he lowered his voice so only she could hear. "Tsukumogami is gone. It's very far from here. If your connection to it is true, you'll feel it before long. I can't swear to anything, but I would bet your best chances at reuniting with the blade is by staying by my side. Now, these two are friends of the one to which I belong." He stepped away, giving her space. "That should, at the very least, make them interesting?"

Mai stared at him for several long heartbeats. Her expression told him she both hated and respected him for the veiled threat.

"Not by themselves," Mai said studiously, turning her attention to the injured pair. She squinted as though she were examining the minds of Tod and Kensie. For all Kitsune knew, she was. After a few precious moments, her eyes lit with delight and her usual wicked smile returned. "But together maybe!"

She kneeled over the unconscious men and shooed away the worried-looking Myobu. He migrated over to Kitsune's side. Taking hold of one of his arms, he said, "I'm not sure how comfortable I am with a yako having sway over my friends."

"Don't worry, Me-oh-boo," she said as she began tending to them. "You've already brought them more chaos than I ever could. Besides, I plan on enjoying them in other ways."

*

Having been controlled by King Oni once before, Captain Pan recovered the quickest. He was able to restore a semblance of order to Kitsune's army within an hour. The prince had been impressed when the quiet man had survived a tortured imprisonment at the hands of the monarch. He was doubly so now. It was no small feat to calm the fears and unease of so many thousands of people, let alone maneuver the mass of troops into a formation that could attack or defend itself as necessary.

As for himself, Kitsune confronted the remaining Kitsunetsuki force. With Myobu by his side nonchalantly throwing around bits of flame, they had quickly acquiesced. They knew their force was easily outnumbered. The presence of so many Yokai, a being most of the soldiers had probably never seen, greatly contributed. The creatures were the basis of their religion, their morals and ideals, and they were clearly on Kitsune's side.

With the help of some soldiers from the north, Kitsune revealed the truth of his banishment and how King Oni was using magic to persuade his subjects and control armies. The explanations were hardly necessary. Their eyes still wide at the sight of hundreds of foxes running amuck through Onger, they were more than eager to pledge their allegiance to the prince. He gladly placed them under Pan's command.

It was well into the night before Kitsune and Myobu came across their friends again. Mai had healed the two men enough for them to move on their own, and they had moved and made camp very near the spot Kitsune and Mamori had spent an interrupted night. The Lady of the Mountain had towered above them that rainy evening. Now there was no mountain at all.

"They'll be fine to travel in the morning. I promise," Mai reported. Her charges were huddled by the fire, uncertain about their precarious situation. Kensie stared into the flame, either lost in thought or just plain lost. He kept stroking his chest where the blade had pierced his flesh. Tod's face revealed a mixture of disbelief, relief, and perpetual grumpiness. Mai continued, "I can't promise they'll be well rested, however."

"She healed me!" Tod blurted out, looking up from the fire. "Not just the wound. The sickness inside of me, too! I came here to live my last days, and I'll be going home a well man."

"It will be some time yet before you see the streets of your home," Mai said, a knowing look in her eye. Then she waved Kitsune and Myobu away from their camp. "Let me become more acquainted with my two new friends."

Kitsune turned to leave, Myobu more reluctantly. Tod grabbed hold of Myobu's cloak as they walked past. Pulling him closer, the grizzled man whispered into his friend's ear. Kitsune was just barely able to hear, "I've shared most everything in my life with Kensie. You know that. He's like my brother—just like you! Does she really expect us to share…her? I don't know if I'm okay with—"

"'Sharing' makes it sound like the two of you would be in control," Kitsune whispered, reaching down and freeing Myobu's cloak, "which would be a mistaken belief. My advice would be to keep her pleased. She saved your lives, after all."

"Are you sure it's best to leave them alone with her? I've seen what she did to her last toy. Not that he didn't deserve it on some level," Myobu said as the two of them walked away. Already on the outskirts of the military camp, they moved farther into the darkness. Ocean waves gradually overtook the sounds of the troops bedding down for the night.

"It's probably not the best idea, no," Kitsune answered. "But she was bored there with the Purple People. Trapped by an obligation and curse."

The prince passed on what he knew of Mai's parentage, loving how Myobu's eyebrows shot up in shock. He explained how Kyubi and her lover Kirin bound her life force to Tsukumogami. In turn, Myobu told all he knew of Kirin.

"He saved your life and was Ninko before you," Kitsune said in wonder. "It makes for such a chaotic story. I know yako are lovers of chaos. They chase it down like it's food for their souls. Mai's connection to Tsukumogami is not the only reason she has followed me all this way. We are heading into even greater chaos. We might even recover the sword along the way. With my permission, she's along for the adventure. She won't jeopardize that. Your friends are safe."

"Is that why you led me out here into the dark, away from the others?" Myobu asked with a sly look. Then his tan face went red, and he said abashedly, "I'm sorry. That was inappropriate."

"It's all right. I know I don't think in the same way most humans do. Why would I expect the same from you?" Kitsune gave a wink as he leaned back against a boulder, but he wasn't certain it covered up the sadness within him. He glanced back at the encampment, which was still a bustle of activity at this late hour. Thousands were asleep, and many more were having their injuries attended to. And then there were the dead.

Indicating several large fires burning on the far side of the settlement, Kitsune continued, "I know you, as one of the Yokai, must have a keen sense of smell. The other Yokai disappeared when we took care of the dead, so I thought I'd bring you out here for some fresh air."

Myobu joined him against the rock. Together, they stared up into the sky.

"How many?" Myobu eventually asked, his voice reverent.

"A tenth. Far too many."

"It's not your fault. Your father was the one who forced them to fight one another."

"I know," Kitsune said. He didn't believe it, though. The storm he had unleashed had been catastrophic, and they had been lucky more lives hadn't been claimed. Some would still argue his actions were the result of Oni's betrayal, of his failure at being a father and king, but Kitsune would no longer blame others for what befell him.

From now on, he would take responsibility for himself.

"So, what happens now?" Myobu said.

"We push forward to Oinari tomorrow," Kitsune answered, looking northwest. "We can get there within two days. Blockade the city with the human army, though at a distance in order to keep them out of my father's mental reach. Then the two of us and the rest of the Yokai can advance into the palace and depose the king."

"Let us hope it is as easy as that."

A golden hue lit up the horizon toward Oinari. The aura grew steadily brighter until it hurt to look at.

"Surely, it isn't morning already," Myobu said, looking at him questioningly.

"Dawn is still hours away," Kitsune replied, straightening up. The warm, golden lights were fading away, emphasizing his point. "I do not know what that could have been."

"We'll find out in two days' time," Myobu said, pulling him back up against the boulder. "It's as easy as that."

"As easy as that." Kitsune grabbed hold of one of Myobu's hands, their fingers intertwining. "Whatever it is, promise me it won't tear us apart."

"Absolutely not." Myobu rested his head on Kitsune's shoulder as they watched the distant sky return to its normal, starry black tapestry. "I'm never leaving your side again, my very pretty prince."

EPILOGUE

The history of Inari Palace was fraught with trouble. Kitsunetsuki's first monarch had initiated its construction, but its completion would wait over a hundred sun cycles. It was an ambitious undertaking for the fledgling kingdom, bringing the royal family to the brink of financial ruin.

The palace was not just a home for the monarchy, and it was more than a symbol of their status and power. The kingdom's first leaders understood the land they were building upon was special. Magical. A species known as the Yokai, the cornerstone of a growing religious movement, congregated in its vicinity.

Just as Castle Verde had been built in the southeast to honor the gifted creatures, Inari Palace was meant to celebrate them. To worship them.

The risk paid off. Kitsunetsuki prospered, religious zeal over the Yokai remained strong in the people's hearts, and the ruling family remained in power ever since. The magical beings became a staple in their culture and everyday lives.

Until they all disappeared.

Now, no one remembered them being anything but relics of an old faith. Many still believed in them, followed their ideals, but verifiable sightings were rare.

Then where the hell did they come from? King Oni fumed. He opened his true eyes, seeing not the ruined remains of the Eastern Gate, but the curved, golden walls of the Boleyn Room.

Located at the very heart of Inari Palace, the Boleyn Room had been built at the epicenter of the magical energies permeating the land. Kings and queens had made it their throne room. Ceremonially, it brought them closer to the Yokai and, by tradition, only a ruler could enter.

They came from Urel, Oni thought, taking a deep, calming breath. *The smell of the whelp riding alongside my son. I recognize it. He was responsible for my defeat that day on the beach.*

Right after I cut down his parents.

The king paced, looking at nothing in particular. Few items were in the room. Two chairs and a table had been shoved to one side. A woman's portrait hung from the wall.

And dozens of golden orbs floated through the air, spinning at various speeds. They contained vast amounts of magic, stolen from others over centuries. It made up the most concentrated amount of power in any single place. Within Inari Palace, a focal point for magical properties, the power was amplified tenfold.

Oni's temper flared again at the thought of how much of his collected magic had vanished. Not only had he lost complete control of the north, but now he was blind to a massive force invading from the east. To make matters worse, the war he was hoping to wage was manifesting in the west. The only tower close to completion on that front had been destroyed along with the Western Pass.

Thankfully, not one bit of power and been sent to the west. What had been scheduled to be installed at the pass was safely within the egg-shaped walls of the Boleyn Room.

All of this is because of Prince Kitsune, the king told himself, struggling to keep his calm demeanor. He was angry at his son for defying his will and intent, but also at himself for not seeing what had dwelled dormant within the prince for so long. *I've always known the boy was part Yokai. How could he not be? His mother's blood flows through his veins, protecting his mind and thoughts from me. The sheer amount of power that must saturate every fiber of his being…the rage that consumes him! If I had only known, I could have taken his magic and already attained my goals.*

Filled with grave concern, King Oni stared at the spheres hovering above him. Just as he had Inari Palace to magnify the magic he controlled, Prince Kitsune wielded Tsukumogami. Oni had once held the legendary Sword of Inari, understood the magnitude of its effects, and knew few barriers existed for those who carried it.

Even more worrisome was the toll Tsukumogami extracted from its various owners. Under normal circumstances, the ones who employed the blade possessed it until their death, at which point their soul was absorbed into it. The sword had been forcibly taken from Oni, however, and with it a small portion of his soul.

Part of his consciousness lived within Tsukumogami, a part he couldn't control. Had it revealed his ultimate plan to the prince? Would it even have a choice?

"I thought I would have more time," Oni said aloud, looking at the portrait hanging from the wall. "Time to assert my control over the region. Hunt down all the Yokai and take their power."

The king did not hate the Yokai. Other than thwarting his plans in Urel so long ago, they had rarely presented themselves as a nuisance. He needed their magic, however. The more he possessed, the easier it would be to command the brass machine.

"Those who oppose me are closing in. The window of opportunity I have created for myself is shrinking."

Perhaps more rapidly than I thought. Oni's recent control over the mind and body of Major Saxma had been illuminating. In particular, it revealed to the king he was not invulnerable. That he had weaknesses. Would his current form fail him, too? Was it already failing him?

I have to act now.

Raising his hands, Oni prepared himself and the golden spheres. Having spent so long damming his emotions, playing the part of a stoic, detached monarch, it took a moment to succumb to his feelings again.

The barriers had been crumbling over the past several weeks, however, and they soon overwhelmed his mind.

Looking at a point in the air above him, the king focused his rage and love. He looked further. Deeper. At the very particles holding matter together.

He went beyond.

And then he found what he was seeking: a miniscule tear in the universe. Using his reeling emotions as a spear, he forced his magic—along with some he had stolen—into it. Bringing his hands down with the effort, he ripped the tear wide open.

For the briefest moment, King Oni saw the churning cogs, wheels, and pipes of the brass machine. It was a shadowy mountain of metal behind curling steam. Then harsh, golden light exploded into the Boleyn Room. The energy pouring through from the other side radiated through the walls of the king's throne room. Beyond the confines of Inari Palace.

I am coming for you, Izanami, Oni thought, blindly searching out the woman's portrait. *I will stop you from destroying your people in the past, even if it means everything here and now will burn to ash.*

What was done to you was wrong. Mistakes were made, and they had profound consequences. I can remedy those errors. Take back what Damian—no, what I—did to you.

I will save you, Izanami.

My love.

Thanks for reading *The King's Fear*. Find me online at:

WEBSITE

www.isaacgrisham.com

BLUESKY

@isaacgrisham.bsky.social

FACEBOOK

@AuthorIsaacGrisham

Instagram

isaac.grisham

www.ingramcontent.com/pod-product-compliance
Lightning Source LLC
Chambersburg PA
CBHW031647100726
47898CB00006B/2008